This story is a "FAIRLY" TALE.
It is like a Fairy Tale, but not quite.

It is a story about "MYTHLES"
which are like Myths, but not quite.

And their adventures are played out
in "MYTHLEWILD"
a magical place that's wild only to those...
...unwilling to step in.

The GLASS EGG

an adventure story for anyone old enough...
...to be young at heart.

by Tom Tate

PUBLISHED BY **T⊒** TAO EDITIONS

PART TWO

CHAPTER 31

Mount White slept under deep spreads of cotton clouds. His brow yawned over the satin sheets of ice blanketing the pleated plateaus below. Each frozen spire of the Snowmass pointed in homage to their pinnacled peer. The old man mountain stirred from his slumbering glacial bed. His foothills woke in snowy baths of rime, while his towering marble summit showered in perpetual warm sunbeams filtered between lofty, purple pavilions and crystal cloudy canopies. Upon one such sun ray, the tiny vagabond butterfly gently lighted atop a rocky lip graved within a massive quartzite hutch and bid her careworn grandfather good morning. However, the gay golden streams did nothing to melt the venerable grandsire's melancholy.

The land lord, Enduros, was as old and hoary as the crust of the earth, which was his domain. In marbled mountain majesty, his bastion of Revrenshrine towered over the realm of Theland. As deities go, Enduros was more successful than most. Mythlewild's kindly citizens still held the ancient potentate in highest esteem, longevity being his most notable asset. His ripened age endowed the lord of the land with tireless patience, the envy of all other deities. Most prominent, and most envious of these was Lust, temptress queen of the underland. Her passion for Enduros' holdings grew, by cancerous proportions, into flagrant hostilities. Her most heinous transgression being the fatal kiss dealt Zeros, god of the sky, put to rest under the black angel's spell. Enduros was still bereft at his brother's loss. His witch sister's aggression severely tested Enduros' perseverance—to the point of constant worry. Depressed in his rocking chair throne, he creaked and swayed like a listing relic of some shipwreck, sheeted and rigged like a cadaver in a white linen toga. A swaddling wrap of snowy whiskers bandaged his rock of ages face. Instead of crown, an ice pack capped his head's peak, which was as bare as his mountain's top. Below, his divine feet soaked in a hot tub lake of Epsom salts and mineral water.

Enduros' attentive wife, Lara, massaged his craggy, stickbone back with lineament and tried to turn a deaf ear to her spouse's nagging dialogue with the hole in the ground—which was his oracle, Oman, the voice of the unknown. It was on Oman's brick rim that the rainbow-winged butterfly danced to a rest.

"My mountain sleeps easy..." muttered the land lord into his oracle, "...why can't I?"

Oman said nothing. Like all true and wisened oracles, it refused to answer foolish questions, or those posed in rhetoric—even at the whimsies of gods.

"Good morning!" said the butterfly cheerfully, just before changing into a scholarly looking caterpillar.

"Good day to you, Creto, my mentor," replied the well-deep voice of Oman.

Enduros just sat and rocked, and creaked and croaked, shaking his bandage beard like a prehistoric woolly buffalo. Another grand relic perched atop Enduros' rocker, hunched as stolid and immovable as its master. It was Palladan, the eagle. The century-worn sovereign of the animal kingdom was a taloned, golden feathered shadow of its mellowed lord. Like Enduros, he was content to roost and roll his year weary head in fitful nods.

"He's growing terribly uncomfortable I'm afraid," remarked the grey haired mistress Lara, in response to Creto's greeting.

"Crotchety," said the deep well, as if to correct the goddess' choice of words.

"But now that you're back, dear Creto, I know it shall boost my husband's spirits."

"Humbug!" shouted Enduros. "These lopsided sunrays have been chilling these bones ever since Zeros' passing. His contrary climate is aching my back, and I'm gripped with this infernal insomnia. My mountain sleeps, but not me! Instead of slumber—I'm blessed with lumbago, gout, boils, bunions, rheumatism, heart murmurs, migraines, and mildew—and my hair is falling out!"

"Escaping," corrected the erudite oracle.

"Perhaps you shouldn't pull at it so much," fussed Lara, ironing down the few faithful hairs remaining. Her milky palms felt smooth against her husband's ragged forehead. The goddess' soft, pastel gown was a comforting lap in which the wrinkled lord might set his woes and worries.

"You've room to talk!" grumbled Enduros, taking no solace when given. "Your scalp is entwined with strands of silver, like a bun of gossamer yarn." Enduros was not prone to dolt on his spouse, so he aimed his ire at Creto, who had just crawled into his mollusk shell habitat so that only his fuzzy caterpillar head stuck out. It was every bit as rutted and convoluted as his grandsire's, and bearded and bedecked with bifocals, and two curling arm-length antennae stuck on for good measure. "And the same to you, butterfly... or caterpillar... or snail—whatever the tarnation you are! You're always switching back and forth between he and she and its... I don't even know who or what I'm talking to half the time! Good morning you say—Humbug I say!" Enduros rubbed his elbow vigorously and then stuffed a thermometer under his barbed tongue, which continued to waggle nevertheless. "My arthritis is flaring up again! Storm's coming—I can feel it in my joints—Palladan too." The old eagle was as unmoving as marble statuary, save for a blink of his chiseled eyes. "And Creto, your hole is as tight-lipped as a nutshell."

"Discreet," inserted the pundit from the well.

Enduros shook a fist full of inflamed knuckles toward the oracle. "And insolent too. You'd think it had a mind of its own."

"Do you 'mind'?" quipped Oman in a show of oracular wit.

"There—you see! That sarcastic stone-lipped... if it weren't bottomless, I'd fill its obnoxious orifice full of lye!"

"Not 'lyes', but truths only fill my gullet," Oman retorted.

"Have you found time to observe Omnus' pilgrim, Grandsire?" interjected Creto the caterpillar, attempting to change the topic, while stretching from his shell so the befogged sire would recognize Creto as the male counterpart to the lovely lady butterfly named, Creta.

"Naturally I've been watching, ever since you left. How else would my ulcers thrive, if not by your oracle's loose lip, or viscid visions. Not that it's been easy; reception has been terrible. However do you get a good picture on this bric-a-brac gap? Must be these confounded clouds that infest my brother's skies of late." Enduros attempted to rectify the situation with a solid oracular kick. But he only succeeded in popping a bunion—and a bit more of his renown patience. "Confounded, infernal ill well!"

"Contradictory... I cannot be 'ill' and 'well' concurrently," reminded Oman unsympathetically.

"A-Ah-Ahchoo!" sneezed the beleaguered divinity.

"'Ahchoo,'" echoed Oman, as the sound of it rattled into the bottomless throat of the mountain orifice. "Bless you!" said the oracle with some sensitivity, as if its god could use some blessings.

"Did you hear that!" grumbled Enduros, peering into the hole and seeing himself. "It's sneezing! No wonder the signals are garbled, it's all stuffed up."

"Impossible," argued Oman. "If a hole is 'all stuffed up', then it is no longer a hole!"

"Perhaps it's coming down with the bug," remarked the caterpillar, hoping to stay any further ungodly outbursts.

"Humbug!" coughed the earth lord. "It's chills that ail it. A spot of vinegar and honey shall turn the trick."

"Don't you listen to him, Creto," admonished Lara, extracting the thermometer from Enduros' swollen throat. "It's not your oracle's reception that's congested; it's my husband. And he's chilled too, sitting under this insidious shade all day, on this drafty peak... and with a nasty temperature."

"Temper!" came the voice from the mountain's throat.

"If anyone needs a poultice, it's you, dear," insisted Lara.

"Humbug!" hacked Enduros again, squinting over the thermometer to read its diagnosis—then shaking it vigorously like a switch. "Why these confounded numerals are too small!"

"Perhaps a poultice for the vintage eyes, Grandsire," suggested Creto. A half dozen caterpillar hands offered his bifocals to Enduros.

"Bifocals, huh..." The stubborn god fluffed his cantankerous whiskers. "I'll tell you one thing I don't need—and that's spectacles—to tell me that Omnus' pick hasn't a prayer of finding my Egg! I CAN see that much! If Oman can't detect my present, no one can. And no poultice will cure THAT malady!"

"All he needs is help, Grandsire," whispered Creto into his lord's ear. "Friendship is the greatest remedy. You could be a panacea should you will it."

"I would first rid myself of my own hoard of afflictions were I so puissant!" Enduros wrenched his spine as he rocked furiously. Palladan dug his talons into the perch lest he tumble. "And had I as many friends to help ME—as allotted to that whippit—then could I manage as well!"

"Befriend him too, Grandsire," coaxed Creto, inching his way into his land-lord's will, "and his allies are then yours!"

"It would seem, Creto, that my allies are already his." Enduros rubbed his nose out of shape. "Sniffles," he sputtered.

"Stuffiness," echoed the oracle bubbling to itself.

"Humbug! Creto, you've been down there from the start, nursing that sprout like a nanny. Withal, despite your henning, he's no closer to my Egg than when he climbed out of that bog in Hurst Meadow. Why Omnus pulled him out I'll never know!"

"Fate intervened, Grandsire. Were I only permitted to step in—"

369

"Interfere? Never!" Enduros stomped his foot down with a splash, into his hot tub, showering Epsom salts and mineral water like a damper onto the conversation. "Observe—but do not intrude. My maker Omnus would not permit it —and neither will I. Gods and mortals—Gad! What a baleful broth that blends!"

"The angel madam, Celeste, was a divinity, Grandsire," pointed out the caterpillar. His whole host of fingers were crossed to aid his argument.

"My glass cousin too," voiced Oman with pride.

"For that matter, your own pet, Creto—whether butterfly or caterpillar—is as common a sight in Theland as flowers in a meadow," mentioned Lara, gently kneading her spouse's jutting collarbone, while studying the sky through intermittent sunrays. A sun-golden stallion could be seen profiled against the distant clouds spiralling downward ever closer to the mountain palace parapets. "And let's not forget our son's winged steed, Paramount."

"Indeed not!" groaned Enduros. "It bewilders me why such a superb mount stoops to bear that over-blown bouncer, Violato, upon his sanctified back—the same back that seats my very son, a crown prince of gods. It's shameful. It's unnatural for divinities to mingle with otherlings—fleshlings especially! Leaves a bitter taste in the mouth, like stirring ashes into ambrosia. By thunder—it's incest, and can only lead to more blight. That bale sows bad seeds I'm telling you—bad seeds! Which reminds me... Creto, did you or did you not plant the seed in that spur's ear to climb up here to my door with his hand hawked out like a bothersome raff?"

"Absolutely not, Grandsire," denied the caterpillar, curling into his shell so that only words swirled out. 'Twas in fact my alter ego, Creta, who attended THAT deed. And the centaur chap played a hand as well. The pony boy's idea set their minds to it. I merely provided a moral boost—like a good conscience..." Two antennae felt their way out to test the waters. "A moral boost wouldn't taste too bitter... would it, Grandsire? Even your fish brother, Isolato gave him audience."

"By no choice of his," stressed Enduros. "He was persuaded!"

"And you, Grandsire... can you not be persuaded? Or do you intend to cave yourself away from the world on this marble slab, like your hermit crab sibling in the brine?"

Enduros grabbed Lara's arm and lifted his prune-skinned feet from their Epsom salt womb. Then he stood up with a deep drawn sigh, and teetered on his corn-plastered bunions. His back was as crooked as a tightly strung bow, and the lord of the earthen deities leaned upon his lackluster scepter as though it were a moldy cane. Had his wife not lent her unyielding support, he could scarcely have taken a single step on his own omnipotent power. Howbeit, the feeble god trembled over to the mountain's palisade. The aged legend strained, but carried himself with a timeless dignity nonetheless. Though his body was bent and broken, and his spirit sapped—his stature remained monumental, and his demeanor undiminished.

Lara's grip tightened as the shaky lord leaned over the summit's edge, shook his cobweb beard and squinted an eye into his realm below. His splinter-thin forearms were still sturdy enough limbs for Palladan, who perched unashamed upon his grandsire; his glinting eyes beamed with piercing pride to serve the durable one.

"Well, Grandame," said Enduros to his wife, threshing out for vocal support. "Am I lord of this land, or just a lofty king crab?"

Benevolent of heart and kindly in her choice of words, the mother of the land spoke frankly. Her eyes, those of the earth, were red and swelled with tears. "My great husband, who is gird of this earth? You are not so long in the tooth that you cannot taste the rancid air, or whiff the scent of death; so nearsighted that you cannot see our earthen flesh flow blood; nor deaf to its cries or numb to its pain. We mustn't condone Creto's baneful medlings... but, perhaps we should help the boy. He IS Omnus' envoy, and travels with our high father's blessing—and under protection of the dove child. Or is Niki another 'bad seed' too?"

"Hmmm... Even our magnified maker—overseer of gods and fleshlings—did surrender to a tampering or two, didn't he? Why then should I sit up here on the shelf growing stale?..." The old lord's curdled mind churned over the possibilities.

Theland's grandame saw fit to expound on her long suppressed sentiments. "And that Lust! How she manipulates you—playing upon your ethics and weaknesses. She turns your sympathies on you as though another affliction. She means to cow you with Zeros' murder—well don't let her! She intends for you to drown in tears of mourning—but don't let her! She wants you to crawl onto your rocker and die like some 'reft and rheumatic fossil under the most lethal potions in her arsenal: apathy, neglect, and fear—you mustn't let her do this to you! Your sister thinks you a withered, decaying, decrepit shell of a god. Are you so aged, so resigned to a premature, preordained death in her tar pits, my husband? I doubt it! If Lust can dabble in the affairs of our kindred—who's to say you cannot? Your devil sister is using the mortals to strike at you. You are the snag, the pea under her pillowed plans. It's your lot she covets—no other. In your seat she can have it all. But look at you... Look at us! Is it our destiny as gods over Theland to sit atop mountain spires watching and rocking and licking our sore spots like dotards while the entire world of ours slides into Lust's abyss. What's happened to us? Has senility sullied our spunk? Our children, Vero and Tierra, are not feeble. They look to you for direction. For their sake, for all our sakes, point the way. Better yet—lead the way! Defend yourself and your home from this peril before its too late—before you meet your end, like Zeros!"

"Speak no ill of my bygone brother, Madam!" cried Enduros despairing for solution to his dilemma. "I loved him. I was so close to him here on my mountain... and I mourn for him hither."

"Will you also die for him, Father?" asked the voice of the sun, striding in upon the wings of Paramount, and mounted thereon like a colossal monument to halidom. It was Vero, son of the earth, and golden prince of gods and men. A star was his crown and the sun his complexion; their radiant light drenched his every feature. Of deities, Vero was a titan—young, virile, and dashing as a comet. Shimmering amber clouds were his hair, and in his eyes an aura of wise, glowing planets set upon a milky space. He dismounted with the fluency of ocean curls. Shooting stars streaked his footsteps. Though his stance was mannered and his voice as softs poken as moon songs, his words owned a particular flair which exacted attention. His forebears were not prone to ignore him.

Enduros turned and squinted up at his son. "I would hear your words, Vero. Tell me what is in your heart. You have always been forthright with me."

"It is as I spoke, Father. I deem to know if you would die for your brother in defending our realms. Or will you die like him—on your trusting haunches in pliant, whimpering repose awaiting the wraith's hugs and kisses." The Titan Prince knelt by his father clasping the brittle hands in his. "I've never before spoken to you thus, Father; but extant happenings preclude past facades. Our souls must of necessity be bared. You've never avowed yourself to Zeros' murder, nor denounced Lust as the cold-lipped culprit—yet you know it. Who else has audacity enough—power enough —to undo a god! Your sister spites you all the more. She believes your power is too palsied to foil her, so she comes caterwauling on your very doorstep. Oman has kept no secrets from you in this regard. What you've observed has been no distortion. Look there—you can see them even now, across so many miles. Like locusts they swarm—Lust's condors—a black blight in our skies. And the Ill-timbers' mildew and worm-rotted armies infest and rape your fragrant, virgin evergreen forests. I've seen it first hand awing Paramount. Enduros, my Father, I have watched with you as the children in Mythlewild courageously feint and parry every bane and wicked misfortune thrust in their face by bitter lions and lustful zealots. But courage alone is no match for spoilage of gods. Your sister—queen of the dead —and her clay-born barghests will rule the day, unless met by us. Only your army of invincibles can resist the goddess of Luhrhollow and check her advances. Only one force can repulse her—Yours! Only one deity is mightier—You! Constantio can challenge DeSeet's grab-claws, but not Lust's. No mortal can fight your battles. Fleshlings they may be, still and all, they are our children—and to a man, they look at the heavens for stock."

"As an egg wants for warm belly," inserted Oman, not to be outdone.

"And this matter of the Egg," continued Vero. "We owe it to ourselves to help young David gather the Glass Egg and return it to the creator. Should Lust be first to gain the Yoke, 'twill spell the doom for all of us.

Enduros shook the cobwebs from his bearded tresses and looked up, glowering and red-eyed from his thoughts. "Yes... my Egg... It must be returned to its intended..." The mountain lord's eyes forged into frozen glares. His words were smoldering cold. "...The Egg was meant for me, not Omnus... and I mean to have it!"

"Father—take care," warned Vero. "The Glass Egg can be as corrosive as Lust, and even more potently destructive. Whether in heaven or hell, it can kill for good as wantonly as evil. Wash your claim from it, Grandlord, else you sink to Lust's defiling depths."

"Perhaps I should assist the yoke of my egg..." reveled Enduros, mulling his offspring's advise. "Can we mount an opposition to my sister, Vero?"

"Most certainly, Grandlord! No sooner had Paramount returned to me from Middleshire with his counsel, than we set about the surface realm of yours, marshalling the warrior gods of Mythlewild to your cause. Your supreme deistic hosts are bolstered by a divine army of gods, all eager to contest your sister's challenge. We wait only on your command and generalship."

Enduros' great eagle clacked his jaw and some sparkle lit his grey-flecked, marble eyes. Alas, his pedestal of clay was not so pulsed. "Generalship?" balked the relic god. "You already have my spirit, would you have my shriveled torso too! Am I expected to sally off into battle with all the sky's young stallions? Have those ages not passed... Or would you hitch a team of horses to my throne and have me rock into war upon a chariot chair!"

"Humbug," echoed Oman the oracle.

"Humbug indeed!" voiced Lara. Her voice was raised above the matriarchal level and her silver strands slightly tossled. "Have we not grown old together, husband? Do you see me living out my days doubled over in a coddle chair?"

"For that matter, Grandsire, you have already risen from your roost," observed Creto, sticking his caterpillar nose out of his shell and into the debate. "Since you are up and about, do you not feel more alive? If gravity pulls you more to sit, let it be upon your throne—and not your bier."

"And let this sit upon your brow." From the ice bucket, Vero retrieved a glittering gold crown beset with sky-hung jewels, and placed it upon his father's age-parched scalp. Enduros bore its weight by rearing his head loftily into the air. "A more becoming fit than ice packs, is it not, Grandsire?"

Peering into his well of wisdom, Enduros faced the image of a magnificent godhead. "By thunder—what a god I was!"

"What a god you ARE," redressed the hallowed well in reverent homage, now that his house lord had returned.

Vero and Lara accompanied their patriarch over to a resplendent platinum throne, chiseled from diamond stone and shimmering like a star cluster. Disengaging himself from his crutches, the earth lord straightened up, and was drawn to the resplendent seat like a wren to its nest. The seating erased countless years, and the feel of it massaged his antique muscles more effectively than his compassionate matron's soothing fingers.

"Ahhh... it fits well too!" sighed the king of the earth. Palladan fluffed his wings and drew out his chest as the lord of beasts proudly mounted his favorite perch.

"If your seat suits you, Father, then you must command the force to keep it under you," said Vero.

"So I will," answered Enduros, without a cough or a sneeze, and twirling his scepter nimbly in between lean and limber fingers. "So I will!"

"Our pilgrim visitor will be impressed," cried Lara, "to meet a LIVING legend!"

"Ah, yes... our visitor!" Enduros cocked his crown and adjusted his posture. "Though it's quite unorthodox, I can hardly rebuff an emissary from the exalted, High Overlord. By gods—I'll do it! I'll roll out a welcome to remind that meater where he treads." And with a spiteful swipe of his bunioned corns, the earth lord kicked his foot bath over the brink. To his delight he found it not nearly so immovable as his oracle's brick rim. "Vero, perhaps you and Paramount might facilitate our friends' arrival with an escort. It's easy to find oneself lost on this crag's cliffs and scarfs."

Like a sunburst, the golden titan was astride his winged mount, and together they streaked through Mount White's cloud bank trusses. Enduros stroked his eagle's neck, and Palladan responded with a breast-pattering 'caw'. "Is it possible, fellow, that we've been looking down from these marble breezeways so long that we've lost sight of our lot?"

"Your head has been so long and often stuck within that recess," commented the eagle with a mellow, pointed voice aimed at the oracle, "that you've lost the feel of our earthen roots."

For once Oman could think of nothing to add. Creto's chuckle could be heard deep inside his mollusk shell.

"Ho! And you—too long a perching on my collar," laughed Enduros. "Fly then, Palladan—to my 'roots' with you! Delve down into my dirt and see what you unearth!"

The shrill screech of Palladan rang from the mountain shrine as a clarion call to arms for all the gods of Mythlewild to rally 'round. Lara and Enduros saw through the misty wisps coating Mount White as they watched the grand eagle spread his massive wings and descend into the hinterlands. Enduros rubbed his toes vigorously. "Confounded bunions still throb... Feels like bad weather."

Creto too, felt chilled in the grey sunlight, and so stayed curled away in his shell. Cold breaths even escaped from Oman's throat. "Ah-choo!" sneezed the oracle quite unexpectedly.

"I've forgotten! It's time for your medication..." Lara instantly produced a lap tray for her husband.

"Vinegar and honey?" exclaimed the earth god. "Humbug!" he roared before pouring the concoction down his well's throat. "This must be for you, old fellow!" crowed Enduros, much to Oman's displeasure. "And what's this—warm milk and toast? Humbug! No more old man's diet for me. I still have my teeth—and some bite too! Today I shall dine on nectar and ambrosia—and at the table with my wife and daughter!" Lara eagerly offered to help her husband to the dining hall, but it was unnecessary.

"Bravo, Grandsire!" applauded the catapillar with a hundred hand claps.

"Humbug!" spat the oracle, a tart taste still clinging to its endless gullet.

376

CHAPTER 32

"You'll never get it!" taunted the hazing voice. "You're not back far enough! Go back... Back... Farther... Farther!" it repeated, over and over, from some distant place. Four lamb shadows frolicked amid star lighted meadow grass, playing catch beneath a spreading ebony tree. It was no mere ball they tossed—but an odder sphere, glowing brilliantly. Was it a star? No... an orb! It was glass—a glass egg! All that played the game chased after it. The most prominent figure present remained shrouded in heavy, mysterious fog-bridled robes. However, the other three were vividly stark. Under fleece-hidden faces lurked more familiar features, which brought a dreamy smile to David's slumber.

Why, they're not lambs at all! The sphere-chasing, cloud rider was too gnarled and thewey for mutton. David recognized him as the king, Constantio, though his mane was wool, his frock was lion hair. And Lo—one face outshined the stars... It was Valentina, berobed and beguiling. Her dimpled glow would never have faded from David's mind, had it not been for the last remaining apparition.

From behind a veil of clouds she stepped, so soft and satin sheer. She was a pastel-girded sky walker, graceful, radiant... sublime. An angel's reflection, only more beautiful; the boy could not tear his eyes from such a vision. Watch out! Another image intrudes—a shade, black-faced and fleeced in red robes. Then, in less than a heart stroke, it departs, cackling. The winds whistled and howled, the ebony tree quaked. Caught in its lash, the glass ball swirled out of control. Seized within a cyclone's whirling hurl, it was vehemently smashed and shattered against the rocking ebony trunk. The four lambs were swallowed in a churning, gusting sky wave which crashed, not like ocean breakers, but with a woeful wailing. "Help me!" it cried. "Help me!" Then it thundered, "Go back! Farther... Go back!" And the dream turned cold.

Was it his own voice that woke him? Or the frosty gust of dawn's breath? David didn't know. The shadow of Mount White spilled over the dewy hummocks while the blooming sun opened his huge, sleepy red eye as if to watch the stirring pilgrims. Startled by his rude awakening, David's gaze scoured the misty morning campsite. In the middle of the snug hillock encampment, Peter prodded a modest cookfire, while nursing a busy fry pan. Niki perched overhead, chirping a morning melody in time with the sizzling breakfast bacon. Fidius sat, as he had the night before, on post upon a nearby crest. David felt under his head for the satchel which had been his pillow, then sighed with relief as his winged toes smiled back from the foot of his bedroll.

"Don't worry, Davy, they're still there. None of your nightmares has stolen any charms from you yet." Peter brought his friend a cup of hot grog. "This'll take some of the edge off the morning. The cold arrived last night to announce winter's coming."

David slipped into the heavy wool jerkin and hose Constantio had provided. They lent warm, welcome substance to his flimsy blouse. A sip of grog and the crackling fire toasted his toes. "It's bitter today," remarked David.

"The grog?"

"No, Peter, I mean the weather."

"Oh, yeah... Looks like it might even snow."

"It's snowing up ahead, in the mountains," commented Niki, swooping into David's breastpocket and finding its wool-lined warmth as welcome as the privacy it provided earlier. "It wasn't this cold when we left Sovereignton two nights ago," noted the dove while studying David's restless eyes. It's like we stepped out of fall and into winter overnight."

"I had the strangest dream last night," uttered David, looking at nothing except the sky.

"A 'smashing' one too, was it not?" The grinning pony boy lunged at an imaginary shape. "Who's got the Egg? Maybe it's that heaven-bodied sky walker!"

"You know?" said David, gulping down the last of his breakfast.

"Sleep talk," chirped Niki. "You had best discipline your tongue about speaking your mind, or no secret thoughts will be safe."

The cookfire snapped the air as the pony boy poured bacon grease into its mouth and commenced to break camp. "Let's be off. I want to reach the Rime River before the snow descends to meet us. Two more days shall see us safely there and into the Snomass range. I'll go fetch Sir Fierce from his sentry sitting. Eccentric old lizard! I'd have thought the bacon scent would've pried him loose of his post. He's been up there most of the night—on vigil, he says."

"Not eccentric—precautious!" cheeped Niki.

"Well, for all his precaution, the chill still crept in—right under his nose." Peter trotted up to the hillcrest with a plateful of foodstuffs.

"I'm disciplined, don't you think, Niki?" pondered David, still immersed in his dream.

"You've proven as much, painter," said the dove. "Have we not both born secrets enough to satisfy you? You can't let cock sure centaurs, nor uninhibited fantasies shake the confidence you've developed in yourself, for both are likely to remain mysteries—at least until you are wise enough to be considered 'eccentric'!"

With their supply cache securely fastened to Peter's back, the pilgrims set off on the third morning of their trek, wending their way steadily along the Rime River Road which branched from the North Byway skirting Serenity Plain at the borders of Phantom Forest. The 'Spookwood', as it came to be dubbed, was so named for the ghost-like images her snow-masked spruce and fir fermented in the minds of passers-by. Their November morning dress however, was still a verdant green. The crooked path bent and wound its way up and through the fragrant evergreen-speckled hills which embraced the Middleshire's northernmost townships that were tucked tidily into her woven shade forests and glens. Below them, in the distance, beneath the watchful spires of Bia Bella, spread Sovereignton, nestled in the mountain foothills like a placid, picture perfect hamlet at peace with the world. Sadly, the foreboding grey sky was not so tranquil. It grumbled and heaved, as unsettled as the clouded mood impounded behind the city walls. In the more pastoral, lulling, southern meadows beyond Sovereignwood and the hedgerows of Downy Hills, brilliant autumn reds surrendered to dying winter bleak and brown. For just a fleeting moment, David recalled the beautiful September landscape he had started when Fearsome first surprised him—and this adventure had begun. Now, however, his thoughts lay ahead, to the endless elegant army of olive and emerald needled sentinels, rigid in their tall mountain saddles, protecting the staid, snow-crowned palace of Revrenshrine with unbending resolve to deter any intrusion.

Niki flew above David's head cooing and singing, merrily unmindful of the environs, and elated to be on track in their long delayed quest. If the sky smeared grey, hopes nonetheless glowed bright pink within the party. David whistled in tune with his dove. And soon Peter began to sing, loudly, while searching for a key. His soundings drowned out his more melancholy memories of the sometimes woesome woods. His last venture nearly took his leg, leaving the wary pony boy wondering what this new sojourn may exact in toll.

Fidius toddled ahead of them on point. With some trepidation and a mouthful of bacon, together with some of his own grubs and lizard fare, he was also moved to music. As he sang, puffy balls of smoke popped from his nose.

"Fidius looks just like a chugging, green locomotive," remarked David.

"A green what?" wondered Peter.

"How silly of me," said David. "Of course you don't have the foggiest notion of what a locomotive is. Well, it's... a relic... from my past. Think of it as a forge on wheels. People in America, used to ride on them—back before jets outmoded the rairoads—"

"Railroads?" puzzled Fidius.

"What's a jet?" asked Niki.

"Where's America?" asked Peter.

"Oh my—now I've done it!" David exhaled. How does one explain the future? It may not even be the future. "Er, just think of jets and railroads as horseless carriages... for citizens of America. That's the country I come from."

Peter puzzled. "You mean these Americans are 'man' kind? You're a 'man' child —is that it?"

"Uh, yeah, sort of. Americans are people. I'm a people... I mean, I was... uh, I still am... except now I'm here. So I'm not American anymore. I'm a Mythle instead... or so I like to think. Er... see?" The boy stopped, at a loss for any word, except exasperation.

Both Peter and Niki looked grossly overwhelmed. Only the dove saw fit to add another note. "I see that whatever they are, these 'Americans' better watch where they sit, for a ride on a roaring forge might blaze some blistering tails!" The ensuing laughter drew a curious glare from Fidius, who led his train ever deeper into the rising Phantom's firs.

The Rime River Road drew ever narrower and more stubborn as it wrestled with the Spookwood. Wayfarers were few and far between at this juncture. Not at all like the more heavily traveled North Byway. Along their way, for the last two days, mottled groups of harried outlanders flocked past David's band: assorted farmers, drovers, herdsmen and hill tenders—all were town bound. The scattered populace of the high Middleshire barreled from the hilltop crofts like their frightened stock. For these refugees, the adventure was begun long ago, when the first dark shadow of Lust blighted their holding, which now lay fallow and forsaken. With families and possessions packed onto carts and backs these stooped souls trudged, with sullen and stern faces as rutted as the furrowed fields, from their humble farmsteads to the granite guarded gates of Sovereignton. There to find refuge, to serve, to fight, and to escape. Left behind was the sweat of past labors, so they might muster some stand against the death queen, thus salvaging some hope of redeeming their lot in life. Passing such dreary caravans struck a doleful note into the merrier melodies of the aspiring pilgrims. In each hollow face and gutted frame they passed, the malevolence of despair bared its ugly soul.

"My word," said David, "These poor folk are already beaten—and the first skirmish not even fought!"

"For these citizens, the battle has been ceaseless," Niki explained. "Day and night they reap life from a dying clod. Now they rally to Bia Bella in droves for the last great battle to be fought, sacrificing all they possess to preserve their meed. Remember these brave souls, painter—they are the reason my master has sent us on this quest."

For every retreating immigrant from the highlands, there was the stout heart —too proud, too stubborn, too rooted in his landholds to yield even a step. To these that remained, the very notion of surrender was worse than death. They could not desert the lives which these hills held—past, present, and to come. If their life's breath be left behind, their bones would mark the victory. Hence, readily and at their plots they stayed, to toil and till the soil—or Satan—whichever claim them first. To these stalwart countrymen, the pilgrims bid good luck and left with them their prayers. That would have to serve as repel to the deathless foe massing their way, a foe who respected neither pride not property—nay, not even prayer—and valued life even less.

Making good time, by noon of the following day, the pilgrims passed the last lowly homestall shuttered and completely abandoned of life. From there the Rime Road shrunk into nothing more than a crooked footpath pecking its way haphazzardly up through the Spookwood's lush timber. By nightfall, the thick fir forest closed in and tucked the trespassers into its needle-down bed. The pace slowed considerably on the ensuing day. Peter was proven correct, the remaining mountain trail was indeed too narrow and impassable for any but the most surefooted of ponies, or pilgrims. Pressing on, strengths waned with the slackening steps. Prior zealousness left them vulnerable to fatigue. How long had it been since anyone felt like singing? Upward they trekked, plodding along endlessly grueling switchbacks and timber-strewn crest and crag. As they ascended toward their hoarfrosted goal, the snow kept hauntingly at bay.

"Despite my stilted gait, we should nonetheless reach the Rime on the morrow," said Peter, panting heavily under his cumbersome load. "We'll find ourselves on Enduros' doorstep thereafter and should see my father ranging there."

"If'n the snow holds off," added Fidius, twitching his nose. All the while it appeared Sir Fidius had fared far better than anyone else on their climb—a happenstance the more youthful members of the expedition admitted with consternation. "Experience," tooted the serpent, gloating over his stamina. "Don't waste breath talkin' 'r singin'—like some a the more 'disciplined' members of our party!"

Peter could find no strength of wit to retaliate with.

"Conservin' yur breath?" puffed the lizard. The trio watched as a triumphant smoke ring wafted above Fidius' head, then dissipated. They continued to stare skyward as clouds descended upon them with the darkness.

"How ghastly the sky looks," shivered David, wrapping his arms around his ears. "It soughs and whines dreadfully. Is it a tornado?"

The stewing, grey sky whipped suddenly into black. Tall pine shadows blotted out the daylight. But there were more intensely oppressive shades. Bullying, black wisps hovered overhead bruising and crowding the gentler clouds.

"Those are no clouds!" clattered Niki, dunking into David's breastpocket and observing with dismay as the forest ceiling caved in.

"No!" screamed Peter, uncinching his pack and scrambling for cover.

Before he could finish, the menacing sky pommeled them from all directions, screeching, clawing, and lashing out with wicked wings into the pilgrims' midst. The giant beasts squealed fiercely in sadistic fervor as their swirling, swooping frenzy sent the pilgrim band a scattering.

"Condors!" shouted Fidius, wheezing with all his energy. "To the trees—it's our only hope!"

Peter ushered a stunned David into the safety of pines and juniper scrub just under a snarling scissor-swipe of condor talons. All the air was aflap; yet dwelling there on the path undaunted, was Fidius. The old, armor-crusted lizard stood alone with his javelin cocked boldly in the face of the diving black torrent.

"Fidius!" David's cry was lost in the screaming din of crakes and caws as a raining flock of massive condors poured down on top of the intrepid lizard.

Despite all of David's frantic pleading the pony boy held him fast. "There's nothing we can do, Davy—just protect ourselves and our own flesh, lest it be torn from our bones by those vultures."

"And who's to protect Fidius!" David cried. "You and your disciplined pony half can stay here and take root within the bush, but Sir Fidius risked his hide for mine once before, and I'll not do less for him now!"

The nerve-shattering squall of the vicious, giant birds magnified and jarred David's senses. Their repulsive carrion breath stifled the tall, trembling pines. Yet David did not cower. Breaking away from Peter, he rose to enter the bedlam.

"Painter—Wait!" Niki's urgent voice checked the boy in his tracks. "Look!"

Together they all watched, and caught their breaths, as the condor clouds began to lift—then disperse in a wide riveting arc. "They're retreating!" said David, gawking into the ejected flock.

When the ferment finally quelled, there betwixt the settling flurry of flayed feathers and dust, was Fidius, standing resolute amid a pile of cold, ruffled condors. The reptile knight, armor clad, and somewhat rumpled himself, was huffing with life just like a true gladiator. Billowing smoke and fire, he shook condor carcasses and singed down from his javelin, then waved it defiantly after the scathed scavengers.

"Unbelievable!" gasped David.

"It seems I was wrong; Sir Fidius has indeed rekindled the fires in his belly's hearth," said Peter sulking, and somewhat ashamed that he underestimated the reptile's capacities, while overplaying his own.

"Only you had the good sense to be cautious, Peter," soothed Niki, "and saved our necks from those witch-wraiths. The grimlings were Lust's to be sure. "The tiny dove pointed into the swirling tempest above. In its eye was a singularly large, loathsome long-necked harpy, soaring in erratic dips and darts, often bumping blindly into his black brethren. Upon his back rode the demonic, blue apparition. "That bird of prey is Odios. His devil master, Horros, gives him rein—Lust's gargoyles both!"

Peter's head shook with admiration and wonder. "To think Sir Fierce was at their mercy—and won out!"

"No!" cried David. "Look! He's failing... He's been wounded!" Without further delay he and Peter rushed from behind their pine shelter.

"Perhaps we should stay undercover," mentioned Niki. "Condors still soar overhead..." But none heard the dove's caution except the fir.

David and Peter were already at Fidius' side. "Are you hurt badly old fellow?" asked David, his voice trembled with concern as he and Peter scanned the lizard's steely hide for any new, unwanted holes or ruts.

"I can't see..." moaned Fidius, who was crawling about the ground on hands and knees. "...I can't see!"

"Oh my word!" exclaimed David. "You've been blinded!"

"Like a post, Dang nabbit! An' I'll stay that a way too, 'til I find my bifocals. 'Fraid I lost 'em in the tussle... Mind lendin' a hand... or an eye?"

Smiles and laughter lent themselves to the search for Fidius' glasses; competing with the clacking of the spiraling, death clouds. With their attention so focused on the ground, the wanton sky lay neglected.

"Above you—It's a ruse! The vultures return!" chattered Niki—alas, it was too late. The steel-clawed curtain dropped swift again upon them. From the forest, Niki flew fast to her friends, but to no avail under the onslaught of this new, more craven, assault. Regrouped and ravenous, Horros directed his bloodthirsty scourge with unrelenting ferocity, raking eye and throat with mortal condors' claws and jaws. Like snared voles, the pilgrims scraped and kicked vainly. They were helplessly trapped, and with no hope of reaching the beckoning safety of the pine cover. This time the pilgrims dug in to stand against the scavengers' smashing brunt.

David brandished his paint satchel like a leather mace and discovered much to the dismay of the ambushers, that it made a surprisingly potent weapon. Lashing out with tempered discipline this time, Peter's steel-edged hooves and rage proved formidable in fending off a whole brood of rakehells. Many a condor wing and pate cracked and toppled under the pony boy's bone-stomping blows.

Repulsed only temporarily though, the pilgrims soon found their foes' numbers too overpowering and their own strength dwindling—and their fate, inevitable. Fidius managed to recover his bifocals just in time to see a monstrous set of blood-stained talons engulf him. His rasping cries for help were lost in the foray's turmoil, and his fiery breath was exhausted to an ineffective flicker.

"Fidius!" David looked in helpless horror as the giant condor sank its vice grip into the green gladiator and lofted above the havoc below. "They've got Fidius—somebody do something!" he shouted, lowering his own defenses to reach the lizard. A black wing swiped him completely off his feet, and the boy grimaced sharply as the cold, packed ground reached up to bruise him more.

Peter crouched in a tangled swarm of screeching vultures and all further efforts to resist seemed destined to failure. Everything was in chaos. Fidius disappeared into the churning cyclone of talons. From David's side, Niki shot skyward attempting to divert the creature of its prey. Alas, with too much success, she fell victim to one of the other lurching predators. Its gaping jaw snapped shut on the doves tail feathers and down she plummeted.

With all his strength, the pony boy sprang like lightning from his knot and galloped under Niki's fall to brace her in his tight grasp. In a deep faint, but with her frail chest heaving, Peter announced, "She's alive—by inches only—but alive!" Then, in a whisper added, "Not that it matters now..."

Still, the words were a reviving gust of life for David, who hugged the ground in desperate defense against the slashing, blood-fowl. A chilling, pain-wracked wail split the air as Fidius sank his javelin deep into his captor's vulnerable underbelly. Still, the talons' grip held, though its body be sapped of life. And there Fidius hung, not falling—but worse. Another of the horde's scavengers vied for the honor of the kill. Its lunging cusps gnawed and gnashed into Fidius' tail and threatened to tear it out by the roots, sending what was left of the poor reptile, plunging to an even more tormenting death.

Below, David could not help but wonder how useful some of Constantio's knights would be right now, or a sword or spear. Even then, without the strength to wield them, no weapon would serve them, be they sword and spear, or satchel and shoe. "Come and get me, you bone-licking flesh pickers!" weeped David in a craze. The relentless pelting and howling became unbearable. The ravaged boy pressed his ears tight, shut his eyes, and prepared for the worst.

Fidius' despairing calls for help were ceaseless—but to what purpose? Who was left to help them? Then, David detected something different, something in the condors' clamor. Their incessant squall was not as victory sounds—but the trill of terror. It was the whimpering whine of the panic-stricken. David felt the gale-swept force of beating wings wane. The reeking, fowl-rotted air cleared.

As the deafening current eased, David dared to open an eye and peek down the trail. He was shocked right out of his shoes to be greeted, not by condor talons, but paws—bear paws! The big, brash and bushy bear's feet were set on two burly black legs, supporting a monumental, white hulk of a bruin body clothed in nothing more cumbersome than a woolen cowl. Powerful and predominant, there was no mistaking the colossus goat tender—it was Pandas—swishing his pine-sized shepherd's crook to and fro at the brutish birds, culling them from the sky as though shooing flies. The condors' pleas for mercy were welcome relief to David's ears. And his eyes relished with delight as the witch's flock dispersed and shrank away. As the hectic swarm thinned, David caught sight of Peter and Niki sprawled on the blood-soaked trail. The centaur's legs were swollen and his russet coat lathered. Niki primped over her defrocked fantail. Shaken, stunned, and scraped—both were nonetheless sound and fit. They stared with David at the spectacle unfolding before them.

Discarding his staff, Pandas was busily wresting fleeing condors from the air and plucking their feathers out; then tossing the naked birds away on the ground as though stocking a larder for winter.

At the giant's feet scooted Milly, the humble little, apron and cloud-clad shepherd girl. She determinedly swat at the condors with her broom. "Shoo! Shoo—

get away, you nasty birds!" she scolded. And once they had finally fled, she tidily began to sweep up all the feathers which strewn the forest floor.

Having no more birds to pluck, Pandas gently helped the pilgrims to their feet and examined their bruises and bites, licking them each just to be sure their wounds were not serious. Thus assured, the bruin cyclops proceeded to inflict further insult on the crippled buzzards by popping the plucked fowls into his mammoth mouth like peeled wildberrys.

"Mercy!" squeaked Niki, quite sickened enough already. The sight of so many cropped cousins, even condors, being devoured without the blessing of a baking, revolted the dove. She hugged the lining of David's pocket.

"We owe you our lives... uh, Pandas?" thanked David, attempting to offer his hand. But the big bruin paid no attention. He squat down on the roadside and supped in aloof modesty, like an over-stuffed teddy bear.

"Pandas didn't save you, mister..." peeped Milly, looking up from her sweeping, "...he did."

David's gaze followed the girl's finger as it pointed to a nearby pine stump, upon which sat the shaggy faun, Liberato, completely immersed in playing his flute. Only now did David's ears pick up on the blaring racket emanating from the goatherd's pipes.

"Did you think a few nasty birds could make all that awful noise? It was my brother's music that drove those pests away. They've plagued us and our flock too. Lucky for us that their ears are not as attuned to Liberato's songs as his sheep."

"Pah-tooey!" Pandas' gargantuan head shook vigorously as the gentle giant spat out a mouthful of plucked condors.

"You foolish loaf!" bleated the goat man as he bounded over to the group on his hooved lower half. The mute flute was tucked mercifully under his armed upper half. "Could've tol' you those fly-beaks would rank—even for your grisly tastes. Maybe that toad over in the hackberry would be more toothsome. My partner likes toad leg!" Liberato spoke aside to David from under his rose-tinted glasses, apparently undaunted by the feat just accomplished. "Say, my horn's still sizzlin', wanna hear some more slick licks?" He scratched his tangled hair perpetually as though strumming a lyre. "Say—you're that dawg's boy, aren't you? The three-

388

headed one... the dawg I mean." Liberato tugged his goatee in recognition of his dinner guest in the wood, while completely unmindful of them during the lavish banquet at Bia Bella only days earlier. David was about to acknowledge the faun goatherd, when a desperate shout broke in.

"Hey! Put me down, Gol' durn it!" hollered the familiar wheeze. Let go a my legs, you claw-pawed clump! Condors come back—take me too!"

"Stop! Please stop!" shouted David, rushing hastily to Pandas' feet. "That's no 'toad', that's Fidius—our protector!"

"Well don't that curl your wool, Pandas," blared Liberato, knitting his bushy brows at such a sight. You was so indulgently stuffin' that bear belly at Constantio's food fest, you don't recognize the king's lockup?"

Fidius dangled upside down in front of Pandas' wide open mouth, like a succulent prawn. "Ex-lockup if you don't mind!" smoked Fidius. "I'm a dang nab knight—an' don't forget it! Not that it matters... right now I'd settle fur bein' a plain ol' land-lickin' lizard again."

"Tsk," murmured Milly sardonically as she shooed the giant off his feet so she might sweep under them, lest they track across her forest carpet.

Fidius dropped into a green, armor-clanking heap, and was promptly swept away with the rest of the pine needles, conifers, and condor feathers by the broom-wielding dryad.

"Dang nabbit!" fumed the distraught lizard, scrambling to his feet grunting and fondling his tender tail. "Git away from me, you Gol' durn wench! First that fowl-chokin' gorilla salvages my skin—then tries ta pluck it fur hisself... as if my legs was nothin' but plumage! Them black, gizzard-necks would only have my tail; but this... this two-toned chunk craves too much—him and his midge maiden!"

"Don't be too mad at them, Fidius," laughed David, as much as he could under the circumstances. "We might all have been plucked and noshed had Liberato not happened by with pipe in hand."

"Haw!" nodded the goat man in a show of false modesty. Then pursed his lips as if threatening to blow his flute again. "We didn't just 'happen' by you all...We live here now."

The faun's news confused David. "But, isn't your home down in the Middle Meadows? How can a shepherd raise sheep on mountainside's slopes and chasms?"

"Easy," tooted Liberato, "instead a sheeps, we raise goats—mountain goats!" Then, the goatherd's rose-lit complexion turned ashen, and his fond face became drawn with fright as he spoke. "The Mid' Meadows have changed since we last met up. Our crofts were riddled with goblins and spooky, sheep-scarin' critters of all make 'n' manner. The pastoral life got ta be a hassle for us down there—hard, hostile... no place for placid, flock-tendin' folks like us."

"Sovereignton's strong gates are spread wide open in welcome relief for war-racked refugees," Peter began, brushing his lathered fetlocks until his coat glistened to match the fermenting glitter in his eyes. "They're trudging past us in droves to the city for safety, just like lemmings. Are you not inclined to join them behind His Highness' protective walls?"

"Us! What for—we ain't mice!" Liberato bleated in distaste, then hastened to add, "'Course, we ain't brawlers neither." The goat man spat through the reed of his flute. "We're flock tenders plain an' simple. We done tried runnin' from foxes, 'n' vultures, 'n' vermin—that's why we're up here exposin' our humble, bareskin hides to mountains' mean streaks instead a baskin' in balmier lowland climes. Strife grazes those clover-coated meadows in the Mids'. It makes no sense ta scoot back down there again, right where all the ruckus is. We peaceful sorts don't take ta violence—"

"Peaceful?!" Peter neighed at the very suggestion. "I know some condors that would argue that point with you, crofter!" The pony boy turned an eye toward Pandas, only to find the carcasses either eaten, or swept away in a feather-dusty cloud by Milly. "For someone trying to avoid the fray, you seem victoriously unsuccessful."

Liberato lifted the rose-tinted glasses from his nose to scan the path for any trace of disarray. Grunting approval to Milly, he shook a shaggy smile to the skeptical pony. "Oh, that... Well, them buzzards do get my goat—if you know what I mean. An' my partner does like ta put the feed bag on; an' he's hard ta cook for too, right, Milly? Quite the little homemaker, my sis'... Say, you're quite a hunk a horseflesh there yourself, yearlin'. Yep—make some mare or maid a fine provider. You 'trothed yet? Ever thought a goat herdin'? We could use a good hand... hoof too! Milly's taken quite a shine to you—I can tell—right, Sis? She's good at groomin' too—real good. You look like you could use a good curryin'..."

From far down the trail Milly toiled diligently under the gradually settling cloud of condor dust. Just the sight of the undainty dryad with dishpan complexion was enough to bring an abrupt end to Peter's dialogue with the mangy faun. The pony boy went discreetly back to his own brushing.

Liberato then retracted his grin and tugged at his wooly, red hair, while musing over his plight. "Guess we ain't been too lucky up here either, now that I think on it. We ain't avoided fowl 'r foxes neither. Strange ta find 'em both so far north. Can't imagin' 'em followin' our flimsy flock all this way... an' this bushwhack's got me buffaloed. You folks don't got nothin' of interest to 'em... no goats, 'r sheeps —just a dinky old pigeon—"

"I happen to be a dove!" cheeped Niki, darting out of David's blouse to twitter emphatically at the goat man's big, ruddy nose. "And if you would comb the wool out of your eyes and remove those dark glasses long enough to look around in the light, maybe you'd notice what spurs condors and vermin into the Snowmass, scratching on Lord Enduros' very threshold. It's not pigeons—it's Lust! The pit queen's general was born upon that horde's wings as surely as their talons clipped ours!"

"I see," said the goat man raising his shaggy brows from behind the rosey, dark glasses. "Some madwoman is attackin' yours 'n' mine with her buzzards so's to get at our land lord? Are Pandas' munchies so scary, or the earth's honcho so frail, that he's tamed by a few tin-eared birds—Haw!" Liberato flourished his flute and shook his shrub head.

Niki's little head shook too, in fearful contemplation. "No, Lust would not send condors against Enduros... nor you, except for mutton. But against us—or more precisely..." Niki swallowed her words as her sad, pink eyes met David's innocent blues; then, after a moment's pause, surveyed the ground where a pair of angel wing-down slippers graced the hazardous pathway.

"Blamed buzzards are after somethin', I gotta admit," scratched Liberato, squatting primly upon a stump. "Just like that blamed vixen. Thought I left her lamb-bone theivin' skin far back in the Commons. Somethin' about my flock has struck her fancy—spooked my poor woolies all over the piney she did!"

Niki's white face paled. "Fox?... It wasn't your music that stampeded the flock?"

Liberato bleated in agitation. "Haw—that's a laugh! My critters are too stupid ta bolt at a little mellow tootin'. They's more cultivated than them uncouth wring-necks." The goat man pounded his fist in his hand. "The vixen's back for more a my mutton—no doubt about it. She's bein' paid for it too—and not with bones!"

"Preposterous!" hooted Peter, unwilling to say more, yet not about to muffle his opinion. Niki was not so shocked.

David couldn't refrain from asking, "Why would anyone have to pay a fox for stealing goats—especially now. The gal's already got the goat she wants... doesn't she?"

"Not goats..." said Liberato, "...lambs! That scamp stole a passle of 'em from me in the Meadows—an' now she's tailed us here. But she'll not get my goats—I'm tellin' you!" Liberato bounded onto his cloven feet and promenaded over to David, jerking his goat beard and shaking a pointed finger toward him, and Niki, who seemed particularly interested in the flocker's story. "Mind, I can't say why, but I know what I saw... An' I saw that mule-eared prince payin' the vixen off with honey sacks, and salt pork and bacon—payin' her for services rendered! An' the thievin' services she rendered was booty of some sort—you can count on that!"

"Vito!" Fidius growled, baring some of his few remaining teeth. "That mongrel dropping has the scent of home in his nostrils!"

"The mule lad is well traveled to be sure," mulled Niki. "I wonder what other vagabonds have migrated north on condor wings... and if it's painter's wings, or something else, that lures them here?"

"With that prince of asses about, you can be sure there's devilry afoot—Yes sirree!" Just the mention of Vito's name had Fidius so ired and fired that he had quite forsaken his tender behind. Peter flicked his tail at imaginary flies at the very recollection.

David's curiosity, and alarm, grew. "I can't imagine any goat that important," he said, so naively he wanted to believe it.

"It wasn't for any goat, or common lamb, they hired her out—face it!" Thoughts of his friend, Christen, pervaded the centaur's mind.

"Maybe it was neither!" cooed Niki. "All booty does not graze in flocks. And a thief, having hit the jackpot once, is he not likely to steal again for greater gain? Mayhap the fox was paid, not for services past, but for the future rendered."

"But if this is the fox which took Christen away, Niki, what prize would top it?" David wondered.

The dove perched upon the boy's feet. "I should say there must be, painter; or so it would seem to the mule, and the fox, and the condors—and the lordess of black!"

The conversation had begun to stray as far as Liberato was concerned. He bleated once, then pulled out his flute and spit into it again. "Well, what's more important than one wooly, is a whole flock. The day's growin' impatient, an' I got a gaggle of goats ta round up. Pandas is givin' me funny looks, and Milly's wearin' out her broom here. Been nice talkin' to you folks—So long!"

"We'll help you," offered David, before Niki could halt him. "It's the least we can do in exchange for all your aid. But when your flock is gathered, we must be on our way too—right, Niki?" The dove contained herself and nodded good naturedly, only glad that her companion had not totally forgotten his prior commitments.

"Say, that's right—you was lookin' for somethin' before when we met up. Find it yet?"

"No, but we're hopeful," smiled David as the pilgrims accompanied the goat man a short way down the path.

"Whatever happened to that three-headed dawg a yours? Would a made a fine sheeper... Better plug your ears; gotta start tootin' so my goats know where we are."

"Once they know, which way do they run?" asked Peter, shielding his sharp ears from the faun's shrill music.

"Say, you got a fine sense a humor for a young colt. Milly likes a feller with wit. Care to stay for supper? Oughta be a special treat tonight—no mutton! Milly can work magic on broasted buzzard. What say?"

Peter said nothing more. After the last goat was accounted for, the young centaur gathered his supply cache onto his back and led the way as the troupe retraced their spiraling steps up the pine and dusk-lined footpath ever closer to the pale citadel of Revrenshrine.

CHAPTER 33

The ensuing dawn's light waxed the slate sky then melted into evening without sight or scent of the Rime River, which lapped the base of Enduros' mountain shrine. The trail steepened below the pilgrims' stiff, aching legs; but they trudged onward, their spirits unflagging. As their pace slackened, their wounds ripened under the sunless winter chill.

Fidius fell behind as he put the finishing touches on a sturdy walking stick fashioned during his past night watch. "Whitlin's sort of a hobby a mine," he puffed, proudly displaying his handiwork.

"Pinewood's easier to ply than Ill-timber's, right, Sir Woodcarver!" said David from up ahead, recalling his friend's bravery in the rose garden.

Peter caught his breath, then looked back at the old lizard and chided, "I hope your pine leg will provide you with pace, Sir Fierce. Darkness gains on us with each dragging step."

"Better save yur own strength fur marchin' in my tracks, li'l' colt!" sputtered Fidius as he whisked up the trail and thrust his staff into the centaur's hand. "As a tad, I was known as Fidius the Fast, so don't pull up on my account. 'Sides, this here crook ain't mine—it's yurs! The northern chill can be harsh to tender yearlin's an' their mendin' joints."

Peter's pride held the walking stick at bay. His face still seemed lost under the lizard's more valorous showing during the condor attack. He could not readily accept the further humbling of a crutch, although his hock did ache bitterly since their encounter. And the additional weight of his pack did press upon his discipline.

"A good solid cane would provide you with some clout, Peter," David pointed out, "to smite the predators and picaroons that cramp your style—and legs."

The pony boy responded with silence as he leaned onto the stalk. Then he wielded it as a rod, and jabbed it towards Fidius. An easing smile etched across his face. "Not one leg, but arms I have now. Tell me, Sir Swift, have you other surnames swimming in your illustrious past that we should know about?"

A tired gout of flame escaped as the old lizard chuckled and rubbed his caloused feet. "To tell you the truth, li'l' Pete, I never did quite live up ta those stories... Fact is, I started most of 'em myself, yes sirree! But I'd be plumb honored ta be known by you fellers as Fidius, the 'Friend'."

"Ho! Well said, Sir Friend. Comrades we are, but fools we were to continue on after our attack," remarked David, kneading his calves as the companions rested by the wayside. "Though my feet feel pampered, my legs are aching numb. Had I a stout pine rod like Peter's I would say fiddle to the fowls and use it for warding off these devilish cramps. We would've been wiser to stay at Liberato's, wait out the storm, and recuperate before proceeding on so soon."

"My tail's draggin' too, li'l' knight," reminded Fidius. "But some journeys ain't meant to be comfortable, an' we can't out wait winter. Like I tell my own boy time 'n' time again, nobody ever progresses who sits out rough weather lickin' their soft spots." Fidius twitched his snout and stomped to his feet. "Now then, night and that sky are lookin' kinda heady. They're gonna dump on us sooner 'r later, and I for one would like ta be on the other side a the Rime when it does—Yes sirree. Somehow the snow don't seem so cold on Enduros' hill and the night, not so thick 'n' dark. You fellers can wait here an' mend—I think I smell water up ahead."

"That leather fossil must stoke up all his pep in that furnace-lined belly of his," sighed Peter with envy. The young pony boy was beginning to lather again. "I'd be willing to pitch camp here and now, but that old frog is right about the Rime's high side. Besides, the farther away we get from that goatherd and his sister, the better! I'm anxious to cross Enduros' border and put this Spookwood behind us. I'm sure its master is expecting us, and has a reception party on the way."

"I'm wondering about our welcome on that bank myself," peeped Niki, to no one in particular. "After all, who knows how the king of the hill will take to trespassers. Enduros may not like the hand we drew for him in this match." David shared his dove's anxiety, yet was glad to hear her twittering once more. She had remained unusually quiet and pensive since their encounter yesterday. It wasn't until a lizard's wheeze rippled down the trail to tickle her spirits that she finally sang out again.

"The Rime! C'mon!" announced Fidius from far ahead. The others quickly rushed to join him.

The companions arrived on the mossy banks of the wide, mountain stream to find the elderly lizard basking his blistered feet and tender tail in the invigorating eddies of water which, to David's surprise, was very unimposing—no river this, but a timid, trickling stream.

Peter chuckled at the sight of Fidius. "So, Sir Swift has feet of clay after all—how edifying!"

"Isn't it cold?" asked David.

"Nah, not for our Sir Fierce," smirked Peter with delight. "He is part frog, remember!

"Perhaps we should hurry on across and make camp," suggested Niki as she flittered over the gurgling gill and lighted on the north bank. "It's beginning to snow."

"The li'l' dove's right; we mustn't tarry. Darkness is sneakin' up on us too." Fidius splashed on over, pausing in midstream to point the way. "Looky, not even knee deep!"

"Better let me ferry you across anyway," said Peter, offering his back to David. "Never can be too careful with your footing in these creeks."

"But your pack..."

"C'mon, hurry, Davy. My discipline may be a fair-weather friend, but I'm still in excellent condition." Hence, with David straddling his shoulders, Peter stepped into the gentle, lapping water of the Rime.

Then, winter arrived—like a cold steel sledge-hammer. The sky suddenly split wide open, unleashing a winteresque maelstrom which pelted the pilgrims with volleys of hard, heavy shots of slicing ice pellets. Hail and snow cascaded upon them like an avalanche of pale stones, trapping the pilgrims between two ever distant shores. From some secret, sinful place, a hurricane wind pounced on the two boys; and in the same breath, sucked them away in the swirling crush of the current's undertow.

Fidius clung to the north bank, looking helplessly into Niki's welting eyes. She screeched in dismay as the placid brook swelled into a torrential wave of foam and froth, with Peter and David sinking in its savage curl. David gulped for air. "Peter!... I can't breathe... I think I'm drowning!"

"Hold onto my neck!" The pony boy gagged as he strained to keep his head above the whelming whitewater. Jagged rocks slashed at his legs while he struggled to find a firm foothold on the tumultuous river bottom. Peter held to his pine staff for support; but, for the moment at least, neither brook nor its bed would relent. The centaur winced as the jutting shale bit into his hamstring in one particularly hateful, heaving eddy. The loose floor slid away and Peter, together with his pack— and pilgrim—were washed away far into the Rime's ravenous gorge.

With Niki's help, Fidius had ambled onto the slippery north bank. Then, without waiting even for his breath, the gallant lizard scampered downstream after his comrades. Niki darted haphazardly overhead just out of reach from the rampaging river. "Over here, Fidius! I can see them—here!"

"Don't worry, li'l' dove, this allygater'll pull 'em out..." With that, Fidius dove into the chopping, growling rapids. The merciless snow thrust down in blustery white sheets, nearly knocking the dauntless dove into its deathbed too. Withal, Niki continued to hover tenaciously; frantic, but faithfully resolute, she resisted winter's most severe blows. As eternity dragged on for her, she paced the turbulent air, barely able to see beyond her own orange beak. How long had it been since Fidius disappeared? It seemed like hours since anyone could be seen above the scrambled water's surface. Niki's hopes sank as surely as her companions had. The tempest howled in salvos of maddening mockery. "Niki!... Niki... *gasp*!" But wait— that was no blizzard. Blizzards don't wheeze—"

"Over here!...Can you see us, li'l' dove?" whiffed the rustic voice. Niki's face warmed to melt the freezing snow when she saw through the squall to the north bank. There, on its icy edge, clung Fidius. Laying next to him was Peter—and David. But as Niki drew nearer, glee turned to gloom. The dove studied the two soggy, frost-coated heaps beside Fidius, who was silent. Earnestly the lizard pounded David's chest with his fist. Niki's tears froze on her pallid cheeks as she landed on the boy's forehead and examined his hoary blue face for any sign of life. There was none to be found. A cold quiver shook the ground she stood upon. Hold on—it wasn't ground—but boy beneath her.

David's chest heaved—and his eyes popped open. Niki bolted into the air in a fright, then settled down to hug her teeny wings around as much of her painter as she could. "Oh, painter... please don't scare me like that—ever! I thought you were a cold fish for sure."

"Boy Howdy! I'm beginning to feel like a hunk of flotsam for all the water I've swallowed of late." Water dribbled from David's mouth as he sat up and coughed. "I'm okay, Niki... thanks to Sir Fidius." The lizard was presently too busy reviving Peter to acknowledge. Niki and David both watched with swelling joy as warm, flushing colors returned to the centaur's cheeks too.

"I declare, Sir Fidius—you're a full-fledged alligator for sure! The way you swam after and snatched us from that crazy creek..." Peter lauded his lizard rival as he regained his feet, shook the frigid water from his hide, and tested his hamstring under weight. "Great galloping horse feathers—I thought we were knocking on the lord's gate for sure this time! That Enduros throws a bitter cool reception at his allies, doesn't he! Maybe trespassers rankle him. If we don't find my father soon, I think I shall be inclined to cross back into the spook and condor woods again—for safety's sake."

"Not me," said David firmly. "One crossing like that is quite enough to last me. The only god I've ever met greeted his guests with a good dousing—it was Isolato. This was his water we forged, not Enduros'. The old sea badger is as cantankerous as ever!" David peered into the rapidly receding river half expecting Isolato's bug-eyed spider fish, Perilgullum, to spit at him—but was not the least bit disappointed when it didn't. "If you don't believe me, ask Niki."

Niki folded her wings and stared out at the peacefully rolling brook behind them. "True, Isolato is crotchety, but he would never imperil Abraxus' father. Futhermore, we have done nothing to irk this stream's sire. Nor would his brother, Enduros, be so infuriated by our presence."

"Yeah, well somebody's sure piqued at us!" observed David. "Mother Nature doesn't act so... so unnatural, not like that creek. And I can't imagine any mad witch stirring up Isolato's waters, nor treading so blatantly on Enduros' mountain."

"Granted, but Lust is certainly beyond anyone's imagination." Niki dipped into David's wet, woolen breastpocket as the snowstorm howled around them. "Brrr... We need some warm, dry clothes. Now that Phantom Forest is behind us, we've the mountains to cope with, and their salutation stabs deeper than any hail in Spookwood."

"Best set up camp right away," wheezed Fidius. "I'll git us a fire kindled afore this blizzard finishes what the brook begat." The lizard had abandoned the river bank in favor of a nearby clearing. In a shallow alcove he busied himself constructing a plump woodpile, which he promptly torched with one billowing breath, then fanned the sizzling flames with his resilient tail. "Good thing the ol' belly burners ain't water-logged; won't be needin' any matches this a way."

"That's good," said Peter. His cocky voice hung lead heavy as he sauntered up from he brook's bank. "Because we've got no matches. And as for dry clothes,

400

and hot food... the river owns them now. It has run away with our supply cache, and unless we all develop furnace guts like Sir Fierce's, we will likely freeze to death tonight... or starve the next." The pony boy's constraint withered into chills. "All we have left is the pouch slung over David's shoulder—and I'm afraid his paints can supply neither shelter, warmth, or nourishment."

No one spoke. They could only peer glumly into the ice-edged night. There were no miracles to be seen, only a sleepy stream of water, mysteriously placid now —but not its brother, the wind. It squalled and vented in ever mounting tenacity. Its bitter, bellowing breaths battered the temperature to its knees, and snuffed out all but the faintest flicker of hope.

In the wake of such a dire turn of events, the pilgrims huddled together around Fidius' blazing fire, which provided temporary respite from the unrelenting Northwind's blasts. Yet it blew something not so fleeting, and even more merciless, into their camp—despair.

David wrung the river from his satchel, then carefully hung it and his canvases up to dry. His teeth chattered and his knees knocked. The only two things that weren't frostbitten were his feet. They remained snug and warm as toast inside his weatherproof shoes. Fidius mealed on some of his grubs, while the others agreed to nurse their hunger before tasting the lizard's vittles. Each chewed on their thoughts for the present and little was said during these first few depressing moments. Someone mentioned that now everyone was puffing their breath like Fidius, but no one laughed, except maybe the trees. The tall, snow-coated firs loomed over them like the tormenting ghosts of Phantom Forest, bending their white-sheathed boughs in a hauntingly depressing ritual. Then, from their midst, out stalked Fidius, presumably to gather more firewood. Insulated with thick layers of reptile hide wrapped around his oven belly, Fidius appeared not only immune from the cold, but stimulated by it.

"Most remarkable toad I've ever seen," mulled Peter, completely without expression.

"At least someone of us will survive to mourn," said David, figuring even morbid talk was better than none at all.

Maybe Niki thought so too, for she flapped out of David's pocket, punching the chilly air with grim, deliberate wing strokes. "And this alcove will be our hoary grave if we linger here! As soon as everyone is dry, we must seek out shelter of some kind."

"A cave maybe," proclaimed Peter, his glint revived. "Father and I often passed coverts in these mountains. If only we could find one now."

"No need ta worry," panted Fidius waddling back into the clearing, his arms full of wood. "I think I've found a humdinger of a hutch, yes sirree—it's a real find!"

Moments later, with strength and hope rekindled, the pilgrims filed into the incessant dark, wintry night to see for themselves what Fidius had unearthed. With torchlight to warm their way against the obstinate northern wafts, the band soon found themselves in a wind-broken grove of evergreens. Fidius had vanished, only to reappear poking his head from out a huge, hollowed, weather-worn hemlock trunk.

"How do like it?" Fidius glowed, obviously proud of himself for being so useful. "There's a cavity under here, tunneled between the roots. Some critter musta burrowed it, then skedaddled. But it 'pears unoccupied now, no sleepin' bears 'r nothin'."

"It's not exactly a cave," said Peter.

"No, but it's just as roomy, and drier—an' a durn sight warmer than where yur standin'. C'mon in an' see fur yurself."

"Niki also was disappointed—and hesitant. "Good heavens, Fidius! It's dead and rotted... and it reeks!"

"A might ripe and mildewy, surely," mumbled Fidius, crinkling his long nose, "but it's here, an' it's comfortable... an' it's all we got. Now, do you want ta come in an' live with the stink, 'r stay outside and freeze under pine-scented ice?"

"It does seem adequate shelter," observed David, sticking his head into the hollow, then urged his heavy-stepping feet down into Fidius' find. Peter shadowed after with no further coaxing. Niki was the last to enter—and when she did, it was with grave reservations.

The blizzard wailed even louder now. In the blinding snow no one had taken time to notice the heart-shaped scar painted deep into the rutted tree bark.

Nor did they spot the large worm-haired cat napping serenely in its stark, frozen branches, her stone skin immune to both the nettles and the Northwind. "All you've got, did you say?..." whistled the icy hemlock boughs as they parted in the wind to reveal a layer of ebony, "... Indeed, it shall be quite more than you expect!"

CHAPTER 34

"The air in here is so heavy and fulsome I think I'm going to be sick!" David gagged as the despondent band hunched together inside the tree hollow gasping for breath.

Peter scoffed, even as he swallowed his tongue. "You'll not want for fresh air outside, but would you fill your lungs with ice? Sir Fierce was right; survival is more sensible—even if it revolts you. It's better to be fetid and warm... brrr, not that I'm roasting in this bole! Better toss another dry log on your fire, Sir Fierce. At least you have plenty of dead wood here."

Turning a most unlizardly livid green, Fidius knelt, panting and out of breath, shaking hand and fist at the fire he attempted to build. "Don't make no sense... Gol' durn fire 'pears to lack air and logic both. In spite a my huffin' 'n' puffin' it burns stale as turned curd, givin' no whiff a warmth 'r comfort."

"A most unsavory place this follicle of yours, Sir Fidius," Niki shivered, her beak clicking endlessly, and her wing tips tinged with blue, "suitable for crawling things and lichen too, but not the likes of us."

"No matter what anybody says, Enduros is the instigator of our woes," Peter grumbled. "This is his hill—it can be no other! My father always said he was eccentric... had his head out in the snow too long I suppose. Let's face it, that crusty old curmudgeon doesn't want us here!"

"Nay, 'tis not that 'crusty old curmudgeon'..." A bone-tingling voice welled up from deep inside the tree's confines. "...'tis I who does not wish it!"

The gloom-edged words grabbed the pilgrims and lured them farther into the sinister antrum, down through the winding, honeycombed linings of the pulp vesseled cavity. And there, at its rotting root base, they beheld him with gaping, glassy eyes. Trussed in a gnarled web of root shackles was a wooly-haired boy, with lamb ears and a round lamb nose. His eyelids were shut, and a pair of gangly lamb legs dangled limp from his wooden bindings. David recognized the boy instantly from Cin's visions. Peter was the first to cry out at the sight of his friend.

"Christen!" For just a moment none could move. Then shock gave way to joy, and flooded all their eyes.

All except Niki. The dove saw something else in this shaft—and it terrified her. She glanced at David's shoes. He stood motionless, unable to move.

Peter surged toward his lamb comrade. "It's a miracle! My Prince, my friend... Or are you a dream?"

"Wait!" squawked Niki. "Something is wrong—terribly wrong!" Niki studied the lamb prince's expressionless face as Peter embraced him, ignoring the dove's warning.

"Christen! Christen, it's Peter... Don't you know me?" The lamb lay stone cold still as the pony boy fought earnestly to wrestle him loose from his bonds.

David stood lead-footed and aghast. "Niki, I don't understand; why doesn't he move? He just spoke to us... didn't he?"

"I think not, painter. My holy brother, the prince, appears to be under some strong enchantment. He has a most odd color about him—as one possessed. We must get out of here quickly. 'Tis not mildew which fouls the air, but the stench of death... We're standing in the doorway to Luhrhollow!"

"Git back, li'l' colt!" roared Fidius. The lizard had been long licking the air suspiciously with his tongue, and now stepped suddenly foward to cut at the knotted roots. "Let me bust the prince loose an' be rid a this durn dung hole at once! I was daft ta step into it!"

At the first slice of Fidius' lance, the roots cried out in pain. Its green, bile-scented sap gushed from the piercing rifts. Peter and David tugged furiously, but to no end. The bleeding roots would not release their grip on the lamb. With even more intensity, Fidius hacked savagely at the pulpy tethers—all for naught. No sooner would he rend one limb, than two would sprout to replace it. Each severed tentacle so rejuvenated, would rebuff the lizard's most efficient clefts, and further entwine its captive. Each stab of the javelin drew forth an agonizing wail of pain, erupting from the hollow and shaking even the outermost branches. This was no dream, but a disheartening nightmare, into which David's band had walked. Fidius' fire was useless against such a scourge, and it left the weary lizard gasping for air. Peter and David were equally sapped of their strength.

"The tree's got him, Niki!" screamed David. "It's hopeless!"

"More than hopeless, pilgrim... purrr, it's suicidal," mewed the malevolent cat wail. Prrrr... Now the Ill-timber has you too!" The feline laughed smugly in a guttural growl. The voice of misery was poised on a branch above the lamb, and from under its press crawled the rock cat, Vexpurra. Her creeping, snapdragon hair hissed and the stone-skinned kitten crouched as if to pounce. The pilgrims stepped backward. A response which brought gloating purrs of satisfaction to Vexpurra. "Your blundering luck has disturbed my sleep, prrrr..." The slinking creature yawned, displaying an awesome set of wicked, yellow fangs. "How fortunate the mutton brat sleeps so soundly. So, you've found Constantio's kit—you think! Prrrr... And do you also think it was by chance you came into my haunt?" The she-cat licked and primped her sand wings. "Now that you're here, just how do you intend to leave with your sheep-haired churl?" Vexpurra's green eyes smoldered with gratification and her tail romped wickedly with the rapidly regenerating roots. Her matted, worm hair hissed menacingly and danced like a self-assured black widow toying with her entrapped victims. Like moths on a sticky web, the pilgrims stood paralyzed, lame with horror.

Then, moved to action by some unexplained prod, David shouted in defiance, right into Vexpurra's sensitive ears. "How? I'll show you how, you... you worm-rotted, rock-headed gutter cat!" David's eyes blazed fueling his wrath as he began to pound and kick the chain-like roots, igniting the hollow with his fiery onslaught. "Like this!" he said, snarling to match Vexpurra, who howled in mortification. Her green glow flared into burning rage, and her tawny body grew taut as the root twines loosened their strangle hold and began to wither under David's battering—just as they had before in the rose garden.

"Quick—grab Christen!" cawed Niki.

Peter and Fidius leaped to follow the dove's orders—but not before Vexpurra pounced—and with such velocity that, even as the rescuers gasped, the demon cat vaulted from the roots. Up, and out of the tree cellar she bounded, airborne upon silt wings.

"Niki cheeped alarm. "Christen! Brother! He's gone... She's got him. After her!"

"Ill-timber, you monster..." wailed the wind with cat's voice, "...take care of them!" Lust's feline had taken flight and disappeared into the cruel and cold-blooded night.

"Hurry!" cried Niki. "She's getting away!" The little dove, her frostbit wing tips now heated to a passion, shot out of the tree in hot pursuit.

Alas, none else could follow her, for on the cat's command, the Ill-timber squirmed to life and barred any further escaped. Its serpentine limbs closed in on the remaining band, holding them fast in a suffocating wrap, not unlike a cocoon.

The sight of it caused Niki to halt and turn back. But David called out, "Don't, Niki! You mustn't stop—go on! After Christen...We'll make out!" There was confidence in David's urgings, no hint of fear. Yet that in itself would not wrest them from their predicament, and so, Niki started back for her ward. David pleaded all the more. "No, Niki—please! We'll follow you shortly. This dead shrub is no match for my weapons—remember!" David stomped his foot down hard and the timber cringed.

However, it was not the sound of pain bewailing from the wood, instead, the force of will in David's eyes convinced the dove to leave—but not without a second thought. Even as the hollow ground trembled under David's heel, the storm relented and Niki felt some warmth return. "I know you will, painter—you CAN do it, can't you! Here, take my hat. Wear it, that you may follow after me. Though I am gone from your side, so will you remain under my protection... Faretheewell!" bid the dove, fitting her miraculous helmet to set comfortably on David's head. Then, without a backward glance, the pilgrims parted hastily. On Vexpurra's trail flew Niki, south—toward the Moors.

"See you soon," called David, his thoughts distracted southward.

"'See you soon'!" screeched the branches, scraping against the wind to send chills up the bones of David, Peter, and Fidius. "I spoke the same words myself... Ssss," rasped the Ill-timber, squeezing its belly ever tighter on the choking prisoners within. "Remember, pilgrims-s-s-ss?"

The whole tree rumbled and shook even as the winter wind retreated. Yet wrapped in root and without the room to breathe, David's blows were becoming ineffective. His nerve, however, was not without kick. From a knothole, he looked out to see the bark-skinned gargantuan. "Show me your face, you double-dealing, dragon-limbed hunk of deadwood!" Though he could see neither face nor features, the wood walls around him vibrated in a vengeance. It was like being sealed in a beating drum as the Ill-timber growled and hissed without.

"Show you my face did you say... Ssss? You've seen my face, man-i-kin, a week past, in your pig queen's garden—remember? Though you would not recognize it to look at me now. I was attractive then, full and budding, my crown twigs lush in leafy green. But anon, a hemlock's hair I have to wear. Look upon me now...Ssss! See my bare black branches...Ssss! See my long svelt limbs...Ssss!! How gracefully gnarled and twisted they've become. And my beautiful skin, once smooth and soft, is nothing but a shriveled, wrinkle-ridden crust...Ssss. I've been scarred, and sliced, and singed by you groundlings enough. My beauty treatment I owe to you, stripling—and now you shall be paid...Ssss! You will be as magnificantly mangled as me—"

"I'll scratch and scorch you again, you ill smelling Ill-timber—unless we are all released at once!" David's voice smarted with a telling courage he could not explain. Yet those around him knew it was not fear which antagonized him. Withal, the boy's plucky rebuff did nothing to stave the sadistic tree snake from its fun. Its coil tightened, and the forthcoming screams brought a thousand smiles to the gang of Ill-timber's limbs.

"Ssss... What's this? A nibble? A threat! Do the mice smite the cobra?" Ill-timber hissed. "Your tattoos scored me once, rodents. And your boots bit sharp as your paints. But now you're in MY thistle bed, man-i-kin, and stifling it is...Ssss! Tell me, how's the air fare now?" The Ill-timber spit with delight as it sucked in its guts on David and his friends, muffling their gasping cries. "The kick in your sole will etch me no more when I've squished the last drop of impudent air from your lungs, you miserable clumps... Ssss!"

"And you'll find a mongoose among the mice, you vine-limbed viper!" Shouted David right back. But even as his companions wrestled within the wriggling gullet, their hopes were rapidly being smothered.

"Why don't that tongue-flappin' tree shut up an' put an end ta this tormentin'," huffed Fidius, jabbing futilely with his ineffectual javelin. "Even my fire don't do nothin' 'cept tickle his innards!"

"Tickled? Yes-s-sss, I am! You shall wait long for your death hug, just as I waited long for this day." The tree droned on unrelentingly. "You were supposed to fly after me into the Misties you know—for entrapment there. Instead, it was that primping prima donna Nordic I decoyed. Ironclad clod—it's nothing but leaves and sap the peacock chases... Ssss. While north comes I to intercept the jaunting plumbs from their pudding—and to conclude our garden interlude! I fretted Horros' flock would finish you first—but no! At last you are here in my cozy bed... Ssss, and it's not your shoes I would fain—it's you!" Ill-timber's branches snapped and crackled in bemused applause at its success. The vice belly tightened still another notch in a spasm of satisfaction.

David had no screams left. His veins nearly popped. His mind also swelled until nearly bursting, and his thoughts weighed heavier still. Was it the dove's silver hat he wore? My shoes! he thought, looking to his feet. Were Niki's thoughts the same? The shoes' wings began to tease his feet. And the wings upon the silver helm tempted his ears. Thus it came to him, and he blurted out, "Fidius! Do it—'tickle his innards'! Set fire to this wooden coffin before it's too late—quickly now!"

"Fire?" Fidius balked. "An' cook us too? Or do we suck in the smoke an' exhale a getaway? Is that yur ointment fur the squeeze we're in, li'l' knight?"

"Do as I say!" snapped David, his voice never more earnest. "Give this rot-belly an ulcer! Tickle him, Sir Fierce—tickle him good!"

As the lizard stoked his coals, smoke began to pour from every crook and cranny in the Ill-timber's cracking bark. It was no more than a cramp it felt in its stomach—indigestion only—but it was enough to make the tree giant convulse. And in the course of its warbling and wiggling, its stomach relaxed—only to catch its breath mind you—yet it took no longer than that for David, Peter, and Fidius to scramble through the knothole orifice, and plunge from the simmering trunk, into the deep, cool, refreshing snowbank outside.

Ill-timber's limbs constricted into tight, gnarling knots. But it was too late to reclaim its dropped morsels—they were out. Out, but unable to run in the snowdrifts. The wooden serpent uprooted its tentacles, and in an instant, an army of contorting snake limbs coiled around the pilgrims, confining them like cold prison bars.

"Ooohhh, what saucy cockrels!" jeered the Ill-timber. "You overripe little peppers have given me heartburn... Ssss. Spicy mouse, tickle me again. Go ahead... No, better yet—trim my finger nails, as you did my toes. Or does your twig cage please you, my little canaries... Ssss?" The gloating branches whistled in leering delight.

Enough was enough as far as Fidius was concerned. The proud old lizard could no longer abide such indignant gibes. "You vile mannered vegetable, I'll pare you into shaven, gol' durn, shards! You'll drown in yur own sticky juices when I've carved you down ta size! We'll make slaw from yur shredded boughs, and toothpicks outta yur whit' limbs—By cracker we will!" Fidius lunged as he spoke.

And each curse cast at Ill-timber was reinforced with hacking, chopping lance thrusts, dispelling severed branches and sticks across the snow.

Each and every remnant cried in pain, yet continued to squirm about until the branch-strewn ground resembled a tiny, twitching, worm-covered forest racking in anguish. Each dismembered shard immediately drew a life of its own—stronger, more vile than before—and more! In their former socket, sprouted still another hideous, gnashing limb. Thus, with each blow dealt, the hewn limbs regenerated into even larger, nastier nest of wooden snakes.

"Fidius—Enough!" David and Peter fought to stave the influx of snarling saplings. "You've sown an army of Ill-timbers... We're overwhelmed!"

"Sssss... My my, what a mess you squirrels have made!" The tree beast cackled in vulgar gulps and pants, not the least bit wounded; but in fact was even larger looming and more powerful, armored in sprouting fresh shoots. It was as if each cleavage gave the convulsing creature new life. It began to pick its bramble fangs with its own splintered spawns. "Who was it wanted a toothpick, manikin... Ssss?"

In defense, David crushed a slithering twig beneath his boot, and grinned to feel it throbbing underfoot—then he laughed blatantly as he mashed it dead into the frozen ground. To the boy's surprise, he was delighted with his feat. Throughout this entire harrowing ordeal, something quite extraordinary was happening to David. Evident in his every move and manner. The timbre of his laughter, the pitch of his voice, bespoke a new audacity, hitherto suppressed. Each flick of his brow uncovered a glinting, deranged sort of daring. Peter and Fidius were too immersed in combat to perceive this most recent and rising, ripping tide. Therefore it brewed unnoticed in the pilgrim's head—until exploding in a fit of unrestrained madness.

"You're a hideous, heinous, horror, Ill-timber!" David jeered, screaming to shake the snow from the skies. "I've branded you once—and will again! I'll wedge my spurs into your grave!" The twisting swarm of stems and stalks began to writhe and snap under the boy's hardened heel.

Peter and Fidius stayed their blows and stood awestruck, while the splintered shoots returned to their stock. Cringing and cracking, they cried out from under the shadow of David's callous trampling. But there was no mercy laced within the ruthless, stamping soles—only David's ranting laughter as he doused out the saplings' shrill cries with mauling, mashing shoes of white. Not so clean as before, nor pure of heart—Ill-timber's shards were wedded with the angel's wing. And when mayhem's dance died down, only a whimpering wooded giant survived. The Ill-timber, horribly maimed, stood alone against the sap-stained shoes and their boy, dripping and crazed by his carnage. The mangled tree hulk was no longer chuckling to itself. Its limbs hung limpid and beaten. And neither did the winter swirl around them, but paused to take notice of this new, more volatile, storm. Peter and Fidius also held their breaths and wondered who this heartless giant slayer was.

A sudden, surging emotion gripped David, then overcame him. It was not fear, nor fearlessness—but something, somewhere in between, and altogether different. It was something not entirely healthy; a fervor—no, a fever. Defiance, rapture, yes... No—the name didn't matter. The fever was indomitable, or so David thought. Whatever it was, this inflammation propelled him with a vicious vigor into taunting the disjointed Ill-timber.

"Would you like another tattoo, tree? Would you get a 'kick' out of it—Hah! Ha haaa! I'm going to kick you all the way back into that spiny fen which bred you!" Then, with claw-edged compassion, David began to prick his foe with his sanguine-soled shoes. Each pain-rending tap brought pleas of mercy, as the Ill-timber shook its branches and strived to keep the maniac boy at bay. But such servility only made him sneer and laugh the louder.

The deranged sound of it sickened Peter and Fidius. Peter called out, "Davy, what's the matter with you? Stop it! It's over, you're killing it. The beast is beaten—can't you see?!"

No, David could not see. The hate flooded his eyes. The voices he heard in his head were not his friends', but they sounded oh so friendly. They were the diabolical wheedling of power. To this enticement, he was neither deaf nor blind. From under Niki's gleaming silver hat David turned a flashing eye toward his companions—and snarled all the louder. "Yes! Yes, I see, horsemeat—do you? This weed is wilted, yet still not dead. But when its life is last drained out, and I've done with it—I shall dance a jig on YOUR limbs next!"

CHAPTER 35

David's menacing words assailed Peter's ears and mauled his senses. The pony boy could not believe what he was witnessing. His friend, David, was drooling as he strangled all life out of the crumpling Ill-timber. "What palling heroics are these, Sir Fierce?" gasped Peter. "Has our knight paragon gone mad?"

Fidius' gaze never once left David during his outburst, and his head shook gravely. "It's the cantrap, li'l' pony; it's got 'im under its spell."

"Lust," assumed the centaur, "I might've known her black magic was at work."

"Nope!" said the lizard. "There's lust in his eyes, but 'tain't the witch. It's them slippers that's got hold of our li'l' knight—or maybe his new hat—or both! All this hoodoo has hexed 'im—an' we gotta snuff it out it somehow, 'fore it starts gobblin' on us!"

David's demented onslaught intensified into a foot-stamping, curse-slinging spasm. The Ill-timber withered, then toppled onto its back jarring the entire mountain slope. And the wolf, David, like any true predator, went for the creature's vulnerable throat in a yowling frenzy. "Does it burn now, Ill-timber? Is it excruciating? I hope so—Hah ha haaa!"

"Ssss... It burns-s-s! It Burns-s-s!"

"What's that—mercy? Ha haaa! Is it mercy you want, snake? Or is that just life I hear oozing out of your pores—Ha ha haaa!" The night air filled with the steeping odor of death, and its blizzard fled under the forest's howling epitaphs.

"What can we do, Sir Fierce?" Peter paced the ground in distraught circles. "It's a duel between two monsters now... and I tremble to think which is the worst."

"There's blood in the eyes I see, li'l' feller—that's a fact." Fidius' breath was icy cold. "An' there'll be more than tree's blood spilled unless we fetch some help fur ourselves!"

Peter couldn't settle down. He refused to believe his eyes. "I can't imagine the mighty Lord Enduros allowing such atrocities—practically on his doorstep. And my father, Paramount... I'd have thought he at least would come to our aid."

Fidius' grey face flushed as he blurted to himself, "Father—that's it! A course!" The old lizard scampered off toward the Rime River in a flurry, leaving Peter alone to muse over his own fate, once their mad pilgrim finished deciding the Illtimber's.

"Well," gulped Peter in a quandary. "I suppose evasion is one way to deal with crisis, unfortunately, some things are unavoidable. I don't relish getting swallowed by a tree dragon—or trampled either, for that matter—but I can't just go trotting off and let Davy lay ruin to himself and everything around him on some insane binge. Niki would never permit such a cowardly, white-livered act of desertion... Come to think of it—neither would Davy!" Peter reared his hooves sharply into the ground and lifted his mane-tossed head high over his staunch shoulders. "And for that matter—neither will I!" Then the centaur galloped to his friend and, locking his arms tightly around David, attempted to restrain the boy from his hysteria. "Stop it, Davy! You gotta stop this senseless slaughter—it's utter lunacy! We have work to do; we have to find Niki... You remember Niki, don't you?" But Peter would have better risked a favor of the devil than of David in his present trauma.

"Let go of me, you hoof-footed stable-snipe!" David snarled at Peter's throat like a rabid wolf and, in a fit of bloodthirsty delirium, he kicked the pony boy viciously against his hindquarters—and the tender hamstring gave way. Peter buckled, and collapsed in a contorted, pain-racked clump upon the snow.

For an instant, his languishing sobs caught, and held onto, the impassioned giant killer. The sight of Peter, writhing on his back in such agony, brought a fire-quenching tear to the 'wolf's' swollen eyes. Then, the beast turned his back on his rabies and the prostrate ebony, and stooped instead to his comrade's side. Even the most obstinate of spells will fray and snap when met by the even more enduring allure of friendship. Peter's cries had cut completely that evil entity which bore on David. The fiend was gone, and the friend emerged to preserve the bond between the pilgrim and the centaur.

From the inner reaches of David's mind, a tiny voice scolded: 'Oh painter, what a cruel and ruthless blow to strike. Your shame shall haunt on you for this.' David blinked in wide-eyed astonishment, and then embraced his good friend in recompense. "Peter! Oh Peter... What have I done?"

Alas, a pilgrim should never turn his back on evil, no matter how benign. For sin so spurned, will most assuredly exact its pound in some shape or form. If not from within, then without—and with regenerated severity. So it was, as David pined and fussed over Peter, compassion, not power, blinded him to all other dangers. The wounded Ill-wood was not so insensibly lost however. It was tempted, not with compassion, but with hate's passion. The wood wraith was here and now, and growing stronger by the moment. It was malice that nursed the creature to its former lowly heights. With vindictive fury it struck like a snake, grasping revenge in the coils of its limbs, and the taste of it was sweet on the foul, forked tongues.

There was no resistance left in Peter, who could not; nor in David, who would not—the pilgrim found self-pity to be more stifling. Even as the sticky, life-sapping branches tightened around them and thorns chewed on their flesh, Ill-timber's lethal embrace seemed a blessed escape.

"Sssss... back at you, man-i-kin!" cackled the Ill-timber, more ominous than ever. Wiggle your toes now why don't you! Are the games over?... It must be time to eat... Ssss!" The bramble-toothed jaws closed in on Peter and David. "If only that toad was here... Ssss. I love toads!"

"Well that's gol' durned splendid!" wheezed the puffing voice from the woods. "Since you got the hankerin' fur the taste of it, I rustled up a brand, spankin' fresh 'toad' fur you!" Fidius zipped into the clearing breathing fire. "Here's a sampling of my specialty: lizard legs, jumbo sized—and served pipin' hot!"

Suddenly, violent earth tremors shook the mountain side. An avalanche of white ice and snow cascaded to the ground. The thick, fir forest swayed, then bent to its knees—bowing before the enormous serpent looming like a great, green, undulating peak behind his father. It was Fidius' offspring, Abraxus.

"Feast on that, sap guts!" gibed Fidius, spitting smoke.

The sight of the two lizards rekindled David's flagging spirits and soothed Peter's throbbing hind. "Sir Fierce! I should've known you wouldn't desert us. I say, that's a long tall shadow you cast!"

"It's Abraxus," said David, "a friend I thought long dead." As if to demonstrate his life, the dragon sprang at the Ill-timber and ground his arsenal of saber-edged teeth into the timber's lungs, sending the nettle beast reeling to the hard ground in cursing pangs.

"Toad!... Ssss, call off your newt, or I'll squeeze my captives into juice!

But the stolid dragon was loathe to liars' threats. Abraxus' steel jaws only ground tighter, and was close to severing the tree's two-pronged tongue from its trunk. Anon, the stump's words were eaten as it cursed... and swore for mercy. "Sssss... Lay off, slug! It was sport, nothing more! Take your groundling squirrels and spare me...Pleasssse!"

Only after the boys were safely released from the tentacles' toothey throes into Fidius' care, did Abraxus loosen his bite. The gratitude of evil is venomous however, and Ill-timber was quick to payback his better. No sooner had the sea drake turned a concerned eye toward his man friend, than a hundred hardwood fists pommeled his spine. The thrashing attack caught Abraxus completely by surprise. With Ill-timber at his throat, the dragon child rolled to his back in defense, reeling under the monster's stranglehold.

The mountain slope staggered and churned, while its frozen forest gasped at the mammoth duelists. Yet the spectacle attracted nary a glance from David, whose attention remained focused on Peter. Even Papa Fidius seemed unusually dispassionate at his son's predicament, preferring instead to fret over Peter's distress. The centaur's hock was terribly swollen again. Nevertheless, he shook off every effort of help or comfort.

"Isn't anybody going to help our big, green friend?" questioned the anguished colt, spurning the efforts of his two 'doting nannys' as he put it. He tried to rub the pounding pain from his inflamed hamstring. "Davy, Fierce—I'm okay! But the drake needs help... Can't you kick that timber off his throat?!"

"Tut," puffed Fidius, and with fatherly pride began to brag on his son. "My fry's got some throttle left. He'll have that backboneless blackguard at bay 'fore you kin stand up—yes sirree!"

No sooner said than done. Turning on its powerful haunches, Abraxus repelled his assailant with swift, ripping forelegs. A team of incisive claws plowed through Ill-timber's crusty pulp, and his lashing tail nearly broke the tree demon in two. It was spiked tooth set into serrated skin—so the contest was joined. Surmising its predicament and then summoning what, to the dastardly, passes for valor the liver-limbed wood worm pulled up its roots and hobbled into the pine cover, where even his kindred plants rebuked him. But Abraxus would not let loose his shifty stalk a second time. Like a stirred chase hound, the leviathan thundered in close pursuit.

Fidius' chest bulged. "We'll soon be warmin' our chilly cheeks over a campfire of 'Ill-wood'!"

"But, Sir Fierce... aren't you worried?" Peter's face was drawn with painful lines. "Have you forgotten—the beast regenerates! Even now his splinters are probably sprouting around your foal."

Swallowing his smoke, Fidius clutched his javelin in alarm and charged into the broken pines after the two battling behemoths. "Take care!" he called back. "An' whatever you fellers do—don't come a lookin' fur me!"

Moments later, in the distance, the rumbling shock of two mountains colliding in a death lock rattled the white mountain and continued to jolt the night. Against that tumult, David proceeded to pack snow on Peter's leg to numb the pain and retard swelling—much to the displeasure of his patient.

"Davy, you gotta help them, there's nothing further you can do for me!"

"I've crippled you," said David bitterly, "that's what I've done for you, Peter—now hold still!"

"You've salvaged this leg once already... Perhaps I fibbed a bit to make this quest with you. 'Twas never fully mended. The trip has dealt it a worse blow than you. It was the river crossing that nearly did me in. Until now, Fidius' crutch has been my best limb."

David hefted the pony boy to his feet. "No more... I'm your crutch! And that's more than I can be for Fidius and his kid. Fidius realized that. You must know it too, Peter—you saw what happened to me when I put the power in my shoes to work. It took hold of me. I was possessed—no, corrupted—by their allurement. They're a jinx! I promised Niki, and her master both, that this would never happen. But I've failed, and might've paid for it with my life—and that of my fellows."

"So, now you're afraid to take any step—unless it be backward? Listen to me," said Peter, "for all the risks you wield in wearing those gifts, you nonetheless saved our lives this night—is that a failure? You've exerted your magic in the triumphant pursuit of your quest—can that be so wrong? What reason to repent? You were not so corrupted, as berserk... uh, that is to say, sick... but only temporarily—and in the head—not the heart! A pilgrim of weaker worth might've succumbed long ago under such a cross. Niki would be proud of you, Davy. Indeed, to my way of thinking, 'twas her ill-fitting hat that turned your head, not your shoes. Beforehand, you had walked a long and righteous mile bareheaded. Perhaps a crown does not suit you—what do you think?"

David removed Niki's helmet, and felt relief as he pondered Peter's words. "Maybe I can think clearer without so much magic on my mind." The painter then placed the silver, winged hat into his satchel for safekeeping. "You're right, Peter; I must exercise great care, and use my gifts to that purpose for which they were deigned. We have to find Niki, return her helm—and locate the Glass Egg at once!"

Regrettably, Peter's silence pointed out one swollen handicap to that plan. Any further trekking for him would have to wait until his hock was healed completely—or at least until daybreak."

David helped Peter back into the alcove Fidius had first spotted on the river bank. A fire still smoldered, and smiled warmly upon being fed by the pilgrims who crouched around her while waiting out the raucous night in relative warmth.

They woke late, to silent lingering echoes; Fidius was still nowhere to be seen. The boys were surprised to find some dried fruit and figs—even a morsel of jerky—among the grubs Fidius had stashed. Breakfasting on their good fortune, the two of them queried the reptile's fate.

"I'm worried, Davy, the ground still rocks. That tree draws its strength from the soil, while the sea lizard is out of his element."

David tested the pony boy's tender hamstring and found it laming. "Isolato will protect his spawn. Believe me, Peter, the most urgent need now rests on your legs."

Peter rubbed his wound, and his chin. "Isolato! Isn't that old hermit neutral in this muddle?"

David almost smiled. "He allowed his prize gladiator to cross out of the water realm into ours in answer to his daddy's call, didn't he? Or is that neutrality nipping at Ill-timber's neck! Lust might just be in over her head after plunging into Isolato's river yesterday. From his lips no less, I know he detests the witch's constant interloping—and maybe now desires to give his sister a purging bath!"

"A pity his burned out legend of a brother is not half as wroth," said Peter. "The gall of that crone—hiding Christen here where you'd least expect it—right under Enduros' stuck up nose!"

"I wonder?..." That thought returned to torment David. "Niki and I both felt something amiss with the lamb prince. My shoes saw through it too, and held me fast. Perhaps it was Christen's trance—but maybe it was more! Ill-timber let slip the condors were sent here, not as sentinels, but to wrest my shoes for their witch mistress. Who then to guard her hostage? None—save for purring rock and a demented, half-dead stump, seething with revenge. Don't you see, Peter, it was a vendetta! It was us that drove them here, to spy or settle an old score, who knows? Whatever the provocation, it was not to safeguard their plunder—if in fact that was Christen!"

Peter's brow knitted with his friend's and sank under the same sinister thought. "But, Davy, if such a ruse is possible, who is it that fled with Vexpurra? Who is it that draws Niki away from us and into the far Morass?"

"It's no lost lamb I suspect," said David, "but black-skinned, red-fleeced, bait. And my dear deceived Niki next on he menu!

"A Judas goat with a 'lust' for greener pastures!" added Peter, stomping his hooves and reaching for his pinestaff. "Help me up, Davy, we've no time to lose. We have to catch up with them before it's too late!"

"Do you also intend to leave your hamstring here behind you?" reminded David, as Peter dug his fingers into his friend's shoulder.

The pain shot through the pony's sinews, but found no escape past his gritting teeth. "I'm not short of legs, Davy," grimaced Peter. "With three of my own, this wooden bolster of Fidius'—and you, my strongest limb... And I've yet another—discipline. Though that one's suffered a bit too; withal, it grows sounder by the day!"

"As we all do, my friend..." A broad smile warmed David's face as Peter leaned onto his crutches and limped gamely from the alcove, then added sadly, "...but how many days are left for us I wonder?"

"It's warmed up a bit; we're in luck!" noted Peter optimistically, looking to the welcome trace of sunshine."

"And when the cold night returns, what then? We've no food, weapons, or supplies," said David, though still smiling. "You call that luck?"

"Of course," laughed Peter, "for who would carry such a load if we had it!"

Despite their plight, the boys' enthusiasm kept them chipper, especially Peter, who needed the merry medication most. "We've a whole pouch of grubs to chew; it's a pity we can't take Fidius' fire with us as well, to warm our way."

"Now that you mention it—I've a candle to light the most sizzling of fires," said David, reaching into his satchel for a brush. "But first, as Sir Fidius will be looking for us in due time, I shall leave him a note, so he may follow the way we mark."

"And how are WE to find the way to mark, if I may ask? Niki has not provided us with any note."

"No—she's left us something better!" David retrieved Niki's silver, winged hat from his satchel and, after placing it upon his head, doffed it at Peter. "Behold, my hunting cap! It has a keen sense of direction for its proper head."

"Just be careful you don't lose it..." scoffed Peter, "...your head I mean!"

"I'm getting good at this," said David, applying a new paintbrush splint to Peter's leg. "How do you feel?"

"Wonderful, Doc," replied Peter, kicking one of his good legs and anxious to be off. "So wonderful it hurts. Look how well I wield your artist's brush!" And with goosebump trepidation the two pilgrims forged cautiously back across the tepid Rime and into the Phantom Forest.

"So long, Enduros... for now at least." said David somewhat remorsefully. He had really been looking forward to meeting another god.

"Good riddance I say," responded Peter. "That old craigtop's red carpet rollout nearly ruined us!"

David dwelt momentarily on Enduros' welcome here, or rather the absence of it. But the sun on his neck melted his mind's wondering before it wandered too far afield.

The grey sun followed on their heels. Behind them, on the slopes of Mount White, heavy snow drops began to fall again, soon blanketing all traces of the forenight's drama—and leaving not a note to be seen!

Though the weather was warmer to the southeast, after many pain-wrenched miles, Peter had found the going not so fair. His discipline notwithstanding, a healthy hind leg would have served him better. "It's no use, Davy..." panted the pony boy. He was lathered and feverish. "If only I had wings on my feet as you, then maybe I could keep pace...Without magic of my own, I fear I'm too lame for this trek."

"Hmmm, so it's magic you require is it." David tipped his hat again, and this time turned it over to Peter. "Maybe a winged head would inspire your feet! Niki's helm fits you as well as I—better, for on my mind it weighs too heavy. Besides, one set of wonder wings is more than I can handle!"

"Incredible hat!" declared Peter, trying it on for size. "How such a tiny cap can fit all our heads!" The dove's winged crown stretched comfortably over the centaur's set of horns dressing head and hind like a soothing compress. So bandaged, the crippled pony boy forgot his torn ligament. The pain of it became a prod, spurring him to walk, to canter, and lo—to gallop—and more! More swift even that his thoughts could comprehend, he raced under strumming wings and on pounding hooves in pursuit of their dove. David had, out of necessity, straddled the streaking steed for fear of being stranded in his track. The multi-legged boys were winged away from the ice-shrouded canopy of Snowmass, down into the lower tors, where even the milder Serenity Plain looked wrought with harsh and howling winter winds. Yet in the melting flake of an hour, it seemed even the Sovereignwood was behind them. Then the wide, windy Windingroot River was past, and the Rollingway too. Even the Common Downs were long gone at day's end. Whether the wandering lasted for a wink, or a week—neither knew. And even the new sun marveled to see such distances as magic had spanned. Regardless, the charm—like the body—will with use grow wane. Thus the next eve's moon rose forlorn to find the low moors spread around the weary twosome like a cold weald sheet, leaving them to wonder where would come some welcome rest and comfort. Somewhere between then and now, either appetite or time had depleted their pouch of its grub. Their cohort, night, fell dark and dismal on the fatigued wayfarers, and bid them halt in no uncompromising terms. Then all wings folded into silence.

"B-Better b-break out that candle of yours, Davy," stuttered Peter, collapsing to his knees lathered and way-worn. "F-For I need some heat and light to reassure me that we are not lost in these pathless hursts—or on some scarp of Snowmass... I know not. Are we snowbound, or is it my mind that's fogged?"

"I don't understand this 'flight' either I'm afraid. How long has it been? It seems but a day, yet I own a fortnight's aches." David pinched his wings as if expecting them to jump back to life. "Surely our flaps would not abandon us here, in the heart of nowhere!"

"Nay, it's my legs that walked out on me," moaned Peter. "My agony feels days behind—only the blisters are new." The centaur wiped the foam from his bulging hocks. David stooped to inspect the injured hamstring, when the pony boy suddenly threw himself into the air. "Davy—look yonder! Unless my eyes are failing me too, I think we've found a light!" He hurriedly grabbed his pine stave then, with David's aid, the duo fought their way through the tangle of scrub.

David cheered at the faint glowing distance. "A campfire—Hooray! Do you suppose it could be Niki? Maybe that's why our wings have folded up."

"Maybe," said Peter... but not too loudly, for likely it wasn't.

CHAPTER 36

The two weary pilgrims staggered toward the heady smell of hot buttered curry which lured them into the warm, glowing ring of a welcoming campfire. The rippling, orange light revealed a scrap of black robes wrapped around a mere morsel of a man—if indeed it was a man. Whatever it was, it wasn't Niki. It hunched nervously upon a log, stammering to itself beneath a lean-to.

"Uh, let's not be too eager, Davy," hastened Peter. "We shouldn't go begging at a stranger's fire, let our wits be as sharp as our appetites."

"Tush!" scoffed the boy, casting caution aside. "He's nothing but a shivering sliver on a stump... Hello!" called David cheerfully, as he took a bold step into the dancing circle of light.

At the sound of this sudden voice, the fleck of a fellow quailed and tumbled backwards off his log, spilling hot curry all over his lap.

"Oh! Forgive me... I didn't mean to frighten you—" David's apology was cut short as he lent a helping hand to the fallen figure and saw for the first time the face of the twitching wad in the dirt.

It was Mors—the bone man. His chillingly livid skull leered up crossly at David and Peter from the campfire pyre. "Drat you vermin! Look at what you've made me do! Sneaking up on me that way...Why, bless my soul—if it isn't the pilgrim, and his runner colt!" Mors sounded genuinely surprised and, upon recognizing his visitors, truly contrite. "Oh, do forgive poor, pitiful me." Mors slapped his jawbone in a show of penance. "You almost frightened me to death," said the skeleton, and began to wring out his meal-drenched wraps.

Though their legs were aching and crumbling, David and Peter remained on their feet, scanning the night as if they expected a lion to pounce from the dark wood curtain.

Mors' black-hole eye sockets peered at them from under their mantle. "Don't be shy... Come, sit down and sup with me. It's a hellish night to be stalking about in these cold thickets. You'll catch your death out there... Ahh, you wouldn't be lost now, would you?" The marrow-lined voice dropped out as if it already knew the answer.

"Why, er... No! Of course not," retorted David, not wishing to appear defenseless before DeSeet's valet. But then he reconsidered, having little recourse except admitting their obvious predicament. "Er, that is... Yes, now that I think on it, we do seem to be at a loss..." David's tongue began to wag. The aroma of piping meal and liquored honey tortured his pride. And the warm fire lashes drew him ever closer.

"This ghoulish brake can be so lonlifying and scaresome at night. Even the moon turns a pale face away this eve." Mors' empty eyes pierced the darkness and his bones clattered. "Join poor measly Mors, won't you? 'Tis only grog, but hot—and my mead has bite. And you must be cold as cadavers. I'm chilled to the bone myself!" Mors pulled his hood high up over his angular cheeks, concealing his skull face almost completely.

Though he looked no more inviting than a tombstone peeping from its grave, David couldn't resist. Stepping underneath the windbreak, he helped himself to the pot of tangy porridge and consumed the warmth. All this while Peter sat in his own tracks, out of the fire's reach.

"Are your suspicions as sating as my meal, young stallion? Or do your lips smack for spite?"

"Fact of the matter is, I am hungry," replied Peter, unable to hide his want, "starving right down to the tip of my tail. We lost our provisions to a gorging mountain stream this very week, up in the Snowmass; not that you'd have an interest in that... lost some curry and mead too, by the way!"

The bone man batted not an eye, though he were able. "The Snowmass you say? A fortnight's journey—Yiii! What a swift-stepping stallion you are—and your broken shank be the fee for your speed." Mors caught Peter rubbing his leg. "An extraordinary courier you are! Mors is impressed. Do you mock me then, by your reluctance to sit at my camp?"

"Er... on second thought, Peter," gulped David, sparing a glance at Niki's miraculous silver hat, "perhaps it only seemed like a week's passage—"

"Horsefeathers!" scoffed the pony boy. "I don't mean to be rude, but my caution is no more a fancy than my words—which are true! This skeleton, on the other hand, still has the flavor of a lion dropping—though it's scented with butter and curry. I'll not step into any overture until convinced otherwise!"

Mors' bones rattled uncontrollably, while David, showing none of the discomfort of his partner, poured another heaping bowl of gruel.

"You seemed especially high-strung at our arrival," continued Peter. "Is it these woods that make you wary, or is it other denizens that spook you so? Lions, for example! Might I ask where your spineless bone master, DeSeet, is skulking tonight? It was thought you both escaped into some distant fen together—to his mistress' cesspool in the Kyln... Or quite possibly, our lion count is closer than we think?"

"Oh yes... yes he is, kind pony master!" Under a dredge of tears, Mors dropped to is knees in a rattling panic. His arms were tied around Peter's waist as he began to plead with the two boys. "Yiii... I beseech you—beg you—implore you! Help me... Help poor, defenseless Mors, please!" The bone man bawled and rattled to beat cast dice, kissing Peter's hooves as he chattered. "Yes... yes, you're right; I am afraid—mortally afraid—for my poor, miserable life..."

While the sobbing pile of black and white ranted pathetically, David sipped the remaining mead, letting its honey-sweet warmth coat his cold insides. He listened intently to Mors' tale and gawked with wonder into the eye sockets' morbid void, puzzled as to where such melancholy tears originated, lacking eyeballs like they did.

"Pray, save me!" wailed the empty eyes. "Save poor, wretched Mors from hateful lion's tooth. I have fled my master count and his brigands... Now they hunt Mors' head!"

Peter wrestled his way from the bone man's frantic embrace and joined David on the log to safely study the mystery unraveling.

"Mors and master made good our escape from dwarf king's dungeon and did hasten for the marshes. Above the South Swards jungles we threw in with my count's colleague, the troll Negare, and his ogre confederates. With their armies so meshed, we drove northward across the Commons and lowland moors in a pillage. Spared not a twig we did—it was lovely!" Mors' voice drooled. "If 'twas in our path— or even out—we made a point to prick it and pain it. Whether by torture, torch, or sword tip, we had our sport. And when no life, nor land, nor property was left to trounce or tread upon, we ravaged farther north to draw bloody pleasure. After Amber Glade and Emerald Bay, 'twas Sovereignton which lit my master's eyes. How proud Mors felt to hobnob with such formidable conquering dregs..." The skeleton begged pause to sponge a hellish tear from an empty eye with his gauze sleeve. "But woe, a curse set upon us and gutted our game. Your royal chip's legionary, under General Affirmare's command, did gather before us—on the plains of Cinnabar it was—Yiii! How the battle did rage! The sun and his maiden moon did wax and wane a set of times before the final bloody blow was dealt... and doom was certain, *sniff*..." The bone man stopped again to change his sleeve.

"For whom! For whom was doom so certain?" chanted Peter and David together voicing their concern. "Not for Affirmare most assuredly," guessed Peter. The sobbing skull nodded, or seemed to. Perchance it chased a devil's tear.

A sharp shudder slipped down David's spine at the thought. "Constantio knew defeat would be the only end should troll and lion throw their might together. Mors, tell us quickly now—who was it? For whom was the fatal bludgeon struck?"

The bone man rattled so, he nearly fell to pieces. "Why... to poor pathetic Mors, of course—that's what I've been telling you! 'Twas on this battlefield of Cinnabar that I lost my head—Yiii! Verily I did beg leave of that life-spilling place. Er... Uh, without suitably begging leave however, Mors begged off... and left. As much as I savor the sight of good bloodletting, I'm dreadfully grossed by the thought of letting my own... I do bleed you know. My marrows are juicy red—and so they intend to remain. Dying scares me to pieces—especially if it's me!"

"You are a gutless, spineless, liver-lacking, yellow-boned coward, aren't you!" Peter demanded to know what transpired on the battlefield.

"If you mean, did the this poor wrap run? Yes—as fast as my joints would bend to that task. Howbeit, with the skirmish paused, the ogres stalk these woods for me, sniffing out the bounty on my bones... Mors is quite the valuable package you know!"

"We know your worth, you marrow-mouthed maggot!" Peter took hold of Mors' cloak and shook it like a switch. "We care not a whit about you. Were I able, I'd have your head and bounty both for myself. Now, that battle... How fared the battle? Affirmare must've been outnumbered three to one at least!"

"Nay—five, or ten, to one more like; but I've no word. 'Twas at a stalemate when poor, jangled Mors escaped... uncertain as I was of who the victor be. Each side sought for reinforcements. My master count beckoned into the swamp for his fire hair queen. And the white cross general sent to his flank for King knee-high. For that reason Negare withdrew, and circled north after me—"

"To outflank Affirmare—that's my bet!" supposed Peter with absolute certainty, and so enthralled with the skeleton's forthright account, he was willing to concede its truth."

"As you say, colt master... Still, your cross-breasted general pursued Negare, though to what conclusion I cannot say, as I lost all interest in the match up. The fragrance of their affray has shaken my bones. Now, poor despondent Mors desires only to survive... to waste away under some distant roof in peaceful solitude."

"Peter, I had no idea we strayed so near the battlefield!" exclaimed David. "We must continue on at first light. Mors looks harmless, too jelly-limbed to be really dangerous."

"If only we could believe him; he's such a cunning coldbone that one. Could it be possible?" quizzed the pony boy. "Is it truth which gives him jitters, and relaxes only when he lies?"

"You'll stay the night with poor, forsaken Mors? Bless my soul, you'll not regret it... You'll see." The skeleton's relief spurred his raving. "We'll be safe together. There's condors about—the witch's birds—I've seen them... come to pick poor Mors' bones for juicy marrow!"

"So—it's for you the vultures flock is it?" Peter now concurred with David. "Not only harmless and frightened—he's quite delirious."

"Oh yes—yes it's true," rambled Mors. "I'm valuable you know... Secrets aplenty lay stored under this skull cap of mine—but my fleshless lips are tightly sealed!"

"Your lips are seeping with secrets most surely," agreed Peter, "for I know the company you keep: that of Lust and lions both... and condors too perhaps, to cross the miles between the mouths? I've seen them 'round you by the by, attracting vultures like Vito's flies. Have your 'flies' spurned your pickless bones?"

Mors moaned at the thought "They have, they have, but I'll be safe with the pair of you—you've power over them!"

"But are we safe with you! You speak of our power over Lust's sparrows—How?"

"There's magic to protect those who travel in the urchin's footsteps... or so my master says."

"Which master: count or crone? Whom do you serve, underling?" demanded the centaur.

"I serve Mors most faithfully, master colt—and those who would lend a magic shield to him, lest condor talons tear out the secrets his locked lips hold."

"Haw!" bemoaned Peter, growing more uncomfortable by the minute. "Your secrets will get you butchered. You'll die like you lived, with your white lips left open in wide inanities, while your pandering bones and their riddles melt into boiling ogre broth pots!"

Peter was again besieged by a deck of ivory-plated fingers. "Nay, pony master! For those who would spare poor Mors from the cauldren, his secrets would be a welcome ray of light on a cold, dark journey. Dispel the gaunt rack you behold in these rags and listen to my words. Then, and only then, shall you find what you seek."

"And just what do your lips know of what we seek?" queried David jumping from his meal. The aftertaste of gruel still caked on his palate.

"Could be a pigeon, perhaps?" speculated Mors, whirling with glee at the pilgrim's rise. "One such fowl crossed my path this very eve—like a snowflake on a coal forest, she caught my eye."

David tried hard to mask his concern with disdain. "And why do think a pigeon would interest us?"

"Because I notice her feathers decorate your halfling's fancy hat—and mayhap you seek to add another!" The skeleton chuckled madly. "Just because poor, pitiable Mors owns no eyeballs, do not think him blind. I've kept the wisdom visions bring under wrap 'til now. Would you listen?" The bone man waited long for the reply. The pilgrims put their heads together, as if they had any choice except to enlist the vassal's aid.

Peter voted against the very notion. "We have Niki's hat to help us, Davy. Let the morning's light find us cut loose of this mummy."

David was, by necessity, of a different voice however. "Our wings are clipped and muted now, Peter; did you forget? For some reason they led us to Mors—perhaps it is Mors who shall lead us to Niki. Or do you shun the mummy's food and blankets too?"

"A skeleton's warmth, and word, are both suspect to me. I can't help but wonder whether it was this hat—or Mors—which led us to Mors. Yet that bundle of bones does seem our only hope. I'll just try and come to grips."

"Very well," decided David at long last. "Unravel your mysteries, skeleton and, if we are able, my friend and I will preserve you from the pot."

"But neither do we intend to boil in your place!" added Peter with a grunt. "Now show us your color, and tell us where our dove has flown. She is a pet we would lorn to lose."

"And your hock?" responded Mors, sidstepping the question to examine Peter's hind leg, which was swollen like a melon. "Would its loss sorrow you too? You cannot stand, yet you aspire to fly after sky riders."

"Oh, that... It's nothing, only a twist." Peter gnashed his teeth as Mors poked the melon swell, and smirked.

"A 'twist'? Yiii! A plump tendon I think, and so tender to the touch you can barely stand it—or upon it—without staves."

"It IS somewhat aggravated," confessed Peter wincing. He tossed away his crutch in a painful show of strength. "It'll pass though. I've traveled far on these legs and need no crook to carry me. My muscles—and my instincts too—are kept well-toned."

"So I see. And you'll likely lose a healthy batch of both, taking your life with it—if you don't ease up, pony master. Unless..." Mors began to rummage through his duffle. "...Unless you will allow poor Mors to help you. I do possess some expertise on the subject of bones. Yours have obviously been cracked rather coldly... A condor, was it?"

"Are you so familiar with those bone-pickers as to credit them for my own clumsiness. I told you—I just twisted it!" Peter tried to be resolute in his charade, but chills massed on his skin as he cast a peek into the skeleton's raggedy poke.

"Can you really help him?" asked David, who fretted by the firelight after gazing at the bone man's kit. He was more concerned with his friend's health, than in any further pretense.

Mors was now thoughtfully reading the directions inscribed on various vials and vessels stashed in his ditty. "Oh indeed!" uttered Mors with a moan of satisfaction as he extracted a pungent smelling cruet. "I believe I have the remedy right here!"

Peter was hardly impressed however. "All the tools of leechcraft—how handy!"

"My humble balms and talismans shall alleviate your suspicions, as well as your pains, master colt."

"Humble balms? Hooey!" scoffed Peter, his whole body throbbing to match his leg. "Sorcery's salves most likely. A poison poultice would cure your ills too—wouldn't it, bonesetter! With Davy and me so duped 'twould set you in fine stead with the witch —and save your head from the lion's pride of ax men."

"As you wish," sighed the ragged pile of bones. "If my master colt is so stiff-haired within at poor Mors' medicines, I shall prove my sincerity without." The skeleton then handed Peter the cruet. He rattled over to the pony boy's flank, and patted it gingerly, while inspecting the swollen joint. "What curious splints I see—paintbrushes!" Mors discarded them like hot coals before any objections could be raised. Satisfied with his own diagnosis, he abruptly clasped Peter's hoof and yanked—as vigorously as he was able. A brittle glass smashing sliced the night's silence. Struck with pain, Peter dropped Mors' vial onto the stone ground, where the ointment quickly bled. David cried out so loud that none but Mors heard the hollow knock of Peter's socket joint popping into place. Peter doubled over, chewing his lip lest a cry escape. David was quick to offer assistance, but the bone man merely knelt by his bag unmoved.

"The colt's leg was grievously dislocated. Now it, and his hamstring, may mend satisfactorily. He may even walk again. As for the pain? It will pass—the more anon to one so hale and hardy as this horse. One of his 'discipline' spits out pain as a trifling seed."

"Bonesetter!" cried Peter. "Have you another concoction for this hale and hardy hurt? It lingers too long. I would digest your poultice instead of this agony."

Mors had already sifted through his elixirs and now extracted another cruet, which he promptly sampled as additional proof of his trustworthiness.

David looked on curiously as the skeleton drank a second capful of the pungent syrup as if sampling wine. He wondered where the fluid ended up once swallowed. "Well, it smells bad enough to be good medicine," remarked the boy wrinkling his nose.

"As long as it works," gulped Peter, downing the syrup as though it were sweet butterscotch; and to his delight, found it almost as pleasant tasting.

Mors meanwhile, had begun to fuss over the injured leg, coating it with a smear of thick, creamy salve. The touch of it cooled the fire in the centaur's muscles, and before long the pain eased, as did Peter's incurable skepticism. "Well now," he said finally, "the pangs in my leg are quelled, it's high time to treat my stomach. I hope your oatmeal works to match your elixirs, bonesetter."

"Oh yes," proclaimed Mors. "Indeed, you shall be surprised at the results, master colt."

With David and Mors lending support, Peter tested his legs by hobbling over to the fireside encampment. There the boys partook of its hospitality, and spent the night under warm, comfortable blankets.

"Your welcome to join up with us," said Davy by way of good nights.

"And you with me," replied Mors, smiling a child's smile as he pulled the covers about his face and appeared to close his hollow eyes.

Peter observed his restlessness with keen interest. "I wonder what other secrets that bone vassal owns in his bag of potions? Even his sleep is on edge."

David rolled over and snuggled into a ball beneath his blankets. "He's just scared of DeSeet, and that troll general. His conscience probably bothers him too."

"It should," said Peter. "As for his lion and Negare, they haunt my thoughts too!"

"Stop worrying, Peter. We would've been victims of the elements had we not chanced upon Mors. Luck is with us I tell you."

"Agreed," said the pony boy pensively while he double-checked the compress on his leg before turning in. "But is it fair or foul?"

Later that night David woke with a start. Something was tugging at his feet. "Hey!" he yelled, sitting up to discover Mors pulling his shoes' heels. "Just what do you think you're doing there?!"

Mors pale face pinkened with guilt—caught in the act as he was. Nevertheless, he continued to pursue his shady endeavor with even greater vigor.

Having no further use for subtleties, the shaking skeleton tried one final, frantic yank on the boy's winged shoes.

David shook the clinging bone man loose with a good swift flick of his leg. Mors tumbled into a heap, wedged in the lean-to's corner.

"If it's my shoes you fancy, it's no use," explained David. "They will not be removed from my feet, except by my hands only."

Exasperated with the corner into which he had been hurled, Mors scrambled from the shelter. And he might have successfully fled into the night's grasp, had his alarm not so thwarted his legs that they tangled in his long wraps, tripping him into the smoldering campfire.

"Boy Howdy! Now look at what you've done—you're on fire!" David was the one hot under the collar as he rolled Mors wildly about the ground to extinguish the flaming gauze. David then held the skeleton tightly by the scruff of the neck, and shook him so hard his bones rattled.

"P-Please stop, k-kind, merciful pilgrim," cried Mors from under a whiff of smoke. "Y-You'll jiggle poor, despicable Mors into pieces!"

"I'll stop when I've shaken some truth out of you! An explanation is in order. It was my slippers that brought you here—wasn't it? On DeSeet's orders?"

"Y-Yes... yes, young master. It was the shoes I sought. N-Now let me down if you would know more."

Maintaining a firm hold on the elusive bone man, David did halt his thrashing, only because of the convincing quiver of atonement in Mors' voice.

"Spare your wrath from poor penitent Mors, and I shall talk freely of that which I know. 'Tis the fire-haired siren who desires your shoes, not her lion. 'Tis Lust I serve, not the governor. I have truly deserted his service in favor of his more consummate consort. For the underearth jinni I have spied upon my count these past years, and would shed no tear if he should fall and rot at Cinnabar."

"If you're as slick a spy as you are a thief, then Lust and lion both will bite the dust of underearth."

"She would've rewarded me well for that pretty footwear... But now—"

"Now your poor, groveling head is in jeopardy from the cat, and the crone!" surmised David with a smirk. "For what can be the fate of such a dismal wretch as you, if not death—slow and agonizingly punitive too no doubt, huh!"

"Oh spare me, young merciful master... Please spare poor, miserable Mors!"

"I wonder..." David scratched his chin, "...can a helot so lacking in scruples serve still another master?"

"You've only to command me, indulgent master!" Mors knelt at David's feet whimpering like a stray mutt begging for a bone.

"Just what am I to do with you? It's plain you're too canny to be trusted. You'll require watching day and night, until we reach—uh... Until we arrive at wherever it is we're going. You might prove your worth to us yet. If you have really seen my little dove. And if, as you say, Lust is your queen, you may lead us to her abode and quite possibly to Christen too—huh? Or would I be better off tossing you back into the fire to warm my night? Your bones burned of fine kindling!"

"Yiii! No—no not that! New more merciful and amusing master... Mors promises to be good! I will take you to the firehair, and find your pigeon, yes... and the lamb too, if that is your wish. I will do this for you—cross my heart. You saved Mors' poor burning bones... Mors will not fail you. He's very valuable you know— He has secrets!"

David demonstrated his trust in the fickle, friendless skeleton by tying him securely to the nearest tree with tight, leather tethers; there to wait out the night. The bone man wrestled with his ties. "I can't breathe," he gasped.

"Skeletons don't need to breathe," reminded David on his way over to Peter's bedroll. A couple of jabs failed to rouse the pony boy from his slumber. From under the pillow, David suspiciously removed Mors' bottle of elixir, sniffed it, then emptied the contents into the fire which drank it willingly like fuel. David's hairs went rigid. "Poison!" he gasped. "Just as Peter suspected all along!"

"Correct, young master," sniggered Mors. "One of my jinn queen's charms. But not the potion, 'twas in the curry... Te-hee! By morning young stallion will have naught but a belly ache, so worry not. Had your shoes not roused you from the spell, you would be sleeping too—with wealthy, runaway Mors gone long away from here—with his brand new pair of boots! Oh how my firehair yearned for your pretty slippers... and Mors? I could have been her favored!"

"You'll be paid for your services, bone lacky," promised David. "Think how happy your dirt mistress will be when you've brought her an unexpected pair: the footwear, and the feet!" The skull's eye pits lit up. "But for now, I long only to put this cold behind me, and conjurers up front!" After double-checking Mors fetters, and reassuring himself of Peter's well being, the pilgrim tunneled into his bedroll, seeking respite from the chilly things nipping at his toes.

"You'll find the climate more tepid in the Misties, master pilgrim," promised the bone man from deep inside his ash-singed wrappings as he and the campfire crackled.

CHAPTER 37

Niki came to a weary rest on the lintel of a window bay beneath the shanty's dreary, drooping eaves. Tonight, beads of sweat replaced yesterday's snowflakes. Her frosty feathers had long since thawed in the sweltering heat of the swamp. How her wings did ache. She had no reprieve from her tempestuous flight from Mount White so many miles and mornings to the north. Vexpurra would allow her no such comfort —not until now, at this noxious place, which Niki prayed would conclude her chase.

Veiled in steamy miasma, the tiny dove hunched under the boiling sulfured press of countless misty monsters, whisking across the glutinous evening air like a fleecy fleet of vapor ships; or more precisely, wispy witch-brewed wraiths—"cloud stalkers!" Niki knew their name, and trembled under their heat. Steeped with exhaustion, she regrouped upon the shanty transom which was cracked and blistered like some parched, pouting lip chafed from too many scorching sights to which its impassive, shade-drawn eyes bore witness. Now its unflinching, glassy panes sat sealed by shuttered lids to all the outside world.

"What a creepy old hovel this is," said Niki to herself as she surveyed her haunting roost. Above her, warped wooden tresses weighed like dank, gloomy brows upon the swamp-eaten, weather-rotted shack. It crouched, bent and bow-legged, on mildewed mangrove knees. Its stilt-like limbs barely prevailed in protecting the splintered, gabled hulk from the relentless, oozing bile called Kyln Morass. Floating in its stifling embrace, the crumpled-up old cabin was entwined in strands of moss-choked mangrove fingers. Peat moss hair hung from its dreary brows and heath vine boughs groped gangly arms around the lichen, fungus-freckled torso, down to its rutted, root-wound knees. Mammoth cypress sentinels stood watch close by, arm and arm with eucalyptus, gum and nightshade, and weeping willow woods. Though smothered like a moldy moth with this eroding web ring, the legume fingers did nonetheless serve to preserve the mortifying shanty from certain death by emulsion as there was little or no solid ground around, at least none that Niki could detect.

For a moment the dove thought she discerned some vague stirrings amid the marshes misty gumwood and giant mangrove guardians, but was quick to shrug it off as the imaginings of one too long deprived of sleep. "Dash that stone-veined cat, Vexpurra!" swore Niki, envious of her adversary's stamina. "That sleepless, tireless gargoyle. How long has it been since she slinked into this decaying hutch with my prince of lambs in her jaws?"

Niki had skirted about the shanty trying desperately to gain access, or perhaps a glimpse, or just a whisper of the happenings inside, only to return forlorn to the sanctuary of the brooding eaves. The door, the windows, cracks and crannies, chimney too, had all been locked shut, and boarded—sealed from any unwelcome scrutiny. For all the silence, Vexpurra may just as well have dropped off the earth's face, behind that shanty door.

As Niki pondered the cabin's mysteries, her weary head began to buzz. "Dratted mosquitoes!" slapped Niki, pecking and pruning her snowy feathers, attempting to rid her sticky skin of the Kyln's mastic pets. Yet it was not the swarms of pesky midges which threatened the spent little dove, but the dredges of fatigue. Her weighty lids began to close like shanty eyes in the sultry air. Evening was nearly settled, and even the foggy full moon, bewildered by autumn's absence from these moors, seemed too sleepy-eyed to penetrate the fen.

"What was that?" Niki asked of the night, which was beginning to stir again. Through her heavy pink eyes, Niki believed the dogwood branches, which had been so protective of her roost until now, had taken on the familiarly sinister specter of ebony—and Ill-timber. Just as a blood-stained, spine-studded tentacle coiled to strike her, Niki came to her senses.

"Oh dear!" she exclaimed. "I can't sleep now, I mustn't..."

A branch cracked. Was it the rustle of a restless willow? And next, a splash... What? a salamander?

"Goodness gracious!" This swamp... These twitching trees... I swear it's all alive!" Niki clattered in a sleepy delirium. "They're closing in on me... Back! Get back! Mercy me; hold on girl. 'Tis only the mist and exhaustion baiting me. I'm plagued by nightmares of that hideous Ill-timber." Niki shook off her jitters and pinched her cheeks; she even plucked a small tail feather to stave off these aberrations. "How still these woods behave," observed Niki. "Woefully so..." Only slowly did the dove's worn anxieties yield to reason, though it proved unsettling as her nightmares. Once acclimated to her plight, Niki finally realized the startling truth of just where she had been drawn. This was more than a swamp. It was the Kyln. Yes, but it was more. With this sober awakening, it soon became apparent to David's dove that not all of the closely lurking shadows were wooden, nor dead. Neither were they altogether living. To these looming, disembodied shades, it was not bark which coated their embalmed trunks, but condor-crested armor. And their death-cured arms, not cypress or willow, or any wood—but the flesh-petrified, graven burrs of sword and ax, and nothing good.

"Clay-born!" cried Niki, in a slip of unabashed fright at the recognition of Lust's ghoul sentinels. All around the clay-born pickets sulphur-scented clans of cloud stalkers crouched, surrounding their sleepless, soulless sergeants; as watchdogs would protect their stoic masters. "My good god Omnus!" squeaked Niki. "I've settled on the very threshold of Luhrhollow!"

As if to confirm the dove's suspicions, a dozen grisly pale shadows filed from the brackish dark's recesses sniffing the corpse-scented night for any breath of natural life. Toward the shanty window bay death's servants massed. Niki pressed into her own shallow niche within the cornice brow—her only ally. From beneath its dark and yawning sills, Niki dodged the livid yellow leers. Nevertheless, the mortifying aura of such morbid, bloodless beacons struck through to her bones, sucked them of their nerves, and penetrated to every downy pour of her body. But looking clear through and seeing nothing, their mood was uncaring, passionless; yet they bore on unrelenting, like the leech-breeding cauldron crypt in which they thrived.

"Oh, how vulnerable I feel without my hat," sighed Niki to herself. "If only painter were here with me. Together we could devise something against the gremlins entombed here. Do hurry after me, David!"

Then, as the helpless dove cringed in the shanty's notches, she bolted—at the sudden, deafening click of a padlock. The door flew open, and out lumbered the demonic, blue hulk—Horros—a giant once again. The front porch swayed under each disquieting step the devil took.

How could such a gargantuan possibly squeeze into this cyst-sized shack? wondered Niki, who just had to peer in from her niche.

Then she saw her question answered. Horros flicked his tail, snapped his bat-webbed arms, and snorted blue brimstone. In the wake of his steam, the demon had shriveled down to the size of a grub, where he stood stomping, puffing and still spewing coals upon the smoking porch. "Mmmmm, hurry Odios, you crook beaked, feather rack! Mors will be needing us!

On the heels of numerous bumblings and stumblings from the cabin corridors, Lust's stork-legged condor jerked his way through the doorway in a spasm onto the porch. He flitted about like a nervous goose. After careening off a railing post, he tripped over a plank—or his gander feet—and toppled down the steps into the soggy swamp where he sank to his knees in the simpering murky mire. Had the devil's hand not been so preoccupied, he would undoubtedly have heaped further ridicule on his nearsighted mount. Fortunately for the fowl, haste was the little demon's main prey now. With the condor so sunken, it was an easy exercise for the compressed horror to step from the porch and onto the bird's back.

"Up, Odios!" snarled Horros, prodding the quilled steed with his trident. "If you can steer into sky instead of posts, let us be off!"

Now Odios was not without his pride. Bearing himself upright, the gangly buzzard shook off the goo, flapped his great condor wings, and stepped forward, head high—and stumbled with a splash, flat on his nib, which was quite crooked enough already. Horros tumbled off his seat and, after only brief thrashing about, soon disappeared under the stinking swamp water.

"Awwk!... my mistake," cawed Odios. "It's me feet... sticks in this mud they does. Yoo hoo...Where you be?" Odios plucked his head back into the thick water like an ostrich, and pecked around in the muck searching for the little blue imp.

A stinging trident bite in the tail reminded the muddle-minded vulture that Horros was quite able to fend for himself. The soppy, satan-eyed beast growled intolerably from Odios' shoulders while cuffing his mount on the topknot. "Brack-dipped, brain-lacking buzzard!" The demon thrust his trident once more into the bird, and did so emphatically.

"Yeeouchhhh!" screeched Odios. He pulled himself out from the morass, tucked in his rangy toes, and cruised into the northern sky, spiraling miraculously past a tangle of heath vines, and just narrowly missing a crowded stand of thatch palm, finally to be lost amid the other fronds and wasps encircling Luhrhollow.

Niki wasted no time musing over such antics. The shanty door had not been open long, but it was opportunity enough for the swift-thinking dove to slip inside before it swung shut and locked behind her. Like a gusting leaf, she was gone from the ghastly, gazing giants which stalked the night beyond the door. Withal, they remained unflinching, and resumed their never-ending vigil with an unwavering obedience to voices only the dead's deaf ears could hear.

Now that she was finally in, Niki was even more perplexed by the baffling swamp house than before. Inside, there was nothing. Not from creaking floor to sagging silent ceiling; not from one peeling wall to the other; nor from the blind and boarded windows, was there even any trace of life—and of light, a lonely sliver. But from where, thought Niki. A glance up the pitch-sealed chimney did nothing to allay the riddle. "This shanty's secrets hold the light of moon at bay, and yet some eerie aura seeps into her parlor and blisters the souls of my feet." Niki examined the cracks which streaked the tepid floor boards. "I wonder... Vexpurra must be somewhere. Those walking weirds outside are certainly not guarding as empty haunt." Niki looked to the walls, but they were not talking. She tried the door; neither did it open under her prompting. Had she not been so intent on finding her lamb prince, she might have owned the wisdom of fear. And, had Niki not been so tired, she might have solved the mystery. Alas, the stale, musty air fed her weariness and, with nothing else to do but stand a solitary vigil, the befuddled dove curled up in a corner of the hearth and let drowsiness devour her. With eyelids heavy and crusty with sleep, they closed like a baggy stage curtain. And even the sloshing of approaching footsteps did not rouse them.

They were fen-drenched fox's feet, and they dripped anger and ire with each spongy step. Out of the morass they tramped, across the groaning porch's planks and into the murky parlor's void where they waited with piqued impatience for direction.

Accompanying the four vixen's paws was a pair of larger legs, which were manly—and fly-specked. This voice 'Hee-hawed' directly into the fireplace. "Friend fox... come," instructed the mule man with a whine. "It's a secret passage—and a most appropriate spot to dry off."

"See here, Vito!" barked the vixen, stepping into the hearth's large mouth. "I've never shrunk from turning your governor a favor or two, for Count DeSeet pays handsomely. Bacon side and honey broth are a toothsome change from mutton and bone... or those raps your cat's steward rations out so miserly. But even for a golden lamb this place curdles my palate. Why I allowed that lion's mistress to fetch me into this decaying mire of hers, I cannot comprehend... I must have let my craving stomach rule my brain. It's disgraceful! Look at what those upstart condors have done to my gorgeous auburn coat. Had I walked all the way from Middleshire through this sludge it would not have suffered as much indignation." The fox attempted to comb her frazzled fur back into its place, and lapped the stubborn mud clods from her pelt. "This stench is ruining my sensitive hunting nose too—it's congested nigh beyond use!" The vixen began to wring the sour swamp water from out her bushy tail. It dripped onto the floor, forming an acrid green pool just beside Niki's beak. Yet the dove still slept soundly, hidden from view in the semi-darkness.

Vito meanwhile, rather than answer any of the fox's charges, proceeded to cuss out a string of raucous commands. The hearth responded immediately—the lava brick floor began to descend. Unfortunately for Vito, his irate companion wasn't remotely impressed; the vixen lavished only grumbles and gripes. And while the one continued to carp, the other slung curses, thus was the chain sustained all the way down into the swamp's thermal defiles.

They descended into the bowels of a subterranean abyss, forbidden to all but the Kyln's most degenerated denizens. This was the home of the undead, and their demented mage, Lust. The vixen's fur began to curl under increasingly hotter air; the scalding smothered even her fuming for the while. Niki too felt her stomach sink amid the rise in temperature and words, and so began to stir.

Vito cocked his donkey ears. "What was that?" he asked.

"I said I was quite happy in the cool North, poaching that faun's mutton," replied the fox in annoyance, more irritated by the heat than with strange noises. "If I could shed my coat, as you switch loyalties I would not complain!"

For a moment Vito said nothing; instead, he dismissed Niki's rousing as a mere echo, and turned his thoughts back to foxes. "And you, friend varmint—you devour your loyalties! Have you no faith in the count's judgment? He bid me bring you here to his queen's court so we may discover the nature of this latest favor—for which you have been partially compensated."

"No doubt its nature be robbery. Why else would a thief be summoned, if not for her talent!" deduced the wily vixen, tapping swamp water from her plugged ears.

"Oh!" peeped Niki, as she woke with a start under the dripping fox.

"Oh, indeed," continued the unsuspecting vixen, before Vito could respond. "Now... we may ask, what is it that must be stolen? And why is it so valuable to our witchy hostess?"

Smoldering sulfur ash and peat ember now baked away the final film of dampness, save for the beading sweat which bound their skins like salty shackles. The sultry heat fried even the swarm of horseflies which clung perpetually to the air around Vito. A flash of firelight seared the darkness as the plunging hearth jarred to a torrid halt. A skin-scalding hiss alerted all who entered this steam-tiered, brimstone palace to do so with profound caution. So warned, neither mule nor fox hastened eagerly to accept their witch's warm welcome.

As for Niki, she remained in the hearth too, trying desperately to wake up to what had happened with that empty parlor where she napped. She recognized Prince Vito—and this place too. Though never here before, it was not so alien. She had seen it in sleepless nights, and tasted its wretched wastes each time she cried in pain. This was the unholy place—Luhrhollow—and Niki knew her search had ended. The billowing steam pillars of swamp drippings bore an unethereal resemblance to her own home in the Far Always. For a moment she longed for a miracle, some overseeing angel to quickly whisk her far away from the torment brewing in this vile crematory.

Just then, what should the steeping vapor reveal, but a large and solitary paragon sitting statuesque with its hard-boiled wings wide spread. But it was no angel It was hideous—it was Vexpurra—set like a tawny, stone-cold panther guarding her pride. Upon an ebony root alter she sprawled, primping and combing her writhing worm hair, basking in her brimstone paradise, tanning her brown brick skin on blazing coke fires. Her siren-chiseled face inflated into a wide, licking leer.

"Prrr... Why fox, you unscrupulous little bushwhack! And Prince Vito, the whimpering fly's ass... what a surprise!" Vexpurra paused only to sharpen her claws on her own grindstone hide. "Either you vermin have answered my prayers and died, prrr... or you've been summoned here for more larceny... Sssst" Vexpurra spat onto the sizzling coal-bedded floor creating another spiral of hissing steam. She despised everyone who was not dead or suffering.

Vito brayed sarcastically at the coke-skinned cat, then stepped brazenly from his fireplace into the pumice lair, ignoring the fiery flouts. The vixen, however, smartly chose to stay safely within the hearth, as her tender paws were shamefully blistered already.

As for Niki, with her presence so conspicuously illuminated, and without a log or stick to hide her, the little dove had sought a more covert cover—though its safety was decidedly dubious. It was from the furry cover of the bushy fox's tail that she and her unsuspecting host watched, while Vito attempted to negotiate Vexpurra's slag and tinder-textured carpet. Sadly though, it was a bit too torrid for the mule man's tender cloven soles. Like popcorn on a skillet, Vito skipped snappily across the coals to Vexpurra's pedestal.

The puma's nostrils flared as the scent of charred flesh whet her senses. "Roast toes!" purred the lava cat, smacking her lips and stabbing Vito's scalded feet with her claws. "How thoughtful of you, sire of flies, but you shouldn't have put yourself out... I'm stuffed!"

Vito fanned his scorched feet furiously and searched rapidly around for a cool place to soak them. "Cat! If you dare to harm just one of my toes, your mistress would ground you up into charcoal and fuel her fires with your brick cutlets!"

Vexpurra shrugged off Vito's distasteful remark and spat upon his feet... Sssst! She then mewed at the spouts of steam it drew. To add to the torment, she then produced a crucible of ice water from her queen's canteen, and began to drink before her dry-throated visitors.

It was all Niki could do to stifle a gasp—not from the heat, nor thirst, nor even fright—but from the lush, fox tail which tickled her mercilessly.

"Where's Lust, you sweet, sulfur-breathed cat litter!" demanded Vito with contempt, as he smugly threw himself upon Vexpurra's root lounge, scooped his fried feet into her ice bucket, and likewise helped himself to a long, cool quaff. "Count DeSeet, my colleague—and your mistress' consort—said she requested our presence here, regarding a boon we might render." Though Vito's words and manner boasted intrepidly, Vexpurra's soul-searing stare scorched the mule prince's thin shell of grit. He started to quiver in the feline's chilling shadow. The seething cookpot in which he sat made him tingle with fear. His implied contention that the witch would protect him dissolved when her lava cat began to purr again, and comb her whiskers haughtily.

"Prrrr... My mistress is not here!" Vexpurra grinned wider and more hungrily than before.

Vito swallowed an ice cube whole, and his audacity melted in his throat. The knobby legs shook like his churning stomach. "N-N-Not here?..." Vito's whine echoed off the steam pilasters. The heat became intense, and he began to sweat ice. He pandered a look at the fox, who merely eyed the donkey prince like a stranger, cooly indifferent to his plight, totally unimpressed with any of this show, and growing more impatient for answers to her questions. The vixen's most salient reaction was to scratch her tail, which was beginning to itch.

"Yes, sultan of flies; she's gone... Sssst" Vexpurra hissed as she spat on Vito once again and reveled in watching him steam.

Guessing this to be as fine a time as any to excuse himself, Vito slid meekly off the stone panther's roost. With one foot still lodged in the ice bucket, he hobbled back to the more accommodating brick-bedded hearth beside his partner in crime.

"Mistress and I had just returned from a wily ruse at the dirt lord's tower, Prrrr..." explained Lust's pet, "...when her lion beckoned."

As she spoke, Niki listened tensely, pouring over the meaning of Vexpurra's words—then, in terror, she grasped it. "A trap! We were duped!"

"Prrrr... Your whining, tomcat count has gotten his mane ruffled at Cinnabar. Stepped into some messy opposition from the runt king's main cross bearer, it seems. Prrrr... and from your lion's account of it, Constantio and that rooster-crested, cock strut of his, Violato, have alloyed to reinforce the cross-breast general's position. "Prrrr... so our compassionate queen has answered her tom count's mewing, and is this very moment rushing to his distress."

Vito's mule ears twitched, and wilted at such news. "B-B-But she wanted to see us... p-personally." Vito stammered from behind the fox, fondling her tail like a furry security blanket.

"My dear donkey-witted fly speck, 'p-p-personally' it's unlikely our queen would ever WANT to see you. Prrrr... with those flopping ears and fly-bitten tail, you're much too ludicrous for comprehension!" Vexpurra paused, and Vito ducked behind the tail expecting another stream of spit. Instead, the wary feline sniffed the sweaty air, and surveyed her guests with a new interest—having spotted a white feather at their feet!

"Mistress did however leave a message for your vixen—the one with the lovely tail..." Vexpurra purred before padding from her settle. She drooled over to the fox, with busy, stalking eyes—and there turned over a sealed note to the hunters. "Be courteous enough to read it on your way out!" The worm-haired cat's wide, toothy grin was gone; but her teeth remained bared, and her sharp, slit tongue danced across her fangs, and her slithering tresses hissed with life.

Vito wasted no time in wailing the appropriate curse which would elevate their hearth—unfortunately, the prince's hopes were not to be so raised. His sidekick felt an irresistible itch in her tail, and the accompanying scratch produced a slight fallout of two or three unfox-like feathers. As if these incriminations could go without notice, a timid little sneeze was soon to follow.

"Ah-choo!" squirted Niki.

"Bless you," said Vito

"Bless you," said the fox—then put aside her note and looked curiously at the mule, who looked curiously back at her.

"Why bless you both!" purred Vexpurra, her yellow eyes sneering wider than her mouth ever did. Lust's cat pounced over to the hearth and unsheathed a set of cutlass claws. At this point Vito fainted in the vixen's arms. But it was the vixen's tail which held the fire cat's interest. She tenderly sifted through the auburn tufts with her paws. How fondly she stroked Niki from her cover, and so wantonly clutched the tiny dove, all but impaling her in a deviously edged handshake.

"How nice! You nits have brought me a present... Prrrr!" A cruel, curdling curse from Vexpurra sent the mule and the fox aloft on their mission without additional discussion, leaving Niki to dangle in the face of Lust's favorite monster. Her every fearful facet attacked Niki's most stout defenses. "I've been expecting you, squab!" purred the hell cat fiendishly.

If Niki could have turned more white, she would have. The only escape from her fright was to shut her eyes; alas, the terror mounted. Sounds and smells of hot hissing steam and wormy, roasted hair suffocated the dove's nerves—and for a while the pain was smothered.

Inevitably, Niki's benumbed lids gathered enough courage to dare open once again. But the image they revealed was not Vexpurra's fire-cast face—No, this vision was a woolly one. It was the face of the lamb prince, Christen. And by the look and scent of him, this one was very, very real.

CHAPTER 38

An earth-splitting clamor raked the warm daybreak, rousing David from his sleep. He looked at the two empty bedrolls spread by the dead fire and rose in a panic. For the past two nights Peter had spent the early morning hours on watch; but now he was gone—and the bone man too, was nowhere to be seen. David raced into the forest in search.

Again and again the sky shook, and the trees trembled under each deafening volley. It was not the peal of thunderclaps which charged the countryside; these were iron echoes pounding and jolting the greenwood like an angry metal tempest. David tracked its fits and tremors onto a nearby crest, where he beheld his first glimpse ever—of war.

On the distant hillside, a pulsating panorama of scrambled, screaming fields of iron men tilled and tore apart the scarlet-soiled flesh of sod and soldiery. However, David was not long to savor the sight nor sound of such distant turmoil, the shocks of a more immediate warfare lay before his eyes.

Churning the field in front of him were two armored giants locked in a mortal duel. Each wielded massive weapons, lashing out in a fever-pitched contest of strengths: battle ax against broadsword. Both were reduced to clashing, silver blurs and neither yielded a foot of territory. Through the gale of dust, David struggled to make out the figures. The entire turf tossed and swelled like a turbulent sea under the onslaught's fury. From a clump of hawthorn trees, David scanned the mutilated clearing, while covering his ears from the abrasive din. He winced at each new salvo, then hid his face in terror at the grotesque image of one battling contestant. A sicker sight than the ravage of war—it was a troll, rutted with festering yellow skin. The thick rind provided better protection than his sword-rented bronze vest. And for a helmet, his yellow-husked skull sufficed. Two red, slitted eyes sneered from within to match his whole defiant countenance, which glared and snarled at his opponent—one who seemed remotely familiar to David. It was a knight to be sure, but a gouged, cylinder helmet concealed his face. The flowing white blouse which draped his chain mail trappings was so shredded and blood-soaked that its crest was completely obliterated. Then, a jolting ax blow staggered the weary, sword-wielding knight. David held his breath as the white figure faltered.

"Hold on, sir knight," bolstered the boy softly to himself. The warrior in white clearly had his sympathies. What an intense contest this must have been, thought David, taking in the ripped and wounded, furrowed field beneath the combatants. The diminishing clouds of carnage on the brawling plateau beyond looked like a storm front had vented its destruction then moved on in shifting, ceaseless fury.

Now, as the dust began to settle, David noticed two elfin squires sparring at the combatants feet, acting out the deadly drama of their larger-than-life counterparts. Upon the one, a white doublet bearing a red cross bordered by the

Decima—the crest of its sire. It was Yang. And the beleaguered knight—it could be no other... "Affirmare!" shrieked David upon recognizing the king's crusader.

"Shhh!" hushed a harsh voice from behind. David spun around and cried even louder than before, "Peter!—"

"Shhh—Quiet!" whispered the pony boy once more, appearing from a tuft of hawberry bushes. "Of course it's Sir Affirmare. Who else but the general of the race of men could inflict such wounds to enemy and earth alike! Now be silent, else your cries distract him to some mortal mistake."

David lowered his voice to match the rustling berry bushes. "Where have you been, Peter? I was in a dreadful fright."

The centaur trotted over to his friend and yanked at the leather tether drawn taut in his clasp. From out of the shrubs jerked Mors, still bound snugly and twitching as wretchedly as ever. "Same as you, Davy," replied Peter softly. "We're watching the doings on the battlefield. Our friend, bone-setter here, has a weak stomach for such close encounters however. He quails like the thumping turf—and with good reason. I see from your flexed face you've noticed the dainty, yellow beauty with the weighty ax—that's the lion's bone-picker, Negare! He's on loan from Lust I imagine. Hobgoblins, croakers and clay born—that cocktooth commands them all."

How well David remembered Affirmare's vivid description of Negare at the king's war council. However, it was not nearly so numbing as the fiendish figure fighting here so frightfully near to him this very minute. Peter's reassuring, brassy talk was all that kept the young pilgrim from keeling over on the spot. David shed his gaze from the violent encounter and turned an ear to Peter's words.

"Only moments ago Affirmare cornered old razor lips in this draw," continued the pony boy. "Beyond the forest rise, on the far plain, contingents from their respective armies are embroiled in unquartered combat. Though it pitches and booms so, neither side has yet found the edge. Only the forest's columns of hawthorns draws back, as if her earth will be the final crumbling foil."

"What a rude awakening it makes." David unplugged his ears as the rumbling bolts rolled inexorably across the plain while its two thunder heads pounded each other unceasingly in its stead. "How is it Affirmare's crusade finds us here?"

"Just who has found who, I wonder?" posed Peter, studying the scene. "It would seem we, and the crusade, have strayed far afield. And in our wandering, both have discovered the whole of Mythlewild to be beset."

David could see the centaur's eyes grow glassy as he watched his fond comrade waver under the force of Negare's ax, then cry in anguish as the merciless double edge found its mark. "Enough!" brayed Peter. "It's time for this pilgrim to take up a soldier's cross—a sword!"

David's stomach was churning, and his heart throbbed like the shaking earth. Not by Peter's words, but by the pall of combat. Its stark spillage stuck on his senses like tight-stretched skin. "I-It sickens me too, Peter, but I don't know what to do... I've not the fiber of a warrior. And of fighting, I know nothing."

"No? Well you've managed to fool me so far," remarked Peter as he began to grovel in the underbrush. "Here, let this be your fiber—your mettle—your sword!" A bold, sudden smile struck the centaur's dark face as he cracked a hawthorn branch in two, and gave one half to David. "You are a knight, remember? Have you talent enough to run and scream like a loon?"

A hesitant, but approving, nod from David was all it took to trigger the ready-set pony boy. Holding onto his silver hat, out from the trees he sprang, under a bone-chilling howl. He heaved on the tether, yanking Mors from the thicket, where the cowardly bone man had been holed up like a turtle. "C'mon, Davy—it's time to try our hands in this tilt!"

David also felt something tug at his feet. So, off into the clearing they charged, like two madmen—three, if you count Mors, who was dragged behind stirring up dust and wailing insanely, if only because of the pain inflicted. Brandishing their stick swords menacingly and casting stone arrows, the pilgrim warriors hurtled themselves into the thick, stirring up clouds of confusion as they laced toward the fray.

Negare had gained what looked to be an insurmountable advantage. Affirmare staggered to one knee, while struggling gallantly to thwart the scathing press of the ogre's ax. Only an unexpected onslaught of hooves and whoops gave him pause, and turned the frothing giant's vicious blade from its target. Had the ogre not been caught in such a startle, he might have taken time to count the advancing heaps. But in the clamor of confusion, the hat-clad pony boy became a mounted knight in full armor, and his stick, a lance pointed at the ogre's throat. David was not merely one, he was an oncoming infantry by the sound of him. And from the dirt Mors stirred, it was a war band for sure bearing down on Negare.

Before the goblin had time to think, Affirmare wheeled about to ward off his assailant. He regained his stance and parried, turning the yellow villain on his heels with a salvo of telling blows. Repulsed at every turn now, DeSeet's troll general had no recourse, save retreat. David and Peter jumped and shouted triumphantly as they watched the yellow grimling and his lacky flee beyond the trees to rejoin their ogre brigands.

"Have fun while you are able today, my friends..." groaned a pathetically weak voice from under the crusader's iron helmet. "...Tomorrow your laughter may lie cleft and broken upon the field..." Affirmare slowly removed his helm and revealed a startlingly grim and ashen face. Creased with cuts and spilling blood with each despairing word, the huge knight released his dulled broadsword and collapsed like a fallen oak.

The two mock soldiers dropped their stick weapons and rushed to their felled general, who was being tended by young Yang. The loyal page stanched his master's wounds and sponged his feverish forehead with cool dressings. Then Yang hastily flung open a saddle pouch, and drew out a flint and tinder to construct a fire. David could barely recognize this torn and bleeding haggard lying in the dust as the gleaming cavalier he had known at Bia Bella's gate. Not so robust now, he was drained of blood and luster both—but not of spirit, as his battling voice bore out.

"Forgive my rudeness, good comrades... I am alright... and indeed much grateful for your timely assistance. I've pursued that witch's deuce for a lifetime, and it's a bitter wound to lie here upon my back, while he escapes..." The crusader gnashed his teeth and grimaced, as Yang cauterized the ripest cut with a scorching knife. David drew in his face. Peter went to turn away, but didn't, as the elfish squire busily packed a tinder-boiled concoction of sulfur and herbs upon his lord's festering scars. Only for this searing second of human misery did Mors show a

453

smattering of interest. His black-hole eyes grew intensely pleased from within his grimy wraps, as Yang administered his poultice like one too well practiced in such medications.

From it all, with florid complexion and furrowed face, Affirmare looked up and found a smile. "Is there only one among you who does not shun the sight of a warrior basking in his glory? What did you expect to find beneath the shining silver suit, but the fragile flesh of man. Look upon this noble gladiator then... and see what sustains him, armored in his chain mail bandages. Behold my bloody tabard... is not so argent now—Aaagh!"

Though the sight and smell of it turned his stomach, David managed to see through this bent and grisly knight, to admire the man who spoke with so much veracity. Even as he suffered, Yang began to expertly stitch together the deepest abrasions, saving some of the body's seeping humors. Then he carefully jacketed them all in soft cotton dressings. The young squire's doublet was wet with his own blood, but he paused not, so one might tend to him—an injustice not unnoticed by the crusader. "Everything—that's what my loyal double will sacrifice for his bleeding white champion... Could I offer less for mine?" Peter and David bent their heads in agreement with Affirmare, then lent what aid they could to each of the king's noble servants.

"Have you lost your way, my friends? Or has Lord Enduros sent you egg hunting back into the lowlands?" Affirmare rolled his eyes in Mors direction. "Or is it a 'scavenger' hunt perhaps? Can that unraveled heap be some sickly substitute for the worthy Fidius?"

"Oh no, sir... Sir Fidius has saved our lives!" explained David. "Atop Mount White we were set upon by Lust's cat, Vexpurra—"

"Vexpurra you say? On Enduros' peak? Doom is surely at our door..." Affirmare's shoulders sank.

"It might seem so, sir," said David hurriedly, renewing his story. "Nevertheless, there is cause for joy. We are not lost, nor have we abandoned our dear lizard. Fidius' dragon child has joined him to combat the witch's hybrids in the north, while we pursue her cat."

"It's Christen, sir!" burst Peter. "He's alive! Unless he be illusion, we've seen the prince just one week past." Affirmare perked his ears and lifted his head at such good news. And Peter was buoyed by the renewed sparkle in his hero's eyes. "Vexpurra has her teeth in him and we've taken up the chase. Mors is leading us to her hideaway. But I fear, as pilgrims, we are woefully ill-equipped to deal with whatever we might unearth there." The pony boy snapped his stick sword and discarded it under foot to prove his point. "Will you inform His Highness of our news, and our distress. We would ask for help if any could be spared."

"For sure," spoke Affirmare, his voice pitched deeper now. "But if you are the fire-eaters I and my king believe you to be, you'll need no weapons beyond those arms pilgrims bear—faith in yourself and feeling for your fellow man. Carry no pretense of being something other than what you are... Howbeit, as witnessed, you are not so far removed from war's dreadnaughts as on the high lord's mountain. Rocks and sticks will hardly harm the queen of Luhrhollow. To slay the evil hunting these wilds, you'll need more solid steel than saplings."

"Those condor talons were dread enough for me as any skirmish waged," said Peter. "Had I been armed, I would have no battle scratch to show you now!"

"From the look of your puffed leg, you obviously lack for more than arms, young stallion," observed the crusader. "Maybe I can provide some insurance for all your precious limbs... Yang, lend your bow and arrows to the king's courier."

Peter eagerly accepted such a fine weapon and promptly tested its efficiency with a twang. He then placed the bow across his shoulder with nodding approval. "A strong yew and full quiver—now I have an archer's supplejack to lean upon!"

"And for our fledgling knight... What?" Affirmare fumbled with his belt, and from the girdle drew his leather-sheathed dagger, and forced it into David's hands. "For the more stubborn sinners which cross your path, pilgrim. Undo those devils with this blade that has made limb-saving mortar of my blood."

David also felt strangely secured by the weight of steel in his hand, and comforted as he stuffed it into his waistcloth, as if to hide this transgression from his conscience's glare.

"Be not so guilty, young knight," said Affirmare. "A prick is as a prayer when in Satan's throes. Would that I could render greater service in your cause..."

"Our cause!" added David, with his hand on his waist.

Affirmare nodded briskly, and held up a sturdy straight arm. "Anon... I am the one in need of help..." With his friend's assistance, the wounded general staggered to his feet, much to David's amazement. "Yang... I shall be needing a mount..."

The little page immediately sheathed his master's broadsword, which he had been deftly honing, then laid the weapon in its stirrup before dashing dutifully away.

"What dandy tales we could wag on here, my friends. I truly long to linger and visit with you brave hearts... Alas, my profession mandates combat over conversation. Though I detect from your story, and those wounds, you've joined in bouts to boast about as well... and allied yourselves to some queer company. Take caution, lads!" warned Affirmare, his dark eyes resting on Mors. "That knave's bones are not to be trusted. No bindings can confine his treachery. Sorcery harrows Theland; its dibble and hoe have turned a different earth—one not want to recognize... All is not as it seems—so be wise and trust no appearance, lest its sham sweep you under! This war has only just begun. I mean to rejoin Constantio and relay your tidings. The news of Christen should cheer His Highness greatly. As for help? Expect none. That has become a luxury few of us can grant to any, save ourselves. According to Folly's last message, the king's situation remains grave. His Highness and Captain Violato have reinforced my belabored command at Cinnabar. But even our combined machines are gradually succumbing to DeSeet. His ranks of warriors and warlocks are mingled with wizardry. I am afraid it is the lion's consort who holds the wild card. Lust's black magic has dealt them the upper hand, and dire omens have been written in the runes and on the sky. How many weeks now the sun has failed to smile—as if to say, even his lord, Zeros, who rules the heavens, has fallen prey to the pit sister's trumps."

"Or died..." uttered David without thinking.

But Affirmare's thoughts would allow no distractions. "No doubt Negare will now gather up his husks and return to his lion cohort at Cinnabar, to seal Constantio's fate once and for all. I'll not let that happen! If I can stave off Negare, there's a chance Sir Siegfried may yet arrive to bolster the royal defenses against the crone's underlings, and turn the tide. Alas, there's been no word from our valiant

Dragonheart. I dare not imagine our fate, if that tree squirm has lured him to his end." Peter and David exchanged looks of dismay at such a possibility. For fear it would confirm their suspicions—and further distress the crusader—the boys kept silent about their dealings with this same scourge in the Snowmass.

David looked up into the knight's taut face. How tall he stood, though bent with pain. The boy wondered if there were any other soldiers in the realm like Affirmare. "Can you tell us, sir, of the sea campaign? How fares Admiral Honos?"

The crusader answered in a sullen, lean voice. "Regretfully, Folly has relayed no dispatches from the fleet. For that matter, we've neither heard from Folly for some time. Our plans are plagued by chaos... We must all rely upon ourselves..."

Yang arrived with fresh steed in tow, and in the company of Sir Affirmare's white-vested knights. Still, the determined general would accept no assistance as he pulled himself into the saddle. Once mounted, his coat of arms—scarlet on a field of soiled white—seemed restored of its brilliance. David was choked with inspiration as Affirmare slipped the still shining helmet on over his exhaustion. His dark eyes reflected a new luster; they gleamed from behind the iron face.

"May your faith protect you, my friends... that may be the only aid you can count on. Albeit, if 'tis great faith, it will suffice—Adieu!" Affirmare waved, and raised his torn banner in salute. Then, spurring his white charger, he and his armsmen were gone again to battle.

"Would that our meeting could have been fonder," sighed the pony boy after the departing warriors.

David stared in another, more distant, direction—south—toward the Kyln Morass. "Peter... do you think my faith is strong enough?"

"Of course, Davy. It's been ample so far, hasn't it?"

"I suppose... Still, the company of some sword-bearing crusaders would be very comforting." Mors grunted as Peter tugged on his collar.

CHAPTER 39

By week's end, and after only a half dozen ill-spent nights, Mors had led the wary pilgrims far into the southern fells. Be it black heart or faint heart, it was a slightly roundabout the battle course the skeleton plotted—and, except for David's unerring shoes, their tracks would doubtlessly have wound much more about. For all his treachery, the bone man had indeed worked wonders with Peter's injury. Progress was nothing short of miraculous. The pony boy had abandoned Fidius' crutch, and felt invigorated be the keen response in his legs.

Fortified with the wondrous winged hat, the centaur carried his passengers swiftly from spans of stark-standing highland hawthorn and junipers, through the rippling brown grass swards of Mythlewild's lower downs, and into the heart of her broad delta. Cautiously they veered around the Bineholt, forested breeding ground of the gruesome Ill-timber armies, which served as a monstrous buttress protecting the larger looming realm of Lust's lair in the Kyln Morass.

They pulled up in a sea of saw grass at the very fringe of the witch's woods. A vast, foreboding hummock of tangled, twisting stands of shagbark and strangler figs wrestled with eucalyptus, gum, and giant mangrove trees. Waving great spiny tendrils of ivy plant and heath vines, the moss-drenched cypress, thatch palm, and willow wood together, beckoned the pilgrims enter, and engage the water-rooted warriors of the fenland. Within the brackish walls, the sweltering waste clacked and buzzed, groaned and growled, and ticked with teeming sounds of birds, and bugs, and beasts galore. All added voice to challenge their callers: 'step in' cried the desolate Kyln under its whisping, misty mask and shrouded shade; the cloud configurations of the Kyln loomed low and leering.

"'Tis in there you'll find your lamb," pointed Mors. His half-hidden face glowered with confidence now that he was almost home.

"Shade at last!" exclaimed David in a burst of glee upon sighting his first tree of the afternoon. He had long ago discarded his woolen jerkin by the wayside on the plains; stripped of all clothing save his shirt and hose, he still fried in the heat. "The ungodly sun is so unbearably hot on this prairie, I feel like a crispy piece of toast. If I could, Peter, I'd lend you my shoes for an hour under Niki's fine hat."

"And had you four cozy slippers rather than two, my aching hooves would gladly trade!" The pony gamboled uncertainly upon the sun-soaked heath which began to sag under his weight. His apprehension mounted as Mors began to strain his tether with increasing zeal.

"Follow me," whimpered the bone man, running as far ahead as his restraints allowed. "Plenty of shade in the Morass... and worthy Mors knows the perfect place. Mind your steps—there's gators and gars and other nasty biters lurking about... Hee-heeee."

"We really have no choice but to follow him," said David, patting Peter's shoulder after noting his disquiet. "Though I share your aversion to this seep, it has, after all, what we seek."

Peter cocked his head skyward as if expecting it to swoop down on him. When it didn't, he stepped with cautious reluctance into the swamp's peat and palmetto confines. The inner breaches of Kyln provided neither path or sign of trail on which to plan a route. Except for the sun, scrub-sedge, swamp privy, and moldy wooded fronds were the only guideposts their environs would supply—and she did so with cruel abundance. The farther into her clutches the boys plodded, the deeper they sank in her plush peat bog and moor grass carpet. A sweaty mist began to rise from her torrid, twining floors. It resembled a fog, only hot on the skin, like steam—and cold to the senses—like the slimy things which swam and scurried beneath their feet and between their legs.

"Where are we now?" protested David, swatting his way through a swarm of hungry mosquitoes. "These insects are as deep as this sticky quagmire you've brought us; and the heat is getting thicker than both!"

Peter pulled the tether taut around Mors' neck, which stuck out only inches above the tall marsh rushes. His chin jutted straight up to the sky, as if salvation dwelled there. "Answer him, bone-setter!" snapped Peter. "We've been slopping our way through this pea soup for hours, past scores of shade trees. Now just where is this campsite of yours—or even some dry ground for that matter."

But Mors was not talking. He remained a silent skull, stuck in the mud with his nose in the air, as if he was capable of smelling its stench.

"Peter, look there!" David pointed to a broad, grassy hummock, which rested high and dry like a verdant island rising from a consuming sea of lea and lime. "A perfect camp. And here's a good, shady spot!" he said, sliding wearily from the pony's back onto the hillock, and rubbing his own hindquarters. "Owww... My seat is so sore; I'll bet your back is bonier than Mors."

"And just how do you think my poor spine feels after cradling your rump all this way," replied Peter, with a half smile, as he searched around their site. "Uh, did you say there was some shade here?"

"Yeah, er... There was. " David twisted his neck to see what he saw, but it had left the scene. "It's not here anymore!"

"There it is," said the pony boy. "No, wait... It's gone again!"

"Hey—look! Up in the sky, Peter... It's only a cloud's shadow. We've been fooled!"

The centaur agreed, and said so in a cry of alarm. "Davy—quick! Get down!" He turned his face from the plunging shadow, then pulled David to the grass out of harm's way. With an ear-splitting screech, the shadow swooped down upon Mors, and just as soon was gone again. In its clenched talons, the bone man dangled from his leather leash.

"A condor!" gasped David, wiping moss and mud from his chin. "The poor, pathetic skeleton. That eye-picker won't find much meat on his bones."

"It got what it wanted," said Peter with disgust and slapped the swamp water, exasperated. "And it wasn't meat it wanted—it was Mors! Odios and Horros are returning that maggot to his mage, leaving us here—lost in hell's hallway, with no recourse but to go rapping on its gate like beggars! By heaven, I'll not be so slow to string these arrows next time!" The pony boy shook a fist at the steamy sky, but wounded it naught.

"I wish we had those armed knights now," said David. "Then we wouldn't be so helpless."

"Who's helpless?" replied Peter. "We're lost, maybe—and green, wet-furred fools—but at least we're on dry footing." The centaur trotted across their hill scouting for suitably solid ground to pitch camp. "Bone-setter was courteous enough to leave us his pack; at least we shall soon have shelter from these infernal mosquitoes." Peter began to set up their tent by driving stakes into the peat bog, which resented such prickly pounding. The result was like hammering holes into a wet sponge. Brown, pasty water oozed onto the deflated mound. Before long their island camp had completely sunk into the wallow, leaving the two boys chagrined, and knee deep in sludge and murky water.

"Are we 'helpless' now?" asked David, too fatigued to be anything but silly.

Peter slapped away the attacking midges with his tail, then admitting defeat, joined his friend in a good, heady laugh. "Ha—in such a balmy pool as this, lunacy may prove our only refreshment! If a pair of woebegones like us can flout and chaff in the face of this predicament, we can surely spit in the eye of any jackanape, nix or nasty Lust spews our way."

"W-What about s-snake's eyes?"

Peter dropped his jaw and stared as David scrambled out of the water and onto a nearby log, while a huge water moccasin swam in menacing circles around the driftwood. "P-Peter... Do something!" shouted David, clinging tenuously to his floating life raft. "Shhh... Steady, Davy. Whatever you do—don't move." The centaur hastily strung his bow and nocked a ready arrow; he then took careful aim.

"Hurry, Peter—he's going to strike."

With a hearty draw, the pony boy released the spur-tipped shaft which landed straightway and deep—right into the log, barely an inch from David's feet—and entirely missing the snake, which slithered harmlessly away.

"Peter!" gasped David in a near faint. He seated himself and tried to catch his breath. "You weren't even close! I could've been killed. If that viper hadn't swum away, I would have been snake bait as well as target."

"You were on death's brink for sure," agreed Peter. "For if that gator you're sitting on wasn't sleeping, you'd have been that clapjaw's bait too!" The centaur stepped over to his comrade and kicked the 'log' beneath him. It rolled over, belly up, revealing a bulbous pair of alligator eyes and an enormous mouthful of jagged saw teeth—and one well-placed arrow in its temple.

David didn't linger there to look, but was quick to hop again onto Peter's bony back, where he sat shaking, and hushed.

"If only Fidius were here with us," said Peter. "Sir Lizard would negotiate this fell jungle. As for us thin-skinned fellows, the twilight is nigh, and we had best find a hardy tree and make our camp in the security of its highest branches, before dusk's blacker brother, night, falls to finish us."

"Must we?" objected David. "I'm not so fond of trees anymore—not like I once was." He hugged Peter's withers and shivered all the more. The pony boy shook his head. "Perhaps you'd rather nest upon another 'log'?" Needless to say, there was no further argument from David.

The boys made their way to a tall, expansive cypress tree, which rose like a rangy, wood tower among the surrounding eucalyptus and thatch palms. After a thorough inspection for thorny teeth and chiseled scars, the pair declared it to be nothing but an ordinary cypress tree.

It was an easy matter for David to climb up, perched as he was on Peter's back. The pony boy however, was hard pressed to lift his equine frame from the soggy brake into the tree's high, moss-draped limbs. But with his set of hands clasped tightly in David's, discipline was finally hefted awkwardly among the sturdy wooden boughs, along with the remains of Mors' pack.

"Humph—a fine place for a horse!" grunted Peter, as he clung like a jay bird to his perch with both hands and all four hooves. Even his tail had forsaken the mosquitos in order to hold on. David would have chuckled at such an absurdity had something shocking not caught his eye.

"Peter—your legs!" He could only gape at the numerous, slimy black splotches stuck on his friend's four limbs.

"Leeches! Davy, help me get them off! Use the turpentine in your paint satchel... and your candle, to burn them off. It's the only way to remove the cursed, little blood-suckers. And while you're at it, better give yourself the once over for any unwelcome tenants." Peter frantically began to pinch and pick the stubborn parasites from his skin. "Is there nothing surrounding us in this god-forsaken waste which is not loathe or hostile!"

Just then, a flowery butterfly lighted on the centaur's shoulder, fluttered its bright wings as if to spite the ugly suckers, then continued on its merry way. Such a brief, but beautiful encounter served to remind David that it was in such a horrid bog as this, that he and lovely Niki's paths first crossed. And now, once more they had been cast—hopefully to be reunited, and released again.

By the time the last leech had been peeled off and the boys' grimy bodies bathed, the sun had begun to duck behind the cypress forest's heights, and in doing so, eased some of its heat. Though the pesky mosquitoes relented, other swamp denizens conversed in ceaseless clattering codes with all their kindred creatures. And beyond the murmurs surrounding them, occasional splashes or rustling of scrubs and woodruff reminded the campers, they would never be alone in the Kyln Morass.

In their treetop camp Peter began to relax. He settled into a makeshift hammock slung over a small, peat fire which dried their feelings, feet, and footwear. David fussed ruefully over the condition of his belongings, and attempted to restore the fine finish of his slippers with a good buffing. "How shamefully I've treated my treasures. Just look at how silt has attacked the soft, supple soles and matted their fine, downy wings."

Peter also seemed startled by the worn state of David's shoes. "I thought your soles were immune to such scourges as the wear and tear which befall most mortals' garb."

"That's true... At least it has been true in the past. But I must confess it has me puzzled. This swamp is so toxic... The whole place seems infected by its own excesses: its heat is hotter, its dampness wetter, and its brutes—more beastly. Peter, though we've just washed, I'm even more uncomfortable and dirty—and more scared than I can admit. If bitten by one more hot lip today, I shall be tempted to heel it right back to Bia Bella, where I'm wined and dined by kings, rather than drowned and stuck and supped upon by things in this reeking wasteland."

"Better not 'waste' your wishes with summertime dreams or reflections of the past, Davy. Regrets might burn you more than this fen. Save your faculties for our tasks in the present."

While David's thoughts loitered in the reticent past, Peter's hied on the more demanding present. The centaur's attention focused on the orange-tinted sky. First he merely rose from his hammock for a better view. Then, in one fleeting motion, he reached for his yew and let fly an arrow. However, it was the woman's shrill voice which woke David from his reminiscence.

"Help! Help me!" came her urgent pleas.

David looked to see what all the excitement was about. There, above him, silhoetted against the sky, was another huge bird sailing heavenward. In its talons, a beautiful damsel clung for dear life. "Another condor!" screamed David, jumping into his shoes.

Peter quickly nocked a second arrow, which was soon to find its way. This one struck home. Releasing the lady, the gigantic bird screeched in pain then plummeted, tail spinning, into the swamp. David hurriedly assisted Peter out of the treetop, then hopped on, as they galloped through the marsh water in search of the lost maiden. The colt muttered under his breath while attempting to negotiate the dense snags of heath and scrub thickets strewing their way.

"Do you suppose she's all right?" asked David.

"She's a strong voice for sure," panted the pony boy. "But lungs alone will not cushion her fall, nor stave off the alligators and vipers, and other infestations in these bogs. We've got to reach her before this paste does her in."

After several minutes of fruitless sloshing around through an endless mesh of reeds, and willows, and woodruff, the advancing shadows of night threatened to end their hunt. The fast-fading twilight cast an ethereal, eerie red light through the misty, marsh curtain; but it revealed no trace of the lost lady.

"It's just too dark now," Peter ground to a halt. "Make us a torch, Davy; this gal might see our light. Or maybe we'll even be able to find our way back to camp, where our dinner guests, the leeches, await their hosts' roast."

"Was she real, Peter?" David wondered as he held his candle aloft. "I had a dream about such a beautiful woman at our journey's outset. Perhaps our lost lovely was a dream..."

"A screaming dream, Davy? Our wisp with a voice cried out for help. If only we could have... Now the quagmire has probably claimed her." With no hopes left of ever finding their damsel, Peter and David turned back to begin a new hunt—for camp. It was only now that the swamp proved merciful towards their frightened figment.

"Here..." sang the soft voice through the darkness, sounding as sultry as the night, "... Come this way," it said.

The two boys shined their candlelight into the brackish glade towards those words. And what they saw sprawled there on the sandy bar of bedstraw, lying just beyond the reach of rushes, cattails, and carnivorous plants was definitely no dream. It was a woman—absolutely. Totally real, and solidly captivating. She was an Amazon, statuesque, with flawless, olive skin that glowed like pale light under the misty moon. Her lank and whorling hair shimmered as brightly red as the gown she wore. David was astonished.

"She's beautiful!"

"Your dream?" asked Peter, as David dismounted, then frowned.

"No... but a vision of enchantment nonetheless."

The vision sparkled like a ruby, and smelled of soft, ripe-scented roses and lavander, amid the swamp-privy and poison sumac. At their approach she arose, unhurt and nearly dry, and greeted David warmly, extending her smooth, slender hand with a provocative smile to match. "Kind sir... Was it you? Are you the archer which saved my life?"

"No, my lady..." responded David with an awkward half bow. This attractive woman was so charming and gracious, he felt obliged to do something respectful. Why, she might even be a queen. "My name is David; but it's my friend, Peter, who deserves your gratitude."

The pony boy stepped politely forward and tipped his hat courteously. Like David, he was infatuated by the woman's spellbinding loveliness.

But the red lady all but ignored his courtesy, preferring instead to address the two-footed boy. "That wretched eagle would have supped on me had you not shot it," she went on, without further introduction.

"Did you say, eagle?" interrupted Peter. "We thought that scavenger a condor."

The lady now acknowledged Peter with a somewhat crooked smile. "Eagle... Condor...What difference? Both are nasty raptors."

Peter smiled back into the olive-skinned rose. "This swamp is chock full of nasty snappers; it's not a pretty place for such a comely one. You're very lucky to be alive."

"Yes. The heavens have smiled down on me tonight. But I'm really quite well now, thanks to you and your friend. As for the everglade, it is home. My house is not far. If your charity could carry me there, you would be welcome to spend the night. That is the least I can offer in quittance for your good deeds." Her satin voice was a fresh sea breeze in the stagnant moor.

Just like a lotus among the leeches, thought David of this queenly maiden of the marsh. Everything about her was so alluring. Her very nearness boosted the pilgrim's spirits—even to the point of humor. "Well, I do hate to forsake our cozy little nest in the cypress... but, it you insist!" David chuckled while he helped the damsel onto Peter's back.

As the boy hoisted himself up, the lady's jewel eyes gleamed brilliantly. "My, what fascinating shoes!" She brushed one of them with her palm, and stroked its wing—then released her grip with a jolt, as though stricken. She raised her brow to David, "So soft... like wearing the clouds!"

David was flushed, then he felt a tingle in his toes. "Hurry, Peter, I think I feel a leech!"

The red lady guided them deftly through the dark shoots of nightshade ferns and leafy legumes of her grasping, thick-grown neighborhood, but seemed somewhat adverse to any discourse. David attributed this reluctance to her ordeal. However, Peter grew edgy at such languid silence. "How did this eagle happen to capture you, madam?" he inquired by way of conversation.

The vibrant, distaff eyes, which had continued to admire the winged shoes, now turned upon Peter. "I was on an errand, and it fell upon me for no good reason. It is a risk one runs when residing in the swampland."

Peter nodded, but didn't understand. "Might I ask why one of such rare beauty desires to misplace it in a treacherous habitat as this?"

"I find it suits me." The lady's red lips imparted a hot sensuous grin at the pony boy, nearly melting his last apprehensions. "You must not trust too fully in first impressions, archer; they can be critically deceiving."

Before long they arrived at a wide, moonlit, willow-walled glade, which spread like a dry oasis in a swamp-washed desert. Crouched in its center was a cozy, cobblestone cottage framed with yellow thatch roof. Sweet-scented lily pads and myrtle plants hugged the wallstones from atop a plump, cushiony heather terrace. Smoke drifted out of the red brick chimney; and from within, the windows' golden firelight cast a welcoming glow upon the soft, dry grasses and revealed a splendid weeping willow more lush than any either of the boys had yet seen.

"Not much like our campsite, but it'll do," commented Peter, feeling more at ease now.

"Why, it's just like home," said David, who was reminded of Valentina's cottage in Hue Dingle.

"Who would've believed it?" The centaur stopped short of the front porch to observe all his eyes and ears and instincts would allow.

"Go on, boys... Step in," coaxed the red woman with her winning ways. "You'll find it's quite a departure." She opened the door for her guests and, upon entering, all traces of the Kyln immediately vanished.

In the middle of the parlor, beneath the lace curtains and beside the crackling hearth, sat a pudgy, diminutive, old lady, with a grey bun of hair set upon her dinner roll face. A homespun shawl wrapped her supple bulges, and the whole sweet package swayed lazily in a frilly-cushioned rocking chair. What there was of a lap, housed a fuzzy kitten, that frolicked with a ball of yarn, which the old woman was crocheting into a muff.

To David's mind, this picture of coziness it was indeed a refreshing change. Once inside, he breathed a deep sigh of relief. Peter breathed too, but shallower— and more measured at the premise he saw.

The old lady acknowledged the callers by adjusting her bifocals, then continued knitting, with not so much as a word of hello.

"Another 'chatterbox'," whispered Peter. But his jeers failed to dampen David's enthusiasm.

The pilgrim had already made himself comfortable by the fireplace and was entertaining himself with a parakeet which chirped melodiously upon a perch above the old woman's ear.

"Let me take your shoes, young man..." suggested the red lady, "...so you won't track mud."

But David kindly explained how impossible that was, and apologized by wiping his slippers clean with one of his rags.

"Suit yourself then," the lady said flatly. "Just make yourself at home," she said, before turning to go. "I do have that errand. My husband's affairs delay him you see, I was on my way to abet him when that hawker picked me. I'm dreadfully late... If you will excuse me, my housekeeper will take good care of you—"

"Wait—" said Peter. "How will you get there? Let me carry you."

But without further explanation, the beautiful red lady was out the door.

Peter was baffled. "Well, where'd our miss will-o-the-wisp run to do you suppose?" He looked out the window, hoping to catch a glimpse of the mysterious lady. Through the lace curtains he saw something move in the moonlight. Then, it was gone. But it was not the lady in red, she had disappeared completely. The willow boughs rustled in the stillness, and something else stirred too. Peter's hand moved to his bow.

The pony boy turned again to David and whispered cautiously to him. "I don't like this parlor, Davy. Something is terribly wrong here—terribly warped. Close your eyes... feel the air in this hut. It's thicker than the bog... hotter, more stifling—yet we're the only ones to sweat!" For the first time David could remember, he saw Peter trembling with fear. "Davy, out there in the swampwater I felt helpless, I admit it. And in our tree camp I felt vulnerable, and yes—afraid. But never in my life have I been as flushed and numb with terror as right now—in this household of jugglery." Peter's lips were cracking dry, his eyes puffed, and his hazel hair bristled. His argument could not have been more convincing.

Other troubling words returned to bedevil David's mind: 'Do not trust in first impressions' the red lady had warned, 'for they can be critically deceiving'. The pilgrim stepped closer to his friend. His feet became marshmallows.

The old spinster remained quiet. She had put down her knitting and began to stroke the tabby in her lap, it was no longer playing—and it seemed larger. David forced a smile. "W-Well it's been nice chatting with you, madam... B-But we really can't stay—"

"Oh, but you will!" came the voice from the rocker. Yet the old woman was still.

It was a sharp, cinder voice; the feel of it moved David toward the door, where he tried the latch—unsuccessfully. "It's locked!" He began to choke on the air. "Peter —the door! Break it down and let's get outta here—I'm so scared!"

Summoning all the strength his strained legs could muster, the pony boy reared and kicked the cabin door hard with his hind legs, knocking it completely from the hinges. To the boys' amazement, the old woman offered no resistance; she simply sat in her rocker as if nothing unusual were happening. As her guests turned to run, they saw why.

Standing before them on the porch, was another door—no, it was a wall—a wall of disfigured and diabolical bulwarks in armor shells and packed with clay. In every conceivable size, shape, and squalor, the misshapen soldiery all shared the same cause, and the same singular trait—death! These were the clay-born: the ghostly guardians of Luhrhollow.

Peter and David froze in their tracks, petrified under the intensely grim and ghastly stares of the walking dead. From behind such an arrant curtain, stepped a particularly repugnant figure—a runt compared to the rest—a wad of black and bone. From behind his hood peeked the empty-eyed skull of Mors. The bone man straddled the threshold and delighted while the two boys chewed on his presence, swallowing it like a bitter pill—and with it any hope of escape.

Stepping into the doorway behind the skeleton was another spook. Secured in this clay-born's clutches was an eagle—felled by an arrow which still lodged in its side.

"Hee hee—This one's too pure for our flock. I believe he's one of yours!" snorted Mors, as the feral picket heaved the bleeding bird at the pilgrims' feet.

"Oh my lord!" gasped Peter. His face paled to match the dead ones upon recognizing Palladan, sovereign of beasts, and beloved pet and protector of the earth father, Enduros. "What in the name of all the gods have I done!" Had he not anger to equal his grief, the young centaur would surely have died then and there. But, while his fate was certain now, he was not going to his grave in shame. As the bone man gloated in the limelight, Peter set his bow.

"You're not leaving so soon?" the skeleton squatted on the battered door like a famished jackal. "You've been very rude to poor, forsaken Mors—Hee hee!"

"Were I not so stale a hostess," spoke the old, close-lipped lady once again, in a voice more rasping and ground in wickedry, "I would have your weapons, bowman." It was the growl of a mongrel cur. And when the pilgrims reeled to face it, 'twas not the least bit cozy.

But Peter was not ready to surrender his arms—not to anyone, or anything. "Take my arrows then, devil!" he retaliated. And through the putrid slough, into the very heart of Horros did his arrow fly—alas, to no effect—save to humor the blue demon, which mocked him from the rocking chair and picked his teeth with Peter's shaft.

The lap cat also purred in ridicule. And their pet bird too joined in, and clacked in condor's tongue. Before the shocked pony boy could recover his sanity enough to notch another shot, he heard the entire room contort with loathsome laughter. It twitched and twisted about him as the hex was lifted. A thousand arrows would not quell it. But Peter was not given a second chance—a cold and bloodless blow sent him into unconsciousness.

David reached into his blouse too late. He was struck down with Affirmare's dagger still sheathed.

"Get those shoes off him!" growled the voice of the devil. "Cut off the upstart's feet if you must—I will have them, and that satchel too!" Those were the last words David heard.

CHAPTER 40

Outside the perpetually stewing swamplands, autumn was eagerly basting Mythlewild with a chilly winter topping. Cantankerous grey clouds jostled for position in their crowded, overcast sky lanes. Each bullying billow jeered menacingly over Folly's shoulder some distance below them. The hippopotamus cherub, momentarily grounded, sat dolefully atop a pile of tree branches and wind-swirled leaves which, like him, had been shunned by November. Now they served as a comforter, on which the rotund angel pod earnestly poured over a large, crinkled map and soberly attempted to discern just where he was.

"Hmmm... Now let me think. If I can remember where I was... then maybe I might be able to see where I am now; or perhaps learn where I am supposed to be, or was... before I found myself lost..." Folly began to chew his thick toenails out of a nervous lack of anything more moist to nibble. He next scratched one of his many unsettled chins. "Phooey! What good is a map—you have to know where you are before you can find yourself!"

The nasty sky chuckled briskly under one gusty gambol after another, and stole Folly's map into its windy jowls, which then delivered the chart to one of its far away, fluffy hecklers in a taunting game of keep away.

"A pox on you—you unscrupulous sky!" yelled a mortified Folly. "May a drought dry out your puffed up truants and bake their badgering breathes!" Flapping the leaves from his wings and climbing ungracefully onto his squat, chubby legs, he shook a mad, meaty fist at the rollicking air. "Is there no calm to your harassment? Your gloomy complexion, and flirting curls have blinded my flight like thick, tar tresses. Your rude winds fling me from my sworn duty and shove me to the ground like a chucked pollen speck. And, as if your persecution was not complete, you whisk away my maps—my only hope... though a hopeless hope it seemed to be. How am I supposed to find my way back to Cinnabar? How shall I ever explain this larceny to my angry king?"

The uncompassionate fronds shrugged their swirling shoulders, moving Folly to retaliate with an ineffective volley of arrow. But the vexing grey nuisances paid no mind, as the rubber-tipped shafts passed harmlessly through their wispy creases.

The grounded cherub sank onto his leafy cushion in a dither. "What a perfect occasion for some sweet apple wine." Folly sighed with some regret upon delving into his quiver to find nothing but arrows. "Pshaw! The king's war dispatches sit idle in my quiver, undelivered and unread, while my wonderful wine well stands brimming, but abandoned, outside Sovereignton's south gate. *Sigh...* Failure is destined to be my only success."

With his spirits as inclement as the weather, and steeped in weariness from all his futile flights, with no direction of his home or Highness—and with no apple nectar near at hand—Folly decided to bury his troubles once and for all. He curled himself up into a big round mound covered in leaves and sticks and took a snooze. And there he might very likely have remained for the war's duration, or at least a good long spell; however, a sudden sharp sting on his blubbery buttocks roused the chub with a hardy 'Yelp', casting the paunchy hippo pile once again into the woes of wakefulness.

"On your guard, you wooded rogue!" shouted a familiar voice. "Taste my metal nettles, Ill-timber!" Another jab on his flabby flank sent Folly high into the air. Shaking off the limbs and leaves, he sought to regain some composure; unfortunately, as was his fortune—Folly failed. He landed once again, like a great-bellied earthquake upon his tail—or someone's tail—and before a regiment of knights.

Rubbing his bruises vigorously, Folly stared with indignation at two kingsmen standing before him: Siegfried Dragonheart, whose brick jaw hung wide open, gawking back at the hippo; and Pax, the griffin, who winced first on one foot then the other, as he tugged on the pancake—which was his mashed tail—the one on which Folly so weightily sat.

"Why, Folly—it's you!" observed Siegfried, returning his sword, Byn Tu to its girdle. Saddened by this setback, and surprised at finding the king's air post thus grounded, he strived to put the pieces right. "I'm dreadfully sorry about this mishap... I mistook you for that sinful shrub, Ill-timber—cloaked in its boughs as you were. 'Tis like no other tree's foliage..." The Northman extended his arm, tree branch in hand, as if it would vouch for his account.

Folly puffed the dry spring into the wind, attempting to assert himself over something at least, then accepted Dragonheart's hand. With an added boost from Pax, the hippo was eventually towed onto his knees, where he busily set about recovering spilled arrows. He was in no mood to discuss this encounter with the king's knight. For while it was embarrassing enough for Folly—for the king's air courier, it could prove tragic. To be caught napping on the ground in this time of national emergency, Constantio would never forgive such dereliction of duty. However, the devoted cherub needn't have worried; the flaxon warrior was too engrossed in reconciling his own shortcomings.

"As you may remember, Folly, His Highness directed Pax and me to pursue that wood worm; hence we set our noses to the trail of loam and dead leaves shed in the beast's tracks. Alas, we were mislead. The wind scattered the sheddings, discarding them to every point in the realm, leaving my band nothing but aimless blades to rook and bilk us out of our way. While we dog after his shavings, the real tree skips off in some opposing direction..." Siegfried paused to locate Pax, who sensed the shame about to come and so picked up his wounded pride, slung it over his shoulder with his broken tail, and returned to their chariot to sulk. "...And my misguided griffin pilot—whose navigational talents amount to nil—has divested my trust in him by leading us on a wasted run to... to here! Wherever 'here' is?"

"Should the dragon's heart not share the failures of his nose? Both lost— both fools I say," philosophized Folly softly. "And was it not His Highness who entrusted the coxswain to YOUR care?" he mentioned by way of correction. This minor point would rebound to haunt the poor hippo, as Siegfried's amber face lit with inspiration.

The dedicated knight slapped his hands together. "Why, Folly, how fortunate we've stumbled onto you! As the king's aerial surveillance, you must know where we are—and you've maps to chart our way out!"

Siegfried had anticipated some kind of response, but Folly just sat by the wayside counting his arrows, silently sifting through their messages. The flaxen gallant then removed his helmet, as if to air out his brain. "Er, come to think of it sky runner... what business has grounded you? Your calling is higher up, is it not?" Siegfried stuck his suddenly stiff face into Folly's, sniffed... then poked his prodigious nose into the quiver. Have you been sipping spirits again, gatekeeper? I can detect nothing... Or, have you also run afoul of that wayward wind?! Tell me true, herald—are you misguided too?" A grin cracked the fair-haired Northman's stony face, but Folly would admit to no more humiliation today.

"Me... lost? Don't be absurd!" Folly rolled to his feet with as much dignity as an albino hippopotamus with wings could gather, then snapped a salute. "Do you take me for a buffoon? Humph! I was simply carrying out my orders, Sir Dragonheart... Waiting for you... on this far flung byway. I have a message from His Highness..." After some fumbling through his arrows, Folly extracted a note which he had just discovered during his reshuffle. "The king is in dire straits at Cinnabar. He beckons you to break off your weeding, and deploy your column toward yon plain to reinforce him at once." The cherub swelled with pride at his alibi; though, in fact, he really was venturing to deliver this same dispatch prior to his turnaround in the cloud banks. And while a boastful grin nearly broke between those somber cheeks, he held his head under the sour note his heavy news had struck.

"This is most serious," lamented Siegfried, crushing Constantio's letter in his hand as though it were the forces of foes he smote. "The king's ranks are surrounded on all sides. Mayhap, my troops are his salvation—we must hasten to him!" Dragonheart donned his silver helm; its gold wings glistened as the indigo-caped champion took flight. "Come with us, gallant gateman. Lead us to Cinnabar! Ride with me, your weary wings must beg for respite—you looked positively dead when we chanced on you."

Though distraught by such an invitation, the hippo had no choice except compliance. If he was to be lost in this war-racked land, it would be more honorable—and so much safer—in the company of a king's regiment. Alongside Pax, Folly plop- ped into the chariot, which sagged moanfully under the added baggage. "Say...you wouldn't happen to have a spot of ale about, would you, chap?"

The languid griffin only stood by the reins and scowled. "Which way?" he wanted to know. And all of them: griffin, and knight, and each of their men seemed to stare at Folly for direction. Even the clouds crouched down to hear his answer, and then—in part to make amends—parted to reveal a glimpse of yellow sun, which was also curious to hear.

"Look, Pax—the fickle sun is back on our side!" smiled the Northman. By its position, a northwesterly heading should bring us back to the Carmine Meadows—and the plain of Cinnabar. Am I right, Folly?"

A quiescent hippo nod was all it took to send them off. Pax cracked the chariot's reins and his team of stallions responded with a whicker, then smartly surged into full gallop, leading the Northman's regiment swiftly to the rescue of their king and kinsmen.

Fourfold nights forced march, and three days of unflagging haste saw Sir Siegfried's chariot roll to a halt beneath the blood-streaked sky over Cinnabar. While his men stole some sorely needed rest, Siegfried panned the bleak slate that was the horizon. The afternoon's muddy mantle of clouds had become pitted and riff with multiple layers of vultures. Though he could not yet see or taste it, from the head-splitting shrill of it, the Northman knew the wold, which stretched before him like cured hide on a rack, was to yield a scene of great carnage and torment.

A steeply rising slope slackened their pace, once the troops continued on. Heads were cocked high at the circling predators, while hearts were held in each man's clenched stomach. The devious wind brought them all the sounds and smells of the slaughter of their dying countrymen. "'Tis good you do not waft about the sky now, Folly. That flock of carrion would pluck out your belly and sink our air force like a burst balloon." The cherub was all set to smile with relief at this harboring thought when the Northman added, "Better to perish here upon the earth with your comrades!"

Up until now Folly had been straining to nap on the chariot's floor, but the mood deserted him. The air turned cold in the condors' shadows, and plump goose bumps charged up his pale hide. Sleep surrendered to the rising clamor, and Folly's nerve became another reluctant victim. As Siegfried beheld the battle panorama, its first impressions etched a mortifying brand upon the once rock features of the warrior's flaxen face. His jutting jaw and burnished, broad shoulders sagged like soft wax; it's mood coating his hardened armor body like flowing lava.

Pax dropped his reins and stood stark still, like a corpse. The twining column of knights became an unflinching array of hollow metal men lined on the hillcrest. From their vantage point they saw the spoil and massacre of Mythlewild boxed in the battle-torn basin below.

Constantio's position was indefensible. The king was hemmed on all sides by DeSeet's insurgent war bands, which were immense in numbers. From every fold and wrinkle of the broad plateau the lion's horde poured like blood from an open wound. Negare had returned from his skirmish with Affirmare to outflank Captain Violato on the west, and had totally decimated the king's most formidable command. Constantio's prized legions lay devastated under ogres' hoof and blade.

Of survivors, there looked to be some. But, for how long? All was chaos. Had it not been for General Affirmare's timely return, the king's own cohort would have been lost entirely—along with the barest thread of hope.

Dragonheart wept openly as he and his witnessed their king's finest knights crumpling under the onslaught. Overmatched, and under attack unceasingly, Constantio's fragmented militia was pressured to retrench—until now. Another ally of DeSeet's, the Rollingway River, wound around behind and poised at the king's back. "Guidon—sound the charge!" commanded the Northman. "Griffin—give rein!"

Pax was slow to respond. His stomach took acute leave, and the bright orange feathers behind his bandanna went pale, then shriveled up like dry leaves. Despite these throw ups, the dutiful griffin somehow found his voice. "Y-You mean attack? With only these few hardbacks of cavalry and tree hounds? I say, sir, do you expect to turn such a tide as... as that sea of sorcery? Death will surely meet our heroics down there."

"Heroes are born in death, coxswain," countered Sir Siegfried, retrieving the reins from Pax. "We shall now be baptized in war's waters. And we cannot accomplish that with our unsoiled backsides saddled up here bantering—with our weapons and guile girdled! The only avenue of approach is the east. Apace now—while there remains a semblance of something worth saving!" Bestowing a pat of confidence on the griffin's iron hat, Sir Dragonheart brushed his own long, golden locks, unsheathed Byn Tu, and raised it above his head for all his men to see. "For My Lord!" he shouted. "For My Liege—For my land!"

And his loyal column of gallants resounded the call, and raised their arms and voices: "For My Lord, My Liege, and my land!"

"And for life..." repeated Pax to himself, over and over again. He was not alone. Much louder was the rallying cry of the flaxen's lusty cavaliers charging into the pandemonium of Cinnabar.

The chariot rumbled as if down the thumping throat of some angry pitfall. Needless to say, Folly was quite awake by now—but not by choice. The hippo rolled himself into as compact a ball as possible and huddled on the floorboards. His hands were folded in a hasty prayer, on the vain hope of placating his nightmare. Unfortunately, the portly tosspot was not to be so easily absolved of his excesses.

Even tucked in as he was, Folly was hardly indifferent to the slaughter snipping above his ears. Nevertheless, he pretended it was not really happening.

The racing chariot tossed and jarred, though over what lumps Folly dared not guess. The violent sway rocked his bones and belly and piled bruises on top of bruises; while the wailing, splintered screams of Siegfried's sword and soldiers dashed his wits. Other cries were heard too—though of what he could not imagine. It was not men's, but bestial howling, like vampire bats, or banshees, or jackal pack at feed beside its kill. The king's offish gatekeeper never wanted war to touch him so intimately—but it did, and cared not a jot or tittle of its martyr's wants. Under such loveless caresses, every inch of the blanched white bulk stiffened with fright.

It had begun to pour; but it was not the cleansing raindrops which speckled Folly. It was the spattering of blood dappling his pure, angel meat. He prayed all the harder that it was not his. Folly's life came and past again before his tightly-closed eyes; not once, but twice, a dozen times or more, until his nightmare carousel was ended—by the touch of something more bizzare. It was squeezing tightly around his skin. Then the rumbling waned. The din drew up silent, and soon more cries—but they were not the melancholy wails of death.

Something serpentine wrapped itself around Folly's leg. One of his eyes dared to open—just a crack; but it was enough to see Pax's tail hugging him with earnest. The trembling griffin squat next to his albino counterpart, and a few of Folly's fears evaporated under a calm and peaceful warble.

"Battles frighten me too," cheeped Pax, clenching his tail as if it could save his life. "Sometimes I wish I had never become a combatant. Then, when I serve at the side of stalwarts like Sir Dragonheart, or Admiral Honos, it strengthens me; and I'm reminded, that in order to conquer my enemies, I must first quash my own fears..."

"And a very good lesson it is too, By Thunder!" said a weighty voice. "As you have so graphically reminded my enemies by your daring gambit. You've breached our foes front lines—now, have you the edge to rise and greet your king, so he may acknowledge his gamecocks properly?"

Both Folly's eyes popped open at the sound of Constantio's words. He watched while Pax hopped from the chariot to take his place beside Sir Siegfried as the High King hugged them both warmly and pronounced in adulation, "Dragonheart—gallant Nordic—what a miraculous sight you are! And brave Pax—you are truly an extaordinary pilot! What a bold and grabbing dash into my camp you made—Bravo!"

Some camp! observed Folly, unable to draw his sight from the devastation encasing him. The killing calm of a hurricane's eye would be more accurate. The hippo remained temporarily secure, hunched on the floorboards, still debating whether the war, or the king's wrath was most to be feared. Thus, it was from this seat he viewed the aftermath of pitched battle. Surely, he thought, this entrenchment of armored corpses could not be the same brassy caravan which had paraded so splendidly from the cheering throngs of Sovereignton, alive with zest and fervor for accolades and honor. Was this graveyard the resting place for such grand a glorious whims? What became of the brilliant, splendor-crested panoply and plumes of the cock-sure crusaders he left but a few short days ago? What has happened to their victory?

The streaming, gaudy banners were all struck down. Tattered hatchments dipped to shroud the battered, bloodied bodies which kissed their coveted colors no more. Death's rampart remained unfurled over them, lapping the scent of suffering and despair. Its black designs hung mercilessly in the red-soaked sky, on the out-stretched wings of condor silhouettes.

Only one royal flag still flew above annihilation to bar their celebration—the Decima Crown. It was Constantio's—around his coat of arms the ragtag army rallied. And now, to the king's standard, Siegfried Dragonheart raised his. It was when this alliance was displayed that their regal king broke down—and wept.

The sturdy monarch sat haggard and worn to the point of collapse, yet still somehow majestic. Though his lion skin raiments be pelted and patched, and his chiseled red torso chinked and chipped, Teak—his club and scepter—prevailed in his firmly locked hands. His war-laden brow, though florid and careworn, was not too numb to carry his crown. And his faithful cloud pedestal tirelessly enthroned its imperishable rider with an undiminished eminence and distinction. Thus was their sovereign still regal, still commanding exhaustive respect, and still shouldering the awesome weight of his responsibility.

"Sir Dragon, your unexpected arrival has temporarily set the enemy on their heels, and what's more, brought us our first cessation of hostilities in nearly a week. Naththeless, as soon as our enemy's causalities revive and rejoin the living hulks, they will be back, as sure as winter."

Presently another rampart appeared and was hoisted to compliment the others. It was the strutting crest of Violato the Red. Though it was not the captain's hand, but his hand servant's that hoisted it. In Constantio's tent, Folly spied the king's lusty champion prostrate on his back and gravely wounded. His bronze war coat expired in a corner all dinted and dull. One arm was nearly gone, severed to match his mangled body, cut open as it was from nape to groin, and stitched back together again before his life could desert him. His broad, powerful chest of bronze skin had caved in on him like a dream gone sour. His robust face was drawn and discolored almost beyond recognition. Yet enough of him was there to recognize an old brother in arms—and rival. As Siegfried embraced his good friend, Violato clasped the Northman's arm and squeezed as if to demonstrate the strength remaining under the sagging red beard.

Folly was moved to recall how often Violato belittled him by the city's gate. At the war council, no one had been more harsh—nor lavished such attention upon him—as that wounded, riddled flesh now seeped of every ounce of ire. Folly wiped his

blubbery eyes, but they would not dry. The ruin about him would not permit that, nor would his shame. This was no nightmare—or it was—a waking one. He would not wipe this sleep from his eyes, nor forget this scene—never! Folly was overcome by the guilt born out of his dereliction. Death had left its mark on him, and all the other living too. The hippo was shaken by what his senses said to him; and he was stirred with resolve—and by the sight of Affirmare.

Over on the west flank the general's crusaders continued to skirmish, resisting—at times even countering—the enemy's advances. Such fidelity to cause, and to men, inspired the whole encampment. Many, more hardened than Folly, were moved to tears.

Some, like Violato the Red, could scarcely speak, except with hearts. "I would be armless, Sir Siegfried—Nay, lifeless, By Gad, had Affirmare not stepped between me and death's blow... and for you, Dragonheart. We had all abandoned hope of ever seeing your flaxen face again... Or that bandanna-masked coxswain, Pax! Kind griffin, the gods have led you to our woeful camp."

"Gods indeed!" said the king, casting a backward glance at Siegfried's chariot. "We had given up on all of you. My aerial communications have proven somewhat uneven. Time and again that shilly-shallying hippo has skipped away, neglecting his duty—and dispatches!"

Folly dipped back down behind his cover, believing he could duck under Constantio's coal-eyed stare. But there was nothing near lethal in the king's look.

"I'm happy to see that time has proven Folly worthy of my confidence—for he has ridden danger's tail—as we all must, if we are to survive this scrape."

"Most assuredly, Your Highness—the cherub is a veritable trump in our cause," complimented Siegfried, disregarding Folly's cowardly behavior during their charge.

"Er... has he been wounded?" inquired Constantio, who had drifted over beside the chariot to inspect the white hulk huddled on the floor. Folly was so ashamed. Nerves clamped his big lips like hard mortar.

"Poor chap is exhausted, Sire," explained Pax, in defense of his compatriot.

"Battle fatigue, of course... a most frequent visitor to my camp," said Constantio. "Yet not so sought after as you and your rolling marvel, Sir Dragon. Your arrival has brought pause to the fighting, and given us a chance to lick our wounds. Perhaps, by your presence, we may yet regroup and stave off the inevitable."

The Northman felt honored by his king's praise, However, his lank features betrayed a more disquieting concern, and would not rest until its burden was dispelled. "Sire, if I may ask..." his face trained on the vast enemy encampments across the battlefield. Their fires filled the sharp chilled night like a thousand icy eyes. "...Such an awesome multitude! Wherever did they come from? Have we so grossly underestimated the lion's following?"

Constantio sat down wearily upon his cloud and invited Siegfried to join him, while he deliberated his response. "To answer your question, sir knight... No. Affirmare's excursions into the South brought precise assessments of Negare's strengths. And of Count DeSeet, we know his strength—and weakness. We have not been wrong—but we have been wronged—and very stupid and naive. When we first encountered that damned pair's combined armies on this plain, it was but a fraction of these current masses. Victory did not seem so elusive then. Alas, witchcraft swept in to swell their ranks tenfold. While our brethren lay down their life's blood, the foe multiplies with walking wounded and undead. Their slain shed the throes of death and rise reborn to strike again against their more mortal adversaries.

"Lust!" said Siegfried with bated breath. "Her clay-born ghouls are resurrected here. 'Twas through their hollow hulks I slashed to make it down."

"Aye! DeSeet's villain dame has been summoned to them; it's devils' deities we combat!"

"We have high and mighties pulling for us too," grumbled the Nordic, "and stronger!"

"And deaf," said the king. "Or dead!" Constantio waved his teak stick across the vulture-clouded sky, as if the scepter was a magic, wooden wand with condor killing powers. Unfortunately, darkness only augmented the sleepless flocks, and they seemed thicker for it. "The crone's buzzards already pick the sky lord's bones. Our prayers and sacrifices to Enduros go unheeded—awry in the cursed wind. The lord of all the earth has left it in fleshlings' hands to vanquish our common nemesis.

"Sadly though, we 'meaty' monarchs require our sleep. The night is upon us, and we should help ourselves to some sorely needed slumber in the battle lapse. Sir Dragon, your knights also look overtaxed, have you given them no rest of late? Let them disperse, gnaw bone and bed down; there are no courtly formalities surviving on this field. As for you, Flaxen—into my tent. Your sudden appearance has not caught my crystal seer by surprise. She and Jo have prepared a gracious gourmet feast for you and your regiment—curry! You do like curry don't you? It's all we have left... Ha!"

Folly remained seated in the chariot, and watched as Siegfried and Pax filed into the king's tent behind His Highness for a brief parley before retiring. The glass lady was there to meet them with a deep, pristine smile etched into her crystalline face, though it no longer sparkled, nor shined as before. The grimy film of battle caked her gem smooth skin and cracked its fragile flawless features, chipping the pearl cheeks and chapping her clear quartz eyes with brittle braking wounds. Yet this durable, delicate lady had not broken. Nor had her billiken consort, Jo. Though a knife and shield now protected his pink and dimpled skin, the bubbly jester still found happiness and humor to be his most effective defense. He entertained Violato with spirit-lifting mimes and magic, and wore a mock frown as though Sir Siegfried had stolen his show.

"Crazy clown!" cracked Violato, trying to laugh. "By Gad—your mummery will kill me before any hostile hand! I swear, I'll not die under the eyes of any happy-hearted halfling—lest, for joke, you dance upon my grave, with rosy glee to match your complexion. Had you any real magic, you'd juggle these wounds I bear and bring back my innards!"

"And while you're about it, Jo," said the king, "erase our opponents also—if it won't be too taxing on your talents. Let us be home again, and feast on food instead of curry, fish and fowl!"

Such a hearty laughter that ensued proved to be a potent tonic to those so riddled with war. And the spirited elixir trickled intermittently throughout the encampment like a soothing roundelay.

"Perhaps you arrival is a good omen, Sir Dragon," suggested Constantio. Earlier in the week General Affrimare brought promising news concerning my lamb son, Christen. Young David has seen him. He and the centaur, Peter, are on his track, headed toward the Kyln I daresay. If only I could spare an arm or two in his behalf. Alas, I've a feeling in my joints... Events tomorrow will be taking a crucial turn. Clariss has foreseen something too—even through Lust's opaque sorcery. And... as tidings could hardly fall worse, they must, by logic, improve!"

"Bright futures seldom come sensibly wrapped in secret shrouds," warned the glass lady. "And what the morning will reveal, even I cannot see. Whosoever destiny it holds—their power is greater than mine."

"The power of gods?" voiced the king, as if in a plea. "Perhaps they are not deaf to our prayers. Mayhap our fortunes wait to rise with tomorrow's dawn."

"In truth, Sire, hope is more likely to settle with the dusk tonight," spoke Siegfried. His words fell like a damper on the king's tent. Even Jo could force no smile as the Northman recounted his dismal campaign. Pax, unable to listen anymore to so sorrowful a tale, gathered up an extra bowl of curry and shuffled outside as his taskmaster proceeded to explain once again:

"It was the false trail of Ill-timber's leaves that brought me backward and wayward until Folly found me lost upon the flatlands, and guided my troops hither. By chicanery, that cagey ebonwood eluded me. Though combing the whole east and southern moors, I could find no trace of your son, the prince—and of the lad, David? This, and only this, did I find." Into the king's hands Siegfried placed the torn, wool-lined lionskin jerkin, which had been David's. "'Twas on the saw grass flat outside the Kyln Morass I came across it... and farther on, a trail of condor quill and plum—"

"Mors!" cursed the king, recognizing the jacket he had loaned his novice knight for warmth. "Affirmare told me DeSeet's bone servant led David and Peter's way... Led them to their doom more like!"

A grievously long second of silence followed the grim realization of the two boys' fate.

CHAPTER 41

While Siegfried Dragonheart and the king's confidants mulled destinies inside Constantio's marquee, outside, Pax had rejoined Folly, who remained piled upon the chariot floor like a forlorn heap of soiled laundry. His eyes were swollen pink.

"I've brought you some curry soup," peeped the griffin. Then his red feathered head turned brighter as he pushed a wine flask into Folly's hand. "Take it —wine will fill your hollowed spirits, and the soup will warm your mood on this chilling night since you choose to spend it exiled out here."

Folly sipped at the hot curry. As for the wine, the repentant 'potamus just glanced at it resolutely and sobbed. "N-No thank you... Poison would taste sweeter to me now, than any brew."

Pax wrapped his tail around Folly in an understanding hug. Its length suited the plump cherub's width just perfect. "Don't feel so sad—or so alone either. I'm ashamed of myself too... but can you hear Sir Siegfried in the king's tent? He speaks well about the two of us. Listen how he accepts the blame for my shortcomings. Our maneuver was a disaster, through no fault of his—but of his guide—me! Some navigator I turned out to be. Even at sea, it was always Admiral Honos that fixed a true course and held her steady." Pax put down his bowl of curry and began to nibble the tips of his wings. "How I wish I could be like them... an admiral...or a knight!"

Somehow the griffin's squeaky, scratch and peck voice was soothing to Folly. He began to relax and wiped the tears from his eyes with Pax's tail.

Pax unwound a bit too after his admission. "I have courage like a soldier—but no stomach for violence. You, on the other hand, have ample tummy—but lack the, er... guts. Maybe we would do well to pool our strengths and pull together." The chariot creaked as Folly sat up beside the doughty griffin. With his bowl of curry he toasted their friendship, then swallowed the sauce in one gulp. His mood was warmed; Pax's too.

Darkness advanced on the retreating daylight and the survivors of the king's armies wearily returned from the field of war. Affirmare was the last to join them as the remnants of the royal regiments clustered around the campfires and reposed with their thoughts. Only after the last of his wounded kinsmen had been made comfortable, did the crusader extend a warm greeting to the new arrivals. Shreds of his once gleaming hauberk still clung to his broad shoulders with abiding pride. Upon sighting the spreading cluster of heraldry displayed on the flagstaffs outside the king's tent, the valiant general was quick to raise his own to that distinguished, tattered family of flags. And by the time daybreak cast its pink light upon Constantio's marquee, it beheld a bright array of rainbow risen rows of proud and princely pennants from every rank and file in the royal legions of Mythlewild.

However, death's paramour was not about to strike her colors yet—especially now—as the slowly rising sun would testify. It peeked sheepishly through the black helix of vultures, which sustained their circle over Cinnabar. It was not smiling. Nothing in the heavens smiled today—nor on the earth. Lust's shadow seeped over the plain like poisoned pitch. It suffocated even embers in the dying campfires, and painted the bloody basin a more morbid shade of scarlet. On the opposite rise she stood: a malevolent monolith to evil, erected far across the way, but high—upon some rocky palisade—so none could miss her, leering with her arms outstretched in sadistic satisfaction at the holocaust she wrought. Her soulless servants swarmed and bowed in trembling allegiance before their queen.

The king's men, more clean of heart and mind, who would not kneel, still quaked at her vision intruding into their sleep. A satanic slab of evil, she was forged in hell's fire and cast upon Cinnabar so death may worship its mistress. Her cataclysmic laughter echoed down the dell and gutted any last lingering remnant of resolve or hope still stranded in the liegemen's broken breasts. The black angel's presence alone seemed to sound the final knell for Constantio. Its tolling lent a cursed, shallow rest to the night's quiescence.

Folly's and Pax's slumber had been sporadic at best, until now. They sat dolefully on a slumping hill of dying clover a few paces apart from the camp, viewing what they supposed would be their last sunrise. Clarissima had joined them in the early morning hours. Requiring no sleep herself, the crystal lady sat up with the dreary pair of exiles, lending what encouragement she could—though it wasn't easy—for sibyls cannot lie.

Jo accompanied his mate, but could lend neither levity or support to the lady, as his wee, billiken body had fallen blessedly into an innocent repose.

Folly sighed, "Peace is sleeping on the eve of one's extinction."

"How lucky Jo is," remarked Pax.

"And yet, he still smiles," said Clarissima. "You two fellows could take a lesson from my innocent wag. Lift those chins of yours up off the ground, or you'll smother in your own depressions. Although, even my eyes can find few pegs to pin a hope upon. You, at least, shall shall find your spunk today—and your stomach.

For now there is no other choice, fight or die." The hippo and the griffin looked quizzingly at the glass seer, but said nothing further as the camp began to stir.

His Highness, Constantio, as always, was among the first to wake. He strode up the hill on foot while his cloud floated faithfully behind, looking more like a clump of soot than a king's puffy stand. "Clariss, so here you are!" Constantio bid them all stay seated as he addressed his sibyl in a sullen voice. "The witch is here. I rise to face my gravestone mocking over me. But has she come alone? I see no monster brood beside the trolls. Surely her faceless fiends have tailed their mother from the fens?"

"Such a vain villain she is, Sire. She is confident her incantations will be mob enough. However, fear is her most cutting weapon. She directs it at us this moment from across the waste, exalting in her victory—high and haughty like some corrupt tower about to topple and crush us all on our own misgivings."

But Constantio would have none of it. He hurled his teak club at the obelisk, Lust—and spat to see it fall short a mile or more. "The witch celebrates too soon!" swore the king. "On my life, I will not lick sod to the likes of that lion's wench! Mark me now, glass miss—that vanity will etch her own gravestone one day!"

"B-But she has us surrounded completely, Sire..." blurted Folly at last, chancing a remark to Constantio. "... We're outmanned!"

"Nay! Not 'manned'—we are only outnumbered. Neither are we outclassed." Constantio turned to Folly, and expressed his belated gratitude by embracing the hippo fondly, which was not easy for the stubby monarch. "Ah, Folly, my dear servant! Stout in heart and paunch. You did not allow me the opportunity to thank you adequately last night. Your courage was exemplary—" The words did not bring joy to Constantio's hollow cheeks. "I hope you've gumption left to give... For now, I must ask of you another boon."

Folly's wings and heart fluttered and thumped. His spirits soared at this unexpected chance to salvage some self-esteem. He bounded to his feet. Then his knees began to knock, as details of Constantio's mission unfolded. And once again, the hippo's wings drooped, and all his chins began to sink.

"The Rollingway at our backs remains a more negotiable foe than what we face from Lust," explained the king. "It is our only avenue of escape. But ships only

—not chariots or charger—can course its waters. I must have my navy! Admiral Honos is overdue. The royal fleet is the only ally we have left—It must be near at hand. Fly to Honos Folly—clear to the Citrine Gulf if you must—but find us our escape, and lead my bull's armada to Cinnabar, as you did my Dragonheart... It is our last chance. "I've dispatched pigeons and runners to Sovereignton advising them of our plight; nevertheless, should they get through, we can expect no help. I've given Queen Superbia strict orders: Prince Agustus is to shore up the city's defenses —and brace for the siege which is certain to commence upon our eventual defeat here..."

Constantio was unable to finish. Folly had burst into tears and dropped to his knees, kissing the king's feet and trying to disown his own portly face. His Highness gaped at Clarissima and Pax in puzzlement, but they were as shocked as he. Even Jo woke and scratched his knobby head at the cherub's woeful collapse.

"Oh, Sire... please forgive me... I've committed a grievous botch!" It was the most difficult chore Folly had ever performed—delving into his quiver, and delivering the message into His Highness' hand. It was short; but its thrust was deep. Constantio read aloud. It was from Admiral Honos:

"Cape Saphire fleet taken—Unable to rendezvous at
Emerald Bay—Both ports and all territories between, lost.
Have engaged overwhelming pirate armada in the Citrine
Taking heavy losses—Require immediate aid.
The Windy's going down with all hands..."

Constantio's crown dropped from his forehead and vanished momentarily in the dying clover, while the king buried his grief in his hands.

"Sniff... The admiral entrusted me with his note six days past," cried Folly. "And I...I forgot to..."

"Soldier, do not forget yourself now," reminded Constantio, looking up from his own sorrow. He was much to battle weary to scorn his loyal gatekeeper. "You still have a mission at the mouth of the Rollingway. We have not given up on ourselves—let us not yet forsake the resourceful bull captain. Rush to him—we'll abandoned neither hope, nor Honos!"

Jo handed the king his crown, and Constantio once again mounted his staunch pedestal to become a sovereign. "At this very moment Lust dissects us with her cantraps," declared Constantio. "But let's not die just yet! Let us instead marshal our strength and take it to her hellions, and finish this fight first, before we lay down in the bloodied soil of this vale. Fly, Folly! Fly fast to Honos—so we may yet upset the death angel's vanities!"

Without any further delay, Folly began to assemble his bow and arrows—and courage. Constantio provided a sorely needed boost when he laid a set of piercing, flint-tipped arrows into the hippo's quiver. "Real arrows!" The cherub blinked his eyes in disbelief.

"Lust will not yield to rubber, brave courier," said the king, "but to keenly chiseled ore. You shall have to cross her skies; these may clear the path—for you're a better marksman than before, brave Folly. Good luck and gods' speed!"

Farewells were quickly exchanged. Weak-kneed and heaving a stomach churning with nausea, Folly took heart from the allied confidences of his king and comrades. It was all the fuel needed to propel the winged warrior into action. Despite a somewhat lubberly take-off, the hippo dutifully ascended into the dismal sky over Cinnabar, armed with pointed arrows and lethal determination. However, the high heavens were every bit as devastating as the hills below. The seething, swarming ceiling of scavengers descended upon the king's messenger.

But this was not the same frivolous Folly that rolled into Cinnabar on the floorboards of a nobler knight's chariot. This was not a quivering belly of jelly plodding across the airways like a bungling interloper. No! This jam would spread himself before no predatory palate. This was a defiant, white hot comet, speeding upon a predestined course—and heaven help any obstacle intruding across his slip stream.

But intrude the condors did. Possessed of no courtesy, Lust's buzzards collided with the impassioned fireball. Wave upon wave of them attacked, raving and clawing in frenzied intensity. Though wheeling and reeling under the clacking sorties, Folly managed to beat them off time and again with fierce tenacity. His arrows were death-dealing darts now—and so was his valor.

The sky bled with dying condors. They dropped from the ink-tainted clouds like black rain. With such pent up zeal did he battle, the inspired hippopotamus may well have conquered Lust single-handed. Alas, Folly's arrows were not so inexhaustable as his ardor. Thus, when his supply dried up—so to the rain. No longer did the condor causalities fall away. The droppings flocked again and, in a wrathful flying line, hove straight for the fleeing hippo hell-raiser.

Dedication paled into desperation. Folly's wings pounded against the sky, slapping the frumpish clouds from his path to find escape. But the intrepid hippo was too bulky, too tired—too slow. His way out lay blocked by bigger, brawnier barriers. They swarmed first—masses of taloned, shrieking wisps—then they struck in force.

It was then the showers began anew. Condor beads dropped dead once more, and victory fell to a different breed of bird—or beast. But how, wondered Folly... Who? As if a passing turn-tail might pause to answer him. Then, out of the dark blue, steering his way through the ruptured cloud banks, was his friend—the coxswain, Pax.

There, beside Folly, the griffin pilot shared a new supply of arrows with his stout comrade. Together they distributed the shafts into the dwindling flock of vultures. The team shot their way through the thinning wasps, until finally a narrow sky lane opened ahead of them.

The triumphant twosome rested only briefly. On a friendly cloud they toasted their victory with a good word. "His Highness thought it looked like 'rain' today," chirped Pax happily. "And he decided some added protection from the elements would be wise."

"How fortuitous!" replied Folly with the biggest, brightest smile you ever saw a hippopotamus wear. "And I could not want for more welcome cover, er... I declare, your color looks somewhat queer, friend 'Griff'."

"I'm afraid my stomach is no more suited to the sky than the battlefield," responded Pax. "I was more comfortable at sea, wrestling the wheel on Miss Windy's rocking poop deck."

"Well then, if you are not too 'pooped' yourself, allow me to repay your heroics. We shall seek out your Windy's deck and cross our fingers she is still rocking!"

Pax gladly accepted as Folly assisted the airsick griffin onto his broad, round back. "Won't I slow you down?" he asked, concerned about his mount's stamina.

"Tosh! Not as much as those condors would have!" answered Folly. "You've the wings of an eagle, do you not? Just flap!"

Their sky lane ahead was clearer for the moment, filled mostly with genuine clouds of little consequence. Below them, the wide Rollingway River pointed seaward toward the Citrine Gulf. Pax had brought a curry gourd along, and though he abstained presently, noontime found the hippo's appetite insatiable as his vigor.

Later, when an afternoon storm front closed in on them, Folly at least was up to the match. He offered to fly around the new menace in regard for Pax's delicate tummy. The griffin however, would not allow it. "Time is too precious," he gulped, "let's do it—to the bow!"

"To the head!" sang Folly. And with no backward steps kindled in his mind this time, the hippo bore into the approaching wind gusts, which soon swelled into a tempest. Folly became an inflated kite, tossing and tearing against the blows of an incessant gale. It spat on him with sharp, chilly breaths of sleet, which cut his wings and threatened to slash him out of the sky. But perseverance was an unbreakable twine, pulling the king's herald through his turbulent flight. The plump cherub never felt more akin to angels than here and now, stubbornly spiraling his way, inch by inch, across heaven's belly ever closer to Honos. The turmoil around him was insignificant compared to the titanic conflict below. Yet it was here, miles above Mythlewild, that Folly found the self-esteem so long eluding him. Now it tied him tightly to his countrymen on the battleground. That drunken fop and failure had ceased to be, for he slew the condor flock. He had not slept—fatigue was cast off too. His life had been a saturated waste. But now it was he who shouldered the fate of Cinnabar. And Folly would permit no ill wind to suppress him. Thus, in defeat—or perhaps in homage—the gale bowed. The pugnacious kite glided by, sailing on the suddenly admiring wind, which escorted him safely over the more menacing misty menageries of the Kyln Morass shrouded below them. All the way, on the current of air, rode the two couriers, until the southern sea breezes smacked their cheeks.

Upon arriving in the Citrine Gulf, Honos' fleet was nowhere to be seen. The ghosts of a great naval engagement still haunted the gulf's mackerel sky. Scudding wisps wreathed around the ribs and wrecks of hulls that could have been the Windy, or a multitude of other sleek-bodied vessels. They were skeletons now, those that were not laid to rest—like the others in their cause—the ones at Cinnabar. From above, the sack of Amber Glade looked complete. Pax became despondent. This time it was Folly's pluck which boosted his chum from his distress.

"Maybe we've passed over them in the storm, 'Griff. Let's backtrack upstream."

Pax hung on as his broad steed sprang about. The poor griffin was terribly ill, and his wingtips were frostbitten from the crisp altitude; but he did not complain. His long, reptile tail was strapped around Folly's wide waist. The ferment of their flight had jostled Pax so, he now dangled upside down like a green, red, and yellow icicle.

"It's no use Folly, I'm so numb, I can hardly move, even to tremble. If I could... I would heave. How lucky I am to have your strength to carry me through."

"'Twas your pluck that pulled us out against the condors," reminded Folly, "and smoothed my wild-eyed run at Cinnabar. And when we reach Admiral Honos, 'twill be to your credit, friend 'Griff."

"I pray we are not too late. If I could just set foot on Miss Windy's deck once more, even seasickness would be a blessing—Folly!" Pax caught himself, then clambered right side up on his hippo's back, and pointed through a break in the cloud cover at the river below. "Look!"

"Ships!" exclaimed Folly. "Oh praise be—Honos is alive! And on his way to Cinnabar to rescue the king. Didn't I tell you, griff—didn't I!"

The hippo glided lower for a closer look. "And see over there, to the west— an army. It's the insurgents. They're moving out—fleeing! Hooray—we're saved! We're saved!" Folly flip-flopped for joy; and Pax's stomach deserted him in similar fashion. Then, his feather-red face turned livid yellow, as his fleeting elation bailed out too. What he spied sickened him anew—all over—and much worse than before.

Folly noted his companion's condition with alarm. "Oh, 'Griff—your poor stomach! I've lost my wits. We can go down now—"

"NO!" squawked Pax, as loud as he could. "No—we can't go back down. It would mean our certain death. Folly... are you still strong? Those ships, they 're not ours—they're DeSeet's! And that army... look closer—the lion's ramparts! They're not on the lam—they're on the march—north. North, Folly—to Middleshire! To Sovereignton!"

Halting to gauge their situation, the two desperate stalwarts fixed their gaze on the distant horizon. The pair's pulsating hearts quit on them. They beheld the Middleshire, smothered under a blanket of smoke and condors—and beneath, a swarm of other grimlings too. The crown jewel of Theland appeared to be a bone to be chewed by ravaging lions. Nay... the siege of Sovereignton was not begun—but altogether done.

"Oh lordy, lordy!" cried a very distressed Folly. "And His Highness is powerless to stop them!" The tearful cherub was beside himself, hovering in dizzy, erratic swirls. The overtaxed hippo teetered on the verge of hysteria. "Ooohh—I'm getting an ulcer attack, and my liver is rebelling... Oh merciful memories! What I wouldn't trade for a sip of my sweet strawberry wine, or even apple..."

Pax nearly heaved again in his spasms—but he didn't. "W-We must keep our heads, now, as never before," he said chewing the tip of his tail, which he fondled for only a brief, uncontrollable moment.

"Y-Yes," repeated Folly. "We must keep our heads... Oh, lordy, lordy! Hold on, 'Griff!"

Pausing only for a quick, silent prayer, the hippopotamus and the griffin steadied their nibbling nerves, then raced on wings of eagles for help—though from what direction it would come, they did not know.

CHAPTER 42

While autumn's golden glazes were rapidly succumbing to winter's hoary siege, deep within and under the Kyln Morass, at Luhrhollow, the season was swealtering. This was the first thing David felt blistering his cheeks—that awful heat. Then, distant guttural snarls, as of bickering wildcats, nipping at his ears. And sulphur, like sharp smelling salts, stung his nostrils. He rolled his spinning head around as if to dodge the pain. His hands would not move to rub the aches away, nor would the rest of him. From the neck on down, he was totally entwined in numbing briar vines. Then he discerned a voice; though miles away it seemed, it was familiar— "Peter!"

Struggling to lift his heavy eyelids just half way, David looked past the steaming mist and saw a blurry vision of the pony boy carefully doctoring some crippled eagle, which he vaguely recalled, as if so long ago. Then something stirred on David's chest. The sensation of it jerked his head upright. Did his eyes ever pop out of their sockets when a lovely dove poked her creamy, round head out of the boy's breastpocket, and tipped her silver hat.

"Niki!" exclaimed David. His bonds prevented him from scooping the little bird into his hands and cuddling her fondly. Nevertheless, she cooed in affectionate response from her linen nest—for she was similarly tied up with creeper shackles.

"Allow me," joined Peter. Bound only by a leash and his swollen hamstring, the pony boy tugged his restraints to the fullest and grinned broadly. He tousled David's fair hair by way of greeting—and examination. "Since I seem to be the appointed physician here, why don't you tell me how you feel, sleepyhead!"

"Ouch!" winced David as Peter thumped the top of his friend's head, then giggled when he noticed a new bump on the colt's forehead. "Why, Peter, you look as if you've grown another horn. Now you have three!"

The centaur just winked. "Don't laugh—you're wearing a handsome crown now yourself. You look like a unicorn!"

"Uh, by the way... Where are we?" questioned David upon settling down. He tried to see past his misty manacles and penetrate the smoke plume pillars.

"A fine question," Peter replied. "Sorry you asked. For the past two days you've been in dreamland. As for the rest of us—we're in hell—or on its threshold. Welcome!"

"This is Luhrhollow, painter," peeped Niki, trying to ignore Peter's flippant attitude. "We're bunched here in its garret like netted herrings. The swamp cabin was merely a portal. 'Twas here Vexpurra lead me. Like a mouse nosing cheese, I followed Lust's kitten unwittingly, right into her trap. Peter explained to me how, after parting with Fidius, you and he became the next obliging pawns, scurrying after me. Christen was my bait—I was yours. The lure of friendship proved catching!"

"That, and Lust's illusions and incantations," said David remorsefully."

"Whatever you call it, we fell for it hook, line and sinker! Our beautiful lady has reeled us in. She, and that cottage we first saw, and its docile tenants... all were masks, hiding the mousers' real identities. We're in their parlor now—or the frying pan I should say. The Christen we saw on Mount White was nothing but an apparition. The real prince remained here—imprisoned as we are—only worse!"

Niki directed David's baffled gaze to the far corner of the steam-shafted hovel enclosing them. There, bound to the wall in roots and vines, was the lamb boy which they sought—and this, no masquerade.

David didn't know what to say. He felt like kneeling, or bowing in reverence, but settled for dipping his chin. "No need for that, painter," warbled Niki. "He's dead to the world, under another spell I suspect."

"But not dead!" marveled Peter. "His abductors have spared His Highness that grief... at least temporarily."

"Speaking of those kidnappers, I ran across them here," continued Niki. "The vixen and her cohort, another vermin—the ass prince, Vito—Christen's own stepbrother! He inherits DeSeet's ambitions, as well as a throne, perhaps. Howbeit, the lion and his black beauty remain the true culprits. They supply the purse, while the puppets provide the prince. And more, the bandits have been paid for their services again! But the deed, or victim, of their freshest swipe remains a mystery. Peter informed me of your encounter with another of Lust's urchins."

David nodded glumly. "Mors! He was the bone which baited us here—as if we had no inducement already."

"Do not be too quick to damn the rascal, painter," argued Niki. "For did the skeleton not feed and quarter you two lost and hungry, homeless heroes, and keep you from a chilling end?"

"Humph!" muttered David. "When and if I see that pile of knuckles again, remind me to thank him for his favors! He brought us in from the cold, only to open death's lid on this more boiling stew."

"True, the crone has saved you for herself," acknowledged Niki. "but the great eagle here had news on another note. Palladan rambled about Vero, Enduros' son, and prince of the gods. It seems the Titan Prince was sent to escort us to his father's house."

"Him, and my sire too!" said Peter. "Paramount carried Vero down from Revrenshrine to welcome us—just like I knew he would! That's another reason Lust sent Mors to snitch us—before Vero and Father found us first."

"I don't understand," said David. "Whatever happened to them? Why didn't they reach us?"

"Who knows? One or the other of us ran a little late perhaps..." Peter sighed as he returned to the eagle's side. "Palladan could say no more before lapsing into his present coma." The pony boy repacked the last of the eagle's bandages. He did not stir, either in pain or comfort—rather, he laid perfectly still. "I pulled the arrow tip from his neck. He wasn't hurt too bad really. The wound mended remarkably fast... yet he languishes so—as if he too is bewitched."

"Maybe he's just asleep," said David.

Niki disagreed with Peter, and scowled at her young pilgrim. "If Palladan is under an enchantment, 'tis by his own god's making—not these witches!"

"Say, who is this bird anyway, some big shot?" David wanted to know. "Do you know him too, Niki?"

"Yes, painter, as I would know my own brother. Enduros' eagle is my kin—and that of all the beasts and birds whose home be earthen. This distinguished animal is Palladan, their forebear. And the earth lord, Enduros, is his loving master."

David looked at the listless bird with new respect. "Well I'll be... What do you suppose he was doing way down here in this peat?"

"You saw his purpose for yourself, Davy, as did I." Peter's eyes began to water. His face never turned from the great eagle. "We were witnesses, as the right arm of Enduros took flight from Revrenshrine and sought out his divine enemy—Lust. On the swamp's surface we both watched from our treetop as Palladan found his prey. Then... before the king of creatures could fetch her back to Mount White... I—stupid, rash, cruel—I shot him down in my ignorance, and... and so saved the life of the red witch, Lust! Thanks to me that 'beautiful lady' could live to desecrate the face of Theland, and ruthlessly annihilate its citizenry. I've brought a curse down on all of you... and Enduros smites us in his wrath. He will never help us now..." Peter had no more tears to weep. He cradled the eagle in his arms as if a shake or two might jar it back to life. "Forgive me, lord..."

"You mean that lady we saved was Lust?" When no answer was forthcoming, David shouted, "Peter, stop it! Don't persecute yourself this way! Crying isn't going to get us out of here. Where's some of that discipline you used to flaunt? If you've really a burr under your hoof, you'll yank us out of here, since you seem to be the only one able to roam around, why don't you untie us?"

It took Peter a moment to recompose, but when he did, it was more like the snorting, stomping stallion the boy had come to admire. Returning to David, the young buck began to tug at his fetters. Whereupon the vines writhed to life and coiled furious and fast around the centaur, entwining him from neck to knees in cutting, nettlesome roots and briars. David was speechless now. Peter, however, only shrugged his shoulders in a complacent manner of non-surprise. "Sorry to disappoint you, old chap, but just how do you untie a tree?"

Niki sighed as David frowned ruefully at Peter. "Don't be mad at the centaur, painter. You see, he was never really free. The yokes were on his fetlock all the while. He was only allowed to tend our wounds, nothing more."

"This brood must not show our incubus any cracked omelets else we're the goose that's cooked. Better to keep our wits and thus prepare for any future tamperings!" remarked Peter. "Did you think freedom was so easily won? No, sir— not with those death-licking lice crawling about outside!"

"Oh, but those 'death-licking lice' are gone, horsemeat!" growled a cunning, catty voice. "Prrrr... and left the mice in the hands of living lice."

David twisted around, the thorns and thistles ripping his wrists and ankles. But it was Vexpurra's toothy, taunting leer that hurt him most; and those guttural purrings with the sound of boiling acid and the caustic bite to match.

"Ill-timber's binds are tight, are they not, pilgrim? Prrrr... almost as snug as your slippers—" David immediately tore his gaze from the stone skin cat and looked for his shoes. He marveled to find them still on his feet—and his feet still on his legs. "Prrrr... don't think we did not try to coax them off, pilgirm," mewed the cat. "Regretfully, your soles—like your toes—balked at severing their ties." Vexpurra angrily displayed a scorched set of blistering stone paws. "And we did't want to slice up our pie just yet... Prrrr! Not to worry though, our fire hair's business at Cinnabar is nigh concluded. She will soon return to persuade them off. She has her ways... Prrrr. She has... Flare!"

Vexpurra's squirming snake hair hawked a load of venom at David's flawless shoes. But the vine-laced slippers repelled the tainting spittle. The slaver instead splashed back upon Vexpurra, scalding her craggy pads again like hot grease.

Only at this moment David detected the tingling in his numb feet. The wings on his heels spun like humming birds'.

They've been 'talking' to you since your arrival here," said Niki. "'Tis Christen, the Prince of Lambs, who causes them to stir. While in the face of Lust's illusionary lamb on Mount White, Omnus' tongues spoke not a word—"

"You should follow their example, pigeon!" growled Vexpurra, licking her greased paws. Have all your master's toys inherited his tricks? Prrrr... well, I've a card or two myself to turn!"

Vexpurra cracked her tail in a whiplash. The steamy veils parted and revealed two wrangling, wild beasts, bent and bickering upon the floor, between the fiery arcs around them. David knew them both by name. The one was seen among the condor flock above the Snowmass. It was the bat-winged demon, Horros—a mere pip now—his mildew blue cheeks grew deep red to burn with his ember eyes. He flapped his webbed arms and slapped his black tongue upon the floor in rage. Squat in opposition to him and his temper tantrum, was another nix—Mors. His ivory skull also flushed with fire at the futility of their task. In their midst was a satchel.

"Oh my!" gasped David, looking down at his root-encrusted chest as if he could possibly find his paint kit.

"Prrrr... not all your slops proved so cussed to our stripping!" snickered Vexpurra, who took a comfortable repose upon a root, nose to nose with the boy. She mewed in delight as her hostage turned green under the stench of her rancid breath. "Unfortunately—for one of us—your satchel is as stubborn as your shoes. It remains locked beyond all meddling—beyond all comprehension—as tight-lipped as your sleepy-headed sheep suckling. Bewitched probably." David cringed as

501

Vexpurra panted down his collar. Her needle fangs gleamed across her face like diseased stitches. "But we'll think of something... Prrrr!"

Vexpurra purred with such catnip mirth, she nearly rolled off her root. Her hair coiled as if to strike again, but thought better of it. The writhing worms contented themselves with reeling into a long braid, then draping around Vexpurra's shoulders like a boa constrictor.

David shuddered to think what ominous thoughts her remarks kindled in the urn that was her mind. His own concerns turned to Christen, across the room—yet a thousand miles away in spell. Poor Prince, look what your secret wrought. Was this cremation to be their fate too?

The lamb boy just sat obliquely in the throngs of the serpentine roots. Then, a string-limbed condor stumbled onto his shoulder, tripped over a gnarl, and tumbled to rest at Christen's feet, squawking and screeching to raise the dead.

It suddenly dawned on David that he was looking upon the same inhabitants of that cozy cottage in the marsh glade: Here was the singing parakeet—a cursing condor with two left feet, and a bent banana for a beak; the friendly kitten—with wormy hair and a heart of stone; and the old woman in the rocker—who was a fire-spitting, cinder-chewing horror, prevailing on his charm to unlock the satchel's secrets. This blistering crock pot was their parlor—Satan's sitting room, thought David. All that survived of his illusion, was the fire. Its insufferable heat was all too real. Affirmare's words of ware grilled his mind: 'Sorcery harrows Theland, trust no appearance, lest its sham sweep you under'. Oh why hadn't he heeded them. David cried out as he remembered another word; he would never forget it again —'Cinnabar'. The voice was like a bellows fanning the flames inside him to new heights. "D-Did you say Lust had business at Cinnabar?... General Affirmare mentioned that battlefield."

Vexpurra's slitted eyes flared in amusement to find a subject which so appalled her victims. "Prrrr... not just a battlefield, pilgrim—Cinnabar is soon to be a hugeous cemetery for your runt king and all his paltry partisans. When they're dead and in the dust, my wing-shoed child—they belong to Lust! Their clay-cold carcasses will serve my mistress like her other stiff-stepping spawn. If only some of your sleepless sibling sentinels remained outside, I would introduce you to your future brothers... Prrrr!

"What's that?" cheeped Niki. Vexpurra's words had roused some special interest in the dove. "Do you mean to say those ghostly guardians are gone! Gone where?"

"Why, to the fresh turned sod at Cinnabar, my pigeon—to welcome their fledgling family; or back into their swampen sepulchers perhaps. Who knows what heartbeat the dead march to? They're not MY brothers! But there's no need to flutter so... I'm still here. You may call me 'sister'... Prrrr!"

"I'll call you damnable, debasing, devil litter!... Oh, if I weren't a lady, you'd hear what you really are!"

Vexpurra's claws raked her root settle so that it almost grimaced in pain. Her back arched in a volatile bent. Saliva drooled from her gaping fangs, and the shear-edged slate hair stood aghast at Niki's guile.

David felt a stream of sweat twining uncontrollably from his temples and into his burning eyes. But he shook away the sting to restrain his dove with a few calming words. "Shhh! Niki... Isn't our stew hot enough already? Don't let your ire stir it up. We'll not live to sample the broth if we're diced beneath Vexpurra's arsenal of carving knives."

However, Niki's wits were not baked dry just yet, and so she tried to convince David. "Painter, can it be that your respect for that cat's cutlery has severed your thirst for freedom? Did you not hear? the clay-born sentries are gone! Their absence—while sealing the fates at Cinnabar—might pave our avenue of escape. We must not tarry here too long. Let's exploit our chances when we gain them, for Lust will bring us none. If she returns with the rest of these root worms' clan before we make our move, any escape will be impossible— and too late!"

"It's already too late, if you ask me!" said Peter in an angry voice, too loud to be a whisper. "Under the crush of these root chains, even a moth would be an insurmountable warden—not to mention the rest of these fire-sucking pawns! As long as they're here—"

I hear my mice twittering," purred Vexpurra, ready for some more sport. "Is your tack too tight a harness for your horseflesh, brother?"

"Not tight enough to keep me from stomping your brick and stone-boned body into rubble! And don't call me brother, gravel guts—you don't have my blood yet!" So piqued by Vexpurra's taunting was Peter that, even despite the squeezing bite of his thorny bindings, he defied the she-cat blatantly. Vexpurra, for her part, felt intimidated enough to seek out a more removed rest spot. She then laid down in a ball of repose and lapped her paws, and purred as the pony raved on.

"Neither my king, my kinsmen, or any of us here will ever belong to your brimstone brood—not in life or death! And you'll not inherit our blood with all this graveyard's garrison of freaks and fiends, nor all your dead-born custodians—nor all of Mythlewild's black magic mixed together! We'll shed our blood, but we'll never give it away, like milk, to be swilled by the likes of you!" Peter gnashed at his restraints like biting a bit in his teeth, such was his contempt for Lust's kitten. The burred taste of his sharp fetters did nothing except spur him on to further provoke his inquisitors. "My words are wasted on your stone ears. What do gargoyles know of loyalty and principle? Your veins are coal, and your minds voids—empty of all rational, except blind obedience to anything more cruel and heartless than yourselves."

To prove his point, Peter called out to Odios, who roosted drowsily over the pony boy's head. "You there—pelican! You seem to me a creature of fowl heart. Release the lamb this instant! His father will reward you with a kingdom's share of wealth!" The wiry buzzard once roused, warbled to himself as if to mull the offer over. "Do it now I said! Or Lust will bite off your head!" Peter smirked as the bird bounced up instantly like a feather ball on stilts, and obediently began to peck away at Christen's roots.

Only a cracking, halting lash from Vexpurra's whip tail sent the down-brain ducking back to roost in a flap of feathers, clacking his crooked beak in a nervous prattle.

"Mindless as a millstone," laughed Peter brashly, "just like the rest of you rock headed, mesmerized magpies! Your muzzled loyalties are nothing but leashes and cantrap—"

"Us 'magpies' will live to gorge upon your wormy meat, my cocky little colt!" Vexpurra was no longer purring. She crouched upon her tawny limbs and snarled

504

back into the centaur's face. "And 'twill be our queen mother, Lust, who serves that feast! She claims an empire which, by the gods' bequeath, was hers, and will soon be again. And I, as one with more mind and meanness than my cabbage-witted condor, will be at courtside when our queen reclaims her reign—while you, my quartered horse, are but viand on the hoof!"

"Your crone tomato and the rest of her vegetable crop will cook in her own soup before she garnishes any kingdom, but coal!" snarled Peter right back. "Not one of you have the strength of character it takes—like that of honest, simple pilgrims. And pilgrims are in short supply in your slough holes!"

"Are they?" mewed Vexpurra, pouting and pacing about to and fro among her prisoners, then stopping before David. The worm-haired puma started to purr again. "We've got us one now—don't we, horsemeat!" Her cold, stone tail tickled against Peter's chin as she turned to sniff at David's shoes—but was careful not to touch. "Prrrr... And with him, we've got his magic feet—which shall soon find us a magic egg. And that will be the end of it—won't it, pilgrim... Prrrr!" Had Vexpurra not shifted her teasing tail, Peter would have bitten it, rock or not. As it was, the cat moved on to the silent eagle. "Prrrr... And we've speared an eagle too, haven't we, Palladan? You remember me, don't you! Enduros' protective parrot—you're not so talkative now as when Mors first brought you to me for treatment... Prrrr!" Vexpurra ran her scathing claws across the eagle's tender wound, eliciting a moan of pain—but no more. "Poor, poor gander, you're not so high and mighty now, are you... Prrrr. Soon your grandsire will be yapping under cat's feet alongside his other nest-fallen chicks. What luck the yearling bowman shot you down, otherwise you might have carried my fiery dame all the way to her brother's roost. From such a gilded mountain cage as Revrenshrine my madam would have never made it to her lion paramour at Cinnabar—and thus prolong her destiny for countless other ages... Prrrr!"

The cruel cat's eyes rolled around at Peter to watch him shed another tear in shame for his error. But the centaur was through crying. Vexpurra spat out her disappointment. Only when her gaze fell on David's breast did her ears perk again. "And, we also bagged this stealthy squab... this pure and pretty poppinjay!" Vexpurra drooled at the very sight of Niki. Moving the petite dove to dip again into her pocket sanctuary. This time, however, she held her face up higher, outside, to spar the cat which looked ready to devour her. "You are a very special sparrow too— No?" With one quick swipe of her paw, Vexpurra flicked Niki's silver winged helmet to the floor.

Forsaking the obstinate satchel, Horros and Mors now began to grapple for possession of this shiny new trinket. Horros grunted greedily and grew several inches more to win the right to don his booty. But no matter how many head sizes the demon tried out, Niki's hat just never seemed to fit. Finally, it caused him such a headache, the gremlin swallowed it in disgust—only to chuck it up again like nasty medicine. The demon chortled only after venting his frustration by pounding Mors on the skull with the hard hat—and when the helm had held against his strongest cuffs and hammerings he used his blue suet fists to box the bone man's head instead.

In the fracas, no one but Niki noticed the butterfly darting from her hat, and skipping unheralded into the group of shackled pilgrims.

"Prrrr... You see, pigeon, how your trimmings confound us. Yet the horse's puffy head was not too odd to fit your cap—was it! These spangles snitch on you, pigeon—as the brat's have betrayed him. Whatever be the source of your outfitter— my queen will have it—as we have its lamb... Prrrr! Quite a special lamb chop too— No?" Vexpurra returned to sit and stretch contentedly next to her pride and joy— Christen. "So you see, pony brat, though we lack your wardrobe—we DO have our pilgrims, my queen and I—and much, much more... Prrrr!"

"You may have more than you can handle already," spurted Niki, feeling a flicker of defiance. "You may have stone vitals and a catty tongue, tabby; but such charms as I possess shall be the trappings of pumice-pawed pussycats as you! Lord Enduros will be after his eagle—"

"Enduros is a feeble-minded, gerbil twit without the guile to venture from his mountain clod—unless by stumbling off! Why do you think my madam waited all these ages before stirring from her abyss? She knew the day would, with time, arise when her older brother's years would cripple him beyond any insurgent's blow. It would seem, dear, little eggling—that time is now... Prrrr! By now you have seen how the mountain master's maladies have kept him from the fray..." Vexpurra paused, her feline face lit with a thought. "... But what of YOUR master, pigeon? And the lamb chops'? This egg maker of yours, Omnus Overseer; he remains a mystery to his daughter and her babies. What do we have to fear from this grandaddy, pray?"

Niki felt compelled to ward off this mewing cat's derision; she would hold in her disdain no longer. Her pride just could not swallow another syllable of abuse—especially on her beloved godsire. So, sticking her neck out as far from David's pocket as possible, she stuck up for their side. "My master is not one to fear; he exists only so his lambs may believe in him, and by his life find hope and happiness in theirs. Because you do not believe—and are incapable of faith—my maker will remain a mystery to you and your litter. Therefore, you needn't fear Omnus; rather, fear us—his flock—for without that trust in the overseer, you can achieve no victory over us, or any of his other lambs—That is what I believe!"

'I believe'... The words flitted across the chamber and through the spiraling pillars of smoke and steam as no others had. And the pitch of them struck upon a pair of spellbound ears, and came back again in a sheepish echo. "I believe," repeated the lamb boy, but said no more.

The reaction to Christen's first words was spontaneous. After a trice or two of graveled silence by all, Niki jumped, then flashed a sisterly smile toward the prince, warmer than the fires of Luhrhollow. Peter and David beamed brighter than the fires, which flushed with rage that their prisoners should find such hope in her passionate laps.

There were others not so elated by the echo's mutterings. "Squawk!" clacked Odios. So startled by the sudden bleat, the condor twisted his noodle neck into a knot, then scrambled to a more distant perch above the hearth. Horros and Mors paid little heed to the disruption, as they still contended with one another.

Vexpurra, on the other hand, was quick to seize upon the opportunity. Like a panther, she pounced upon the lamb, as if her embrace were more permanent than witch or wooden wrappings. "What's the matter... couldn't sleep?" wondered the puma, feeling out her prey. "Too hot? Bad dreams maybe... Prrrr!"

But there was no answer; not an echo, or even a twitch of a response from the lamb prince—just a glassy-eyed stare into nowhere.

Vexpurra mewed with pleasure, feeling crass and cocky once more. "As I thought... only a chime. Lust has him forever. Get used to it, pigeon—you've lost your lamb. My mistress is his shepherd now—you can believe in that... Prrrr!"

"No! It can't be!" Niki refused to accept it. "That's what Christen was trying to tell us—we mustn't lose faith. He knows we're here... I'm sure he does!"

As for David, well, he didn't know what to believe. The lamb boy certainly looked as entranced as ever to him. Still, that echo nibbled at his wits—while simultaneously, something else nibbled at his wrists. For some time now, David had experienced a peculiar tingling sensation in his hands. He attributed it to the vein-constricting tightness of the thorny manacles, or a taut imagination. Only now, with Vexpurra occupied by her new woolen 'mouse', did he have time to explore his bindings. To the boy's surprise, he discovered that they had been cut—or chewed—by a downy, candy-colored caterpillar. Its fuzzy face was busy munching through the roots cuffing David's hands.

"His name's Creto," whispered Niki into her painter's ear. "He's a friend of ours—and especially yours! It seems he's been an integral member of our adventure, in one form or another, almost from the beginning. I've been keeping him under my hat for you. I first discovered him there when Peter returned it. While the bat and the bone man bickered over it, our friend Creto has been brunching on our bonds!"

"Good show, Creto!" remarked David. "What a fleeting fantasy you turned out to be." But the intent caterpillar neither smiled, nor paused gnawing for pleasantries.

"It's a big task for a tiny caterpillar," explained Niki."

"Boy Howdy! I should think so," agreed David, wiggling his hands attempting to assist the busy bug. "These vines have been immune to any chomping, until now... er, where does he put it all, Niki? This many roots would upset the stomachs of even the most voracious pack of woodchucks. Is his bite big enough to free us all?"

"One freed pair of hands will suffice, painter. If you still have Affirmare's dagger under your blouse, you'll find Creto's prickly bite, and your sharp blade, can be very cutting. We'll soon see just how thick-skinned this unflinching fern really is. And Peter too, looks to be busting at the seams."

David stealthily snipped the centaur's chains, only to find him wanting more. I can shake these roots now, so what!" said Peter, more dour than enthusiastic. "I've been listening, fellows—but I'll not budge if it means leaving Palladan behind to these hellions' twisted mercies."

The eagle's limp body drew forlorn looks from the plotters. "Now don't go bruising your gums about that one," buzzed a chipper little voice from behind. It crawled up onto Peter's shoulder with a mouthful of pulp. It was Creto, or at least it was for the moment. "Palladan can take care of himself—and us too for that matter!" touted the fuzzy catapillar, just before he sprouted a magnificent set of radiant wings and turned into a gorgeous butterfly.

David's fantasy arched across the muggy steam room like a rainbow, and lighted on Christen's woolly head; but the lamb boy paid not the slightest mind. "And you needn't worry about this fellow either. Just take his hand and coax him along. He wants to come, really. Believe me!"

So much impromptu chatter prompted Vexpurra to have a closer look at her captives. Imagine her shock at sighting a butterfly—here, of all places. Lust's cat would have none of this tomfoolery. "Prrrr... What's going on among my mice?" she wanted to know, and commenced to sniff and ramp around and betwixt the prisoners.

David stuffed his dagger back into his britches—but not soon enough.

"Ahhh... What's this I've found?" asked the cat of David.

Just then, the chamber door crashed open. Into their midst crept a charred tangle of ashen ebony roots, and writhing limbs. All were gnarled and knotted, and stooped in pain, and flaked with burnt black bark.

Vexpurra stopped in her tracks. Her worm hair coiled and hissed in affright. "Ill-timber?... Is that you?!"

Ever so slowly the scabbing, serpentine trunk stood upright. Grotesquely blighted, it was without a single growing twig or leaf to conceal the unparalleled specter of the all too familiar tree wraith. The pilgrims' hopes collapsed to see it enter.

Vexpurra arched her back in recoil, then calmed. Horros and Mors froze in the heat of their quarrel, and tossed away their differences. The blue demon choked on his fire and smoke, and Mors retreated into his black shroud rags.

It remained for Odios to be enamored with his cohort's startling arrival. The nearsighted vulture flew instantly to perch in what seemed to be an attractive bough of dead and shriveled ebony branches.

As the huge plant flexed its limbs, the prisoners gasped in shock—except for David. The creature's presence only prompted him to pull tighter on the stubborn remnants of his bonds.

"Prrrr... Why it IS you, isn't it!" meowed the cat woman, almost spitefully. "Been playing with the scribbler's paints again?"

Vexpurra's crack brought a howling warble from Odios. But a fast falling branch fist put a deep kink in the condor's cackle. "Sssss... Out of my hair, you bumbling crow!" snarled the Ill-timber, shaking the spindly fowl off like a fig. "I've no mood for nestings... Sssss. That churl's lizards have been my latest playmates. However, hacking my limbs and toasting my skin did not provide the sport they sought. Now the game is over. I seek to settle an old 'score' with the waif myself, and have a whittle at his bark... Sssss! I'm mad and mean and back from the mountain to finish my meal of horsemeat, hen, and him!"

David should have been terrified. Yet somehow the ranting gargantuan no longer intimidated the boy. He trembled only at the thought of other fates—those of Fidius and his dragon son, Abraxus.

"Would a saltier entree suite your tart tastes, Ill-timber!" retorted a suddenly imposing voice. It was the eagle! "Shake me out of your hair if you can," he cawed defiantly.

"Palladan!" gasped Peter in amazement...You're all right?!"

The great bald eagle was suddenly poised high upon some jutting branches, his talons choking the coiling advances. "You're a better physician than marksman, centaur," said the eagle. "I'm fully rested now and ready to forgive past indiscretions, to repay your current kindness. This scrub has told us the game was over—so we shall leave. All his guests seem eager to go! Are we not?"

510

"I didn't like their rules anyway," added David and exclaiming, "What are we waiting for—let's go!" Upon the butterfly's prompting, he was the first to leap from his sticky web. He sprang over to Christen and, with dagger drawn, cut the lamb's bindings, grabbed his hand, and made for the doorway behind the humming wings of the butterfly who led the way.

Uplifted by the sight of Palladan and his two chums bolting for freedom, the pony boy made his own bid. "Disagreeable hosts do make the deadest parties—I'm leaving too!" And so he did—with a gallop.

Seeing her comrades safely out, Niki then cast off her ties, doing so with no flippant comments—but rather a great deal of haste—she joined Palladan.

With an earth-shattering screech, the great eagle soared to a stand at the portal, where he stood usher until the last of the prisoners had cut and run. He then sped after the butterfly, who guided them through a steamy, stretching corridor to the outside.

Alas, freedom was not to be so easily won. The Ill-timber was the first to squirm after them—but he did not hurry. Neither did Vexpurra, who was the next out. But then, she knew what awaited the escapees beyond her parlor, and it made her purr instead of panic. Horros knew that secret too, and so blew himself up a couple inches more as he followed his tabby across the threshold in eager pursuit. Odios couldn't remember what was outside, so after first colliding with a pier of steam, the curious condor pecked his way through the dark veiled halls like a hen scratching for feed. Meanwhile, Mors remained behind, delighted to be left alone at last with the satchel and the silver hat. He remembered what awaited those outside —and so stayed safely holed away inside and played.

The prisoners ran with all their worth, but just how far was it to the 'shanty's' front porch? "Shouldn't the entrance be right here," panted David, "instead of this tunnel? Doesn't anybody remember... Could we have chosen the wrong door?"

Hell's house is a deceiver, painter," reminded Niki. "We took the only exit it handed us. Freedom was beyond this passage once. If such a blessing still exists, it will be waiting for the faithful.

Then—as if to verify their trust—a thread of new light, and a breath of air, waved temptingly before them. Next, just when the pilgrims seemed on the verge of reaching the porch outside, Niki cried out. "Painter—your satchel! my helmet!" And in the same breath, she dashed back into the hovel's inner sanctums.

The band hesitated only briefly before moving on under Palladan's insistence—for a pair of green, glowering cat's eyes were closing in on them.

David was the last to move. He probably would have gone back for his dove —would have—had he been able. Before he could take another step, something hideous and powerful grabbed him about the collar and put the clamp around his arms. And it did not feel like freedom ought, unless even that treasure felt of monster's claws here in hell.

Even before turning to face the forbidding apparition of 'freedom', David braced in the rumble of his companions' cries, and caws, and bleats—and that new and awful noise—the one that freedom makes when it is dying.

It was the roar of an Ill-timber David heard. It was the acute touch of its yoke closing on his neck. And there, dashing all hope of escape, loomed the awesome behemoth. Only this one was more immense, more defiling, more abhorrent than the sizzled crock that was the She-timber's other half. She stood as a perpetual sentinel over her queen's swamp palace. No more the gangling, mossen mangrove tree, with a hutch tucked in its knees. She was a more gigantic genre, with a frightened family of frantic, fugitive 'squirrels' hunching in her shadow.

CHAPTER 43

"Someone's been nibbling on my toes... Ssss," bellowed the She-timber. "And it felt like suckling's teeth to me... Sssss." The tree engulfed the entire porch with her callous tentacles, surrounding the escapees in gnarly wooden walls. When her mate emerged from down under, she began to shake her uppermost branches in tasteless mockery of her mutilated he-half. "Why look at you! Has some rose garden torch lit a romantic fire under my prickly partner... Sssss? Or has another mountain lightning bolt burnt an embellishment on my poor, blistered darling... Sssss?"

"It was that lizard's leather-livered shoot that sparked my madness," hissed the He-timber in self-defense. "Had I not smarts enough to plunge into the Rime and let that stream's wood-curing eddies flush me from those fire drakes' breaths, me and my taproots might not now be nursing on home soil."

The She-timber felt not a sliver of pity and wasted no opportunity to exploit her more humbled he-half. "Blackness becomes you, you char-broiled, bare-boughed bramblewit... Sssss!"

During this face-off, the cornered 'squirrels' huddled together on the porch as the Ill-timber veered from the attack, and began to spat with itself. All the while blocking the doorway and effectively plugging the pursuers inside. This allowed the pilgrims time to put their heads together in a hurried strategy session between the haggling tree halves. Unfortunately, solutions were as scant as miracles. For the moment, only the hassling lockhorns stood between their getaway and their grave.

"Sssss... How would you like to have some of your boughs blackened and bruised too, sweet vegetable heart!" With that, the He-timber began to pluck and pare his she-half's leafy tresses.

"Sssss... Take what you can, baldy! The only green you'll e'r wear is envy, not ivy!" begrudged the She-timber, snapping off a dried twig from her other half.

A howling, hateful outcry from Vexpurra brought an immediate end to the Ill-timber's tiff with itself. "OUT!" wailed the furious cat from the doorway. "Out of my way, you yelping logs! Plug that incessant squalling and grab those vermin do gooders—or I'll have Horros breathe your way, and blow you both into kindling!" The blue demon huffed himself into a few more inches growth, so by the time he reached the porch, he would be able to charge full blown into action.

"The churl!" groaned He-timber. "I want that slipper-whipping churl... Ssss!"

With particular vengeance, the She-timber reasserted her lock on David, and plucked him from his huddle. Christen slipped from the pilgrim's grasp, but it did not bother the lamb boy—nothing bothered the lamb boy anymore.

"Hear that, suckling?" growled the She-timber. "My bitter half wants to play with you... Ssss. Are you game?"

"We are indeed!" cawed Palladan with wings outstretched. "But I've more a sporting chance—especially now—the rules are changed!"

By this time Odios had flapped and pecked his way from the cabin's corridor on Vexpurra's heels. Now, in a stroke of blind and stupid zeal, the nearsighted buzzard set upon Palladan. However, the huge eagle proved to be quite capably recovered from his wound, and checked the vulture's blitz with a feather-ruffling shriek of warning, that this was not the crippled fowl who laid near death upon the chamber's slab. Such an unexpected resurrection caught Odios wholly off guard, and sent him scraping in retreat. In attempting to redirect his attack, the squinting bird accidentally slammed into Vexpurra, and ricocheted off her stone wall fur like a hot pepper hopping in all directions about the porch.

"After that moth!" spat Vexpurra, aiming Odios in the vicinity of the tiny butterfly lofting swiftly away. "A bug is more your match than a bird—if you can only find it!"

The flitting insect had been the first one out, and the only captive to escape over the wooden reptile's broad reach. She flew, not as a fragile, fluttering petal on the wind, but like a streaking shot, catapulted into the clouds, intently seeking its mark—and without a backward glance at the bedlam below. She never saw the spindly condor tearing erratically after her.

Following everything with his keen eyes, Palladan immediately took flight. The great bird clawed past the bedeviled Ill-timber, and soared into the sky. He so wanted to fly to his cousin's aid, for no creature in his animal domain was more dear to him than his sire's butterfly—but cries from below gave him pause. He circled for an instant's thought. Others were left who required his strength: there was Niki, and Christen—and the non-beasts too. One final look to the tiny insect revealed a rapidly gaining condor. "May Enduros take you under his wing, brave flower. As for your friends... I am their only wings. I cannot desert them." So, it was with a leaden heart and utmost resolve, that the king of creatures turned and plunged back into the Morass.

David wiggled and reeled around in twisting gyrations, trying to squirt out of the She-timber's clinch. But on the advice of her twice-bitten other half, the monstrous wraith held her squirrel tight as a nut in a shell, despite his most fervid flailing and kicking.

"Ssss... mean little scratcher, isn't he, hon!" hissed the She-timber.

"The rat's a real chewer, for sure, luv... Ssss!" replied the He-timber, embracing his more vile and verdant half. Dried leaves brushed against David's cheeks like flaky, mildew fingers. The putrid wind murmured through the timbers' boughs. Their combined wailing made David's flesh crawl, as did a crooked set of wanton, wooden knotholes. Brown and cross-grained, these were the mammoth's eyes, and the boy shunned to see the sight of them.

With the pilgrims' huddle torn asunder, the shanty porch became a flurry of activity, especially for Peter, and certainly for Vexpurra. The worm-hair beset the furious pony boy as he assailed the trees' base at full gallop, striking with a salvo of denting blows in an effort to unsnarl his friend. But in a flash of tooth and claw, the cat woman pounced on him, savagely clawing and gnawing, and whining in a fitted rage. Peter wreaked—then cried out in agony, as he reared to shed himself of his pain. For a moment the centaur youth was a blur, a wild mustang kicking his hooves into the air, stomping and biting, thrashing around like an untamed bronco. Yet, for all the dustup, saddled with such a fierce fighting machine as Vexpurra, Peter's back and strength were soon broken. The pony bolted first, then staggered and fell onto his knees, before heeling backward twitching and jerking. His blood spilled across the floorboards. Whetted by this liquor, Vexpurra's nest of worms uncoiled and sank a dozen mouthfuls of venom into the pony boy's gaping wounds.

Christen was the only one left on his feet, right where David had lost hold of him. The listless lamb saw no reason to move. Unfortunately this proved a temporary state, for Horros was not so sluggish. The docile lamb looked so delicious, the blue beast hied with the speed of a vampire bat, onto Christen's throat. Landing viciously, he drove them both over the rail and into the thick sedge mire. The stale water quickly soaked into the lamb's plush wool like a sponge. Then, as if even in a stupor Omnus' prince might prove more than up to trouncing vexing little pucks, the demon bat began to huff and smoke and spit—and grow—to improve the odds. And as the horror grew, he growled and grinned. The bulging blue giant bloated into the heights where there was no roof, and only sky to confine him. "Mmmm... How big shall I grow!" laughed Horros to himself. "Until the sky looks up to me!" he boasted. But when the trees were his peers, the evil-inflated imp settled himself, and gloated with arrogance. "I am large enough for lead-headed lambs!" he bellowed, hoping to wake his prey and hear a plea or two before the sleep was finalized. Flames cascaded from his molten lips like ruby rivers. His black tongue stoked the red fires that were his eyes. With his heel, Horros pressed Christen down into the pasty mire and held him there. Thus, weighted down by behemoth, bog, and black magic—the languid lamb soaked up the infectious poisons and began to drown. Without so much as a whimper or a bleat, he sank— until no more of him could be seen.

David watched with heart-wringing torment from the treetop's tendrils as, one by one, his companions succumbed under the perversions of Lust's mongrels. The sights wrenched him so much more than his own travail. The two Ill-timber halves were now reconciled and grafted together in mutual hate to form a single mammoth monstrosity that continued to bicker and haggle about how long it would take to squeeze the life's breath out of their catch. David's energies drained with every press of the pulpy sinews. This would not take long; there was no resistance left in the young painter. In his mind, there was nil to gain even if there were. Peter resisted, and Christen once resisted; but it got them nothing—at least nothing good. What had happened to Niki? He tried to think—and then tried not to think, about her fate beyond the door.

And Palladan? Of him there was no sign. David searched the sky, praying that he may be wrong—And then rejoiced to find his prayers answered! Spiraling right towards him was the eagle—strong and noble, and on his way.

With all of the pilgrims so desperately outmatched, it was Enduros' great paragon who proved the equalizer. Down he came, comet swift, and screeching hard upon the mewling cat woman, crouched like a lioness over her prey. But this cat would claim no kill today. Before Vexpurra could draw last blood, it was her adamant back that broke. The once solid shape was pulverized into grains of sand under the impact of Palladan's forceful strike. His long talons sank into Vexpurra's splintered spine and yanked her off the bleeding pony boy.

The wretched feline whined in agony, mewing and pleading for mercy as the eagle sovereign carried her by taut strands of hissing, hollering wormy hair. Her womanly face was stretched so out of proportion that at times she seemed to smile as she begged for life, yowling like a stuck pig. "Spare me, lord of beasts!" she yelped. "Master of cats, let me serve you... let me be your slave. I abhorred that witch, that fire spawn, that... let me go, noble king of eagles—I'm begging you...

Prrrr... Don't do this to me! I am not wont to dying—my fate is not with that pit queen's dregs and dead souls... I'm affraid—can't you see? Prrrr... They'll give me no peace, no respect... I'll be nothing! I beseech you, great Palladan... Prrrr, trust me. I will not disappoint you! On my honor... I will never do another evil deed again—as long as I live... Prrrr. Just release me!"

"As you wish, kitten." Palladan released Lust's cat. Her writhing rock carcass plummeted into the deepest sump, where the miserable feline sunk permanently like a hidiously etched tombstone. "If only the Kyln Morass were as shallow as your honor you would land high and dry, Vexpurra. Natheless, your last promise is the only one you will ever keep: your arrant deeds are truly done forever! Let the clay-born beneath the moors have you now. You will be more welcome in death than in life."

"With one mad devil thus dispatched, Palladan was now attracted by other rabid urgings. Horros persisted in his sadistic wringing of Christen. The utterly helpless lamb was sinking perilously close to the realm of Lust's clay shadows. The giant bat had already buried the prince under his heel, yet was left to vex and toy with his victim, attempting to extort some drop of plea or begging from his locked lips. But the senseless, sheepish head was satisfied to disappear one last time under the sediment, unresisting and uncaring. He surfaced only at the diabolical whims of his tormentor. But not so much as a bleat of mercy surfaced. So incensed was the blue bully at this lack of response, he dropped his own guard. The giant vampire did not even see Palladan, so fast did the eagle dive into the stale water for his lamb prince. But the bat did feel the thrust of a tempest lift him off his feet and send him toppling into the fen like an avalanche of hair and bone. And he did see the great eagle pluck the prince from his burial, securely gather him in—as though fishing for salmon—and then gently land the lamb boy safely upon the porch.

Horros did not wait for any further show. One piercing glare from that great taloned fisher was all it took to send the whey-faced fiend fleeing into the braken heath, eager to get his colossal body aloft on flimsy hobgoblin's wings—and more eager to escape Vexpurra's fate.

But Palladan had no time for sifting out swamp vermin, when his own peers were in over their heads. Christen and Peter lay side by side upon the porch, both were conscious—however, the lamb boy's breathing was very shallow.

"Don't worry about us," said Peter, sounding sturdier than he looked. The centaur had been licking his own wounds, but now began to tend his best friend. "I've only lost a little blood, that's all. As for Christen... He's alive at least—just waterlogged. Once he's wrung out and dry again, he'll be fair as ever. Well... almost." The pony boy wiped something that wasn't water from Christen's eyes. Palladan too was grievously concerned over Omnus' only son. Shortly, upon Peter's pressing and pumping, the lamb's chest heaved, and he began to cough. The swamp flushed out of his lungs. Although still stiff from Lust's enchantment, he was again among the living. The eagle's mind eased somewhat, but not Peter's. He looked up into Palladan's steel eyes, and past them—stopping only in the Ill-timber's sprawling branches. "Davy is in most urgent need now..."

The swishing, whistling arms of Ill-timber whacked away at David. His feet were wrapped tight in a tangle of branches. "Stop beating him... Ssss!" growled the she tree. "Let me have him now. I want to hug the little acorn some more—real good and tight... Ssss!"

"I'm not finished pinching him yet...Ssss!" snarled the he-tree. "I want his shell as cracked as mine... Ssss!"

Through it all, David appeared to be passed out—if not dead. The faces of those on the porch were mortified at what they saw. Palladan sailed away, driving at the Ill-timber's core. Alas, there was little of the fury left in his attack, no spark in his eyes—his earlier wound had exacted its price, leaving the mighty wings weaker. His sallies, though forceful, were less effective against the big weed. It was all the great eagle could do to escape the flurry of slashing, stabbing limbs and nettles.

"Sssss... What was that?" smirked the He-timber. "Another nester?"

"Sssss... a sparrow I think," chortled the She-timber, "looking for mites probably!" And the tree pair folded fifty arms around its treat and would let not a sparrow—nor even an eagle near.

Palladan dropped to the porch just like that sparrow with clipped wings. "It was as I suspected... with its roots in home soil, the Ill-timbers are invulnerable. Without stronger magic than mine, I fear the worst."

"Davy's shoes cut like an ax" sighed Peter. "But they're lost to us."

"How about the painter's satchel then!" chirped a tired, but chipper voice from inside the shanty. Everyone looked to see Niki emerge onto the porch with her silver hat on her head, and David's satchel under one wing—and a bundle under the other. "His paints were lost; but I've got them back now—and they're just as sharp on that overgrown stump as his shoes!"

"Niki!" shouted Peter, as loud as he was able, "how did you ever get through to wrest that stuff away from the bonesetter? You've got your helmet, and Davy's paints, and... whatever is in that bundle of rags? What's happened to Mors?"

An almost sinful sparkle lit Niki's round, pink eyes as she emptied the bundle's contents onto the porch. From out of the black wrappings spilled a pile of assorted bones: some knees and knuckles; and elbows and toes; and ribs and wrists; and lastly—a round, but warped, skull bounced out. It landed in the pale pile of other parts, then rolled off the porch and into the swamp water with a 'ker-plunk'.

"Mors?" guessed Peter.

"In the clutch, he just fell to pieces!" cheeped Niki preening with pride. "His blinded bedfellows were too busy falling over themselves to get out after you; they never noticed little, ol' me rushing in to bag the boner." Despite her success, the dove did not cheer long. A pained look at the Ill-timber told her the whole story.

"There's no time to lose, Niki!" warned Peter. "We have to attack the tree beast with David's paints and do it now—no other weapon will phase it!"

"Impossible—only painter can open his pouch!" Niki pointed out, then paused only long enough to sling the kit over her small shoulder.

"Have you wing enough to deliver the goods, little sister?" asked Palladan.

"I have, big brother—if yours have strength enough to o'rsee my flight from that feudal fly swatter." And so it was, with an eagle escort, Niki darted and dodged her way between the groves of flailing branches to arrive at David's side.

The sound of the dove's frantic twittering was enough to rouse the boy from his faint. The sight of his best friend brought David new hope. But his strength was being rapidly squeezed right out of him; and despite Palladan's most strenuous lunges and incursions, there was nothing the eagle could do to penetrate that arsenal of spiny arms hugging David so obstinately.

But there was plenty that those thrashing, thorny tentacles could do to the unwary, the worried, or the harrowed. Remembering well the pain contained within that paint satchel, the He-timber seized upon his first opportunity to swipe the poison from Niki's grasp. Victory was not long in coming.

Niki had extended a hasty wing to reach her painter. And David, upon seeing the glimmer of hope she offered, succeeded in freeing one hand to accept his paints.

Alas, between the wing and the hand, were the wooden limbs of Ill-timber. It was one of these that snuffed out any lingering glow or hope in any eyes—any except the knotholes of ebony. Niki, David, and Palladan, and Peter all—even Christen, with empty eyes—watched from their slough of despond as the magic satchel slipped from Niki's wing, or was it David's hand? It might well have been a hundred hands, or more. But even a thousand hands, or eyes, would not retrieve the satchel from the Morass, where it had plunged—and sank with a most profound, and dolorous splash.

Palladan and Niki both dived deep to fetch it—but who can see under such a meer—certainly not the birds—or trees. No one could speak. No one wanted to—no one, that is, except the Ill-timber.

"Sssss... What was that sound, I wonder?" said the sneering She-timber.

"Sssss... Another nester methinks," replied the hooting He-timber.

"Thick as midges they are, hon... thick as midges!"

"The fen, lov... it's been gluttonous today!" said the he-tree to his other half.

CHAPTER 44

To the pilgrims, the loss of the paint satchel was the most distressing calamity yet befalling them. For David it was far more tragic. The realization that his paints were forever lost was a death blow. Without the confidence his blessed kit provided—the surety on which his whole course had been laid—he saw no reason to continue his bout with Ill-timber, nor his quest for the Glass Egg. For that matter, even living seemed a pipe dream in his present pinch. Thus the painter saw his vision drown, and so passed out in a faint of bleakest despair. The ever tightening arms of Ill-timber were content to hand him his final wish.

Below, on the porch, an equally strangling gloom enfolded the rest of the fellowship. Only Palladan had life enough to spread his wings. His unflagging perserverance would not grant the stubborn eagle the mercy of giving up so easily. In exacting circles he meticulously scanned the cress pond and privy-padded water hole. His unflinching gaze appeared to penetrate the muddled mire; but his final pass saw nothing resembling a satchel, only alligators, gars, and green swill.

"Some razorback might have swallowed the boy's case thinking it a fish," reckoned the eagle. Such a possibility did nothing except spread an even heavier melancholy across the porch—that is, until one of those brackish reptiles surfaced with David's satchel in its jaws. Palladan immediately swooped down in a killing dive—much to Peter's dismay.

"Stop!" screamed the centaur, so loud that it reopened his worst wounds. But he wasn't hurting now—except in the best way possible. "Palladan, don't do it! That's no 'gator—it's a friend!"

The eagle abruptly drew in his talons and veered away, missing the armor-plated lizard's spectacled snout by inches. "Gol' Durn!... You do extend some hand in reception—Yes sirree!" Then, with a cautious look around, Fidius the Fierce ambled out of the water, pounded the mud from his ears, flicked his moss-crusted tail, then held up David's satchel. "Did somebody drop this poke?"

Though Peter was not quite up to walking, he did sit up sprightly, and let his expression welcome his good friend Fidius, as the lizard stepped onto the porch dripping. Niki rushed up to the old turnkey, and planted a big peck on his cheek and wrapped as much of her teeny wings around his leathery neck as she could.

"Well... Me oh my, this is more like it!" grinned Fidius, hugging right back.

"Sir Fierce, praise the gods you're alive!" rejoiced Peter.

"Oh dear me, yes... that is, I think so—thanks to them gods!" wheezed the lizard, wiping off his spectacles.

"We thought for sure the Ill-timber had eaten you," said Peter, with new color in his cheeks.

"What? Ol' Fierce put away by a mere stump! Not on yur life... er, speakin' of life, you boys seem a tad worse fur wear. An' li'l' Davy... My oh my! That hungry stump's fork is no place fur him, I kin tell you... Why, master Christen! How do.

It's so good ta see you again..." Once Fidius had his glasses in place, the sight of the lamb prince brought a wide alligator smile to the lizard's face—only to vanish into a scowl, as he eyed the king's son closely. The lamb boy merely returned the look with cool indifference. "Say, what's a matter with you? Yur eyeballs are a mite lackluster." Fidius now noticed that Niki was all a twirl and twitter.

"Fidius, listen to me! We're alright... It's Christen... And David. Both are smitten under enchantments. We have to get this satchel to painter. Without its magic, both may be lost to us!"

Fidius puffed some smoke balls to be sure his furnace was not doused by swamp water. He seemed surprisingly undaunted by their pilgrim's plight. "Shucks, li'l' dove, you kin unwind now. Davy don't need magic—I brought somethin' a whole lot better... Looky yonder."

Over their heads, almost obscured by mist and mossen cypress towers, was a magnificent golden palomino, sailing on wings of pearl and heaven's hooves. It was Paramount steering in and out, betwixt and between the flurries of slapping, slashing limbs and ligaments of ebony.

"Father!" shouted Peter, struggling to find his feet. He could lie still for no more excitement.

"And Vero too!" proclaimed Palladan. The sight of the Titan Prince brought out a squawk of unabashed joy from the staid old eagle. The sun-haired child of Enduros, prince of gods, and pride of the earth, swept down on the thrashing Ill-timber astride his fleet-winged steed in an all out effort to break through and reach David. "Ho—Prince!" cawed Palladan. "Wait, save some for me!" And off he flew to aid his master's child. The eagle, and the stallion, and the son of gods assaulted their opponent with all of heaven's zeal.

"Now ain't that a sight!" admired Fidius.

"Just splendid!" cooed Niki, with reserved optimism. "Do tell us, Sir Lizard... How? How did you ever survive your mountain bout to manage this grand rescue?"

As Ill-timber grappled with Enduros' deities, Fidius laid out his tale: "Well sir, let me tell you... My boy, Abraxus, an' I had quite a tussle with that stick up on Mount White. We was gettin' trounced, but good. So I says to my boy, 'Boy, you can't kill this thing, 'cause it just re... regener... it just grows right back, like any weed worth its salt. Use yur fire' I tol' him!" Fidius paused for some smoking chuckles before continuing. "Well... our dragon flames made firewood outta that root's rotten pulp. That put a sure-fire end ta his regener... re... ta his growin' back again! Would've been nothin' but an ash tree now 'cept fur jumpin' in the Rime. That river saved his skin an' doused our victory, let me tell you. Goldie an' me traced that driftwood all the way here. I doubt Isolato approved of the taste a that torch in his realm water. Goldie says his fin-tailed uncle ain't gonna take this dip sittin' down, neither—No sirree!"

Fidius stopped to observe the titanic duel in the trees. However, his rapt audience plagued him to continue. "Let me see... where was I? Oh yeah... We dove right in after that log. Would've tailed him all the way ta hades—or here—'cept my boy was called away by urges, or love, or somethin'. Said his gal, Windy, needed him. So off he went, with his heart tuggin' his tail, leavin' his ol' man ta fend for hisself. By the time I crawled outta that hoary stream, I was lost as a post in a pile a pines."

"Didn't you find our note?" Peter wondered. "We left you some directions to follow us."

"Pshaw—who had time ta look fur notes! 'Sides, more 'n likely it was buried under the snow an ice—just like yur daddy was. Found him an' Goldie frozen solid as ice cubes in that sinful snow. Once that bonfire was extinguished, the blizzard come to a halt real sudden. So, with my natural fires, I thawed out Enduros' boy, and we sort a joined up. He said the blows we all run up against was Lust's doin'. She meant ta put the golden prince on ice permanently—an' us too, almost! Anyway, I might a been lost fur good if ol' Goldie and Paramount hadn't flown me outta there. We saved each other you might say. Goldie promised ta help, an' true to his word... well, he's here ain't he!"

"You helped each other—and us!" tweeted Niki. "How did you ever manage to find us down here in this chowder? When you stopped for Vero, the timber shook you, didn't he?"

"Well sir, li'l' dove, his smutty trail did thin out a speck by the time we got down ta these flatlands. Luckily, we happened onto a top notch guide." It was here that the rainbow-winged butterfly flickered into view and lighted on Fidius' broad

525

nose, waving her speckled wings in hello. The bright dots sparkled like a cluster of wonderful, wide eyes.

"Creto!" said Peter, recognizing the artful bug who had drafted their escape.

"If you please, centaur, my name is Creta. I am Creto's distaff. When I choose to resume my life as a caterpillar, you may call me Creto."

"Quite the stickler ain't she... or, he?" mused Fidius. "In the skyways, this li'l' hummer met us over the Misties, and lead us ta this garden spot. That's when I saw that stump knock li'l' Davy's poke into the drink. So I took after it like a duck... 'scuse me, like a 'gator takes ta water. Just glad I could be of some use. It gives these tired ol' bones a real tingle, yes sirree! Looks like I missed out on the big brush though."

Niki chirped at the lizard's understatements. "It's not what you missed, Sir Fierce—it's what you did! And that makes you invaluable, not merely 'useful'."

"Vero and his mount are of some help too, don't forget," added Palladan as he glided to rest from his sorties against Ill-timber. "Those two youngsters put me to shame."

"You're a wounded, winded gamecock, brave Palladan. And no warrior of god, nor man, nor beast can surpass your prowess," spoke the butterfly of her comrade.

"Ho, Creta, you describe some youthful hawk! Nevertheless, for my tired heart, you are truly a welcome sight. I prayed the condor would not eat you, little sister."

"He very nearly did," replied the insect. "But a heaven-sent wasp crossed Odios' flight path and that buzzard swerved to give it furious chase, thinking it had the look of a butterfly I guess. He must have swallowed it too because, soon after, an awful caterwaul jarred the sky. Then, here he comes, hooting and shooting out of the clouds zig-zagging this way and that like a crack crossing glass. The last I saw of that bird, he was clutching his stung and swollen string bean neck. And, with no arms left for flapping, well... he soon sank somewhere out of sight, which, for that vulture, was more than appropriate!"

"Agreed!" cawed Palladan in a hearty laugh. "And soon Vero shall send the vulture's roost packing far out of sight and mind."

"I wish I could share your confidence," said Peter, staring at the fiercely dueling titans before him, and wondering if someone should pitch in and help. "Can anyone possibly slay that miscreation on its own turf?"

"Vero can, my brother," spoke the eagle with assurance, "just you watch!"

And so there they all stood, on the porch with their hearts in their hands, and all eyes planted skyward. The Titan Prince and his nimble mount repeatedly out maneuvered their foe at every twist and turn. Vero reined the golden stallion into a daring, dizzying vortex in and around the frustrated wood worm, successfully evading its most deliberate swats and whiplashes, like an overzealous mosquito. Soon, Ill-timber's heads began to spin.

"Hold still, gnat!" roared the behemoth. "Come to me... Sssss! Let me grind all your bones into fertilizer so my roots can drink your nourishing blood and grow lush on your thews... Sssss!"

"Sorry to spoil your game, big twig, but you've grown quite full and foul enough already at my friend's expense." From his waist cloth, Vero produced a silky lasso. "My companion, Creto, has woven you a fine, strong going away present. Let us see how it wears around your pithy neck." With one carefully aimed toss, the youthful deity proceeded to hogtie the Ill-timber, branch by branch, winding it tightly in Creto's strong caterpillar twine, until the beast was netted within a cocoon wrap to envy any tree high chrysalis. "Now, you shall have your drink, my bloodthirsty twig—but you'll settle for saltwater this time. Nor will your roots gorge themselves in the good earth. I intend to carry you away from this bone meal bed, where your toes will not touch ground. Fish will be your fertilizer, and brine your only sustenance!"

Awakened to the peril at last, Ill-timber finally released its grip on the boy to put its tendrils to better use. Down plunged David, toward the Morass and certain death.

Yet it was not bog, nor gator, nor death which claimed him, it was Palladan. The unfaltering eagle had found yet another wind, and swooped in on fleet wings to catch David and return him safely to his friends' warm embraces. Nevertheless, the pilgrim remained unconscious, oblivious to the uprooting of evil around him.

Ill-timber had become a serpentine fury, writhing wildly in contorted gyrations meant to shun the titan's attack and wrest itself from his trappings. Vero parried the haphazard flailing with deft ease, pulling his rope taut about the timber's throats, pressing He and She-timber's gnarled and knotted faces closer together than they had been for ages. Another couple might have endeavored to make amends—but not these two. Cursing the gods, and each other, the Ill-timbers screamed to blister the ears of any one, or thing, unfortunate enough to hear.

Their blasphemies were blessedly choked however, in one final gag, as Vero sliced a pathway through the misty soup and all its lurking vegetables. He spurred Paramount high and far away into the eastern heavens. Streaking across the skies, with a mighty tug he uprooted the shrieking tree serpent from its ancestral loam for good, and whisked it rapidly out to sea beyond reach of its clutching cloudy cohorts. The screaming boughs wailed like a distant whistle as it vanished into the waning horizon over the Citrine Gulf.

The demise of the Ill-timber was a sweet sight to behold. Yet no one on the shanty stoop could pause long to relish the victory—nor catch their breaths. Niki was a sobbing, twittering wreck. Despite all efforts, her painter remained unconscious and shallow-pulsed. "It's no use—He's dying! I know it... and there's nothing we can do about it!"

"Yes, there is!" declared Creta. The butterfly had just completed an examination of Christen. Satisfied that the lamb prince was uninjured, save for his spell, she devoted all her present energies to the faint figure of David. "There is a cure... But we must be gone from this place. It is rank with seeping dangers; and to remain here a moment longer will endanger us all. We have disturbed the dead ones' slumber. They wake now, and will be coming for us—"

The butterfly's words had not even settled on their ears when, without warning, the Kyln Morass closed in upon the pilgrims. The swamp slaves, dozens of them, then hundreds—and more—appeared from their murky entombment, clay-cold and putrid, and lifeless to the bone. Out of the sediment's depths they rose, and surged through the rushes toward the pilgrims clustered on their moldy beds. On they came, marching, not as before—with creeping, patient resolve—but in lurching, lunging steps that throbbed and tramped, and stomped at random as in a spasm of great havoc. It was like an army of frenzied, giant ants.

"Lordy!" exclaimed Fidius, who began to smoke nervously. "Where did these customers all come from?"

"From their grave vaults below the earth," replied Creta. "This fen is a gate to Luhrhollow. The clay-born haunt the halls of her deepest defiles."

"That's just fine!" said Peter. "Here we are, stuck with one foot in the grave—theirs, not ours, I hope! So what are we supposed to do now?" The centaur struggled to his feet as if ignorant of his lanced and lacerated hide. His pony hair was on end and his coal eyes swelled to a bulge. "I'm fit enough to run, or resist... or whatever. But what of Christen—and Davy? If we move him, we could kill him—"

"We're all out of magic! Can't you see!" cheeped Niki, still chattering on the verge of hysterics.

"Nonsense!" cawed Palladan, who was in no panic. The grand eagle had compassion for the dove's distress and lent his calm to ease her burden. "It has been fortitude, not magic, that's kept us alive until now. Let's keep out fate in our own hands. If you ask me, these clay-born deadheads are as guileless as they are lifeless. Take notice, if you will, how they're all running amuck! And why, I wonder, did the goons wait until now to attack us?"

But there was no time left to ponder. For now the clay-born were upon the pilgrims. A score of the ghouls plopped onto the porch like sacks of meat. Palladan shielded Prince Christen and David, then spread his broad wings and braced for the kill. Fidius drew back his javelin. Peter grabbed a rail post for a club. Creta tried to tow Niki into the air to resist as stirred hornets do—but the dove balked, and so the pair stayed by David to grapple with the rest. For this occasion the butterfly switched to her male counterpart, figuring they could use some of Creto's extra hands. Together, the staunch band was primed for one last battle—But this was not to be the day.

The dead hulks overwhelmed the shanty in slapdash fashion—yet, much to the defenders' bewilderment, they found their foes too spooked to stay and fight. Instead, the clay-born horde scrambled on aimlessly, then off again in one rabid wave after another. Their gaunt and livid faces betrayed no emotion to be sure, but this was a panic-stricken mob without a doubt. Apparently, the only threat posed to the pilgrims was being trampled under the stampede of death's steps.

"Why, they're not attacking us at all!" proclaimed Creto, who had taken a position upon the roof. "They're running... But, what from?... OH! Oh my!... Look out!"

Before anyone could ask why, the stale Morass swelled into a torrential curl of foam. Had the pilgrims not been high above the squalling quagmire, upon the stilted porch, they would have been flushed away like grains of sand in the tide—like the clay-born crawlers.

"Onto the roof with Creto!" commanded Palladan. "Quickly, before another wave enlists us yet into Lust's sod slave army."

Ever so gently Fidius and Peter hoisted David onto Palladan's back. Niki remained close at hand, but ineffectual in her sorrow. While her painter was gingerly lofted to safety, the lizard and the pony boy helped Prince Christen up, lest he just sit lifelessly by and drown a second time.

From their new sanctuary atop the roof of Lust's shanty, the clustered group watched in awe while the tired and tepid moor was purged into a tempestuous spate, as savage as any grudging sea. As the twirling water rose, there was not a single clay-born body left to behold.

"Slave corpses, like dead fishes, won't swim in this bath," remarked Palladan, in a fitting eulogy to Lust's drowned dreadnoughts.

"Are they truly dead?" wondered Peter.

"Or just homeless, with no more beds ta sleep in after that gullywasher," suggested Fidius.

"In all likelihood, they're both," guessed the eagle.

"We needn't worry about death's cast offs any longer," said Creto. "For now, nature is our archest enemy, and as a foe may prove more lethal than any bane or animus of socery."

With aloof unbias, the rising highwater kissed corpse and comrade alike with her wet, rippling tongues; and hugged them with moist, caressing arms inching ever higher. With each gurgling movement the menace mounted. The rank water lapped at their toes and licked their firmest resolve. By now the soggy shanty roof was nothing more than a life raft, bulging with desperate survivors of previous disasters, praying—each and every one of them—to stave off yet another. As they prayed however, their numbers multiplied; but not with such pious minded pilgrims. The swamp encroached upon their craft—as did the swamp's denizens: the venomous vipers, the blood-sucking leeches, and the gluttonous gators. Each sought separate claims to the shanty raft.

"If only we could steer our way into the high mahogany trees," thought Creto, before sprouting his butterfly wings to skirt the danger. "Or a lofty cypress should survive where its gum and thatch palm peers do not. Such a seat would see us safe from beast and heath."

"And what would protect us from the trees?" puffed Fidius.

Peter too shuddered at the thought of trusting his life to another of the Kyln's shrubs. "I've had my fill of this bracken's broth for life!"

"The mortals are right, Creta," confirmed Palladan. "The timber in this fen is rot and wicked, and has proven too hostile to be hospitable. Should it be uprooted —as has been demonstrated—'twould seal our fate as sure as floodwater or tidal squall."

"You must fly us to safety then!" said Niki, asserting herself at long last, for David's sake. "You can handle most of us... if painter and I remain behind. We'll wait for your return. Who knows, the water may even recede..."

Palladan screeched his displeasure, then grabbed a viper in his talons and crushed its poisonous head. "And what of these dastards! Will they recede too?"

"I'm not goin' anywhere without, Davy either!" sputtered Fidius. "I swore ta protect the li'l' knight, and by cracker I'm gonna do it!"

"I'm not running out on my friend either," added Peter. "Davy saved my skin a time or two, and I'll not desert him to this tar pit!"

"He rescued Christen too," added Creta for good measure. "And were the poor Prince of Lambs able, he would surely stand by his gallant, as I and the rest of us intend to do!"

"It seems my painter's one up on each of us," peeped Niki, ashamed for even suggesting the fellowship abandon her young orphan. "I guess this squash has saturated my brain!"

"It will saturate everything else anon," commented Palladan, as he calmly pecked away at the leeches squirming at their feet. "It's too bad your friend can't pull us out of this predicament too." As the eagle snapped at what appeared to be another snake, he was startled to find it was something else—it was a silken rope! Palladan jerked his head heavenward. There, above them all, soared Paramount, holding a taut line as Vero descended onto the sinking roof.

"Why, bless my soul!" squawked the bright-faced eagle with astonishment.

"Hooray!" exalted Peter, rearing and kicking his heels for joy at the sight of his father. His wounds cried out too, but were ignored for more euphoric tears.

Fidius flicked his tail with spry enthusiasm, while Creta and Niki danced a jig amid cheers and plaudits. Prince Christen just looked on with his customary passive exuberance—even as the approaching alligators gnashed their teeth.

"Easy does it," cautioned the Titan Prince, stepping gingerly aboard the 'raft'. "Your celebration is rocking the boat. Let us not be swamped by our delight!" Vero checked the injured pilgrims, then raised Christen onto Palladan's shoulders, securely draping the lamb boy's arms around the eagle's neck. He next gently eased David up to his waiting stallion, which dipped low to accommodate his special passengers. Peter and Fidius were next, followed by Vero, who was the last to mount and haul them away. Once they were airborne, their places were promptly repossessed by jostling salamanders, snakes and other snappers. All of which were swiftly swallowed up by the uncaring Kyln Morass.

"So long, brothers!" wheezed Fidius. The old lizard spit fire as the band of refugees streaked high above the treetop web. Though the cloud beasts still brewed as thick as heath vines, the misty mongrels molested not the fleeing conquerors and chose to keep discreetly distant.

"I apologize for the cramped seating," said Vero. "But I think you'll agree, Paramount is a safer craft than that you left."

"I'm not complaining!" said Peter, patting his sire's thick flanks and relishing the uncommon comfort of his back. Indeed, no complaints were heard."

Niki and Creta flew beside Paramount. The little dove was solaced by the sight of David once again securely astride the lordly alicorn—like their first meeting upon entering Sovereignton. On the winged steed's opposite side, Christen was still tucked tightly to Palladan's shoulder. This relieved Niki too—although she continued to dwell on their fate, and hers, should this pair succumb.

"How good the fresh air feels!" said Peter, as the sky massaged his tender cuts with healing breezes, bathing his matted skin free of the swamp's filth.

"This air tastes sweet as fresh honey," breathed Fidius, inhaling the sky, and filling his lungs with clean, invigorating, fire-stoking gusts.

"Bask in the heavens, my friends," encouraged Vero, "but spare a gaze behind to the oblivion from where we came." Looking earthward, the escapees were all enthralled at what they beheld. The rampaging floodwaters had totally obliterated the Kyln Morass. As dreams at dawn dissolve, so too did the dreaded Kyln. Sunlight poured on the scudding shades of mist, evaporating their flesh like steam pelted under a cold shower. Underneath, all that remained of Lust's jungle was a howling forest of drowning mangrove, shag bark, and strangler fig—and who knows what other swamp-privy, plant, predator, or poison. Whatever vile vegetable or vermin met their end beneath the deluge, it was not to be rued by anything wholesome. The surrounding Moors and delta countryside, for the most part, escaped the decimation, depending on the proximity to its shallower neighbor. It was on these more elevated meads and marshlands that the surviving remnants of Lust's clay soldiery issued forth to rally en masse. There to stand in idle idiocy under the scant shade of a pared and withered Ill-timber grove—a squelched and sponged out army of mindless monuments to deprivation.

"Where will they go now, Creta?" wondered Niki.

The butterfly's soft features hardened. "Like all disease, those maggots will seek out their sore—Lust—Mythlewild's most avid abscess."

"That's why we must make haste to Revrenshrine," explained Vero. "Once the lamb prince and David are safe, my grandsire and I can attempt to remove Mythlewild's cancer. And we'll have some help disinfecting it too—from Enduros' briny brother no less! What you've witnessed today is Isolato's revenge. Lust had tested her salt water sibling's patience time and again, abusing his oceans, rivers, and swamps with her tampering and devilments. Finally, my hermit uncle lost all patience—and the 'dam' burst! With the Kyln Morass so purged, the sea lord is vindicated. Although Luhrhollow still smolders, blood no longer flows in Isolato's water arteries.

"Isolato, as lord of all waters, claimed dominion over these Moors too," added Creta. "It was never Lust's to reign. She was but a squatter here, from her rightful realm on Ebon Isle, in the Dark Farths. She and her clay-born family have been evicted by their landlord—or rather, their sea lord!"

"And us too—almost!" said Niki, trying so hard not to be sad.

Vero cupped the dove in his hallow palm. "Do not grieve, little friend, the gods protect their kin. Isolato would not harm innocent folk in his wrath. With Ill-timber drained of sap, I cast the dry, dead twig into my uncle's ocean. There I was forewarned of the tidal waves' coming and hurried back to salvage the only decent inhabitants remaining in this swampland. The evil will abate here, and Isolato's marsh will grow again, lush and thriving with life as its rightful caretaker intended."

"Does this episode mean the sea lord has taken our side in this cause?" asked Niki of the Titan Prince.

"It means Isolato has decided to protect himself, and his deserving watery subjects. Just as his brother, My Lord Enduros, has decided to protect his. As you are aware, Lust has overstepped her subterranean bounds and crossed my father's borders as well, plucking at his whiskers, and resolve. She's gone so far as to poison another uncle, the sky lord, Zeros, who lies in death's coma much as the lamb prince does now—"

"And you too, golden one, would lie stiff within her numbing crypts," flapped Creta. "Unless she's thwarted, that fallen seraph will murder us all!"

"It may already be too late..." Niki swallowed another tear over David.

"Take heart," cheered Creta. "Our team of wings will have us at Revrenshrine erelong. There you may all find relief. A warm welcome also awaits you. Your courageous examples have served to inspire the immortals. No less a deity than the king of gods, Enduros, is anxious to thank you personally."

"Some inspiration!" grumbled Fidius. "Yur daddy an' his clan of eternals are more 'n match fur Lust. But instead a takin' up the ol' gal's glove, you all squat on yur deistic distances—on mountain tops or oceans' bottoms—an' did nothin'... 'cept maybe peer into some ol' oracle once in a while as though watchin' a joust or game!

An' all the while, you leave the burden of the contest in woefully weaker hands, like fleshy kings—or on the backs a boys, like li'l Davy—Didn't ya!"

"Fidius! That's not true," objected Peter. "Where would we be now if Vero had not uprooted the Ill-timber! And just whose back is this you're sitting on anyway! Paramount has yanked us from the swamp's jaws, hasn't he. And didn't Vero and my father make a somewhat less successful bid to find us last week on Mount White?" recalled the pony boy. "Or was it some other lizard who defrosted them from Lust's ice casket! And another thing—whose eagle was it that lay bound with us in the crone's root cellar? Was it not the same which saved our skins against her motley misfits! Was it Palladan's crime my arrow sprung Lust and nearly spit himself—"

"Nor were Palladan's the only wings sent down on our behalf," interjected Niki. "Creta has been a member of our quest even before you, Sir Fierce—though with considerably more discretion than some others. As for me? I didn't just fall out of my nest you know! And have you asked your scion, Abraxus, who lent sanctuary for me and the painter when a heller's gale would rather have us? Are these the acts of apathetic gods?"

"I believe your case has been amply made my friends." Vero pointed out that poor Fidius was slumping sorrowfully under the outspoken disproof of his two colleagues. Even their earnest apologies did little to boost the lizard's sagging spirits. It wasn't words that fueled his remorse, for he knew they were right. It was not for himself Fidius languished, nor even David or Christen; they were all in good hands now. It was for his king, and country, the reptile warrior suffered. "Yep... we've been saved, sure 'nuff," acknowledged Fidius grimly. "But how does Constantio fare? Or our kingdom? Who'll help them?

No one could answer readily. Who among them had not lost sleep mulling their nights away for solution to such questions.

With all attention so diverted by dilemmas it was for Palladan's peeled eyes to notice something in the sky below them. The eagle descended towards the mushrooming shadow that was trailing them. He then squawked to see such a sight as it came burgeoning into focus. Only Christen and David remained stoic as the hippopotamus floated up to meet them.

"Folly!" exclaimed Peter. "It's Folly! And would you look down there everybody—at the Rollingway River. I think I see a miracle!"

The others had already caught sight of the flotilla, churning its way up river in a hard tack. "Lordy, lordy—It's Adm'r'l Honos—an His Highness' fleet!" Fidius gulped, nearly choking on his smoke. He adjusted his spectacles, just to be sure his old eyes were not deceiving him.

Paramount's ascent had leveled off momentarily, and before anyone could ask a question, Folly maneuvered himself alongside Paramount. He took hold of the stallion's tail to spell himself, and a broad ear to ear grin spread across his vast hippo face. He was panting terribly, and the cherub's two, tiny wings drooped like wilted cabbages from overwork. "My, my... it's certainly a long way up here, isn't it? ... Thought I'd never catch you..."

"Folly, what is it? What's happened?" asked Peter first.

"How on earth did you ever git so high off the earth?" Fidius wanted to know.

"Because... I had to... That's how..." panted Folly, who was now leaning on Paramount's flank, figuring, why deny his body the rest his grateful wings were getting. The grand alicorn bore the added load without complaint.

"Why, Prince... It's you!" Folly gasped gleefully, looking past the lordly eagle to spot Christen. However, unable to contain his news a moment longer, he began babbling, unmindful of the lamb's plight—nor the least impressed by the presence of the son of the earth, whom the hippo ignored in his excitement, along with his steed, who's croup was proving so invaluable. "Oh, Prince, you would not believe what I have accomplished of late... If Griff were still with me, he could tell you... I left him with Admiral Honos... He was airsick you know, but he's happier now... He and the bull had such a fond reunion...We thought the fleet was sunk for sure! So, with no place to turn, Griff and me began to search the coast for any survivors of the scrape in the Citrine... And what do you think we found 'neath a cloudy bank and knocked off course by a few notches? Why, it was the whole doggone fleet— that's what! There they were, holding out against a whole task force from that yellow toad's armada, (puff)... Then this... this colossal giant, (pant)... with a seaweed beard and fins, pops out of the ocean and 'swooshed' the blackguards away!...Next thing you know, a humongous, fantabulous sea lizard comes along—"

"My boy!" blurted Fidius proudly.

"Fidius—don't interrupt!" admonished Peter, along with everyone else.

"Do continue, Folly," urged Vero. "Only slow down. You're much too overwrought, and making little sense. That was Fidius' spat, Abraxus, who responded to his true love's distress call, and arrived to save Miss Windy and the other ships as well. The raging, green-beared giant was Isolato, the sea lord, venting his aggravation."

"Yeah! Yeah, that's it... Why, Your Lordship!" Folly nearly lost his grip when it occurred to him who he was talking to. "A-As I was saying, sir... Once the Admiral was free of those knaves, and Amber Glade was safe and secure, well... he set sail up the Rollingway to overtake the remaining pirates and liberate the other settlements like he did at Emerald Bay. Then, on to Cinnabar goes the Windy to rescue the king. T-The big lizard lead their way into the channel while the other big guy—the green-whiskered one—blew on his waterway, stirring up a swift, strong upriver current speeding the Admiral's ships along to reach Constantio in time..." Here the bubbling cherub had to pause, else tears trickle into his story. "... Oh, Your Lordship, H-His... H-His Highness is in dire need of help... and Sovereignton too! DeSeet's lions have marched on the city some nights past. With Cinnabar in his pocket, the count goes there now to take title—me and Griff saw them! A-And if you could just come with us, sir, back to Cinnabar... what an impressive figure it would cut—enough to turn the tables maybe. Imagine... a titan god on our side: Enduros' prince! That's why I had to climb up here... Help us, Your Lordship; how it would bolster moral. Lust has cast a baleful spell over the battlefield.. .and it would be so encouraging for Constantio to have his son beside him again!"

A deep frown cut Vero's stern jaw. "Alas, Folly, I alone can turn no tables. Moreover, your king would take no encouragement in beholding his son in this present malaise. Christen is touched with bewitchment too. We journey now to my father's White Mountain dwelling. Only at Revrenshrine may he and the pilgrim hope to find themselves again—"

"Pilgrim?" The hippo's popping-eyed stare shifted from the lamb boy, to David, who lay still upon Paramount's back, completely unnoticed by Folly in his flush. "Why... it's that boy! Is... is he dead?"

"Not as yet," continued Vero. "But the longer we delay here, the more critical the situation becomes. I fear this black magic perpetuates itself. As for Cinnabar, the lion may have stolen that plumb and put it in his pocket—yet, until upon his palate, it still belongs to us! You must hurry on to your king without us, Folly. We'll pitch in when we are able—this I promise! However, take some good tidings with you. Lust's concoctions have suffered a severe blow. As you have observed, her sea brother has risen to smite her. Isolato's tides have purged her lair at Kyln Morass. She can ill afford to tarry at Cinnabar now that her home front is breached. Even as we speak she is retreating into her earthen oven to dry out and cook up some new vengeance. With your help, brave Folly, and that of Admiral Honos, Constantio will carry the battle at the 'Bar, and live to defend his sovereign citadel—and take his title back!"

Folly looked so forlorn; then finally, his vast, resolute smile returned. "I'll tell His Highness that Prince Christen is in your care... And help may be forthcoming..." The hippo cherub flapped a feathery wave of farewell, then released his grip on Paramount and dropped like a sack of overstuffed potatoes to rejoin Honos' fleet. Paramount turned carefully under Vero's deliberate rein and soared full out into the North.

"How I long to join Folly," said Peter, looking down sadly.

"Is Sovereignton really on the ropes, Goldie? Asked Fidius of Vero.

"Even more than any of us can imagine, Fidius," came the grave reply. "We've an enraged lordess to contend with now. Don't let her sunken status mislead you. My aunt jinni is a deity—just as my father and uncles; only she is younger, and bitter, and ambitious—and perhaps more potent! She fears nothing—not even gods. She preys on them, casts spells on them, and their lambs. We must first break her hold over Christen."

"And the painter?" Niki had flown over to the boy and nestled near his closed eyes. "He mustn't die either—not now. It's not time for him to go... so much of our task remains unfinished. Can you cure him?"

"No, Niki, I cannot. We will be close to heaven at Revrenshrine—but not that close. If your mentor was inclined to patch things up so easily, then he would have done with all our ills. But can there be purpose without the pain of error? Or life without risk of death? Who wouldn't endure a hurt or two to pluck some happiness off the vine? It's the empty-handed heart that never knows for fear of losing. And our best odds lie on Mount White. There is a maiden there, Tierra, my sister. She will nurse your painter, and the Prince of Lambs."

Dusk held back night's curtain until the chaste silhouettes of the Snowmass rose miles ahead of them—and once again David crossed into the realm of Enduros.

CHAPTER 45

Cushioned below the bleached shadow of Mount White in her stark autumn foothills, the bleak and heavy trodden face of Middleshire was enduring a similarly swift migration. The forests were losing more than leaves this season. For days she observed impassively as her hying citizenry shed their pervasive, but remote, pine-walled protection for the sterner wood of Sovereignton's strongly fortified gates. No abode was more reluctant to lose her lodgers than the Elder Ambrose's manor house in Hue Dingle.

The picturesque little cottage, nestled in the wood hollow, watched as uselessly as a spent beehive, while her lodgers divested her of honey. The lovely domicile was soon to be a lonely ruin. Only a last flicker of fervor remained for this war orphan. The entire household was a bustle, packing and wrapping, lifting and loading—all of their earthly possessions that could find a fit onto their already overcrowded ox cart.

Ambrose grunted as he hoisted Celeste's loom into place atop the crunched divan, then carefully stuffed cushions across the antique to pad its unblemished cheery wood finish as though it were a chaffed child. The elderman's own skin had become sorely cracked and peeled from the toil of war's labor. His official vestments were soiled and laced with leather strappings, which sheathed his sword and vitals both. Patrick remained unencumbered with worry, though riff with anticipation. He tossed a trunkful of belongings onto the mountainous furniture heap which grappled with itself and other heirlooms for each precious scrap of space on the wagon.

"How long will we be in Sovereignton, Father?" inquired Patrick from under an armful of toys and dirty leotards.

"Until this realm's turmoil is settled and we may safely leave the city's walls to return home—and not before," declared the winded elder, puffing harder than he should have. The prosperous smile was now slumped into a frown of sagging folds. He hurriedly tied everything securely into place, while earnestly trying to be honest with his son. Yet realizing in his heart the full truth might never see them home again, Ambrose concealed his most candid thoughts.

"Careful my loom doesn't jostle, Papa—remember, it's an antique!" Celeste rasped her instructions from behind a tipsy stack of bundles, which toddled out of the kitchen on two dainty angel feet. Then they halted on the veranda as a snowy, round head popped into view supervising each and every move. Her glowing halo was somewhat dimmed; and it did not sit so high as before. But still she winked with a certain vim and vigor—and voice. "Patrick! You don't need all those toys... I swear, we'd be better to hitch the ox up to the house and take the whole kit and caboodle!"

"Let him keep them, Mama. We shall be needing any comfort we can manage to take with us. I dare say, Patrick's toys take up much less room than yours —and they're much lighter on the back!"

Patrick finished stacking the last of his mother's bundles into whatever nooks and niches survived in their cart, while Ambrose shuffled up onto the porch, joined his wife, and paused to catch his breath.

"Poor dear, you've worked so hard these past days." Celeste rubbed her husband's tender collar with her plump, soft fingers. "What the Queen hasn't demanded of your time, your family has."

"I hope I get ta fight some a those lion's brigands, like Davy has!" exclaimed Patrick, bounding onto the porch in one giant leap. "Can I get a sword in town, Father? Everyone else carries one now—even you!"

"Patrick!" Celeste scowled, her halo dropping another notch, "you promised not to dwell on infidels and brawls, or swords and such. It only thickens the boil."

The elderman gathered them both into his arms. "Mama, we have to face the fact that, like it or not, our son—our family, each and every one—is going to get soiled by this nasty rumble. The boy's twelve years old now, and you'll see that war will age our young man faster than years. Cold steel cares no whit what age it cuts. At all costs, it is virtue that must be preserved—even at swordpoint—for youth cannot."

Patrick beamed as his father extracted the blade, and instructed his son with a smattering of rudimentary moves. It was a poniard, not a fancy sword by its edge. It was unburnished, untempered, and untested—like those who wielded it—until now. "Don't like the feel of iron too much, my boy; you mustn't abandon your toys for mine just yet. Childhood is a more patient tutor than war."

Patrick surrendered his weapon for the moment, and Celeste's angelic glow returned. "Will Sovereignton be lots safer than our own house?"

"Our daub cottage is no protection from DeSeet's huntsmen and warbands," answered Ambrose. "All but the most die hard of our neighbors have already moved into the city. Even now I feel we may be too late in quitting these sinister woods. Her Grace, Superbia, has warned that insurgents abound on the kingdom's borders. That's why we must hasten to reach Sovereignton by nightfall."

But dark things do not always wait until the black of night in which to hide. The daylight has its shadows too. While the rest of her family scurried in and out and all about, in the back yard Valentina kept a watchful eye on her baby sister, Jing

Jing, who was playing with something from Fearsome's pile of 'toys'. The three-headed pup was sleeping comfortably under the doorsteps tied to his leash as though all were right with the world. One of his heads occasionally stirred to lick at one of the numerous bones dotting the yard. Valentina was the only one who seemed on edge. Her pixie wings flicked and flinched while the elf maiden fingered the nape of her neck, nervously feeling for a canvas pendant which was no longer there. Maybe it was November's disquieting chill which made her cool today, or the duress of moving perhaps—or something else. "Jing Jing!" she screamed, quite without thinking, and quite startling the napping pup. "Must you play with that filthy bone? It belongs to Fearsome and it's dirty...Wherever he found it, I wish Patrick would have thrown it back!"

But Jing Jing, undeterred and persistent, decided what was good for the pup, was even better for the babe. So she began to munch the dog's dirty morsel. The toddler soon decided it was too hard on her tender gums, and too big for her tiny mouth. Nonetheless, she saw fit to explore its potential—until big sister spoiled her picnic. Spotting some flies on the infant's pacifier, Valentina promptly wrestled the smelly joint from the child's custody and tossed it aside in the grass—where it attracted another pair of envious eyes.

Fearsome cocked all six ears and sniffed the wind three times. Valentina hefted Jing Jing into her arms. "Come on, Jing; I don't know where all these horseflies are coming from—and so late in the year—but it's turned too cold out here for us.

Nearby, leaves rustled, while sparrows took flight. Valentina glanced across the yard, shivered, then went to check the gate. It was unlocked. Behind her, a twig snapped. Fearsome sprang to his feet, and for one bristling instant stood rigid and foaming. His hackles were spiked on edge, tense and snarling, and three times more vicious than any dog you can imagine. He lunged to attack, straining his chain tether to its limit.

But the wily, vixen eyes glared back spitefully, then padded away with Fearsom's old bone—because it pleased her thieving appetite. The fox's accomplice subdued the larger prize for which they came.

Jing Jing cried violently, drowning out the braying laughter. There was no word out of Valentina, however. The mule-eared shadow saw to that.

The intruders were efficiently done with their deed by the time the family arrived from the front. They found Fearsome howling incessantly, and Jing Jing left in tears. Valentina was gone. The dark ones had taken her away—deep into the forest—and beyond. A veil of clouds fell across the sun's sky so there would be no other witnesses.

CHAPTER 46

Over countless cloud and snow-filled chasms; and beneath the sky-blessed pinnacles of soaring, marble spires; past many misted parapets sailed the pilgrims atop a sea of rocky crests. A dense and endless layer of armored luminaries capped Mount White. Rows and reams of iron-towered guardians watched their way as Enduros' son approached. Vero had trained his deistic army well; parades of soldier-laden chariots flew from out of the cliffs to greet their golden prince of gods and men. The titans escorted Vero through multitudes of immortal men-at-arms. The stately, spiraling gates of Revrenshrine opened their arms in welcome, and the immense mountain walls embraced their son. The tiers and turrets, and sun-tipped columns of lords and stone, stooped down in homage as Paramount carried his charges in a proud canter through heaven's halls.

Peter and Fidius gaped in awe about them, all but unscrewing their necks to absorb such wonderment. Even Niki was impressed. Alas, the lamb beside her was not—nor the boy. The limp, lethargic figures of Christen and David marred the occasion. "If only painter could see how the gods welcome their guests..." lamented the dove.

"And a military welcome at that!" observed Creta.

Vero was equally surprised—and pleased. "It appears my father has ventured from his rocker and his laxatives long enough to muster the numen—and the nerve —to be lord again!"

"And has discovered a tonic more potent than all the herbs and earth's elixirs," cawed Palladan.

Vero reined Paramount to a halt before a flight of diamond stairs curling, as the crease of angels' gowns, with folded wings which were its bejeweled balustrade. At the apex of this pillared promenade loomed one particularly resplendent visage. From his crowned head to his platinum-pleated toes, gilded in white gold battle attire, he stood alone. One fist clenched a freshly polished scepter. The other gripped a well worn sword pommel; and none had to guess it enfolded a blade as broad and keen as its experience. Age itself had fled its post upon his brow to kiss the ground beneath the mountain god. Enduros—supreme lord of all the earth— looked every inch the godhead of legend: a lofty, lordly zenith to his mountain empire. Looking over his domain, the legend extended an arm into the air. Palladan took flight, straightaway to his master's gleaming mantle. Cheers and flourishes erupted in Revrenshrine.

Vero met his father's face and, through the bearded drapery, saw joyous tears. Dismounting, the Titan Prince ascended the stairs of starlight with courtly reverence only to yield to a parent's embrace.

The imperial escort assisted the pilgrims in laying David carefully in a litter. Prince Christen remained as listless as ever, yet he did gawk toward the reunion at the top of the staircase along with his companions, as if aware of its portent—but of course he wasn't. Neither did he react to the great fuss which his presence

546

commanded. In the midst of gods, the lamb boy was being venerated. Heaven's horde was kneeling before him. This show of devotion, while eliciting no reaction from Christen, certainly raised the brows of his companions—all except Niki, who regarded the right arm of Omnus in even higher esteem. There will be much to talk about on this hallowed hillcrest; no doubt many questions would be answered—and raised."

Suddenly silence descended across the mountain peak. Enduros held his celebrated sword high into the air, unsheathed and glistening to blind the sun. The aged lord cried out and rocked his mountain's brows. From the peaks and pits, from out its deepest defiles, to the highest precipice, he vowed—and it was no old dottard's thunder. "Praise to you, Father, my most revered High Lord, Omnus—overseer of our Mythlewild, and of gods. My son has been brought back from my sister's frozen jails. Now we make ready to ride out and cool her craving. She wanted one—we'll give her our all!" Ovations and cheers orchestrated the land lord's words. "Our black sheep mocks me, Lord, and she blasphemes you. That siren of Satan sins against us both. My beloved brother and your god son, Zeros, has been offered on his back to you, Lord. And by your law—or ours—his transgressor must be rebuked and hewn away as any other infectious crop. Thus, I intend to carve our ravenous red sibling down a size or more!"

Enduros' sword became a lightning bolt flashing a fiery arc above all their heads. Then a clap of thunder as the wielder rammed it home into its scabbard. And when the fireworks waned, the lightning tamer raised his scepter and bid his guests enter into his house. Taking Christen by the hand, Creta advised the band to follow. Peter and Fidius gathered the litter in their hands and proceeded slowly up the sparkling, sloping stairs. Niki removed her hat and, from David's side, cooed a greeting to her master's eldest son.

Upon observing their distress, the land lord descended the steps to meet them, just like a doting parent. "Prince..." Enduros enveloped the lamb child in his hands and gazed into the dull eyes. Yet, even in the hollow of a god's touch, Christen could not stir from his spell. "It is worse than I feared, Niki," said the earth lord sullenly. The lamb has escaped, but the prince lags behind in Lust's clutches. I can be of no help to him here. His fate has been entrusted to pilgrims, while his cure lies off in some witch's recipe. Guard him well, children."

Niki did not act at all surprised at such grim news. Instead, she turned away and bent over her boy. "And the painter, Lord... is he also beyond your help?"

Now the god of Mythlewild knelt down upon the steps beside David and raised a heavy brow. "My dear pilgrim... What has happened to you this time? Have you fought yet another lethal brawl on my behalf, for the sake of a glass egg?" Enduros' furrowed cheeks betrayed a trace of a smile. "No, Niki... I cannot heal our brave friend. His wounds are too ripe, and my powers too old. However, I know a younger potentate who will have him back on his feet." The venerable lord then spied David's footwear with some envy. "Perhaps I should say, back on his shoes! But have no fear; here there is refuge for both body and spirit. Your master, Omnus, need not worry about his pilgrim—nor his lamb son—nor any of you. You have all been greatly burdened in my service, and you shall be duly rewarded."

Both Peter and Fidius were quite confused by all of this. They couldn't understand why Enduros referred to Prince Christen as Omnus' son. As they muddled it, the earth lord turned to face them, and caught them before they could bow down in homage. Enduros extended a warm handshake to both.

"Peter, king's courier and archer extraordinaire, ease your mind, and your pains. You see how my eagle has recovered from his wound; yours are also on the mend. How often your sire, Paramount, speaks of his colt's steadfast discipline to our cause. We are both proud of you. And, Sir Fidius! Constantio's faith in his turnkey was certainly well placed. My oracle has shown this household how you gird and protect our pilgrim and his property like a suit of alligator armor. Moreover, you have unlocked my own son. Lust's bewitched ice cloister would have immured him from my magic, and sealed his death as well. But I'm here to tell you, she has tested my jurisdiction for the last time. That fell blizzard was her final blow!"

"I believe you mean that this time, Father," observed Vero, as he scanned the celestial ranks arrayed before him. "The pilgrim boy and Omnus' lamb must be tended here. Meanwhile, we march—I am committed to the High King's cause at Cinnabar."

As are we all, my sun-tempered child," stated Enduros, extending a hand toward his house. "The immortals are nearly fitted out. Until the time is nigh for stepping out however, why don't we all step in. Enter into Revrenshrine and prepare yourselves for what is to come. Though guests are seldom seen under my roof of late, consider it yours, all of you—and know you are welcome here."

Vero carried David up the remaining diamond steps, and into the most sumptuously splendid palace any of the pilgrims had ever seen. Everything, but everything, from ceiling to floor, and wall and windows, and doors—all shimmered and sparkled like highly polished mirrors. Only, instead of glass, this house was jewel! Its every face, a lacy new filigree of jewelry and prismatic glowing colors. What a precious place to live. Not dazzling, nor blinding bright, as you would expect of such a shining treasure; rather, it was warm and welcoming, and altogether wonderful. As the guests made their way into the sunny loggia, Peter and Fidius remarked how Constantio's palace was too confined by mortal thinking and earthly limitations to be truly spectacular. "We've come a long way from the dungeon cellars of Bia Bella, huh, Sir Lizard," marveled Peter.

"Tut!" grunted Fidius, pretending not to be astounded. "Too flashy if you ask me—an' too fragile. One tossed stone an' the whole works'd shatter like a punch bowl, yes sirree! Fine crystal maybe, but too brittle, practically speakin'... Don't you agree, li'l' Prince?" asked Fidius of the silent lamb, not desiring any argument. Besides, Christen probably did agree, for he was even less enthused by such luxury, and seemed to see right past it all.

As for Niki, she was only slightly more impressed. To someone nurtured by a less pretentious deity, the little dove considered Enduros' lavish fixtures as both unnecessary, and unnatural. To her, the mountain was a more auspicious house. Her sire was the master architect, and she saw no need to embellish his snow-capped handiwork with a jeweled roof. Furthermore, her thoughts were more on one pilgrim than all the palaces in the world. Until the painter was well again, she would be able to think of nothing else, not even in the company of gods.

From the splendor of the reception atrium, Enduros guided his guests into a more modest sized sitting room. Vero carefully laid David upon a plush and comfortable divan, which was as soft and coddling as the walls were bright. "My children," said Enduros, "let us surrender our patient into the care of a genuine angel of mercy. May I introduce my daughter, Tierra."

From behind a curtain wisp, entered the fairest beauty any of the pilgrims had ever beheld. Neither Fidius, or Niki, could fault this exquisite goddess. Her sheer and satin-spun gown adorned her figure like pastel hues cling to a flower petal. Slender and graceful, she moved effortlessly as morning dew to David's side, saying nothing, yet smiling to out sparkle the stars' shine. Her features were even more flawless, her honey hair more rich, her immaculate skin more soft, and her charm... divine. To whom would the gods pray for a daughter so sublime.

"Lordy!" gasped Fidius. Smoke leaped from his snout as the lizard wiped his foggy spectacles. "I can't recall ever seein' such a fetchin' female—No sirree bob!"

Peter concurred wholeheartedly. He brushed his bushy brown hair out of his eyes to view the vision unimpaired. "Bless my soul, Sir Fierce, she must've stepped out of a dream... no, out of heaven! No, by golly—she IS heaven—come down to this mount to save us all. Why, she's even caught Christen's eye!"

She hadn't of course. Though the lamb prince looked her way, he saw naught of the goddess, such was his plight. But Niki knew Enduros' daughter. He knew Tierra to be no illusion, nor was her healing charm contrived. The little dove held her hat and her heart under wing, and watched as the beautiful princess caressed David's brow and dressed his wounds.

At this point another equally elegant, if somewhat more time-honored goddess joined them. Her hair and complexion, both streaked in the refinements of ages past, merely underlined her maternal dignity and classic beauty. Enduros' gracious wife, Lara, invited everyone into the grand hall. "I'm sure you will agree, your friend is in good hands, but he does require rest. If you will follow me, I've prepared some refreshments. Were you fed nothing but fire and fear in the Kyln? You all look in need of nourishment—and then, some convalescing!"

After some persuasion, the weary group left David in Tierra's tender care—except for Niki that is. She would not leave. The faithful dove passed the next several moments perched in a tireless vigil by her painter's ear, carefully observing the lovely idol, and whispering encouragements to David all the while. Niki just knew he could hear her, so she thought out loud. "How many times in the past weeks have we hung so perilously close to death, painter... but always together!" Tierra noted the affectionate bond between the boy and Omnus' dove, and worked all the more fervently so the love bird would not fret. "Ill-timber's tendrils squeezed his bones so hard, I know they must be broken..."

"No. It is not his bones that are broken, Niki—it is his spirit." Tierra's voice was a song-scented elixir. Yet her words were a sad lament. "Ill-timber has pressed more than life from his veins—it has sapped his faith. His complexion has turned to chalk—a ghost already. Why isn't he wearing the satchel Omnus gave him? He must have it around him. It is his best defense against this affliction."

"Mercy!" Niki cheeped in dismay. Then flew quickly to Fidius and promptly returned with David's most prized possession, laying it softly on his chest. Even in unconsciousness, the innocent boy slept easier with his arms around his paints.

"And look at his shoes," said Lara. "They're positively hideous, all caked and coated with this mud. Lust's morass still possesses him. No wonder he can barely breathe. We must wash away the evil clinging to him at onceThe shoes resilience fades in step with David's faith." The beautiful goddess hugged the boy in her creamy ivory arms. Then, with a cleansing mineral water, freshly gathered from the stars, she tediously bathed away every last speck of the swamp's silt from shoes, and satchel, and any pour it might hope to hide.

Still, David slept, much to Niki's mounting anxiety. "Isn't there any kind of... er... medicine, or something you can administer him?"

"Of course," replied Tierra, in a lullaby voice betraying no hint of worry. "You see how he suffers from Lust's affections. Perhaps mine will treat him better." The earth's daughter cradled David close to her bosom and whispered into his soul a loving lyric, such as a mother might recite to her injured child. "I believe in you, my innocent little one..." She then kissed David on the lips.

Inhaling the affections of the earth, the pilgrim woke from his malady upon this soft and silk-skinned comforter, and gazed into the sweet smiling face of the beautiful maiden of his dreams.

"Hello, David," said Tierra, smiling. "Ill-timber's cold, cruel limbs cannot compare with mine—do you think?"

David shook his head and shut his heavy lids again. They would remain closed through the night. He returned to his dreams, where heaven's beauty kept him company. Niki cooed with relief, then joined her painter on the cushiony pillow in a deep, deserving slumber.

Tierra rose, as the dawn's mist does lift for daybreak. "In the morning, you will be renewed in strength, body and soul. I hope you will be able to leave your dream long enough to survive reality, which treats you less tenderly." So spoke the honeyed goddess as she softly slipped away like melting dew.

Daybreak welcomed David's rising with two of the most breath-taking and lovely sights ever to greet his eyes: the radiant mist princess had returned to shine on the pilgrim like dawn's light; and nesting peacefully in her lap, was Niki, still sleeping soundly. David didn't know what to say. First he rubbed his eyes. "Why... you're not a dream after all!"

"I am Tierra," said the morning goddess, "Enduros' daughter, and a servant to all worthy pilgrims. And in this place, your dreams are often real—as are the nightmares. But you are lucky to be blessed with friends such as this to share them both."

David leaned over to Niki and stroked her wings ever so lightly. The gentle touch, and the fond sound of the boy's voice, roused the dove from her own dreams. Needless to say, she was soon all aflutter with loud cooing and clapping. The racket promptly attracted David's other friends to his bedside. What a contrast to his last waking visions in that monstrous Kyln. You can guess his surprise at seeing all of these happy faces—some of which were brand new to him—Enduros for example.

The ancient lord stooped over David and peeked down the boy's throat. "Feeling better, little fellow?"

"Why, er... Yes, sir," replied David, not knowing what to make of the imperious old gent. His gown was illustrious, and these quarters grand, and being as how everyone else faded in his presence, the boy figured him to be important. "Is this your house, mister?"

David's question provoked a roar of laughter from Enduros, followed by a volly of chuckles from his retinue. "Why, yes, I am, sonny. My name is Enduros. This is my house... as is the whole earth."

Well, at this shocking news, David tumbled off the divan and onto his knees. "Oh, My Lord! Forgive me for my impertinence!" he begged.

The earth lord just smiled broadly and scooped David up in his arms. "Forgive you? Why, my child, I shall entreat you—exalt you—and not the least of all, immortalize you! For you are well—and soon we will all be well again!"

Enduros' stare drew David's attention to Christen. The lamb prince stood lamely between Fidius and Peter, alone unsmiling among the gaiety. "Isn't the prince cured too?"

"Not as yet, child, but soon the flock will be restored." Palladan cawed in robust support of his master's declaration. Creta fluttered her rainbow wings. And Tierra agreed, as did Vero and Lara. Following the deities' example, David and his companions all smiled optimistically. Enduros and his family then led a hopeful procession into the breakfast chamber as Niki introduced her painter to their newest allies.

It surprised David to dine on such ungodlike fare as toast and marmalade, and truffles with tea and honey. Nevertheless, he was delighted, for as delicious as nectar and ambrosia sounds, this table suited his tastes just fine. Afterward he felt truly fresh—like a new man. He slid down in his seat just enough to be perfectly comfortable. With his friends at his elbows and his cares far below him, David remarked to Enduros, at whose side he was situated, "How good it feels here, Your Lordship... This is really paradise!"

"For mortals maybe," replied the earth lord, cursing mortal's victuals as he fought vainly to rake out some honey stuck fast in his flowing beard. "But this 'paradise' is imperfect. Gods have more substantive wants..." Enduros' eyes fell again on David's shoes. In the after meal repose, the earth lord set his hand on David's shoulders. "I am not your master, sonny—but your friend. Call me Enduros... and tell me about this mystifying footwear of yours. Can they really find my magic Egg?"

"Well, uh... they haven't yet, Your Lordship, But I think they might." David was slightly shaken by such genial advances—and by a god of Enduros' prominence! It made him feel very important, and embarrassed.

However, Niki was not so receptive, and looked at any undo attention on her pilgrim's shoes—even a deity's—with suspicion. "The shoes will guide the painter to the Glass Egg, Your Lordship," asserted the dove, "so that it may be returned to its rightful owner—its creator and my master, Omnus Overlord—"

"But it's MINE!" screamed Enduros, slamming his hands down hard against the breakfast table, spilling honey all over his lap. "You fleshlings limp up to me begging for alliance; I know you do! And yet you refuse your lord the slightest rap in return—a pittance of tribute which, by right, is mine. Omnus crafted if for me—and I mean to have it!" The lord of Mythlewild, losing every ounce of his renown patience, leaped up and kicked his throne out from under foot. Palladan was sent flying. And everyone at the table rose to their feet in deference to their lord's authority. "I MUST have it! It will bring me my youth again... and my strength... and glory..."

David and Niki both fell silent and trembled before the earth lord's wrath; for when a god is angry, calamity often ensues. Even a relic like Enduros is capable of the most awesome, fearful feats if chafed. Fortunately, Lara intervened in the pilgrims' behalf. With Vero's help, she restrained her spouse and coaxed him back into his seat. Palladan perched again over his master. And order was soon restored.

"You must forgive my husband," apologized the matron goddess. "Try to understand the insufferable stress which weighs upon him of late. The poor dear takes himself to task for Lust's emergence, and for her virulent pounce upon his brother, Zeros—"

"Lordy!" gasped Fidius. "It's true then: Lust HAS snuffed the sky!"

"She stole her way into the heavens on a cloudy day and, masked within a red fog, sucked his very breath away with a terminal kiss," related Lara sadly.

"May all the gods be beside whoever crosses her path!" said Peter.

The grey goddess nodded. "Naturally My Lord relished a boon with so much promise as the Glass Egg. But, in truth, he realizes the great error our grandsire has made in creating such a corrupting power, and concedes that it is only proper for Lord Omnus to reclaim his gift... don't you, dearest?"

Enduros did not voice any agreement; but neither did he deny it. The lord of Theland simply sat sulking on his throne, and peeled some more honey from his whiskers. He had waited for this opportunity, this golden moment, to win the boy— and thus the Egg—to his side. Alas, he lost the handle on his sentiments. So the dove, and maybe right, won out instead... for now.

A brief pall fell upon those gathered about the table. Although Enduros finally offered an apologetic, if somewhat sticky, hand to his guests, Niki's feathers were still ruffled—and with good cause—as her seating companion, Creta, was quick to mention.

"You notice it don't you, Niki? How spoiling paradise can be. Even now, in the advent of his son's return, and the arrival of the lamb prince, and not the least of all, you and David—whose shoes are sorely tempting to behold—Enduros has already mislaid the urgency which bestirred him to amass his multitudes and equip and arm them with weapons and words of war. See how he sulks... Soon it will be the rocker for him again, unless he gets his way—or finds a new fire to fight!"

Niki understood only too well, she could not preen away the discomfort. "Creta, I'm worried about my ward too. Although it gladdens me to see painter so happy and well, I'm nevertheless disturbed to watch him and our fellowship basking in such divine and careless comfort, while our countrymen suffer so much and so far below them: at Cinnabar, and Sovereignton... and all Mythlewild. My pilgrim does not belong to this paradise—at least not yet. He is too happy here. He is also tempted—and in submitting, forsakes his prior purpose."

"Perhaps we should remind them both, Niki," said Creta, "and the others too!"

So, before breakfast had become entirely devoid of enthusiasm, the prism-petaled butterfly proceeded to flutter across the hall, assembling the household around her oracle for the morning's reflection. Such is the custom among Theland's gods to consult with their oracles before advancing on the day unprepared. They all filed into Creta's cloistered courtyard by her quiet, sky-lit study which was filled with volumes of books and not much else, save for some sunbeams in hiding. Oman, the oracle, was situated outside. The well lay at the very center of the mountain domicile, delving deep into its core, and beyond. It was bottomless, and so was its store of knowledge.

The butterfly sat upon the well's rim like a proud parent describing her first-born child. "For our guests, let me present our oracle, Oman. From his deep gullet pour great, if sometimes saucy, wisdoms that ignite the imagination. It is from this pundit's lips, that the gods know what they know..." Creta could easily have bragged on her baby all day, except for Enduros. The earth father began to tap his feet impatiently, waiting for his tinder to strike a light. With that formidable urging, the butterfly waved her bright, gorgeous wings and, after a few fleeting incantations, summoned a rapidly unfolding vision in the oracle well. Everyone, gods and mortals, leaned and looked into Oman's mouth. They watched in silent awe, and were reminded that even paradise has pitfalls. They gazed down upon the bloody, bludgeoned battleground that was Cinnabar.

CHAPTER 47

Streaming up from the well's walls was the Rollingway River, which laced the eastern skirts of Cinnabar like a wide winding ribbon—a blood red ribbon. The whole field was wrapped in shrouds of silent murmurings. Constantio's once grand encampment was massed into a battered island of haggard survivors from the ten realms of Mythlewild. None were without scars; they wore them like wounds of valor. These were their only medallions. These, and the filthy, gutted cuts of war. Above this fallow field of men, flew their capitals' flags and ramparts—still.

Still to be seen was the white, ice-capped pennant of blanch;

The grey, clouded cloth of Dunn

And the blue, water-stitched linen of Woad.

Also unfurled was the green-leafed flag of Beryl;

The yellow, sun-beamed banner from Flaxon

And the rich, red-flamed device of Rouge.

The orange stone standard of Guild was there;

The brown, earthroot bunting of Sepia too

And the storm-eyed purple banner of Puce,

Together with black: the smoke-stained ensign of Sloe.

All were whipping there still, stirring in dignity under the dingy Cinnabar sky, less starched perhaps, and ironed or scented with nothing but death. And though their colors had faded from facing sights so paling, they were never more brilliant or bold as on this day. Thus the ten trigon hatchments of Theland embraced their rainbow blazoned Decima. And beneath the tattered canopies of armorial bearings and splintered halberds, the kingsmen knelt—what was left of them.

There was no furrier, fog weaver, baron, or smith;

They may have been lost, or captured, or worse.

Wind-rider, woodsman, and mason are dead—there's no doubt.

The jobber and fisherman are alive, in part.

And of the ten standard bearers who once issued forth,

Only the yeoman is standing erect.

But his scars be as mortal as any who bear

The crest of Theland above Cinnabar.

Siegfried Dragonheart and General Affirmare were among the surviving field commanders. Captain Violato still clung to life, but only by the slenderest of threads. Clarissima and Jo remained close at hand, though their perpetual optimism had been bled dry. Exhausted or not, there they all knelt beside Constantio and before their gods, praying for guidance before taking up their arms yet again, for what was expected to be the final assault from Negare.

The ogre warlord was in total command now. Lust had dealt her wizardry well and effectively. Her dismembered minions caked the plain like a sinful plaque. There was left this one, final sweep—then it would be all over for Theland's stalwart clansmen. The extinction of Mythlewild would ensue. The ogre's soul-searing wail signaled the beginning of their charge. On all fronts the bloodthirsty earth began to close upon Constantio. The black, condor-soaked sky also fell upon the king, like a noose. From the river, that tide too began to swell, as hostile sails swept onto the scene. The ribbon tightened around the king's neck. And so he rose from his knees with teakstick in hand, stepped onto his cloud and, with his loyal band behind him, mounted their defense.

"Can't we DO something?" wondered David into the oracle, interrupting Oman's vision. "Your hosts could swoop down and vanquish that Negare..." he suggested to Enduros, "...or maybe even a well placed lightning bolt or two?"

But the gods did not reply. And David's companions could not. So entranced were they by what they saw, none would divert their gaze from the well. As spellbound as Christen they had become. Only Creta was put to answer the boy.

"Had you been awake to sit with us last night, you would know too, David—Cinnabar is lost. My master's sister, Lust, rules it now. Her hold on that earth is too rooted. While she lives no god can usurp her claim. 'Tis up to men to save men at Cinnabar."

"Look!" chirped Niki.

David clutched his breath when he saw the condor ceiling break and scatter. A furious fat, white cloud lunged into play—it was Folly! The hippo's rampaging appearance had signaled the arrival of other welcome faces. Down river, Admiral Honos and his fleet churned into battle, slashing and slicing through Lust's river choke hold. At the point of their attack was Miss Windy, breathing hard into her sails and plowing past the most treacherous, death-drenched jetties with even stronger magic—the currents of life and hope. Sleek, trim, and steadfast as ever, Windy was still the proudest vessel in the king's navy, and at the helm, the proudest griffin in the king's navy—Pax. The dedicated coxswain steered a true and tenacious course right through the enemy's artery. Their thrust could not have been more lethal had they prows of iron and hulls of honed steel, with their yardarms swinging mace. As a mighty and magical current from Isolato clove Honos' ships to the very banks of Cinnabar, a volley of cheers erupted in the king's camp—and also a thousand miles away, on the summit of Mount White. They all exalted over this new wave of hope.

"You guys knew this was going to happen, didn't you!" David beamed toward Enduros. But the elder of gods stayed rapt in his oracle, as did all his family and guests. "Look, Fidius!" he exclaimed, hoping the lizard at least would listen.

The only response forthcoming was, "Not now, li'l' Davy—Hush!"

It was Fidius' scion, Abraxus, who stole the show. The sight and spectacle of the colossal sea drake, so intimidating, so indomitable, and so violent in his stormy rage, was awesome. The dragon vanguard led the rout of the insurgent armada. He was a serpentine whirlpool, with an arsenal of hurricane fire and ship-splintering jaws. One slap with his claws and mastheads toppled. A swipe of his tail, and keels cracked and drowned forever into their river beds. Abraxus, prized among Isolato's ocean children, flooded the sea lord's river with his father's unbridled fury. Those of the pirate fleet that could, fled, as if the sea god would allow it.

With his foes at bay, Admiral Honos poured his bullish fury onto shore in rescue of the king's castaways. There was as little left of Honos' royal navy as there was of Constantio's vaunted legions, but it was enough to rekindle some sorely needed hopes. The bull admiral's arrival ignited His Highness' resolve. Moreover, Folly's news of Christen's safety stirred his blood. "I'll spill no drop of it more!" He was heard to say, with confidence restored. So, pumped with fresh and greater strength, Constantio rallied his defenses and stepped forward under rousing battle cries to retaliate—and attack!

His Highness and his lusty hippopotamus knight spearheaded the assault on Negare's stunned stormhorde. General Affirmare and his column of crusaders took charge of the western flank, while Sir Dragonheart's regiment maintained the east.

Southward the scrappy army marched, then charged, all afoot—and right at the ogre army's throat. Even Captain Violato, crippled and limp as he was, propped himself upright on Jo and Clarissima's arms in order to see, and lend what moral support he could provide. Morale was an abundant ally now. The sight of their fallen comrade in arms—the red knight risen again—was a sight to behold. What a stirring drama! It rang the hollow plain with such a boosting quake and clamor, even Oman's oracle image shook.

"I can almost hear it from here," said David. He doubted anyone heard. But oh, how they watched!

Then, from their lofty vantage point, everyone gasped in heart-bursting dismay as Lust assumed the field of war. War's guardian angel was not pleased. Her smoldering, crimson hair bristled and blazed around her brown, burnished face. The witch's festering presence on the battlefield assumed massive proportions. Her indignation magnified into teeth-gnashing rage.

David choked upon recognizing sin's champion. "Why... T-That's the beautiful red lady... from the swamp!"

"That's Lust, and no other," corrected Niki, "The seraph of evil, queen of the defile, and lordess of Luhrhollow."

David gulped, then shuddered in his shoes. "She looks ever so much more horrible... like this."

Before the boy's eyes his red 'beauty' became a monumental maniac, a fist-clenching figurehead for her goblin swarm. But it would take a hotter head than hers to have the brave and brazen band of kingsmen who now battled Negare measure for measure. The ogre's angel watched her yellow hulk's fleet of burning slivers sink into the Rollingway's watery lockers, and his stampeding throng of plaque and scale trampled into the bloody mud of Cinnabar.

"Why doesn't she use her sorcery now?" David wondered.

It was the witch who answered his question. With violent slings and slurs, the black angel cursed Isolato's favorite son, Abraxus. Then with obscene glares she assaulted the sky. Looking far up, through the tunnel that was Oman's throat came Lust's graven, leering face—right into Enduros' wrinkled grins of pride.

"Why, of course!" remembered David. "She CAN'T use her magic—not now! The swamp woman's all 'wet'. Like you said: it's for men not magic to vie for Cinnabar."

"Your brethren have not failed you, sonny," said Enduros, finally paying some notice to his guest, "now neither will your gods. My misguided sister has forgotten her old sibling has some tricks of his own—and my fish-scaled kin in the sea as well, it seems! How I've longed for the day when we might unite again against all odds. If Lust wants a tourney—let her take the tilt to her house, not mine!"

Lust began to shrink and sizzle as she saw her insurgent tide ebbing under Constantio's irrepressible advance. She had underestimated her opponent, and this fanned her fire. Constantio was the giant now, mounted on his cloud and buttressed by his pounding, thumping hammer. It was the diminutive monarch who was truly monumental, supremely statuesque. His comrades gathered by him as the poisoned wave dried away and the rancid, red waters faded, like the dirty sky, then broke into pristine blue again.

Siegfried and Folly rallied around His Highness' side. They stood as one, with Violato, and Jo, and Clarissima, and the ten shires of Mythlewild—and they held! And on Miss Windy's surging deck, Pax and Honos signaled victory. The Decima Crown never flew higher!

There remained only one more pocket of resistance—Negare. Cruel and ever cunning, the troll would not relent. Whether his endurance flowed from the witch's wand or his devil's blood, none knew. One thing was certain, the monster would never yield, nor would those moguls under his thumb.

"You've got to kill him..." coaxed David from his ringside seat. "...you've just got to!" He naturally assumed his companions were too enthralled to express themselves—but he was very much mistaken.

Niki managed to frown slightly at her ward's bloodthirsty call, while shamefully wishing the same fate, silently.

"Affirmare! Affirmare!" shouted all the shires of Mythlewild, as the king's champion set upon Lust's yellow-scaled goliath.

"Affirmare!" exulted David from above. He was so excited, he almost toppled into the oracle. Not even pausing to consider the consequences of such an accident, the boy continued to root for his team. His enthusiasm proved contagious. Soon, even the most staid and demure deity and down-to-earth began to loosen up and find voice.

"Trounce him! Stomp him, Affirmare!" shouted Fidius and Peter.

"Pulverize him!" joined Niki uncontrollably.

"Go Affirmare!" cheered Vero and Palladan. All of them, even the earth king himself, and his family, could not resist.

"Affirmare!" they all resounded. Only the lamb boy remained calm and sedate. Yet, even through his cool raisin-eyed stare, David thought he detected a glint of enthusiasm.

If it is true that thunder is the voice of gods, then the chorus of encouragement gushing from Mount White was an ear-splitting thunderstorm—one that neither Lust nor her clay-hearted heroes could ever hope to combat.

General Affirmare responded to the energy from above with a thunderclap of his own. His broadsword, Byn Un, was his lightning bolt. Flash after flash, it struck in unflinching peals past the battle ax into the hard, clay-thick hide of Negare. Nothing would repel its edge until it had cracked and shriveled the yellow gourd into a mound of dried, bloodless scraps. The ogre's lackey hastily gathered these lobbed off rinds into his armor vest and dragged them away to stow in some deep, dark treasure trove like so much spoils of war.

Affrirmare's own dedicated page, Yang, supported the weight of his wounded liegelord until swarmed over by a merry handful of appreciative comrades in arms.

"Hooray! He did it!" yelled David in wild abandon.

"They all did it!" chirped Niki.

"We won!" declared Peter, who began to prance and dance about with Fidius. How they longed to join their king in his moment of triumph. They all began to celebrate—all except Creta, who was posted atop Christen's wooly head.

"'Tis too early to caper around like carefree lambs," cautioned the butterfly. "History seldom ends with a bloody victory, it merely begins. Watch—all of you—we're not yet finished with our war." Once again the gathering encircled the oracle, and looked to see what climax could possibly equal the last.

"All I see is a field of jumping, jubilant soldiers," said David.

"Oh, but you're not looking close enough!" counseled the butterfly. "Peer beyond the bliss—and see the bizarre. Examine it well, young pilgrim, so you will know its face." David strained his eyes, and an image gradually came into focus—all too vividly. Once more he saw the visage, Lust. She was no longer on the plain of Cinnabar.

"She has retreated to her subterranean pit at Luhrhollow, in the earth's recess," remarked Niki.

But Enduros corrected the dove. "Not 'retreated', Niki, my sister never shrinks from her cravings. See—she goes to gather her spawn about her."

"Horros!" shrieked the dove. "I thought we were rid of that devil!"

The reaction from the others was the same—alarming. "It looks like Lust is giving him instructions... What are they saying, Creta? Why can't we hear?" David was dying to know.

"Much of the mage's hollow realm is kept secret from us, David. Her magic is most powerful there. I am truly surprised Oman has revealed this much—" Suddenly a more caustic-colored voice bled across the butterfly's rainbow.

"Did you ever think I might WANT you fools to see!" wailed the cursed snarl. "And I want you to hear me too—you stupid, interfering old hilltop prune—And you especially, pilgrim!"

Somewhat confounded at such an intrusion into their conversation, the oracle's audience watched and listened as Lust glared up at them from the fathoms of her hold with an anguishing reality even the gods could not ward off.

"I underestimated your resolve, old spook—and yours, pilgrim. But no more. Your sawed-off sovereign thinks he has won something—well, he has not! He has instead lost a city—his city! Sovereignton is a fallen shambles, a pulverized mound of dust and rubble, wrested from its hog-headed defenders by your runt's chancellor and conqueror, Count DeSeet... Or should I say, His Majesty, King DeSeet! I've flown my purring consort north to celebrate the capture of your besieged city. The lion claims your capital for his own now. The hog queen and her suckling, and all that sty's panicked piglets lie buried in Bia Bella's deepest pen, with the cockroaches, and whatever other jail rats rot in those catacombs—"

"Liar!" screamed Peter. "You're a loathsome, wretched liar—"

Fidius attempted to restrain his hoof-stomping friend. "Here, here, li'l colt, there ain't no call fur that... especially now. His Highness has set sail to relieve any siege, should any a that mud tramp's word's square with the truth. Sover'nton'll be recaptured—don't you ever doubt that—No sirree!"

Lust only cackled vengefully. "Listen to that split lip, palfrey; then weep for your city. It's too late for all but tears. There is nothing except wreckage to recover in that hutch. And with what force does the royal rabbit hope to win his wounded digging? His army of moles is buried behind him in the warren that was once Cinnabar. And his navy is farther down—at Ocean Botton!"

"Was it a dead army then that mashed your yellow general into dirt!" countered Peter.

"Were them sunken ships my boy brung with 'im ta plunk yur dories outta the Rollin'way!" roared Fidius, spitting fire down the well as far as it would reach.

But the witch was not one to wince or shy away from flames. Her plume of furnace hair only fueled at the fiery darts from Revrenshrine. "Tsk... I'm hardly bested. Your royal remnants have escaped me there, but my lover, death, waits for them at Sovereignton—and dead, they belong to me!"

"You could use some new recruits couldn't you!" squeaked Niki as loud as she was able. "Isolato has purged your coffin coffers of their wealth. Where do your clay-born sleep now, witch—since their hideous roost is bathed clean again?"

"My children sleep in the high, dry meadows of Middleshire, pigeon!" cackled Lust. "Death is at your doorstep, old spook—so you might as well come out of hiding and joust with me. You've unlocked your door once already, to accept my castaways. Will you also welcome me? I'll be waiting for you, brother! And, unless you open up for me... I shall come a knocking. My lieutenant, Horros, is already on his way with a drove of his own demons. But first, I think he will stop to spell himself with the lions in Sovereign'hutch'. And when your midget monarch noses in—he will lose it—life and burrow both! But he'll live long enough to see heads roll: his sow, the pip and fallow, and any else within that fallen fold."

"You witch—you butcher! You'll never succeed!" Peter began to rejoin and pound the well wall. No one moved to stop the young centaur this time, particularly Fidius, whose fires were fully stoked.

"We're gonna stop you... you crock-skinned crone!"

"You bet we are!" added David. "A host of horrors won't stop us. We've got more than numbers to match your menace..."

The boy looked to Niki for assurance. Niki turned to Vero, who in turn studied his father's decimated brow; and was heartened to see the steel scored will within and without. This time the lord of the earth did not hesitate. "The chosen of Omnus are in my care, sister, and they do not cast idle threats. Do them harm and, upon my word—I shall open the gates of Snowmass and fill the skies of Mythlewild with a celestial draft to swallow your demon flies, and flush them forever from the face of my land. So I swear!"

"Drown out the air with whatever you want, fossil—if you're not too feeble of breath to tread upon your own soil! The pork queen, her piglet, and her pygmy spouse will be hunting their heads all the same. So shall any of their damn race—run them all through for what I care! It's no matter to me who lives or dies on their trivial broils and brawls. It was the lion's dream, not mine. I aspire to greater heights than a groveling dwarf king can climb. And an egg shall hatch my ambitions for me... Won't it, artist!" Lust laughed bitterly and cast a debasing eye at David. "And to have the Egg, I need shoes—pretty shoes—pilgrim's shoes! Do you hear me, waif?"

David heard, but he didn't react; he couldn't. He was paralyzed with a leaden fright that would not release him. The witch's pitch and fire face seeped up from the oracle like a penetrating venom. Although the boy couldn't move, he could still hear. And he would never forget the words that stabbed his soul.

"I want you, pilgrim," murmured Lust, "you—and that lamb! I'll not harm the pigs. Instead, their fate will be left to the whims of war. But I will have you two—here—in Luhrhollow, with me! That is my condition. We must talk... you and I. Perhaps you can be 'persuaded' to see my side. We might even arrive at some... accord."

"She's a temptress, painter—don't listen to her!" begged Niki. "We've already seen her sides, and they're all as black as her soul!"

Alas, it was David's eye Lust held. And now the jinni bared some claws. "If you'd rather, we might spar a bit... a contest of sorts—a duel! How does that sound, pilgrim—"

"Painter! Turn away—don't look at her!" Niki tugged vainly at David. Yet even with the others help, she failed to move him.

"Your friend is right," hummed Creta into the boy's ear. "Lust's lurings are killing, and her contest, cursed. Walk away from her!"

But David was immovable. No urgings could jolt him from dismay. It was inevitable. Niki knew it, yet could not face that fact without crying for her painter.

"Heeee—you have no choice do you, pilgrim," bellowed satan's voice, howling its way up from the well bottom. "We all know that, don't we! You're only choice is to come to me. No power in the world, not men's nor gods', can foil me—none but one. Your sidekicks will tell you that. Hurry, pilgrim... I'm waiting for you —Heeee!"

Smoke filled the oracle and rose like a tart gas, poisoning the sweet, scented air of Mount White. When at last the well was emptied of its purls, a rackety chorus of negatives arose to fill the sky. Everyone spoke at once, echoing the same warning: "Don't do it, David! Don't do it!"

In their midst, only one voice alone drew the boy's attention. It was soft and enlightening above the din. It was Tierra. David was drawn to the fair goddess. Her beauty erased the lines of worry underscoring his apprehensions and flushed his pallid face with wonder. "Princess... What did Lust mean by that, 'no power but one can stop her'?"

"Why do you ask me, David?" Tierra responded. "Was it not you the Overlord summoned to his side and bequeathed this pilgrimage? It is you who keeps company with his progeny. Only you hold his sacred instruments: the shoes are your armor, and the paints your weapons—remember! The Glass Egg is for you to gather; but in its path is Lust. Your burden is inescapable. You will confront the black seraph of Luhrhollow. You must—and you know it, don't you?"

David was unable to move or speak; such was his dilemma. Moved by this sight, Tierra took him by the hand, and walked with him, leaving everyone else behind. "Come," Niki had heard her say, "perhaps I can help ease your anxiety. Since it is inevitable that you must leave Revrenshrine, there are some things you should know." Then, David and the earth's daughter were gone from view.

"Don't be jealous of her, Niki," advised Peter. "We could all do with a little counseling. For my part, I believe my father and I should have a word together. There's been so little time to visit since our arrival, and we've a lot to hash over before..." Peter wiped his eye, for he knew farewells were imminent. "Look at me, will you... I honestly don't know what's happened to my discipline. Must've lost it somewhere along the way I guess. Maybe it's gone the way of Davy's Egg..." The pony boy cantered outside and down the steps where Paramount was waiting, as if already harnessed for his departure.

"Tsk!" mumbled Fidius. "If you ask me, the young colt's found more discipline than he ever lost."

"I believe so too, Sir Fierce," smiled Niki. "Now, who shall be OUR counsel?"

"How 'bout the li'l' lamb," suggested the lizard. "He won't lie ta us. An' there ain't no better list'ner on this mountain. Correct me if I'm wrong, Yur Princeship..."

The silent lamb boy could not deny it. So, squeezing what spirit they could from their sullen mood, Niki and Fidius headed for the diamond stairs with this meekest of souls to await David's return. Creta, meanwhile, had fluttered into her studio to settle on a huge open-faced tome, and there she waited too.

As for Enduros' family, needless to say, Lust's conversation posed a most serious threat to them as well. Vero had stepped into the main hall with his parents to discuss what solutions, if any, existed to their plight. But Lust left little doubt what their next move would be.

"We can delay no longer, Father," insisted Vero with a most pressing tone of urgency. "I will muster your hosts together now." The Titan Prince waited only a respectable moment for word of disagreement. When none came, Vero was gone to his steed. "Fly, Paramount—fly!" he bid, mounting the golden alicorn. They both exchanged farewells to Peter and his friends. Soon, the rolling rumble of war gods filled the mountain stronghold.

Enduros stood arm in arm with his dear wife. Palladan circled anxiously overhead. The sky heaved and swirled with the flurry of beating eagle wings. The aged godhead straightened his oft' bent back, and adjusted his white-gold garments as Lara evicted a family of moths from their platinum nest and dressed her husband in his armor mantle. "Well... I suppose I must go on down into that hodgepodge and make a showing at least..."

"You'll be spectacular, dear," said Lara. "Your battle raiments fit you just as fine as ever. You should have donned them sooner; Mythlewild is your realm too. Even your brother, Isolato, has awakened to repel Lust's green-eyed incursions."

"True... and despite our differences, we are still family, and must stand together to right our misguided sister. The young pilgrim said my sea brother asked about me, and bid me well. My hermit feels sorrow for our rift also. And of our departed kin, Zeros, he is bereaved."

"A sad comment it is, but perhaps a sister's sins and a brother's loss may tie us all together again to celebrate a victory."

"Just like the old days... Lara, my devoted treasure," began the earth lord, his eyes awash beneath the cloudy brows. "It's been such a long, long time since I've sallied off to battle... I've quite forgotten how to say good-bye."

"I prefer the sound of, hello—here's to that day." said the grey goddess, handing her husband his thunder sword.

"You will have a warm mineral bath ready for me when I return?... And my rocker? My bones already begin to ache..."

"We'll all be waiting, dearest," soothed Lara. "But I believe this campaign will do more to allay your pains than any bath. And your throne does make a more soothing seat than any rocker." The subtle-faced earth mother massaged her consort with settling, grace-saving words.

After a long, emotional embrace, the earth's father, girded for war, and poised as time immemorial, braced up then strode down the diamond staircase to a cheering multitude and stepped onto a pearl-decked platinum chariot, drawn by a fain and lively team of winged chargers. The god of Mythlewild took up his reins. His team remembered what was required of them. Palladan was aloft on one side. Vero, astride Paramount, held the other. Nothing was said, no barking commands, no more deafening cheers, no brash trumpets. Peals of any voice were unnecessary. An exodus of gods is flourish enough.

The tall granite gate gave way, as out into his world charged the Lord all lands. The cloud-spun spires of sacred sentinels came alive, dispatching an army so vast the mountains could not hold them. The profusion of gods with eagles' wings soared from their pinnacled heights and issued forth to glean Theland of her immortal gods—and then to the earthen floor below.

CHAPTER 48

Tierra had led David into a pleasant antechamber of glass. Like a greenhouse, fruits and flowers and plants of every description grew in abundance. It reminded David so much of Queen Superbia's rose garden, and Valentina, and... he glanced over his shoulder, then chuckled. Of course there was no Ill-timber here! The boy relaxed under Tierra's coaxing.

The lovely goddess sat down beside a sprinkling fountain. A watery umbrella squirted into sunlight creating a soft rainbow on her saffron hair. It was winter in the mountain's stronghold, and elsewhere, but David felt warm all over. He was moved to sit beside Theland's daughter. Her charisma imbued him with an inner calm unbeknowst to the young errant. "Beautiful, isn't it?" spoke Tierra, in her song voice. "Of all my father's estate, this is my favorite place." I come here to plant, and to play... and to think. It's so alive—yet serene."

"I know what you mean," commented David. "I've got a favorite place too, a dingle in the Fairlawn Forest. It's a neat spot... like this."

"I'm glad to hear you say that, David. You are happy here also?"

"Oh yes, Princess! This is about the most perfect place I've ever seen... Why it's like being in heaven."

"Are you not still distressed by the oracle's vision?" Tierra noted a paradoxical dullness in David's eyes. His face was drawn and pale by the time he found an answer for his dream lady.

"Of course I am... That is, I was. Uh... but now that she's gone, the witch I mean... it's not so bad."

"But Lust is not gone, David—and that IS bad. The bane of mankind can never be gone—not until she is dead. And she is deathless... except for a solitary pilgrim, who alone possesses the power and perseverance to vanquish her—"

"Stop it!" shouted David. "Oh!... Excuse me, Princess. What I meant to say, was... now that I'm up here at Revrenshrine, with you... I feel so comfortable and secure and, uh... safe."

"And 'safe' you shall remain, David. Your are welcome to stay here with me for as long as you wish—or until Lust intrudes into my father's house too. In which case, we will be neither safe, nor comfortable—only dead."

David began to scowl and sweat. "I don't know what you're talking about, Princess... I just know I'd be glad to stay up here forever... A-And I intend to. I'm going no further. I quit—and that's that!" Tierra sat quietly and listened to David as he rambled on. "I can't stomach any more of this... this 'quest'. I'm tired... I've lost count of all the batterings my wits and skin have endured, all for... some 'egg' I've never even seen! I'll ache for the rest of my life because of it..."

"A most cumbersome yoke to be sure, David. But divest yourself of that of that 'egg', and we shall all ache for a long and painful time to come."

"I don't care anymore! Don't you see... I preferred being an orphan to this stuff. Life is too hard on heroes. I'm just not the type. I'm finally ready to admit it.

So find yourself some other boy... If I can figure a way out of these shoes, he can have them. I'll walk easier without wings, that's for sure!"

The earth's princess knew the young pilgrim was speaking out of desperation and not sincerity, and so studied some means to reach through to him. "What of your paints, David? Would you also surrender them—along with your shoes, and your integrity, and the Glass Egg?"

David's arms had been folded around his satchel. It had become a frequent pose. The artist looked at his beautiful gift. As he ran his fingers over its supple surface, he remembered that night when he was chosen by the Overlord himself for this odyssey. He was reluctant then too. He could recount trying to peek into Omnus' deep cowl, thinking to catch a glimpse of the grandlord's face. The silliness of it made him chuckle out loud. For a moment David was ashamed of himself. "It's not that I don't cherish these gifts, Princess—they're terrific. Only... just that a set of paints, even these, isn't going to turn a ragamuffin like me into anybody's savior. Let's face it... Why, I can't even save myself half the time!"

"There are those who would disagree with you, David: beginning with our own grandsire, Omnus, who bestowed upon you his blessed gifts and his confidence, all because of your heroics in pulling his dove from death's snare in Hurst's Bog—at your own risk. And there is my father. Your example has moved even the gods to action. And what of the others you've saved along the way: Peter, Agustus, Fidius and his dragon son, Abraxus? How many are there? Omnus' lamb, Prince Christen and Affirmare, the king's noblest hero—all of them owe their lives to you, 'ragamuffin'. Not a bad record for a few weeks work! No wonder Constantio saw fit to adopt you into his family of knights. And what have these friends done for you lately? They are with you—still—that's what they've done! While Fidius gladly forfeited a thankless life in the dungeons to serve you, others, like Niki, foresook paradise to live in peril protecting you. Why? Because they believe in you."

Throughout Tierra's discourse, David remained pensively mute. And then the daughter of gods got through to her guest. "Valentina believes in you too, doesn't she? Furthermore, it's not just admiration she feels, is it?"

Now the longing swelled up inside David. He was greatly touched, and so very homesick. "I do miss the Fairlawn... and my own Pastel Park. Though it's not so comfortable as Revrenshrine, Val makes it a perfect place, for me at least. I guess there's nowhere else I'd rather be..."

"You would not miss it now, David," lamented the goddess. "Your woods are no longer 'fair', and far from perfect. The forest has been sacked by winter. It is bleak and bare, and stripped of summer. And spring may never come again to dress her. Howbeit, what of your task, David? Do you not yearn for that too? It is unfinished. Will you not find the magical Glass Egg, and return it to its maker before Lust plunders it all? There will be no paradise then, no place to hide. Lust is the vilest of cancers, incurable, and spreading unchecked over Mythlewild. Do you really think the mountains are safe? Even the sky has been pillaged. You saw its dead lord for yourself. The cancer has you marked, David—you and all who aid your cause."

David was growing more and more confused—and perturbed. Tierra's melodic voice had begun to strike several sour notes. But he could not shut it out; his conscience would sing similar dirges in his sleep. Then it began again, Tierra's—or was it conscience's—questioning?

"Can you be comfortable here, David, among my flowers, doing nothing? So far removed from your convictions? Are you complacent... or afraid?"

"No! No... I'm not complacent!" screamed David. Then he lost his breath. "Yeah... I am afraid. I'm stone cold terrified, Princess. And I feel like curling up in some hole and dying—That's what I feel!"

This admission seemed to satisfy Tierra. She squeezed the boy's hand warmly, and her voice grew even more assertive. "And do you also feel mad, David? Mad enough to 'curl' up in hell's hole and NOT die? It isn't enough to be afraid. You've strength, and a gentle nature too. But are you a warrior? You're a good pilgrim, but are you angry enough? Violent enough?... Can you kill?"

David's mind buzzed at the very thought of anything so drastic. "I-I don't know... I only know I can't stay here. I really couldn't. I never intended to... I just feel so... weak."

"Your strength of character is your greatest weakness, David. You are, after all, a moral person. And Lust, above everything else, is evil—prime evil. She will fight you tooth and nail with malevolence—the devil's tools. Her eye, her voice, her touch, indeed her very nearness is leprous. Beware all senses in her house. She will bewitch you. And when their thin purpose is done, they will undo you. She will set your own fears against you, your nightmares... your doubts. Nevertheless, these will fail her, David. For you have just risen above your fears and recovered your senses —as a pilgrim must do in the face of evil incarnate. Now, fear for your virtue; Lust will turn that against you too, intimidate you, tempt you, scare you. But don't let her. Resist her. Show her. Challenge her... Kill her!" urged Tierra in a most unsainlty tone. "Remember, the witch fears you also, David. She fears you above all other things. And for good reason—because you can kill her. You can—and you must! Don't ever forget that, painter."

Some color slowly returned to David's cheeks, as did his confidence. His eyes shined again with that sublime zeal only a pilgrim may know. Yet, his voice still quivered as he spoke. "S-She has so awful much power, Princess. I've seen it, and it frightens me. I've never been more scared in all my life than I was, staring down into that oracle well. Still... it made me mad too!"

"Mad enough to complete your task?" Tierra was smiling again.

Yeah... Sure. If not me, who?" smiled David right back, though he shook slightly amid all his qualms. "After all, I've got some heavy duty weapons of my own!" Momentarily the boy's apprehensions yielded to ambitions, which gushed over him as it had in the Snowmass against Ill-timber. "I have my shoes, and paints —and Niki too...Why, I've got all kinds of magic!"

"No, David, not magic. You have faith! It is your virtue, your integrity, that must triumph—and will—as long as you remain true. Do not lose that edge, that hope. Above all, never doubt yourself. Trusting in your own strength of faith, and not magic, you can fight your own battles, and win. Lust is lacking in those qualities. Without your tolerance for adversity, it will be she who resorts to ruse and magic. That is why sin's siren is doomed to failure—if you but go there and stand up to her... and, of course, survive her bout. All of her black powers will be directed at you, David. She is cornered now, in that vault of hers below the earth. You are going to her, aren't you—to seal that defile forever, and consummate your indenture to Omnus Overlord?"

Lust's image refused to quit David's mind. His thoughts molded goosebumps all over his body. "Can you help me, Princess?"

"Can I?" admonished Tierra in reply. "You already possess help in abundance, from your friends, even the deities. Yet our help has not eased your burden one mote, nor can it ever. You must help yourself, David. You must defend yourself. Even now Lust has begun to weave her clinging web around you. You were faltering; that is why I brought you into this atrium with me. At the outset of your journey a king ennobled you. Upon leaving my house, you shall be beatified. However, as of now, your duel has begun. You cannot turn cheek or flinch away."

Tierra saw that David was growing anxious to rejoin his friends, and so rose to accompany him to the doorway. Before parting, they exchanged confident smiles. "It seems I'm always jumping into bogs," he said.

"And jumping back out too—even retrieving a wondrous dove in the process," the Princess pointed out. "Who knows what other marvels lurk for youth within Lust's pit... Perhaps beyond dark's threshold awaits a man!"

David felt heartened. These moments with the daughter of Theland—the lady in his dream—had been another reawakening, a redeeming balsam for the ails guzzled by a tired pilgrim. He was soon to take another dose.

CHAPTER 49

Returning to the cloistered courtyard, David paused for just one more glance into the oracle, perhaps hoping to find calmer waters. He frowned to find the well was dry, holding only darkness. Although eager to be off, the curious boy was drawn momentarily through an open door leading into Creta's studio. Like the courtyard, the musty chamber looked empty—except for a vast array of books lining the four walls. He tried to turn around, but something lured him to the bookshelves where he began to browse across the endless rows and volumes. Most were history books by all appearances. "How I wish there was time to pause and read a good book," he sighed, thinking no one would hear.

"Why don't you then?" replied a silken, flittery voice. "There's a most absorbing story right over here." David swirled around and spied Creta, the butterfly, sitting on the open pages of a gigantic tome mounted upon a lectern by the window bay. "Your friends have gone to watch the immortal exodus. Before you depart too, come sit with me; I've earned a turn with you too, have I not?"

"Well... yeah, sure... but I'm kind of rushed right now, and don't think I can sit still any more... though I'd sure like to... No, I better not. Some other time maybe... Uh, if there is one—"

"Sit down," insisted another voice, mysterious, calm, and deep—like still water. The words rose persuasively from the oracle outside the window. It startled David at first, for the last noise to come out of the well was Lust's. But this voice was not hers; it was too humane.

David hesitated to look, but his curiosity bested him and he was soon through the door and stretched out over the well's edge, peering down into... into what? A hole? Or was it a pool? Whatever, a reflection looked up at him from the depths. But David could not discern it. "Hello?" he said. "Who are you?"

"Tommy, Tommy... Tommy..." echoed the reply.

"And just who is Tommy? And where did you come from? You weren't in there a minute ago, were you?" David queried the image while scratching his head.

"Why, you're the loud mouth that gabbled all through my vision this morning, aren't you!" chided the oracle voice who, upon recognizing the boy, began to scold him for what, in his estimation, was rude behavior. "Silence is still golden, young man. One of these days you'll learn to be quiet and listen to your oracles. You still haven't sat down, have you! Just like you brushed by, took a quick peek, and seeing nothing, popped away—Humph! You think its easy to drum these visions—Humph! Even I can't answer to the whims of man at the drop of a hat."

Creta had begun to chuckle from her book. "I tried to steer you clear of that blurb, David. Perhaps if you will come back inside and join me, Oman might heed some of his own impudent advise and hush up. He's a very wise oracle, yet can be so bumptious at times. Come, I've something here you should read. You might just discover who Tommy is."

David seated himself upon a high stool and bent over the lectern to study Creta's huge book. "Why, you've been writing. So that's what you are—an author!

"Go on, young one, read, then you will learn what I am." Creta made herself comfortable on the overleaf as David began the text. It was called, 'The Passage'.

One enlightened morning a boy happened upon a caterpillar inching slowly across his path. "Excuse me," said the boy. "I'm looking for the 'Otherland'. Do you know where I might find it?"

"The Otherland?" pondered the caterpillar without stopping. "Oh yes, you mean Mythlewild, that place where Mythles dwell. 'Tis over there," he said, pointing toward the horizon with a gaggle of arms.

The boy squinted into the sunrise. "Over there?"

"Where the pavement ends..." the caterpillar continued, "...that's where you'll find the Otherland.

'Tis but wilderness to most men, child
That place where Mythles breathe.
My ancestors call it Mythlewild
And to know it well you must believe.
Follow me, then you shall find
Theland of Myths and Otherthings
And Othertheres and Othertimes
And other folk, which you call Otherlings.
And should you yearn for sight of home
Or dwell too long to understand,
I shall wake you from the land you roam
Be it reality or Otherland.
Call it what you will, my child,
You shant forget the Mythlewild."

And before the boy could think to speak again, the caterpillar was gone. So, spurred by the notion of 'Otherthings', the boy followed the pavement into the sunrise until there was no more.

"What a nice verse," declared David. "Is it a parable?"

"No, David. You'll find no fairy tales in those pages, for that is a history book. Those events which unfold before you, no matter how incredulous, are true and unalterable. Fate is the author of these histories, and I am his scribe. I record events in these journals. It is my job, as caretaker of the past and—and at my oracle's caprice—the future, to know everything about everybody in Mythlewild."

"Boy Howdy!" marveled David, looking about the room, at the crowded shelves laden with thick, fusty books. "Gosh! You look so pretty and uh, young... like fresh jasmine. Did you really write all these books?"

"Yes, David—me, and my ancestors. These volumes contain the history of Mythlewild since the beginning if time." Creta paused here so the boy would be sure to hear what she had to say next. "And I don't intend to be the author of its final chapter—if you get my meaning."

David did; but he thought it best not to dwell on such dire happenstance, lest its portent smother him like Tierra said it might if he were not wary. So he studied Creta, so lithe and delicate, and finally asked, "How can a butterfly write so many books anyway? You haven't hands enough."

Attuned to David's doubts, Creta batted her long lashes. Then, with a single flap of her silky butterfly wings, fresh jasmine turned crusty. In her place, curled atop a mollusk shell, was a more vintage and very distinguished bug. Fuzzy and whiskered from tip to tail, Creto—the caterpillar—wiped his bifocals in his long, nappy torso. Right before the boy's eyes she had changed—a complete metamorphosis. It was that simple. "I've arms aplenty now, what!" said Creto, displaying his many rows of limbs.

"I've been meaning to ask you about that," remarked David in amazement, recalling the insect's magic transformation in the Morass.

"And I've been meaning to explain..." began Creto the caterpillar, as he squiggled around, almost standing on his shell podium, "...about this book. Since my job as historian requires a supply of lore to record, I hope to ensure Mythlewild's history does not expire with your demise. I doubt Lust would require a scribe to document her deeds, should you fall before her. Therefore, I have taken it upon myself to, how shall I put it... look after you. And so I have—from the very beginning of your story. Do you recall the butterfly Fearsome chased in Hurst

Meadow? Or again in the Boscage? I had a seat at the war council too—remember! Sometimes a caterpillar was more discreet. Or a chrysalis was subtler still. And at Ocean Bottom... Oh me oh my!" Creto laughed so hard he nearly tumbled from his shell; luckily he had several good footholds. " Ho—at Ocean Bottom, I nuzzled into my mollusk shell, and pretended to be a slug! You see... all the time, it was me! You'll never want for guardian angels, young one—except possibly, now. Because this last leg of your journey is banned to me. However, you have your other friends; no magic made can keep them behind. And then there is Tommy... He'll always be with you—whether you know it or not!"

David wrinkled his nose at the mention of Tommy's name again. "Tell me, Creto, who is this Tommy? I didn't see his name in your history book. Was he a myth?"

"Do you believe in myths, David?" asked Creto before answering.

"Of course I do," came the positive reply, which delighted the fuzzy old caterpillar. His bifocals straddled the top of his head; he wasn't going to need them for the next few minutes. He began to talk.

"Then who can say if Tommy is real, or myth? Does it matter? Is there really any difference? Sooner or later we all believe in myths of some sort—I do! Ogres and giants, dragons and dwarfs—there are some who would consider all these, myths. Yet you know them as real, because you've shared your life and your thoughts with them, for better and worse. And what of the rest of us 'Otherlings'? Am I a myth, David? Are you? You're here aren't you, a man among myths.

David wasn't sure he followed all of this. But he did know that, no matter what else, he at least was real—and said so. "Of course I'm not a myth!"

"Then neither was Tommy!" declared Creto firmly, slapping a dozen hands onto his book. "He's as real as you and I. He's the boy you read about in The Passage... the one who chanced upon the caterpillar on the roadside. But it wasn't really a chance meeting. That caterpillar was me, so I should know! And I can tell you all about Tommy. He wasn't a Mythle, or Otherling as he was fond of saying, at least not by birth. He was an ordinary boy, just like you, with a typical boy's imagination. One day he got a notion—to touch a real, live myth. Before he knew it, he was here, in the Otherland, Theland—the Mythlewild, this place where Mythles dwell. He became one of us, a boy no longer, but a genuine Mythle child. He discovered the 'passage' into Mythlewild, that only myth chasers may know: that place as near as your thoughts, but as far away as forgotten dreams; that place lying just beyond the horizon—on the sunrise side—always; that place we call Mythlewild. Though 'wild' it won't remain. Once we're rid of its witches and gremlins, Theland will be civilized. Thanks to boys like Tommy... and you, David, it will be an enviable place to live; a magical, long ago world found only in fantasy—which, in Mythlewild, is real. Or you may find the Mythlewild in one of Tommy's paintings. Like you, David, this boy was an artist, an extraordinary artist—as you shall soon see! Tommy could illustrate Theland's charm with his paints, and depict its history with images, as I use words. Like most boys he had imagination, but more—he could define those feelings and portray them in pictures, so others might see the intangible. Tommy was truly creative—that was his gift! His ambition was to be a great artist. That's why I brought him to Mythlewild—so his dream could be realized!

"You see, Tommy and I are both dreamers. I often imagine myself to be a beautiful young butterfly, looking like a lotus, a flower among the bugs. That's my dream. That's all Creta is—a fantasy. We all pursue our own fancies, David. However, before our dreams come real, we must acquaint ourselves with reality. Look at me; it has taken me an eternity to grow old. I was born when the first dream was dreamed, and suckled in the womb of children's imaginations. The simple faith of innocents sustains me, David—faith such as yours. You believe in dreams, like me. That's why I brought you to Mythlewild. You don't remember, do you?... No, of course not. It was long ago. It was the beginning of time—your time at least. For me, it was yesterday. Age is measured differently in Mythlewild. Not that time is slower here, it's just... different. Hurts always last longer than happy times, don't they. How long has your journey taken? What's the measure: time, or miles? Like anything else I suppose, time is what you make of it—or, in the case of dreams, it's what others make of it. Well, whatever my age, I'm still an ugly, old caterpillar; there's no denying that. Yet before I die, I'll become a beautiful butterfly, for real, just like the one you've seen. Though it be for a single day, or an instant, it will be a glorious lifetime nonetheless!

"Fortunately, not everyone has to wait a lifetime to become a butterfly. For some, like you, David, 'tis but the passing of a single season and falls like an autumn leaf at your feet. You're a chrysalis already, about to emerge from your cocoon. Mythlewild will emerge with you, beautiful and glorious. And the ugliness that used to be, will die—as all caterpillars must, when dreams come true. You know, David, folks today need someone to remind them that impossible dreams—just like myths —can be real. But we must be daring—we must imagine! So close your eyes, myth seeker, and you will see your grandest adventures fulfilled. Then sleep deep, so you may wake—in dreams! It's time dream weavers, like you and Tommy, got the recognition you deserve. That's why I'm writing this book. So that after we're all resigned of life and breath, someone may look upon history and know that—for this one wonderful moment—the butterfly dream really lived!" Creto was all unraveled around his shell. It took only a brief spell for him to recoil, so David thought if he was going to comment on any of this, he better do it now.

"For a decrepit old caterpillar, you certainly have grand dreams!" David had listened to Creto patiently, and was eager to hear more, especially about Tommy. From his earlier haste, he hesitated here, in this odd study. He now realized there was much to learn from this old bookworm. "I suppose if you're going to dream, you should dream of grand things."

"Exactly!" smiled Creto, springing back into form. "And Tommy thought so too! I once heard him say that butterflies were just caterpillars dreaming. And the bright designs on their wings were eyes, through which they see all there is too see in their brief, but grand, lifetime. And a chrysalis is the passage between caterpillar realities and butterfly dreams."

"I believe so too," said David enthusiastically. "Tommy sounds like someone I should meet and get to know. We've got a lot in common."

"More than you realize, David," mentioned Creto under his breath before belting out his next string of surprises. "You will know him, though you two can never meet. Tommy is dead now."

"Dead! How sad," sighed David. "How did he die?"

"You could say his curious nature killed him, David. He was lost... lost on some fatal exploration into an unknown, faraway land, beyond the reach of those too old to be children. But do not feel sad. Tommy is much happier now—I know! He will become famous, like other storybook heroes, as soon as I write his saga in my history books."

"Why haven't I heard of Tommy before now?" David asked.

"Because his chapter is not yet complete. And because that's the way he wanted it. Though he was but a modest orphan—as yourself—Mythlewild's citizens cradled him in their hearts and adopted him as one of their own. From the moment he arrived, as a stranger from a strange land, Mythles gave him a home—and a new name, to fit his new role in our history. We gave him one name, as you know one is plenty for a land the size of Mythlewild. We called him David, after a giant-slaying hero that he admired in some popular scripture from his prior home..." Creto paused here again to see if his audience was paying attention to this last piece of information, and if the boy was ever going to grasp it.

"Hey—that IS a coincidence!" said David. "Tommy and I do have a lot in common. You know, MY favorite hero is David too—the one from our Bible back home—" David stopped short and leaped to his feet, tossing Creto the most bizarre, bedazzled stare you ever saw. "YOU!...You brought me here—to Mythlewild—didn't you! If that was you in the Passage... then, that boy was ME!"

There was no need for the caterpillar to reply, nor to continue with his recital. Suddenly, all of David's dreams came real: his past before the Passage, his memories... and his name. Though he would never remember that life as real, he knew his name—it was Tommy!

Creto nudged the stool under David, as the boy's rubbery legs folded under him. "Boy Howdy!... It CAN'T be true!" he argued with himself. "You said Tommy was dead!"

"Isn't he?" said Creto. "Were not his steps into Mythlewild his last? And were not his last, your first? Just as you had the notion to travel that path, it was a notion of mine to cast you as the leading man in Fate's drama—as it must be written —by me."

"B-But who am I?" implored David. "Certainly no leading man. I'm just me, David—I mean Tommy... Oh, I don't know who or what I am anymore! All I know is this isn't at all what I imagined. I thought the Otherland in my dreams would be a peaceful and cultivated world, a charming, happy place of harmony and repose..."

"David, David... you ARE a dreamer!" sighed the catapillar, as if he didn't already know. "But, so am I. Therefore, let us not wake up just yet. Shall we see this night through until the dawn?"

David merely sat. He was too befuddled to even fidget. Creto could delay no longer. After all, he hadn't enticed the boy in here simply to fill his head with vagaries, and send him off to settle up with destiny in a state of confusion. No, there was a choice to make and, with the substance of it thus laid out, it was time for the pilgrim to decide.

"It is as you have said, young one; the reality of Mythlewild bears little likeness to Theland which you dreamed about. Perhaps your mind deceived you. Perhaps it was I. But as I brought you into this land, so I can take you out again. That is my offer to you here and now: stay or go—complete your dream or wake—be Tommy or David. You may be whoever you want—but not both!"

Now you might think a choice like that would be a ponderous one for any boy to make. However, for the painter, it was not. His decision was made in Tierra's greenhouse, and before—long before, when Tommy first stepped into the sunrise, where the pavement ended. "Heck... I just wanted to meet Tommy—not BE Tommy! I think I know him well enough already. If I really wanted to run away from any old witch... well, I've had my share of chances. I could've become a hermit, like Isolato, and hide with the sea lord at Ocean Bottom. Or I could've been a noble prince, had I remained at Bia Bella. But those were fragile refuges as it turned out. Now Revrenshrine—here's a sanctuary! Or so I thought. Earlier today I was beatified, and invited to live with the gods of Mythlewild. And here I have the chance for a retreat I thought impossible to find—my own homeland—that asphalt-paved metropolis where everyone wears shoes, and I fit in. That would be my only true escape from Mythlewild. But I didn't really fit in. I was an orphan there also, and so I left. That place where we first met is no longer mine. Mythlewild is the only home I remember now. Besides, there I was merely a foundling—a cast off. Whereas in Mythlewild, I'm an adopted storybook hero—a 'leading man'! And all my friends are here... and Valentina. I probably don't have anyone like Val back in that other place, or else I never would've left. I may have been living there—but I belong here. This is what a home is to me. I'm a dreamer alright, so I guess I'll just stay here in Mythlewild with my dreams, even if there is a nightmare or two to dispel. Which reminds me, I've got some unfinished business to take care of... Uh, there weren't any more questions were there? I'd like to talk about this a lot more... except, I really have to go now—"

David started to test his numb legs and began to rise, but Creto caught his attention with one final note of interest. "Off to do your duty, David? Good! And good riddance to your nightmare I say! But first, listen up. Just as the dreams of youth sustain my kind and yours—the nightmares of maturity feed Lust. Though you triumph and slay her, her specter will never die! The world, any world—real or written—must have its frights, to hold its fantasies in check. Therefore, child, don't ever hope to erase or rid my Ebon wraith from history—instead, expose her! Spike her, and hold her up for what she is, for all the rest to see. And in this way, let her own nightmarish trappings undo her. If only I had the answer on my lips to give as easily as my advise. Or if I could spell it out for you... Alas, I am not that gifted a writer. I wonder, can you possibly understand the meaning in any of this?

David nodded. He didn't really understand yet, but he had learned not to worry about it. Too many other things needed sorting first, not the least of which was how Lust, Theland's nightmare as Creto put it, will still live, even though he kills her, like Tierra said he must do. Throughout his adventure things had come together. He had no doubt that this puzzle would fall into place as well. More urgent than these riddles was the fever he felt inside for putting to rest this odyssey of his.

With this finally decided, David slapped his lap anxiously, and not in the least bit hesitant, he stepped toward the door. This made the caterpillar scribe very proud. "By the way, Creto..." said David, recalling the roly-poly gent and the changeling he had met in the butternut grove in Sovereignwood on the king's fox hunt, "... you said I was brought here to play this role in Fate's drama—as it must be written. I was just wondering... is it ever possible to go back again, once your history is put to the page?"

The caterpillar raised his woolly brow and twitched his long antennae. "Well, my young grind, you will find those that argue that point, but dramas are fickle; and histories, by their nature, are irrevocable. Yet both do possess loopholes: All dramas can be rewritten, and history must always remain incomplete. So, I would have to say to you—yes, it is impossible to go back again, into the past, or into futures, or into dreams for that matter... unless you have imagination!"

"Thanks, Creto. I'll do everything I can to make the next chapter in your historical drama... imaginative!"

"See that you do, David, for I'm very inadequate with epitaphs!" The caterpillar waved a hundred good-byes to the young pilgrim as he passed through the cloisters, without giving the well a second look.

David arrived at the top of the diamond stairway to find his companions waiting anxiously for him. Prince Christen sat limply on Peter's back, while Fidius thanked Tierra and Lara for their hospitality. Niki dipped back into her breastpocket nest, like she used to; she then perked her head eagerly to hear what had transpired. But David didn't have to say much. The whole story was graved on his face like an iron bound book. His azure eyes had turned steel blue.

"Everyone's gone now except us, painter," informed Niki. "It was a stirring send off!"

"Well then," said the boy, petting his dove endearingly, and grinning at his companions, "we had better make an exit of our own!... Coming?"

"Boy Howdy—er, I mean, are we ever!" shouted Peter, stamping his hooves on the jeweled promenade. It's tuneful clinking reminded him of the songs they had sung at the outset of their trek, from Sovereignton, and at the very beginning—when he and Niki and Fearsome frisked out of Patrick's house. He wondered if anyone would want to sing on this departing.

"We're all set, li'l' knight!" puffed Fidius, examining David's new 'look'. "That is, if you are?"

David's grin widened, and he hugged his friends while nodding to Tierra. "I've never been more ready for anything in all my life. But you, my devoted comrades... This is not your contest. Lust challenged only me to face her. Mayhap, you could stay behind to take up the cause... if I should fail."

"What!" fumed Fidius. "I ain't about ta let my king's cub slip inta the depths a Luhrhollow 'naked'! What would His Highness think of me? 'Goll-durned, turnkey' he'd say, 'back ta the dungeons with you'!" But no thanky, I'm stayin' with you, li'l' feller—Yes sirree!"

"Sir Fierce speaks for me too, Davy," said Peter. "If you should fail—what cause would be left to take? That harpy's foe to all of us. You shall not take it to her alone and without your kinsmen!"

David's heart thumped with confidence, like a mellow drumbeat. He knew it was neither fear, nor even patriotism—but love—which commanded such loyalty. And he knew better than to ask Niki. She cooed in his breast like his own pounding heart. "We could hardly desert you now, painter," cheeped the dove. "You may need someone to pull YOU from the bog!"

"You gotta have someone ta tend our poor li'l' lamb, that's fur sure." wheezed Fidius.

"And someone to carry him too!" added Peter.

"And you can't possibly leave Prince Christen behind," reminded Niki, "for only by Lust herself may he be purged of his hex!"

Suddenly David felt ashamed; he had never considered the lamb boy's plight. So involved was he in his own predicament, the son of Omnus had been almost completely ignored. David's gaze fell upon Christen, as though drawn by force. For one blinking instant, he thought he detected some faint flicker of encouragement gleam through those dull, glazed, raisin eyes. The pilgrim boy needed no more prodding; not from his friends, not from gods and goddesses, and not from Lust—who had been most persuasive.

"Well spoken by you all," said Tierra. "If your valor be as well-knit as your friendships, David, my aunt will stand no chance. If you are all ready then, I will show you the way."

"The earth mother, Lara, gave each of her guests a farewell kiss before her daughter guided them down the slope of sparkling diamonds, and past the soaring marble-pillared edifices, to the very brink of paradise, where she stopped. There, on the White Mountain threshold to Revrenshrine, they all looked into the languid, lovely land spread beneath them, and beheld the spectacle that was Mythlewild.

The Snowmass, and the Phantom Forest—that paling emerald, fir-scented canopy which nearly froze and felled them—now cloaked their view of Constantio's fair realm of Middleshire. Somewhere under those icy sheets, lies Sovereignton, thought David. A sick and suffering place in need of a miracle. And Fairlawn too, and miles beyond, to the west and east and south—beneath a batch of bloodied skies—was the rest of Mythlewild: its vast canyon vistas; rich, rolling meadowlands; the wooded glades;   lush ravines, deltas, rivers, waterfalls... and all. Past the distant Moors and all the way to the sea—it was laid out there for them to sense. And they each took the time—while it was theirs—to taste it.

David couldn't discern the Kyln Morass, but he knew it was still there. The painter could see lots of things now that had always eluded him from lower perspectives He saw through the crust of Mythlewild, and into its more mawkish innards. Embedded deep inside it all was the slough, Luhrhollow—Lust's lair. The boy could see so far; it was so unbelievably clear. He saw his past, before the Mythlewild: he saw the way home. Then he saw his present: it was here with Valentina. And now he could almost spy the end of his long journey—but for one opaque and oppressing shade which blighted his way. It was black and it was defiling. It was his future—it was here and now. It was Lust—and she was waiting.

"Where are we going, Princess?" asked David. He was ready to light into that witch then and there, but he didn't know which way to turn. "How do we get there?"

"Is it far?" inquired Fidius. These ol' legs might kick out on another long sojourn."

"We've no provisions either, save for fond farewells," mentioned Peter. "And Christen is looking most queer."

"You've all the provisions you'll need, my children. Trust me," spoke Tierra, in a lamenting, lilting voice. "Hell is not so far from heaven, if measured in moments instead of miles. It will not take long to reach your destination. And you needn't fear getting lost, for I shall be with you—to guide you—remember that."

"You, Princess! You're going to take us to Lust?" David's heart danced momentarily, then skipped a beat.

"No, David, I cannot go with you, though I shall forever be your guide. You must believe that. Now follow your shoesteps—and begin the last leg of your quest!"

David and Niki exchanged wide-eyed expressions, and their hearts hunted rapidly to find their pace. Then Niki flew from her breastpocket, leading the way out of the mountain's marble gatewalls. Fidius was the next one through, followed by Peter, with Prince Christen holding tenuously to his back. Tierra's words had been a great comfort to David. Any remaining insecurity was allayed by the feel of his paint satchel clutched under his arm, and by the humming prompt of his winged shoes. Thus he stepped confidently across Revrenshrine's threshold, and looked behind at the goddess' beautiful face.

"I do believe!" said David loudly, so his voice rang down from the mountain palace. "You are the lovely lady I dreamed about, Princess. Even without knowing you, I believed in you—and ever since, you've been a miracle to me."

"Make your own miracles, young one—you have that power!" The daughter of the earth did not venture past the gates of Revrenshrine. She merely smiled and waved good-bye.

David then turned to his companions and called out at them to wait for him. But he was shocked to discover they were gone! He spun quickly around toward the gate, only to find that it had also vanished. Tierra was no longer there—but someone was.

David turned to ice. He screamed coldly at what he saw, screamed fearfully louder than he ever had in all his life. But this earthen goddess would not go away. Her fangs gleamed white against pitch black lips as she grinned, not beautifully, but dark and wicked and ugly—and stinking. It was Lust! It was her black face, and her stench—it was her domain. David was no longer in paradise.

CHAPTER 50

In just one giant step, David had plummeted from the lofty White Moutain spires of Revrenshrine into the bottomless, bleak defiles of Luhrhollow. It was a sultry, smoking inferno, this abyssmal slough into which he had fallen—and so repugnant that all light was afraid to enter. Even the steam and fire were black.

Though David was soaked and hot with sweat, his skin crawled with chilling horror. That which he could see in this burning darkness terrified him. But that which he could not see, frightened him more. His companions were nowhere to be found. David called out to them in a start; only to be answered by stone-hollow

591

echoes—echoes, and the foreboding cackle from the shadowy figure flickering in front of him through the acrid vapor curtain. His friends were gone.

David reached to his breastpocket with heart-throbbing realization—even Niki was no longer with him. For the first time in his arduous pilgrimage, the boy was alone—totally—completely removed from his world.

Only the single, breath-halting presence of Lust squired him now—and a terrifying attendant she was! He cringed to look at her. His cheeks blanched under the sinfully pitch black face and coal-complected eyes which parched his confidences, wickedly bewitching and swathed in swirling curls of crimson. The fire-plumed, python hair coiled about her snake skin body, draping every inch of it in sizzling, steamy tresses, so that only her smooth, scaly head could be beheld. Her green, glowing eyes fixed their gaze on David, while her viper voice hissed in exultation at their visitor.

"Your friends are disposed of, pilgrim," spoke death's suitor, unleashing a venom-soaked tongue. "You will face me alone, little snippet, who has taxed my patience. What a maddening, meager mortal you are, tack! You prick my brood, even to the point of death. You trumped their plans, and with their demise would stick my ambitions too. I think I won't permit that, little thorn. You would also steal my lamb from me, no? And what a prize mounting this prince of sheep turns out to be: my old man Omnus' only progeny! And you—the suckling snipe—his only champion. Now I have you both! I trust you'll be more cooperative than that bleating dummy. You will help me find my Egg... or must you be 'persuaded' too? Come closer, you snot-nosed stray, pay the tithe, and taste my wrath!"

The black lordess said no more, but rather held David in her eyes' embrace, and let him tremble there to quake amid his new found fears, and revel in despair at his unsavory surroundings—and massed together these wretches assaulted David's flagging senses. His skin crackled and stung under a stinking barrage of rank, revolting sulfur breaths. The nauseating fumes flung through the boy's nostrils and drenched his mind with panic. His blurry eyes were too tender to hold out the soul-shattering terror of ghastly visions, whose ugliness became Lust's most lethal weapon. How he tried to close his lids and turn her away, to rebuff the profane advances with shouts and pleas of mercy, in a pathetic attempt at self-preservation.

But his persecutor was fire, and she had no heart beyond her smacking lips. Resistance met with futility. David was imprisoned in Lust's vise grip vision and was compelled to submit. With a whimper, the overlord's champion begged for relief.

And Lust—uncompromising, uncaring, and unscrupulous—responded like the true mongrel goddess that she was. The black angel pounced on her helpless victim... With no words, no warning—and no mercy—she unveiled her secret weapon. In reviling relish, hell's harpy molted and spread wide her tress and cinder-coated arms to reveal herself uncloaked, as the embodiment of all evils. The malignant, malevolent crush of it so mortified David that he yielded to an overwhelming numbness. More piercing than the sharpest sword's edge were the malicious whorls and convolutions of her grotesque body—a horror ultimately more staggering than any blow or blade. The searing, scorching sight of it all ripped David's confidences asunder, until his only release from its unyielding grasp was to explode in a crescendo of scream upon scream.

Louder and louder he wailed for his life, until his lungs—like his soul—were bled dry. With no lingering trace of resolve to be had, the bitter taste of Lust's buffeting poured past the screeching and into David's drained defenses. In one uninterrupted outpouring of wrath and debasement, Lust shed her mortal guise. Once disembodied, she became a living, lava-breathing nightmare—terrifying, malign, and excruciating to all the innocent's perceptions. All of the hobgoblins, banchees, and boogie beasts; every demon, denizen, and shade or spooky shadow that imagination could conjure pounced, swooped, slithered, crawled, and crept into the dreamer's exposed unconsciousness. The incubus was vicious and unrelenting with its fiendish fury. In one final flurry of contempt, Lust erupted in vile laughter at the utter helplessness of this boy—her arch enemy—who seemed but a pip about to be put blessedly out of its misery, crushed within a blackguard's ruthless grip.

The vulgar crowing evoked the tumultuous din of a million dead souls crying for respite, begging release from their torment. But the witch would not let go. Utter despair coursed through David's veins. Unable to shun the grossest of god's specters, his stomach heaved. All his fears retched onto the foul smuts that composed Lust's shadow in this domain of perpetual dark. Only when her victim dropped in a limp heap at her feet did Lust relent. When Omnus' knight was completely disarmed of spirit, and only barely conscious, did the harpy of sin gather in her arms, and clothe her bare and frightful figure with the red-haired wrap and black-skinned mask of the Amazon siren. Only now did the pit queen extend her cruel respects to the collapsed boy who lay gasping in her throes.

"Welcome to Luhrhollow, pilgrim," gurgled the menacing tongue of Lust. "Perchance, has my dark reception persuaded you to see the light?" The snakeskin face contorted and recoiled as she spoke, as if her infectious soul was struggling to escape its demonic shroud. The toxic smoke and ash of her breath encrusted David like reeking, foul fetters, and he had no strength to respond or break its hold. "Oh—but you're uncomfortable," hissed the hideous voice of ash. "And your throat must be terribly dry... Daddy's disciples usually find my climes a touch too torrid. Let me offer you some 'refreshment'; it might revive you enough so we may chat!"

Strands of serpentine hair enveloped David and thrust him to the brink of a deep and gaping pit, whose innermost confines glowed with fiery embers. Lust's blistering laughter scorched his ears. "Here, pilgrim—wash away your thirst with the sight of this!" The boy's eyes fought their way open, only to recoil under the wincing blow of what he saw. There, in the rift below him, were his friends: Peter, Fidius, and Niki—embroiled in some deranged ritual. Each of them ran around and around in frenzied, erratic circles like madmen, holding their ears and ranting with lunacy. In the midst of their insanity, sat Christen. He alone remained quiet and so very, very still. Black magic proved to be the best constraint for the lamb prince. The steep chasm walls were too towering for Peter to jump, even though his tender shank had gained on its three stronger members. The bewitching heat boiled even Fidius' thick, lizard hide. And Niki's wings were too singed to fly. All were confined, either by pit or pain.

Lust's roasting ridicule drowned out the drone of her raving captives. The sight and sound and stench of it all sent David reeling back onto is knees. "When you've drank your fill, pip—I've another surprise for you—a real hot item! But first... I want those shoes!" Lust's viper tongue curled out of her reptile grin and lapped between layers of twisted cusps. Her hissing, acid voice gnawed at David's ears and frayed his weary wits.

Then lo and behold—just when havoc had wrought its worst—a soft and gentle hand touched David's shoulder. He saw it not, yet it was there, in pressing comfort. The pilgrim plugged his ears, and tore his eyes from the wieldy spell of Lust's leer long enough to find a portion of his sanity, therewith retrieving some grains of courage. With his eyes and ears closed to Lust's allure, the winning vision of Tierra rose in his mind and recalled her words to him, 'Lust will turn your own fears against you'. I must not be afraid to fear, he thought. Don't let the sorceress intimidate me with imaginings. Face her. Challenge her. I have power too—stronger! 'Believe', the mountain's princess had said. 'I will be with you'! "I DO have power!" David said to himself, lifting his chin from the dark hold of Lust's hole and replacing the horrific image of her ugly slag with the comely strength of the daughter of the earth.

Slowly he rose from the shadow of lava dust, shook off its stinking sulfur soot with vigorous determination, and stood as tall as he possibly could—like a pilgrim—like a knight. "Witch!" shouted the gallant of deities. "You poisonous, putrid, contemptable crone—now it's my turn. I also have teeth to bare... and a 'bag' of tricks under foot!"

Lust's charred brows arched in chafed disbelief at her prey's sudden resilience. Her tongue squirmed back behind a toothy wall of lava fangs, while her mouth gaped wider than any cavern's jaw. With the witch so taken aback, David took time to study his adversary and repossess his wits. How enticing this smooth, snake-skinned siren was. This chocolate-cheeked seductress of virtue, so gorgeous— yet so gruesome, proved more bawdy and more beguiling than David ever could have imagined. Yet... she's alone too, he thought—and the next move, mine!

"So... you want my shoes, do you—hag!" retorted the painter in his most brassy, defiant tone. "Well, they're mine—and you can't have them—unless you've spine enough to take them off! And I doubt you do. From what I can see, you've no backbone at all—just coils of curls and smoke, and a face as blighted and blotched as it is black!" David could hear Lust seethe and simmer like a kettle ready to boil over. With his courage rekindled, David stuck out his chest and began to strut audaciously around and about the spuming enchantress. His retaliation continued with increasing dash.

"You've displayed some entertaining tricks for an old crone. But I don't like your match, or your rules... and especially, I loathe your fabricated villains and air-drawn daggers. Most of all—I abhor their fulsome, canker-gouged wench! The sight of your repulsive, bestial face turns my stomach... but your your threats and throngs don't scare me anymore. They can't harm me anymore; because your magic is as guileless as your gumption. Furthermore, without your pets or threats or tricks to tempt me, you're powerless—as beaten as yesterday's rug!"

David paused as though he detected a pent up burst of ire under Lust's teeming cauldron coils. Yet the witch, like a cobra, revealed nothing before striking. Rather, she waited as her mark made boast.

"Me and my shoes are gonna walk all over you—you crock-skinned, fire-shocked throw queen! We'll wipe our heels into the nape of your black pile face. A little dirt shouldn't soil YOUR fiber—"

David's mounting brash and boldery halted abruptly, then shifted into a rapid reversal, either from the realization that his shoes can corrode even the most steadfast souls; or perhaps by the sudden awareness that this Ebon snake, though speechless, was not without her portion of poison and bite. It was this leaven concoction, so salted and spiced with David's spunk, and stirred to a boisterous boil by his bravado, that was now fully steeped and ready to explode into a...

"Goliath!" gasped David, as the writhing wildfire assumed gargantuan porportions. A hundred horrors hulked into one, growing and swelling in size until her giant, red braids filled the entire cavern. Lust's black face was bruised red with rage and bellowed viciously as David paled and shrank before her in contrast. Once again, her monstrous presence engulfed him and enslaved his senses.

Shrieking, drum-splitting screams and screeches, squeals and squeaks battered and bounced back and forth in his ears. A sickening, stinging silt soaked the rank and rancid air around him, while his skin bristled in waves of hot and cold, like icy hot liquid lead pouring onto his crawling flesh.

The sight of so large a Lust crowded David's resilience. All of the boy's fears were now lumped into one ultimate nightmare. But there were no bed covers to hide under. No refuge could he take, not here. The hideous, distorted vision grew more grisly, and the pilgrim gagged for any breaths he could steal. But the air was too heavy, unsavory and sour, like thick vinegar. A pungent, palling nausea churned anew in David's belly, until he could take no more of it. So he spit it out. Not in the cowering, cowardly way of a faintheart—his spittle challenge was hurled in defiance—right into Lust's angry coal eyes.

A pilgrim's poison it was, to the queen of venom. And like a snake bite, it toppled the night's angel from her frightful heights, as it had felled the giant Ill-timber and the demon Horros before. Onto her knees went Lust. Onto the lava floor she spilled, like seeping hot wax.

Alas, a viper on its belly is no less deadly, as David was quick to discover. For no sooner had the boy disgorged the leviathan Lust, than a legion of Lusts rose up to engage him, forged from the melted mess around him. A multitude of red menaces gnawed at his nerves, surrounded him—then consumed him—with a hundred more molten monsters, conjured up from some dark defile, or recess of the nighttime. Such was Lust's reprisal. Her black magic menagerie evolved into a swirl of infinitely changing creatures. Flashes of swiftly moving myriads, each designed to dash David's last lingering defense. All the beasts of all the worlds, real or imagined, from beetle to behemoth, whirled fiercely in his face—each one vying for the kill.

Yet, as the horde of horrors thrashed and raged ominously around him, David found himself immovable. Not by choice mind you; for if he were able, the terrified boy would surely have run straight for the cover of Fairlawn Forest, or his home beyond the Otherland. Even it had never housed such haunting creatures as were stalking him now. By necessity, the young orphan stood fast upon his bandy legs and bore the brunt of the savage squall of sorcery. His feet could not move—Omnus' shoes would not allow it.

Thus, it was the Overlord's errant who remained unwavering. Frightened all the way through to his souls, his knees shook, but not his nerve—or his faith—not now. Undaunted and disgusted with Lust's gaudy exhibition, and clutching his satchel so tight it became a part of him, David sought and found a counter punch. Whether by fear, or flourish, he stomped his foot down hard upon the lava bed.

597

And again. The blows rumbled throughout the vast cavity. The report rang full, to fill even the bottomless foul of Luhrhollow. Like a heavy, hollow claps, its reverberating clangor crumbled the lure of Lust's last lingering enchantments. With that one, audacious, foot-stomping knell—the whirlwind rout vanished. The whole of it evaporated like the ominously-shaped fronds which haunted the steaming Morass, only to dissipate under cold affronts. The titanic conflict was over. The duel—done!

Time, who had held its breath in battle, now breathed for relief, that it might live a minute longer. A long, lurid pall fell upon the underground basin. For endless minutes all was silence. David's companions had ceased their rambling hysteria and settled into mute shock within their trench. The only banshee remaining was Lust, who, upon witnessing her embroidery unravel at the hands of a more worthy weaver receded like a trapped cobra arched in self-preservation. She now coiled upon a jutting precipice and swayed ponderously in front of a fly-eaten coverlet, draped high over the yawning abyss.

Just what mystery lay shrouded by the dismal canopy, David was left to guess. For now, another pair of glinting, vermin eyes drew his attention into the shadows. He spied another creature cavorting on the rocky shelf projecting from the curtain's hem. A tabby... and it frolicked with a bone or something... No, wait!... It wasn't a cat at all—it was a fox! And it whined in glee with its gobbet. David recalled Niki's mention of Lust's dealings with foxes. Up to more mischief, he guessed, but did not dwell on the matter. There was another, more vulgar vixen to deal with first.

Lust's ember eyes glowed dimly from the shadows of her pitch face. Her steaming, streaming trail of hair settled like a misty veil, plaiting her ebony body with a red woven gown of lanolin. Satan's smile rested on a tempting woman's torso now. Howbeit, the pearly teeth shown duller than before; their biting edge, blunted. And the irrepressible, tantalizing whisper panted rather than purred, as she began to speak once again.

"Sit down, pilgrim..." she said, sadly, not sinister; and in tones more pathetic than perilous, "... let us both bargain for a spell. You have exhausted me... and for a briar, born of bone and meat, not magic—that is a marvel I did not foresee. As in the Kyln, you have surpassed my expectations again—and finally! For I shall not underestimate you ever more."

David recognized the ebony and scarlet shape before him as the alluring red Amazon which so captured his fancy—and friends—in the Morass. The illusionary vamp, and her vixen kit, both sat sedately beside themselves, apparently appeased, though why, David could not figure. But he was not about to wait passively by and let this mage compromise him further with her catty coaxing. He shrugged off the siren's new cordiality and chose to stand on his numb legs rather than stoop before hell's hostess.

"You only flatter yourself, hag. Weary I may be, but not too worn of wits to parley with the devil's dame. You sit perched over your dint, crowing and strutting and sticking your neck out, fluffing your stuff like some grand swan. But you're a black one! You've lurked too long in mud and mire. Your lake is lacking in life and light both. And the blackness has made you blind, like worms and other crawling things whose homes are holes and under rocks."

At this, Lust's vixen growled and yipped like a pup, but nothing more. Omnus' paladin would tolerate no raillery until his words were laid. "I'm not another of your creeping swarm. I'm here to remind you that a swan you're not. You're nothing but a lost shadow, who extols yourself complete and whole—when in fact you're nothing, a blind shade without worth, or substance, or sight..." As incensed as he was, David probably could have stood his ground and insulted his adversary for hours. Up until now, only the fox's yelping echoed to counter his rebuke.

Lust remained still as stone. Only her nostrils flared, as the witch gorged herself on deep, sulfur breaths. Her eyes' grossly glowing glare intensified until they blazed demonically. It was now that David swallowed his tongue—as Lust plucked out one of those frightening, fiery eyes and tossed it to the boy. Out of reflex he side-stepped the bizarre offering only to have it bounce off his shoe and roll to rest beside his feet where it continued to gaze up at him spitefully.

"Yeee—it's 'blind' I am, brat!" cackled the one-eyed witch. "My neighbor the devil lent me his lenses; now I dole one out for you to see my light!"

Lust and her vixen both yowled at David, who shuddered at this real horror. His foot kicked Satan's eye away and into the nearby pit where it tumbled into imprisonment with the other captives. His mouth would not move to speak his fears. But the one-eyed woman was not lacking. Her words were bitter, her temper... still tempered.

"Yes, pilgrim, I have lived too long in the earth's fissures. Their midnight labyrinths are my realm. Dirt is my domain, worms my subjects. I put it to you: is that fit kingdom for my kind?" David knew the answer, though he did not speak it. Lust began to quake like molten rock. Her voice betraying a grumbling reticence, or a snippet of truth perhaps. "Young, and beautiful too, am I not? And a fair-skinned angel, once... like my elder siblings—Hang them all! With the earth and sea and sky dealt out to those gaffers, our grandsire, Omnus, saved nothing for his daughter deity, except the deep, dark dirt of Mythlewild. You see how the black mud of the Dark Farths has soiled this fair-skinned seraph—"

"It's not the bountiful soil of Mythlewild that's blotched you, hag—it's your black soul!" spoke David, though just where he found the voice he couldn't guess. Still, warding off his adversary's play for pity, he continued. "Your dreary, hungry heart has feasted on your fair skin in search of light, and in the dining dyed it dark to match. And now your divinity—like your humanity—is rotted and worm-eaten in this soot's squalor."

"Damn you, pilgrim!" spat Lust, hissing fire and crackling her lungs. Once again her single Satan eye glowered. "It was that senile sire of mine who rebuked me —not my soul! I was disowned for wanting more than worms! I was deemed mortal for desiring to see the light of day... Am I a monster for that craving? And would my father turn an ear to my cries? 'Twas his shoulder he turned to me—no more!"

"A cold shoulder is generous chastisement to a child so spoiled by greed and envy," responded David unsympathetically. "Your warped, witch! Your mind is bent and your character is corroded. Maybe it's the temperature in this neighborhood, or the hotbed you dream in. You've pitched your tent too close to the devil, dearie—and he's come a borrowing hasn't he?"

"And a better neighbor than nanny I had!" fumed the pit queen. "He at least turned a willing ear."

"And eye too, didn't he!" David was roaring now. "With your own eyes sealed, you opened up your heart to the malefactor."

Lust was shrieking steam. "It was my choice to make, kern—malevolence or mortality! Satan is my chosen sire, and the light of day is my poison. Black suites me anon. It soothes me, and cheers me... Yes, black is my favorite color—and my favorite mood!"

"Your choice of colors is abhorrent," grunted David, composed and no longer afraid. "Your father shunned that color. His world of sky and sea and grass and tree is absent of black."

"Indeed, my father shunned me and my color. My world is nothing but swart, and it is sated by yours. The night is black, and I own the night! The old begatter gave me that much. The sea and sky and earth go dark on its approach. Soon night time will coat Theland like a shroud of permanent dusk. My sibs have grown too senile to preserve themselves or their dominions. I shall soon strip those realms of shine, and snuff out the light of the worlds of sea and sky and land—until all Mythlewild is as black and beautiful as this worm-holed world of mine. And you—you egg-poaching pip, who thinks himself a godling—you DARE to cross my path! Do you fancy our combat is complete? Or your opponent tamed?" Lust laughed a hollow laugh and her vixen whined in amusement.

The snake-skinned sorceress leaned down to David and left a lingering leer in his face with her solitary evil eye, before slinking from her rock. "Our duel is only just begun, upstart! I shall not be beaten as long as I live—and that, my little candy-eyed egg-sucker, is going to be a long, long time! Sweets spoil fast in my rot-glutted cavity, and you'll soon see how heat such as mine can sour your sugar-clad charms!"

The fox scurried out from under foot, her bone tucked in her cheeks. Even the earth trembled under Lust's steps as she strut over to the curtain, which David had earlier shrugged off as drapes. Upon further reflection, he realized there were no windows down here. Horseflies buzzed busily about the cloth. The boy's teeth and knees started up again, rattling like a nervous symphony.

"W-Well... I'm not giving up! he said finally, out of spite.

"No? Well maybe you ought to!" Lust hissed back at him from the coverlet hanging high over the crevasse. Then angrily she pulled open the curtains in vindication, revealing a lovely, sun-haired pixie all bound in red fetters, and dangling upside down over the deep chasm below.

David was struck blind with dismay and his white-hot blood froze in their veins. His lungs had not air enough to vent the shock of it, though one syllable did surface—it was enough. For the name echoed against the cavern's ears and back to his in a hundred acrid, jolting chords: "Val! Val!...Vaaal!..."

CHAPTER 51

The elf maiden did not respond to her suitor's chorus. Her mule-eared watchdog had her gagged; and her sheer wings were strapped tight and still. David didn't even notice Vito prancing around Valentina, braying and hawing pridefully at the accomplishment of this kidnapping. His foxy cohort abandoned her bone hoarding and rubbed her back against Lust's legs, purring in satisfaction like a tabby. Then, for the first time since this milling match began, David's hand was forced. In an emotion-crazed charge, he rushed towards his sweetheart yelling and scrambling up the firestone slope with dagger drawn.

The mule prince clutched Valentina and pulled her out of the boy's reach. He nickered and neighed loudly at such petty rescue attempts as the elfin damsel dangled just beyond her Galahad's grasp.

Lust bellowed with sadistic satisfaction at the futility of it, while her vixen bayed and barked like a jackal. To see such sport was better fun than any toy or chew bone.

Losing his footing in a last ditch desperate lunge, David toppled down the ledge onto his back, and finally rolled over onto his stomach with head in his hands —sunken, sobbing, and disheartened. With more hate in his heart than tears in his eyes, he met Lust's stare with an overpowering contempt that he had never known until now. Words eluded him. His throat was too dry; his voice, if it was there, was hoarse.

But not Lust's. Her mutterings were whet and baiting, and so overpowering. And that eye—that one, beguiling, bewitching eye—it would not quit. "The shoes, pilgrim... I want the shoes! Give them to me. Your freedom, and your sprite's, in exchange for those slippers. See how easy it can be to have an end to your ordeal... The alternative is the pit for you and yours—forever!"

David shook off the siren's beacon gaze, but still her words blazed in his mind, torching all reason. His only thoughts were of Valentina, who looked down to him with pleading eyes; she was shaking her head violently.

Adding to the boy's dilemma were the outcries of his companion's from the fissure below. Voices with shapes he could not see, but recognized, and knew the consequences should their champion falter in this contest. "Davy—painter—li'l' knight... Don't DO it!" they all shouted. "You mustn't... You've beaten her... She's desperate—can't you see! Don't swoon under her lickings! She needs the shoes to best you... Once the witch owns them, she owns you, and it's the end for all of us!"

David lifted his face from the hole's confines. "You WILL release us... all of us?"

"All of you will go together!" assured sin's mistress, without batting that eye. Her hissing was barely audible above the fervid whinnies and whimpers of the mule and fox.

Then, in one irrevocable act of blind emotion, rationed from despair, David abandoned his senses and surrendered his reason—and his shoes—into the clutches of hell's bane. With wings spinning, the lordsdown slippers glided off without resisting. The pumice stone blistered David's bare feet as if to dress him down. And the young pilgrim cried out in anguish, as he watched the witch snatch up her victory.

"Take them, beldam!" sobbed the barefoot boy. "But you won't find their fit so soothing. And you won't find the Glass Egg in their steps. What wretch could find so righteous a gift! You're a godless, black-hearted bat who's sold her sight to Satan; and one so broke and blinded by the infernal can never hope to find the good. Were it under your nose, or at your feet, you would only trip on it and curse it down!"

But Lust did not listen. The belle of blackness was much too preoccupied with her new acquisitions. Squeezing her sooty tootsies into the shoes' soft angel hair lining, she sneered ecstatically at David with calculating menace. "Yeee—You're wrong again, pilgrim; they fit snug as a hug! You flesh and bone brats just never learn, do you!" Lust chortled to herself. Vito and the fox frolicked at their mistress' new feet. It was then that David felt the devil's hand shove him into the dismal, deep defile.

Down into the pit David tumbled, upon and amid his companions. Niki, Peter, and Fidius were all there to brace his fall. Prince Christen just looked on with sheepish eyes. David found his feet in a fit; shaking his fist and dagger, he yelled up furiously at the queen of delusion. "Keep your bargain, debaucher! Give the girl to me—or by my maker those shoes will seal your fate!"

"Damn you, pilgrim!" spat Lust, laughing. "You have my eye... now pluck your own flower, if you can!"

It was this final realization of his betrayal that ultimately conquered heaven's knight. David slumped into a weeping huddle, ashamed and heart-shattered, surrounded by his band of consoling friends. But there was nothing left to say or do. It was over now. No one was about to deny it—no one, except maybe Valentina.

No one's predicament seemed more thread bare than that of the fragile nymphet, as she swayed tenuously high overhead, suspended by her feet.

Nonetheless, the sight of her admirer's downfall did nothing but incense her to the point of reckoning. Gnawing through her gag, the elfette spit it out, and bit into Vito's arm as the donkey attempted to restrain his feisty prisoner. She then shouted down into the abyss beneath her. "Davy—your dagger—toss it to me!"

The sharp sound of Valentina's voice was a trumpeting call to arms for the whipped pilgrim. Thrown for yet another loop, he gazed upward with a new gritty guile in his cheeks.

"Hurry!..." grunted the girl as she continued to snap at Vito. "...Get the lead out of your britches and heave me your blade!"

In the next instant, David was standing on Fidius' shoulders; the lizard in turn, was tip-toed astride Peter's sturdy back. Still far from the trench's brink, they were nevertheless several precious feet closer to the fair dangling girl. With careful aim, David cast his dagger Valentina's way, baffled as to how she would ever grab it, pinioned as she was by hand and foot.

Everyone watched in amazement as the precocious pixie swung wide from Vito's grasp like a lithe pendulum, and agilely latched onto the blade with her teeth. Having the weapon clamped tightly in her round jaw, Valentina first freed her wrists, then slashed all remaining ties, save for her ankles. With knife now firmly in hand, the dimpled lark swayed with ferocity back to her frustrated captor, quickly dealing the mule a retaliatory blow, ever so deftly hacking off a donkey ear from its head. And while Vito stood shocked and simpering, holding the severed ear in his hand—the lissome, little minx proceeded to slickly slice off the other ear before her pitching hobbles carried her out of reach once more.

"Abduct me will you! This'll teach you to keep your mulish mitts to yourself!" By the time she had swung back again, the earless ass had deserted his appendages and his prisoner, and turned tail—which made ample enough target for Valentina, who quickly cut it off, so the mule reached his mistress minus that tuft too.

Cheers rose from the pit, nearly drowning out Lust's snarls. However, the witch still laughed. "Amusing little flower that one—eh, Vito! And wields a nasty nettle too! But see how long your pretty petal dangles before she drops to her doom like autumn's golden leaf. It's been a long, cold fall, has it not, pilgrim?"

"Davy—listen to me! Heed MY voice, not hers!" Valentina hung like a tiny golden grape on a vine far above their heads. "I'm neither a soft flower petal, nor a withered leaf. I'm Valentina—daughter of an archangel warrior—and I don't belong up here, hampered like one of the mule's flies in this black widow's web." So said, one more consummate cut by the facile fairy severed the last of her bindings, and down she plunged toward the gaping chasm.

David's gasp heaved louder than the rest. He followed his heart's fall with affright, and only belatedly raced under her before the jagged brimstone bottom caught his fancy first.

"A lover's leap, how fetching," snickered Lust. "The poor, pugnacious poppet has fallen for the barefoot knight!"

"Touching, " purred the vixen.

Vito only whined from the dark corner where he hid.

But their jeers turned inside out and into fear, as the sun maid spread a dainty set of elfin wings and halted in mid fall; then, brandishing her dagger, veered at Lust, a vindictive glint blazoned in her bright blue eyes. Upon hell's queen she swooped, with the blurring speed of a mad hornet. Her blade hummed like a wing before the witch could duck or defend. The next thing you knew, Valentina had lighted in the pilgrims' midst, a blur no longer, and laying there in David's wide open and unbelieving arms, presented the fellowship with a flowing armful of wavy, red-cropped hair.

"Dang! The fledgling fairy's gone an' plucked herself a foxtail too!" sputtered Fidius, clutching his own appendages protectively.

"There are no foxes in this burrow, maiden. We sin you not!" Peter's self-assured smile narrowed, as his own tail dipped between his legs.

Valentina shrugged off their remarks as sport, while Niki examined her trophy. "No fox's fur this... It's the coat of viler vermin."

"The hag's hair!" exclaimed Valentina. "Hellfire is the fur that witches wear. That vulgar vixen, Lust, is the real culprit in my abduction."

The scalped villainess glared down at her lost locks as if to convince herself this degradation was not more joggery or perhaps some canny sleight of hand. A retorting glare from the magical maiden so convinced Lust of her derring-do, that she shrieked away from the nook mortified, cloaking her naked head in shame to join Vito in his corner and in his whickering.

"Had I a sword, 'twould be Lust's head held in your hands. But a hairless vamp is nearly as humiliated as a headless one!" Valentina threw back her own head in haughty pride, then slipped from David's stiff arms, oblivious to the horrified expressions pasted on his company's faces. They gawked at their friend's adroit little angel as she brushed her bloody, blond hair from her eyes, and casually wiped David's blood-stained blade on her soft satin skirt, and returned it to him neat as a pin.

No one spoke. Lust's tresses were twiddled from hand to hand like a hot silk that everyone wanted to touch, but not hold, else they get burned. However, its touch was neither hot, nor pleasing. At last it was pitched, like so much lint, into a wad on the rocks atop Lust's discarded eye.

David's eyes remained on Valentina as she demurely folded up her sheer wings and tucked them away like napkins after tea time. "Well, what did you think they were for anyway? Decoration?" She couldn't resist chuckling at the sensation she had caused. "I'm afraid they're singed rather badly in this fissure's heat. I'm grounded for awhile... just like you and Niki." Valentina patted the little dove affectionately. The tiny bird shrank from the fay's bloody touch, while managing naught but a feeble 'coo'. A scowl betrayed Valentina's hurt feelings. "Would somebody PLEASE say something! It's me—Valentina—under this red-splotched hair! Davy?... I kept telling you I was no whiffy wall flower. My matriarch is Celeste, a soldier seraph among angels. It's her blood I wear in my veins—not Lust's!"

You wear it well," cheeped Niki at last, breaking the heavy silence with a perturbed chitter. "And now that you're grounded like the rest of us, you'll discover yourself still at the end of you rope... for our plight is no less foreboding."

"Niki's right," said David finally, and with sorrow. "How I had hoped and prayed you would be spared from that harridan's stew pot. When I saw you strung up there, I... I just..." the boy had to wipe his soaking brow.

"What the li'l' knight is tryin' ta say is, we was all scared fur you, ma'am. We never expected ta find a soldier sprite armored in such chaste an' soft elf skin." Fidius swished his tail as he explained.

Peter's also wagged agreeably now. "A titan warrior would envy your gallantry, maiden. Who needs a magic egg, when we are in the company of such fully hatched hawks!"

Niki frowned at so much praise. Valentina merely shrugged it off. "Fooey—no exploits compare to Davy's. I simply shaved an over-weened prig—but he cut her down to size. The day truly belongs to him!"

David was just about to rediscover the comfort of a well-fitting smile, when that baneful voice cascaded down on them from the pit rim. "Take pleasure in your day while you have it, pilgrim, before it smothers in my defile, devoured by the night—which is mine!" Lust's figure stole into their confines again, like an evening shadow, oppressing and ominous. Though thwarted, her hairless, eyeless shame still shimmied under a black and blighted snakeskin sheath. Recomposed and revolting, and hissing more poison than ever, she displayed her pair of white-winged feet, which continued to hum vigorously. "Mine... as are these enchanting shoes, which you so eagerly gave away to me—lest you forget!" Lust's scaly cheeks creased with serpentine satisfaction. "They solace me... make my toes tingle... itching to find my Egg, no doubt!"

"My master's shoes will cramp you style, hag!" screamed David, embittered by his gross indiscretion. "No soothing salve for your soul will they prove—but a morbid balm at best—Believe it!"

The racked expression on the ogress' twisted, contracting face bespoke David's warning. Rendered speechless by throes of stabbing pain, the tingling toes first twinged then turned suddenly into a tortuous affliction, which knocked the chagrined blacker onto her rump in a prostrate swirl of screaming anguish. "OFF!... Get them OFF!... They're strangling me!" Tearing and clawing at her throbbing feet, Lust snarled at her cronies for help. Reluctant as they were to handle such cursed wares, Vito and the fox nonetheless plunged into the dirt they stirred, and lent their wan and wailing queen a hand.

Lust's pangs became excruciating and her shouts intolerable as her mule and fox fools each grabbed a foot and tugged for all their worth. Needless to say, their results were negligible. The enchanted slippers were in no great hurry to accomodate their wicked wearer, who swiveled in crazed circles in the swarthy vortex of lava dust.

But having taught their lusty lesson—and taught it well—the shoes reluctantly released their grip. Off they flew, back into the deep rift, beside the pilgrim's feet where they belonged. The two hangers-on were flung into a tussled heap with their mad madam, who lay in a shallow cranny crying like a deprived child.

"Put your foot into it this time didn't you, queen of hags!" laughed David with disdain. He felt every bit a match for the mighty mage's magic now, as he laced up his precious slippers. They were a panacea dressing for his blistered feet and wounded pride. The pilgrims' frumpish contempt brimmed from the dregs of their underground cavity. So intoxicating was the moment's victory, the abiding pains of their predicament languished. It remained for Lust to remind them.

So incensed with rage, she sent the walls and roofs of Luhrhollow crashing down in a vengeful avalanche—fully into her prisoners trench. "Go on and chirp, you cocky little roaches!" hissed Lust with her poison voice. "Split your sides, and fill your lungs with lava dust! Choke on your amusements—and when you're dead, you will know it is I who am master here!"

An evil, tumultuous laughter drowned out the pilgrims' joy. An execrable rumble of rolling rocks and splitting stone shattered their brief revelry. The crumbling cavern crucible closed in around them, collapsing into the basin like a gravel sky. The mule and the fox scrambled for cover under the brimstone scree, while the wight remained transfixed on the brink of her defile, staring down with fury. Aghast she was to watch her cascading havoc miss its mark.

Far below her—safe and secure in their trapfall—the pilgrims witnessed a miracle. For not a single stone or clod of dirt dropped down upon them. The crescendo of falling earth gave way to softer sounds, as a gently melodic voice sprinkled their midst. "I will be with you," echoed Tierra to David. The earth daughter's beautiful image spread across Lust's cavity like an awning under a rocky rain. The goddess' protective visage remained until the cavern's clouds were settled and dissipated, and the stoney sulfur shower subsided. In the dusty mist, the rainbow icon of Tierra hung like an arch over their heads, shielding the pilgrims from any further catastrophe.

A diabolical howl from Lust faded David's rainbow into a wisp. "So, my hole has become your harbor, has it?" She growled scornfully, sounding like a pack of werewolves. "Keep your shoes, and your day, until morning. You'll need all the magic you can invoke to ever get out of my pit, godling. The steep, rock walls around you are no illusions—and neither am I! Nor is the war which rages at Sovereignton! My armies are arrived—and when the sun makes its final rise on the morn—it shall be 'a wake' to see, and will not shine e're more on Theland. By dawn, Mythlewild will belong to my lion paramour, and you will have no one, or nothing, to fight for. When the runt king and his retinue arrive to lift my lion's siege, he will find his holding leveled, and looted—and lost!

"Never!" yelled David. "Constantio will never yield to your toothless kittens. Nor will I fold up in this stinking earth bottom garret of yours!"

"Then ROT in it!" stormed Lust. Lightning laced her words. "My grandmaker will have cause to worry—fear is for him, not me. I have his progeny, I have his pet—and I have his pilgrim. With or without your shoes, Omnus' Egg and his estates will be mine and all his sheep, slaughtered! Only one hope does your king have—and I've got him here in my sodden vault, together with his foster prince, and all those talismans of yours. They'll work for you, that's proven. Now, if you want to see your home again; and friends again; or if you long to cast an eye on Mythlewild again, you'll exhort your luck to mine. You have until morning; I can wait no longer—neither can your king! My lion's trolls will roast him and his high-born bandsmen for breakfast. And my deepest trough will be your grave tomorrow... Yes, I WILL have my Egg, and my three sibs' realms, with or without your favors!"

Lust turned her back on the pit, and in her haste to leave nearly tripped over the vixen, who had become quite comfortable at the witch's feet, and there continued to romp with her plundered joint. "Damn varmint!" cursed Lust in frustrated indignation. "Get out! Go back to your meals in the woods and be gone from my sight!"

A frothing kick sent the critter scurrying away, out of the dark, humus crypts of Luhrhollow, and deep into some far thicket. The ruffled fox zigzagged this way and that, to dodge the scattered, bloody battle remains strewn about the earth

611

above, lest she taint her sheep-stealing paws. "Lambs are more fain to foolery anyhow," she whined, like a wet stray baying at the distant moon.

Lust snarled after her, "And take your damn fodder with you!" The mad harridan would have pitched the vixen's plundered bone after her, had Vito's mulish whining not distracted her. With loud and vulgar heehaws, he displayed his approval. The poor mule prince, having no ears left, was deaf to his queen's demands that he cease and desist; and so wore on unwarily. Lust had little use for Vito, especially now. With his dirty deeds completed, he was of no use whatsoever. Thus, it was with nothing but disdain that the annoyed—and very angry—slit-tongued angel flicked the repulsive royal ass into the abyss amongst her other livestock.

"Here's more sop for your stew, pilgrim!" cackled Lust. "His incessant braying will prove more tortuous than any of my devises. Until morning then... Sweet dreams!" In a crackling burst of bright scarlet smoke, mawkish and steeping with wrath, Lust was vanished. Left behind was the scarred darkness, a lingering memory, and coated with the witch's red smuts—the vixen's bone.

"Haawww—Mistress!" squealed Vito from his knees, dirt pouring from his mouth. "After all I've done... I deserve more than this."

"Indeed you do!" responded Peter, cantering over to the mule man with his fists clenched.

"Easy does it, li'l' colt," calmed Fidius. "Our elfin angel's done pinned his ears back once already. He'll be hearin' no more threats ever again—no sirree. 'Sides, he'll be gettin' his just deserts at daybreak I reckon..."

"As we all shall..." added Niki with gloom, "...though they won't be 'just'."

"But are we not protected here by the earth princess, Tierra?" asked Valetina, looking into David's worn face.

"Do prison bars protect the condemned, or merely preserve him for his fate? True, the gods have gifted us, but even they can't save us here—certainly not until this yoke I bear is shed... Or found." David enfolded Valentina in his arms, where she recounted the details of her abduction. The boy in turn explained how he and his band had fallen into Lust's diggings.

Thus, with their grim tales told, and the prospects of the dreaded dawn haunting their night, the weary lot drifted into an unsettling slumber born of fatigue and apprehensions. It wasn't until now, that he who slept the longest began to stir. Upon waking from his spell, a demurely moving shadow caught the alert lamb boy's wide open eye.

CHAPTER 52

David's sleep was plagued and shallow, beset with remote, muffled screams. A sultry, sulfur scent roused him in the quiet foul of night. A harsh word or two awakened him—and David opened his eyes to find Valentina tugging at his feet. Niki twittered above her bobbing and reeling in a dither.

"Painter—she's after your shoes! Stop her!"

"Don't be silly," coaxed the darling fay in soft, succulent tones. "I'm just trying to make you comfortable, Davy. You'll sleep much easier without these cumbersome togs... or this poke—"

In another instant the pixie maiden would have removed the satchel from the boy's shoulder—would have, but for the watchful dove, who pecked at the girl's slender, stealing hands. "Don't let her have them, painter!"

"Ouch!" cried the nymphet, withdrawing her dainty arm in pain. "Damn, cursed crow bait!" she growled curtly, grabbing Niki by the throat, and slamming the tiny bird forcefully into the pit wall.

"Val!" gasped David in shock. "W-Whatever's the matter with you?" He crawled on his hands and knees to where his faithful dove lay battered, but still chittering in alarm. Her pink eyes bugged wide in warning as the boy looked up into his sweetheart's evil, elfin face.

Her crafty cat eyes glared back at him. "What's the matter indeed, you miserable, mortal-born brat! I'll have those shoes and paints for a start! And for desert... I'll gnaw your pesky, pilgrim bones!"

Saliva drooled from the fairy's foaming rosy lips as she wrenched David's feet to get at her prize. But the painter clung to his possessions with desperate and dumbfounded ardor. "Val! What's happened? What—"

"What's happened, you straw-brained, goody-two-shoes, is that you've been smitten by a witch's pet!" The snarling, sulfur-stained words spewed in David's face, strapping him with indecision. "I tried to be nice, churl... civil and cooing... wooing you all along to wheedle you out of this foolish endeavor. But you wouldn't listen, no—not you—you meddlesome rake! Well, maybe THIS will persuade you!" From David's waist the lewd angel daughter withdrew his dagger and, brandishing it with her proven proficiency, addressed it at the pilgrim's ankles. "You'll feel how coaxing steel can be to stubborn soles as yours!" David was too chagrined to budge an inch. However, a less paralyzed companion pounced upon the girl before her severing blow was rendered—it was Christen!

The Prince of Lambs, no longer lame beneath Lust's spell, wrestled the dagger from the hate-crazed nymph, and bleated loud into her ears. "Begone, wench! Cast off your holdings on this brood. Take leave of here and tempt no more of us!" Then, with all of the companions awake and astonished, the suddenly impassioned lamb boy did drive the dagger deep and straightaway, into the young sun maiden's chest, splitting her heart in twain.

615

Everyone was horrified to see Valentina's limp, lily form sag to the dust, spitted and squealing like a tender suckling. Fidius and Peter restrained David as he cried out at the maniacal lamb who had so ruthlessly stabbed his love. "My lord! What... what has he DONE to you...Val?" The boy broke down and sobbed over his lifeless dream. "That slumbering Prince of 'Devils' is still cursed... He wakes only to tuck his victims into their death beds!"

Vito, who had been quite deaf to all of this heretofore, now rustled at the scent of blood, and broke into unrestrained nickering at the havoc wrought. But for David, this was too much to bear. With Niki limp at his knees, and Valentina's bleeding body by, he lunged at Christen while the lamb boy still stood over his kill with drawn, burdensome eyes extracting the reddened blade.

"Murderer!" screamed David in a seething fever. "Murderer!" The words struck like hammers against the pit walls, ringing blasts onto a fiery anvil. The pilgrim bore into the unresisting lamb boy and, with his hands knotted around Christen's throat, would have strangled the life out of him, had not a sulfur-breathed hiss harnessed his wrath.

"Damn you, boy!" growled the milk-cheeked maiden—undead—and undaunted by her gaping wound. "Damn you for your stupidity!" repeated the haloed face, in devil's slang. Crawling to her feet, the elfin form approached David with arms outstreatched and wanton, willful, ember eyes. "Embrace me—not him... I am what you're after..."

"Val?"

"Don't listen to her, hunter!" hastened the lamb, gulping for breath under the boy's choke hold. "This time close your ears to her bidding. Listen to me—I am the lamb you seek! Take stock in my counsel; cleave to me... Shut out temptation. That is not Valentina! You must kill her—kill her now!" Christen heaved as David's grip loosened while staring into his oncoming angel's eyes. He clasped the dagger as the lamb pressed it into his drenching palms.

"Would you murder me, Davy... my dearest?" whispered the sun-faced sprite, stepping ever closer. "Would you have my blood on your conscience?"

David could feel the icy touch of her clay-cold fingers... and twisted the dagger blade towards his own chest. "Val?" he called. But Valentina didn't answer. Only frozen sulfur breaths he felt.

"DO IT!" shouted the lamb prince.

Peter, Fidius, Niki—all were hushed—except Vito, who whinnied and stomped the dirt in a stupor, wondering if his eyes were as failing as his ears.

"Oh my god, Val... I can't!" David cried out, and his grip loosened, as the sweetly smiling specter enclosed the daunted pilgrim. Then, a buttery, blandishing voice he knew to be Valentina's called to him, seducing him to commit murder. Next, with a startling air of anger, the heart-tossed boy pumped his steely blade and, with a blow sewn solid and sure with zeal, did slit the slender starlet's throat and severe her fair head from its fairy body once and for always.

A lasting curse spilled from the petal pale lips as the pixie's life and blood ran dark and thick, curdling in the black mud. The horror of the deed held David in its mortifying clinch for endless moments; and there he stood, oblivious to anything else—save for his Valentina—who lay asunder before him. It was her sweet, refining voice which culled him from his trance. It was her soft, velvet touch that caressed him back into reality. Her sparkling blue eyes smiled down at his, and streaks of sunshine hair lit her pure and creamy face like a million, sunny summer days.

"Val!" David gazed at her first, then reached out to feel. Finding her to be real—and very much alive and wholesome. He held her close and wept again, for joy.

"Steady," urged Valentina, returning her suitor's hug before straightening up. "No need to fall apart... like some!" she added, while stepping over to the remains of her beheaded facsimile. She took the severed head sedately into her petite white hands, and held its ashen face next to hers, as though it were a mirror's image. "Merely a fancy phantasm. It would've fooled me too—though I'm much prettier!" she giggled.

David shook his head and rubbed his eyes, feeling for some sense to what he saw. "Val?... er, it IS you, isn't it?"

"Don't be silly—of course it's me," she replied, admiring her boy friend's handiwork, then winked affectionately at David lest he doubt.

Peter and Fidius lent reassuring nods. But, it was the sight of Niki chirping cheerfully in Christen's palm that put his mind totally to rest. "Another of Lust's transformations, painter, to deprive you of your wares—and life too—since neither fit into her plans."

"Luckily Valentina—the real Valentina—called out to you just in time to bolster your will power," explained the lamb boy.

"In time to kill yourself a witch!" said the pixie, snubbing her nose at the face she held.

"Grrrr... Look again, my pretty poison!" snarled the severed head, which began writhing with a life of its own.

Valentina shrilled frightfully as she dropped the grisly grinning thing and darted back into David's arms, just like a skittish school girl spying a rat in their midst.

The whole fellowship was transfixed at what they beheld. Not even Vito chanced an utterance, as the fair-faced figurine melted from death's husk to mold into something more sinister and serpentine, with features bare and black as pitch, and shining smooth as snake's skin. It was womanly and witchy, with a wickedly hissing cotton mouth, and a single scathing eye. It was Lust—the wight—whole and unholy. The fairy tale vision was no more. To the crevice rim she lurched, lest dark's angel manifest herself into a hostile hole.

"'Killed yourself a witch' you say?... Damn you all say I! You've killed nothing but time. Morning will break and find you woebefallen nits here, still clinging to some misbegotten fancy. Cling then! Cling to your paltry charms... What's this?... The mutton!" Lust suddenly took notice of the awakened lamb prince. A startled, but satiated smile, saturated her profane face. "Impossible... Or could it be?" Then, in a sulphurous flash, the lordess of Luhrhollow was gone. And nothing more was seen or heard of her, for the present.

For the longest time frigid silence was the only voice to be heard in the sunken crypt of Luhrhollow. Deep, hot breaths were the only breezes. David felt for his heart, which beat a mad, melancholy theme to the companions' nightmare.

All the cast sat—a captive audience—in the dark, pithy stage. "It's no use," he said sadly, slipping into a squat on the grimy ash and pumice pit bottom. Niki cuddled up under her master's chin, cooing softly. "Is this my lot, Niki? To slay that... that sullied scarecrow—or be slain by it? Why, she's still a goddess—invincible, and immortal—with more lives and shapes than I can count. And who am I? Some high-strutting foundling who feigns to be an artist, and pins his hopes on worn heels and dull hues! Can there be weaker weapons? Or will morning bring another miracle?"

Niki sheathed her displeasure at David's flagging spirit with sage words. "A keen edge does not a dagger make, painter. You have seen how evil defies sharp steel. Nor is there magic imbued within your swag or shoes—'tis within you. Your talent is what all others lack; perchance, that is why others fail where you fare well. And of your miracle? You have that too—the miracle of faith. That is a blade to bludgeon Lust. Don't lose it now, when it's needed most. Remember, only two things are immortal, painter: good and evil. Nothing and no one under heaven is indestructible. Even that scarecrow is naught but straw, and can be burned, if you can only find the match to touch her off. Although evil cannot die—it can be spurned—by good. Lust is no god; what divinity she once claimed is but dust. Destroy her, and her evil at least will be quashed. Your victory, and ours—won!"

"But how?" The question pommeled David's haggard mind until he could no longer think. "If such a sorceress is vulnerable, where is her weakness?

"Here!... Here is that hay woman's 'match'." bleated Christen, seating himself beside David, and offering his handshake by way of introduction. "You are her weakness, Egg-hunter. I believe I owe you my life, and most ardent appreciation. Though bewitched under that crow-skin's cantrap, my mind has not been sealed from the happenings around me. You and your damsel's derring-do enthralled me as a trance... and Fidius! And Peter! My good friends—what solacing sights for spellbound eyes." Only now did the long separated kinsmen spare a moment for reunion. As the good comrades embraced, the lamb and the dove also exchanged the warmest of glances.

"Surely our Overlord is smiling at this sight," cooed Niki.

"As would your father, Constantio, if he could see," said Peter.

619

"Tut!" coughed Fidius, next to tears. "Can't see no blamed reason fur smilin', or thanks neither. Our reunion'll be our ruin fur sure, 'less someone comes up with the torch ta cremate ol' straw guts! The li'l knight's her sore spot alright; but she's still spoutin' sulfur gouts and spittin' it down our necks. Now just how do we cut ourselves free a this ash-skinned warden? Answer me that if you can, Prince."

Christen was not quick to answer the lizard. "Who can say? If the gods cannot rid themselves of her specter—if my father cannot—how shall I?"

David's face puckered into a puzzle-worn knot as he blurted, "But, Christen —I mean, Prince—you MUST have the answer! You're awake!" The startling truth of that matter struck everyone speechless. David was the first to remark on that neglected miracle. "Lust's spell...you broke it! But how?"

The question echoed back and forth between them. And they each in turn, or out of it, offered their own opinions on the subject. Even Vito, straining to hear, voiced his own in mulish banter; though he couldn't make it out well enough to know what he, or anyone else, was talking about.

Through it all, only one voice remained silent—knowingly silent. That voice was Christen's. He alone had heard the witch's words which cast him into limbo— and he remembered. Only he among them knew the two possibilities for his sudden awakening. Although the words were welcome as life itself, even he did not believe the implications of what he spoke. "According to my spell, I would wake only when Lust was...dead."

"Dead? Lust... dead!" David's reaction was spontaneous—and euphoric—as only a despondent, suddenly salvaged from his fate, could be. "Lust is DEAD!" he reiterated. And the accompanying wave of cheers and smiles splashed across the faces of the fellowship like an intoxicating tonic of mirth.

"The crone is dead!" exclaimed Peter, rearing onto his hind legs and bucking like a wild yearling.

"The li'l knight's done it! He's gol' durn done it!" wheezed Fidius, his voice cracking with gouts of glee as he joined the pony boy and danced a jig, spry as a newt. It would seem even Vito had no trouble discerning the news, and reacted with clapping applause, or he may merely have been slapping at flies.

Valentina showered her hero with hugs and admiration. "I'm so proud of you, Davy, I knew you could do it. The witch is killed—you've beaten her!"

Niki was the first to notice Christen's vexed expression—It was hardly happy. Then, eventually it struck them all. In a slow, creeping ripple, the elated madcap mood dissolved. David put their thoughts to lips when he mumbled the haunting reality and, in the telling, laid their joy to rueful rest. "I didn't do it, did I. Lust isn't dead... She was just here, with you, and us... Alive!" The pilgrim stifled any further comments and sank back into the ashes.

Niki did not settle into any depression though. The dove flapped her parched wings in an all out panic, as she guessed the crushing alternative from her lamb's sagging brow. "Christen, my prince, tell us... What is it? You do recall... don't you? Can you repeat the rest of the incantation?"

The lamb boy nodded with reservation, and hesitated to speak. But it wasn't because he could not recollect Lust's curse—but because he could. In Christen's memory, the witch's vivid words came effortlessly to mind, for they were the last his waking ears had heard. But on his lips, the siren's syllables were sores. He struggled to say them, so painfully would they be received. "'You will be still...' she had said. '... still as lead, until the end of time, or until this mage is dead'..." The last line lodged in the lamb's throat and would not be revealed. Only upon the insistence of innocents' ears was the truth coughed up. The words fell thus: "...'Or until the Egg I find!'... So it was said unto me. And so it has come to pass..." moaned the Prince of Lambs in very hushed tones. "My sleep is broken... Lust has it now. That's why she lurched off so unexpectedly—and leered so smugly at the sight of me revived. She knows the Glass Egg is hers!"

CHAPTER 53

If gloom and despair were weapons, David and his companions would possess the ultimate arsenal. The pilgrims' hopes were bottomless, plunged far deeper than the darkest dungeon's defile. Failure was etched into David's harrowed face. Recovering the Glass Egg had always remained uppermost in his thoughts. Now, any chance of success seemed dashed.

"Impossible!" scoffed Valentina at last, lifting her gladiator's chin out of its rut. "Lust CAN'T have that Egg! That one-eyed harpy couldn't find anything good! If she fell over it, she'd probably throw it away... wherever it is." Like the others, Valentina had long suspected the Egg of being something most sacred and beyond any comprehension, yet she never pried into its nature. Now David searched her inquisitive eyes, wondering if such stalwart supporters did not deserve more of an explanation. But Peter, for one, required no such recompense.

"Valentina's right," agreed the centaur. "If blackie did have this Egg, why's she wasting her time in this sweat box with us 'fleshlings'?"

"Suppose our hostess has this here Egg that everyone's so hot after..." wheezed Fidius, swishing his grey, scaly tail in thought, "...but don't KNOW she's got it!"

"Sir Fidius—that's it!" chirped Niki, hopping over the old lizard's flicking tail. "She's stumbled onto the Egg sure enough, else Prince Christen would still be dead to the world. And... while Lust is definitely not dead, if she KNEW she had her prize, we all certainly would be. She left us so abruptly, not to fetch the Egg, but to search it out among her vast holdings. What elusive plunder it must be!"

Rushing over to the lamb boy in a flap, the dove asked excitedly, "Christen, you never have told us... Whatever did happen that night—the night of your abduction? What did you do with the Glass Egg? And prey, why has it been so onerous to locate?"

Shaking is head, the lamb slowly recounted in whispers the dire events of that long ago night; though reason for his caution seemed belatedly inane. Alas, the telling exposed no answers; instead it hatched only more questions. It was as Cin's oracle pool had portrayed at Ocean Bottom.

"Before that vixen carted you off to the Ill-timber, you hid the Egg under the tall meadowgrass... That's all?" peeped Niki dejectedly. Her bent expression reflected all their disappointment at such an unrevealing story.

"But, Niki... we scoured that meadow on our hands and knees—and turned up nothing." David's chin dipped once again under his collar. "It just wasn't there!"

"Or, it was... and we didn't recognize it!" Niki's little round head was swimming. "According to the field flowers, no one disturbed the pasture after that night, until our arrival the next morning. I was wrong, painter. The Egg was there—we just failed to distinguish it. Perhaps it is not for lack of sight Lust cannot see, but like us, she's hunting for an egg—when what she has, is something else!"

David raised his voice in quizzical fashion. "You mean the Glass Egg is not a glass egg anymore?"

"No, painter. A hand is still a hand, though it may look to be a fist; or some breed may call it a paw. Simply put, it is not the Egg which has been lost—but us! We have been shortsighted. We have looked, but have not seen!"

"Perchance, through an extra eye you would detect the Egg, and also discover a loophole from this ditch," squalled Vito, sticking his mistress' cast off eye into the side of his head, where an ear used to be. He groveled through Lust's hair, which was his bedding, and pretended to hear. However, the scrawny mule man remained as blind as he was deaf, a pitiable sight if ever there was.

"Shut up, you harebrained, donkey-witted ass!" shouted Valentina irritably. "Or I'll slit your tongue out too, and silence your mulish mouth once and for all!"

David frowned to see his angel so embittered and bedeviled. Though the elf maiden had ample cause to despise her abductor. "Bear Vito no more malice, Val," he urged. "He's had a bad time of it too, wrung through Lust's ringer and betrayed by her as we all have. We're each up to our ears in ashes together now. Lust is our mutual scapegrace. Who of us is not guilty of our own indiscretions? I, for one, am willing to accept Vito's errors as experiences best forgiven, together with my own."

"Well said," spoke up Christen, rising to embrace his stepbrother, and guiding him into the companions' midst with a sincere sibling hug. It was a gesture which even the earless ass could not misinterpret. "Vito, my brother, I've always considered our blood to be same. And both veins be as cherished to our foster father, Constantio."

Such an overt display of kinship was more than Vito's fragile mind could withstand. Weeping and whining, he dropped to his knees and kissed his lamb brother's feet in atonement. "Boohoo... Oh, brother...I swear to you, I'm truly sorry for my deeds! I was stupid, and desperate, sniff... Y-You do see that, don't you? I so love Constantio, like a real father, as you do... sob. But I was always left to feel like a freak, and an outcast. The count, DeSeet, promised me prestige and power, and... You MUST understand! Sob... I do wish to make amends. I want to change. I can—and WILL! You'll see, I swear it!"

"I believe you, brother," said Christen forgivingly.

"Me too!" said David, offering the pitiable prince of donkeys his hand. The bawling mule man bathed the boy's hand with kisses and a vow of indebtedness.

Niki was quick to offer her sentiments as well. And, after some further deliberation, Fidius and Peter added two more tentative handshakes.

Finally, Valentina, under some strong urging from David, extended a restrained and reticent pardon. "Sorry about your ears. Now stop blubbering... that's no way for a pilgrim to act!"

Such comradery moved Niki to chirp, "Vito's transgression was of weakness, not treachery. A common villain now ransoms all our souls. And the only important question remains: what can we do?"

"Whatever it is, we'll do it together," said Christen.

"We could all die together," uttered David, turning his back again to brood at the steep, firestone wall as though its lava cinders were the only faces he could look upon without shame. Yet, the wall made him weep as they brought to mind this hellish verse: 'Abandon all hope, ye who enter here'. From whatever dint in David's past those words were culled, they bode no joy, but made the boy cry out. "There ARE no solutions! I've failed you, Niki... and you, Prince... and your father. I've failed everybody! What an awful pick I was. A real pilgrim could help you now —but I can't... not with all my trinkets and magic wares. There's no escape... I cannot paint Lust away with my pigments; nor can I fly from her trenches in my angel shoes!"

"Well, one thing's certain," spoke up Peter, who had begun pacing in circles about the shaft like a caged wild beast. "Even our muley chum, Vito, was flapping the same nonsense through his gums. We've got to conjure our way out of here by sunrise. I've no intention of sitting here, sleeping here—or sweating here—any longer, just waiting for the dawn to cremate us in this soot queen's urn!"

"Tsk," snorted Fidius, fluffing up his sagging tail and sitting upon it to add some luxury to their accommodations, the old lizard being quite accustomed to passing time underground. "The folly of youth! Was I ever such a naive tad. Go on, li'l Pete... you sprout wings an' fly out, like doves or fairies. But wish fur fireproof plumes, else yur flight on fancy'll be grounded too—yes sirree!"

"Better to have a singed dream than a burned butt, you old croc! You'll never realize anything but blistered backsides sitting on your duff, that's for sure—"

"Fellows!" Bleated Christen, distracting his two spatting comrades from each other. "Your crocodile tears are dousing your horse sense. Suppose one of us COULD fly from our cage—what then? Seek aid? Where? Who is left that can help us? Is there any parcel of Theland unblemished by Lust's smutty shadow? The south and eastern lands' light lie extinguised. Our Commons' heartland now is fodder for feeding scavengers. Even the North Holds and Western Reaches will eventually crumble under press of the dark jinn's clay-souled minions. No soil or sea or heaven is refuge for us now—nor any man, or god. Were all of us to flee this minute, what freedom would we gain? By tomorrow, the whole of Mythlewild will be a blackened cinder!"

"The Prince speaks sense," sighed Niki, lighting on her lamb's shoulder. "We were not captured here. 'Twas by our choice we came. Hence, escaping this brimstone basin is not our highest hurdle. We've a deeper, wider chasm to cross and always will have, as long as Lust lives. The queen of this hold must be stopped —killed... Someway!"

"How?" mumbled David in a languishing careworn groan. "The ageless crone obviously holds herself together quite well."

"True, but she's not indestructible," remarked Christen. "Were she a god, even then would her omnipotent grandsire, Lord Omnus, have eternity over her."

"Okay, okay! The crone is killable... So?" David conceded, even as he recalled Tierra's words: 'not even the gods know how to slay her'. He argued, "Do you expect us to succeed where gods have failed?"

"No, hunter," replied Christen, "not us... I expect YOU to succeed, For you are their champion!"

David didn't even look up. Another dungeon wall, he thought, and put an ear to it, as if listening. Is it true that walls hold the wisdoms garnered from ages past? Talk to me, he prayed. Yet, except for murky memories, he heard naught but cold stone silence. So foiled, the boy stomped his foot into the ashen floor raising a black dust cloud. "Me? Sure... I'll stomp on her like a roach; that ought to snuff her out."

As the air cleared, Peter ceased his pacing and clapped his hands together. "Why not!" he exclaimed. "Davy, you CAN stomp on her, just as you won your duel. Kick her black bones back into oblivion!"

"Yes sirree!" spouted Fidius, raising some smoke of his own. "Your heels cut a brand on that Ill-timber sorely enough. An' the shoes did take a big bite outta that ol' tigress' toes!" Vito heehawed his affirmation, though to just what, he wasn't sure.

The idea did have some merit enough to pry David from his wall. However, he was not smiling yet. "And just how do you propose to get our hostess back down here at our disposal? A cordial invitation perhaps...or, do we throw a party..." the boy's voice raised in futility, "...our 'going away' party!"

Niki watched sadly from Christen's shoulder as Valentina sidled up and offered some comfort to the distressed boy crouched on the cinder floor. "Lust is no mere Ill-timber," reminded the dove. "The shoes were only a passing discomfort, like her haircut—painful, but wounding only her vanity. The slippers' magic, and the paints', is not in destruction, but preservation—of faith!"

Valentina squeezed David's arm. "Davy... you're other gifts—the paints! We haven't tested their permanence yet." Then, as if expecting them to jump to life, she poked the satchel, still slung inconspicuously over the boy's shoulder.

The only reaction to such a silly idea was David's, and his was half-hearted at best. "Such a nibble these could make would hardly be lethal," mulled the young artist, exhibiting his long pursed array of painting stuffs. "How deadly can pigments be? Do I impale Lust with my palette knife? Erase her from the canvas of Mythlewild with a swipe of my brush? Or blot her out of existence with a splotch of flake white perhaps?" David simply sighed at his own frivolity. But his dove did not.

"Possibly..." Niki mused with all seriousness into Christen's ear.

Valentina pillowed her amber head in David's lap thinking to calm him. "That old wart! I can't believe anyone is so abhorrent. If only she realized how revolting and fulsome she really is under that umber-colored coat she calls a complextion..." Valentina broke off her aside. A golden chain dangled from David's neck and glittered in her suddenly smiling eyes. "Why, Davy... my picture! The one you painted. You're still wearing it!"

The boy clasped Valentina's locket in his hand and gazed fondly at her portrait. The sunbeam face smiled up at him from the miniature painting. Momentarily, David was lulled back into Queen Superbia's idyllic rose garden. That moon glow evening his heartthrob had left her likeness on his breast. Oh, to be in that lush and languid garden just one more night... alone with Val... and safely out of this hellish hole... The pixie's conversation became a mute whisper as David escaped for an instant into his painting, losing himself alongside sunny images. How sublimely beautiful she is, compared to the insufferable manes shed by Lust... so forbiddingly ugly. Like Val said, 'uglier than sin'! Then he cast a hardened stare at the wall. 'Abandon all hope, ye who enter here'... How vivid those words appeared now—not from David's past, but from fables'. They were etched above the entrance to Hades according to some legend. In his revelry, the young orphan recalled other ancient stories from his history books. Immemorial tales of Greek myths and their heroes. How dramatically their exploits sprang to mind—in particular, the one called Perseus. Wearing a cap of invisibility, and armed with other godly-given charms—including a pair of winged shoes—he slew the Gorgon, Medusa, a hideous monster so revolting, all who bespied her ugliness turned stone. Yet she was struck dead when falling prey to the squalor of her own vanity. Perseus had cleverly polished his shield mirror-bright, thereby petrifying Medusa when enticed into beholding the reflection of her own grotesque image. So immersed was David in this dreamscape that his thoughts took voice. "If only the Gorgon, Lust could see herself, behold her own god-awful horror... If only I had a mirror, I'd show her! Then maybe, like Medusa, the forbidden sight of her own reviling face would frighten her to death."

None present could make sense of David's pattering. The young boy's Greek fables were unknown even to Mythlewild's own deities. Nevertheless, they all huddled around him as he turned his ears from the pit wall's revelations and proceeded to empty the contents of his satchel onto the ground.

"Davy... Are you alright?" Valentina's question went unheard as the painter roamed his own thoughts.

"So, these are my weapons? No cap of invisibility here... but who knows what shape the muse might take!" David sighed and shook his head. Out spilled a wide assortment of various pigments and oils, and binders and brushes, along with motley odds and ends long laid forgotten by the boy. Most were rags and such; but among the oddments lay a peculiar looking waxen orb—a candle. Handcrafted and without any wick, it required neither fuse, nor match to light its perpetual flame—an illuminating glow, fueled with faith and kindled by necessity. David's memory burned, though the precise words of its inane maker had long since escaped since presenting the creation to him in DeSeet's dungeon. Howbeit, the boy's attention lingered, not on this unique candle, but fixed upon numerous rolls of canvas, new, and used. It was this conglomeration of paint-splattered parchments which he riffled through as though a pile of dirty rags. Occasionally he would hold one up at arms' length to contemplate with wrinkled nose and raised brows.

"Ugh!" was his most frequent, and literate, critique. "How awful! I wonder how this stuff got into my satchel? Have you been playing with my things, Niki? It's not been opened, except in your presence, has it?"

"No, of course not," twittered the dove, bemused at her painter's ignorance, and glad to see him once again addressing his friends. "None may delve into your kit but you, painter; you know that."

David combed through his hair, straining to remember. "But I don't recall doing any of this. Why, it's nothing but a... a mess, and a waste—just garish blotches of paint smeared on good canvas."

Niki postured herself as an ivory carving amid the artworks and explained. "Painter, these pictures you call a 'waste', are some of the most important paintings of your life. You don't remember them? When you lent your skills to their creation your memory was lost—sucked from your former life by Isolato's spawn, Perilgullum. The one called Fate intervened on your behalf, and restored your yesterdays, in order to preserve the present—and insure the future. So cherish these works of art; somewhere in their framework is the fiber of your life. You found yourself ground in these 'splattered' images, and comprehended meanings none but you would ken." As Niki chattered away, David explored the mysteries of this collection and discovered new worth in his renderings. "It was your unique talent that saved you then, painter. THAT is your strongest magic—and keenest weapon!"

The pilgrim was clearly moved, not by awe... but something. "Just the same, I'd trade all my satchel's works for one ample-sized mirror."

David's wish struck upon fay and pointed ears. Of them all, only Valentina understood their tenor. His thoughts were graphically illustrated on the linen ground for all to behold. "Davy—you DO have a mirror! Here!" she exclaimed, pointing to an empty canvas. "It's even more perfect. Mirrors are no better than eyes —they can be deceived by appearances. But these fabrics can be magic, and when adorned with an artist's eye, they can be extraordinarily perceiving!"

David scanned the floor for only a moment longer, then pondered the lava walls of Luhrhollow for his muse. And from the earth's dungeon troves it came back to him in articulate whispers of rats and roaches: 'all walls are wise...' raved the voice of despair. Old walls especially, are seeped with timeless secrets. Tthe prison louse had taught him that. 'If only we would listen to the walls confining us, we would learn the way out...' No walls are older than the earth, thought David. And so, with his palette knife, the artist scraped the world's wisened insights off the gorge of Luhrhollow and into the ground of his painting. With his hands full of powdered clay, he proclaimed, "These abysmal walls do not imprison—they liberate us! Maybe I was mistaken... perhaps I CAN paint Lust to death!"

"You can, Davy; I know you can!" said Valentina. "Your talent will save you again—and us!"

"That master meddler, Fate, has not deserted me. I'll spend the remaining night painting... and this will be no mad scribbling!" David's spirits vaulted from the ashes. After kissing Valentina gratefully long on the cheek, the eager artist gathered his arsenal around him. He then put the 'mirror' to easel, lit his wax-woven orb with a wish, and went to work.

The dark, dreary trench which gloomed around him scowled its deep jagged jowls, and surrendered to the softly shimmering candlelight. Though the night was wept with woeful midnight tears, and evening's ink black blood drenched the Mythlewild, the pain-soaked cavities within her soil were boiled and hissing hot with Luhrhollow's smoldering coals of a luridly ethereal light. Save for just one ulcer rift in its deepest gullet, therein glowed a rare wax light burning brighter than the bleak of evil. The noxious scents of brine and brimstone balked under less pungent and more insatiable perfumed scents of linseed, turpentine, and sweat.

No one slept now. All eyes could but stare fixedly over David's hunched shoulders as he stirred his multi-hued palette with mixed emotions, and touched his sable swords to gesso shield, thus beginning the most important portrait of his life. The stillness of heavy breathing cried out in courteous admiration. The only noises now were not the jeering hiss of burning embers or raucous steam, instead it was the silent stroking sable hairs deftly daubing muted shades of burnt umber and raw sienna.

None of the artist's advocates dare intrude upon his concentration, so consumate was his endeavor. Niki nested atop Christen's wooly head, as the lamb positioned himself discreetly beside his gifted rescuer. Valentina sat curled at his other hand, resisting all urges to speak. Behind them, Fidius had propped his wearying lizard bones on Peter's durable flanks while the pony boy constantly pranced from hoof to hoof. Of the prisoners, only Vito remained aloof and alone, in a far dark-lit earthen crease; whether from sadness, shame, or sinfullness, no one knew. The mule man surrounded himself with strands of Lust's hair and uncovered her abandoned, glossy eye, with which he toyed in brooding dallyings.

For all their silent respect, the band may as well have been boisterous, for David would have heard them not. His ears, like his lips, were closed that his eyes and mind would open wider. These senses were not shut as he attacked the canvas foe, which to all but him, was a battlefield.

David poured intense care and deliberation into the construction of his work of art. This portrait would be his masterpiece, there was no denying that. A colossal cloth and color monument dedicated to simple pilgrim's ethics, sculpted from pigments and perspiration, accented with endless hues of spilled blood and sacrifices shed, a creation bound with a veneer of valor and undiluted faith—this work was to be a true vision—one which would never fade away. This single, lasting treasure would never hang in any great museum, or displayed in any kingly colonnade, only here, in this lost crack of the earth's cellar—its gallery. And for patrons? An audience of only eight: seven desperate souls—and Satan's soulless servant, Lust.

"Our li'l' knight's doin' okay, ain't he," whispered Fidius to Peter, unable to muffle his respect at the vitality which his friend devoted to his craft. "He's a real burr when he's wound up—yes sirree! Wonder if he ever gits an itch ta use that magical motion fur hisself?"

"He did once," said the pony boy, rubbing his shank, "but then he discovered fealty was a worthier wonder."

Eternity passed before so much as a single other word was spoken, and that, but a bleating whisper. "What an unusual candle!" remarked Christen to Niki, after long pondering the hypnotic, burning orb by David's knees. "How many hours work has passed, yet the wad, no bigger than an egg, holds to its round form without a drop of wax surrendered to fire. It continues to burn, and so brightly, like a chunk of sun. Such a glimmer is reminiscent of our father's Glass Egg. Tell me, how does it work? Is this ball some other magical giving?"

Niki, though familiar with David's candle, was nonetheless lacking an answer to her prince's questions. For she had not been present when the marvelous lamp was bestowed on her painter.

"The candle burns as long as those it illuminates have faith in its light," spoke David without flinching from his task. "A bewildering bequeath to be sure, but more a curiosity than a charm... I think?" Now the painter turned to pause, and noted his ever-flickering torch. Its exotic spindling aura recalled an old, forgotten friend from DeSeet's tower keep. "A cell mate deemed me this, far beneath your lion count's chambers. He fashioned it himself, but not entirely of wax. From some satin, spider twine it was spun. He was kind of an insect you see... a phenomenal fleck of a fellow really—if indeed a 'fellow' it was. The little bugger was a captive most of his years, though still a youth, I think... and peculiar to the point of inane madness. Or so I thought. But, looking back, who knows?"

"An unconventional sort you say?" queried the lamb prince, scratching his chin. "And long held hostage by DeSeet?" Perchance, do you recall his name?"

Though Christen's voice had surged steadily with interest, David remained unphased and, after some light thought, shook such introspection from his head and leaned back into his brushwork.

However Niki hastened to add, "He had no name left, my Prince. I recollect that odd crawler vividly. There was something queer about him... No, not queer—but singularly exceptional! The poor, pathetic roach remembered nothing of himself, yet was unceasing, and unerring, in his babble. Do you know such a discard?"

The lamb boy contemplated the lapping candlelight and flicked his ears in agitated thought, only to find few answers. "A droning, dotty little tick?... Perhaps I knew such a nondescript exile once, but then my mind has born and lost some many weights of late. I can't say, but that the candle's glow speaks to me. If only I could recall its language..."

"The king's jail warden should know his tenants," theorized Peter, nudging a drowsy Fidius to attention.

"Humph! Scalywags!" wheezed the grey old turnkey. "An' beggars too, bedded in my cells. Nothin' else. Then again, as I think on it... In that deepest hold, the lion held a poacher once, but never more. Nowadays, if not the roaches, 'tis the rats which scurry there... uh, unless I'm wrong that is..." Fidius snorted towards Vito, but DeSeet's donkey was not talking. From under his stinking, crone-hair blanket, the mealy mule continued to fondle Lust's jade eye as a miser hoards gemstones, then ducked beneath the shock as Valentina glared his way.

"Whether worn by witch or wretch, those wormy tresses gall me!" she said sternly.

"Shhh—Valentina!" Niki flitted over David's head in a tizzy.

Her painter had broke from his easel again, and sighed as he flushed his palette for new colors and direction. Added glances at his canvas bespoke the intense ordeal wrought upon the young pilgrim. For many minutes now, no new strokes did grace his work. Nor did his enthusiasm mount; rather, it waned, until now. David sat with back to all except his art. He scanned the canvas, peering into it for guidance, but none did appear. He sullenly set his sable sword aside. His muse had perished, felled by fouler forces than inspiration.

"Painter... what's wrong?" twittered Niki, staring at the fabric as though to know its secrets. "Go on... There's not much time! And you're not nearly finished... Are you?"

"No," replied David distantly. "I've but scratched the dark surface of that... that... Oh, Niki, it's no use! Search my soul as I might, I can draw no fresher inspiration, nor squeeze out the talent to depict such a baneful atrocity as Lust. I've tried—truly I have! But I can see no further. The witch has sealed her soul to me. Her real nature might never be perceived by mortal's eyes like mine."

"What you need is a 'window' with which to view the warlock's soul." remarked Valentina, strutting over to Vito's nest and wrestling his bauble from the burrowed bedding. "Is it true our eyes are windows to the soul? Behold, the artist's eye!" Into David's hand she thrust Lust's discarded glass eye. "Let the heller's lens draw you into the innermost secrets of its socket's soul. Take up your arms again, sir painter—portray and slay that fire drake, Lust!"

The witch's eye was like a magnifying lens. Though tinted black, it did expose, in all detail, the ugly inner evil that was hers. With intensified revulsion, David looked through Lust's eye. Stripped of ashen flesh facade, her peccant, sin-plaqued soul lay bare, disembodied and decaying before him. Decrying pain spilled into the boy's head and heart and heels, to see so explicitly the excrement of Lust unadorned.

Gnashing his teeth so they would not quiver, it was with rejuvenated vigor David addressed his toil; and was not to face his friends again until his task was done. So earnest was his labor, that he paused only to reflect upon the progress being made; and to rest his overburdened eyes, which strained almost beyond endurance to handle all the horrors they beheld. Yet once restored, the warrior would set upon his canvas foe with even extra energy, attacking with twice the intensity, and tenfold the flurries of furious sable-stroke salvos. Right into Lust's hideous heart did his brushwork barrages thrust.

The companions' could no longer take in Lust's likeness, so vexing to their eyes it proved. Yet so close knit was their kindred spirit, David was able to reach beyond his palette and into each of their thoughts, soaking his brushes in dabs of their impressions, vital insights on the true nature of Lust as each of them perceived her. The pilgrim was tireless, the night breathless. Thus the vision of Lust was born in oil on canvas. Even the enduring candle flinched its constant glow. And after the abiding light had dimmed, only vivid colors lived to illuminate their den in haunting, horrid hues. Finally, under his portrait's mounting gaze, the artist's lids clamped shut in self defense.

Only the linseed Lust's eyes remained open to espy her demise. From memories David painted now—and from his marrow too. Yet his assault was no less fatal. Out of throbbing experiences gained, he plied his piercing tools in telling duress. With such sensitive emotions as heart-felt love, and soul-searching hate, he groped to touch the witch, capturing each expressive naughty nuance, and subtle sinister shade, and terror-tinted tone; blending it all into one malevolent masterpiece.

What time it was, no one knew. It did not matter now. The ordeal would end when it was done, and not before. Only when that final dashing stone was hurtled across the giant cotton demon did David drop his sling and sighed, weakly— as drained and exhausted as the scattered scores of depleted tubes of paint around him. Squeezed so empty dry by the grip of his calling, he was unable to rise or move. But his eyes broke open now, and fixed their gaze upon his wonder work. In that brief eternity of contact, a war raged—more bitter than any battle waged— and infinitely more dreadful than their prior deadly duel. Yet only an instant did the painter and his painting clash. The 'brat's' eyes refused to yield again, as did his will. The war was won when David embedded the witch's eye into her oily face. "So you may have the 'eye' for art, to see your sinful self as others do!" With a clap of his hands, the pilgrim painter rose wearily from the ashes. "Finished!"

The sharp sound of David's confident voice was a clarion, calling the fellowship in arms to open their eyes and find cause to hope again. With poised reservations, each lifted their eyes and approached the painted personage of Lust; but even in the semi-darkness, they could endure the fashioned figure's face for only a trice. Christen's fleece sprang stiff on edge; all his soft lamb wool was bristled burrs. Niki lit on her artist's shoulder and icy goose bumps bubbled up the dove's tiny spine. Valentina grabbed Davy's hand after screaming in fear, yet could not turn her gaze. Peter's discipline sweat from his russet hide in a cold lather, and he bolted to look at it. The more fragile half of Fidius' spectacles shattered across a newly chased network of wrinkles cracking across his brittle skin, dried all the more by the lizard's foaming stomach. Even David's candle flickered to life, glimmering again in wonder with a warm approving commentary of light.

Meanwhile, still cowering under his hairy sheets, only the mule man bemoaned viewing the artwork. It stung his eyes, and the fear of losing his sight too, was more than he was willing to risk. Then David lent a compassionate hand. "Vito, will you not come forward and remark upon the frame I've fashioned from your mistress' eye? I drew on your impressions too, and would have your say in this viewing."

The reluctant donkey was slow to move, until Valentina made a less compassionate, though more pointedly effective, gesture toward David's knife. It was with such genteel prompting that Vito inched his way to the easel, and pressed his nose, but not his eyes, against the canvas' dark ground face. "I-I-Is that what she looks like?" he stuttered, his eyelids still tightly shut.

"You should know, donkey, you're closer to that miscreation than any of us!" Valentina spoke in harsh words, finding it most difficult to absolve the differences with her abductor and feign friendship.

"Easy, maiden," said Christen. "My stepbrother is not so close to Lust as you would place him, though now it seems he's quite attached!" The lamb laughed as he scrubbed a gob of wet paint from Vito's nose.

"Do let us be more temperate," cooed Niki, to no one in particular. "We wouldn't want to 'rouse' such an extraordinary portrait!"

David set his picture up against the pit wall for display. But there was no audience for the likes of Lust in this fallen gallery, save for one, whose stare it held without release. It was David, alone among them, who could not turn away from his creation. As he had captured Lust, so his subject threatened to collar him—and would have too—had another imaginative head not lent a helping hand. David was too long oblivious to his friends' callings, when Christen stepped forward to break the portrait's mesmerizing hold. A simple flip of the canvas was all it took. With her face against the wall's ashen lips, her luring, lurid looks would intimidate them no further. The pilgrim once again heard friendly voices and turned to meet their smiles.

"Your linseed lover woos you still," said the lamb prince. "Now let the searing cinders kiss her burning mouth, and fuel the fire in her evil eye. Lust's lava kiln will bake its clay-cold model to brick and stone, and once the inferno cooks her oily venom dry and dead, no painted poison will flow through those pigmented veins to tempt nor torture us again."

Such a reaction to his painting left David quite stunned. "D-Did I do that... that portrait?" he asked dumbfounded.

"Nay," said Peter. "No mere portrait—but a masterwork—and by no other hand than yours, Davy."

"No sirree!" corrected Fidius. "More 'n a mere masterstroke... that there's a bloomin' creation!"

"You're both wrong," added Christen. "Nothing creative about it! No muse could conjure such evil. It's a replica of a witch's heart, right down to the last birthmark, bone, and blemish on that black blotch's soul!"

"A mirror could portray no image to equal it," agreed Niki. "No skin and painted mask is this we see, but a reflection of the essence of sin itself. 'Tis Lust stripped inside out, so maleficent that even its mistress will be repulsed to death at the very sight of herself."

"Your paints aren't magic, Davy," commented Valentina, "but your talent is, for you've painted us a marvel!"

His friends' and fairy maiden's words worked a miracle on David. A wide, pearly grin stroked across his lank depleted face. While the painting's countenance was thus turned away, Vito's eyes were now safe to gawk about, and so found some nerve to speak his mind too. "Ahh, what if it doesn't... work? This painter's prank that is." The question was posed innocently enough. But no responses were forthcoming, at least none that he could hear.

"Shut up, you despicable ass!" shouted Valentina, finally loud enough to impress even the earless. "It will work!... Tell him it'll work, Davy!"

"It will," hummed the happy artist. The feverish yoke was lifted now, framed and mounted on hell's wall. And David celebrated his spell of freedom by cleaning off his tools as though he might live to use them again one day. "Medusa fell for the same ploy. I'll bet that on Lust especially my 'mirror' will work its charm—even better than the shield of Perseus! These oils have the smell of truth in them, and such visions as they form will prove toxic for Lust's eyes to touch."

"Hee-haw," brayed the donkey prince. Whether or not he heard or understood any of David's talk was anyone's guess, but his questions continued to be discerning. "And by what device of ours do we seduce the prime seductress of souls to rejoin us in this soil and cinder cellar of hers? Have we not already impressed her as to its dangers and pitfalls?"

"By no device of ours," retorted David with a whistle, slapping Vito's back gaily, "but one of Lust's! Her vanity shall turn her head and tilt the tide of war as well... If only it's not too late!" The boy's whistling wilted as thoughts of dawn encroached to rekindle the fever David bore. "Does anyone know what time it is?..."

"The time is NOW!" snarled the forbidding voice of Medusa. At that moment a foul and reeking breath of sulfur air killed the candlelight, tossing the ditch once again into the dim and livid light of Lust's. "Damn candle!" cursed the dark angel from the rim above. "It sears my eyes! You'll need it not today or any after. What need of light have the dead!" cackled the jinn. "Blackness is our lamp this morn—and what a wonderfully wicked morning it is! The sun is rising shade, and Mythlewild is falling into my hands. Your new goddess is arrived, and you soot-lickers are mine! I am done with vain searching. My destiny—and yours, pilgrims—bides in this pit. My Glass Egg is found. It is here—with you—there can be no other place. Now... Give it to me!"

CHAPTER 54

Lust had torrid talent too, to conjure pictures in her own sulfuric style. No pretty portraits either these—but a grim genre, gross and ghastly enough to match her grisly gifts.

Long before the sun had summoned courage enough to show his paling face, Folly hovered in the ashen morning sky over Sovereignton in a delirious wamble. Even as dawn's harbinger hid behind the murky horizon, its trembling light lit upon the dimly devastated landscape of Lust's composing. Constantio's city, built and risen around the dreams of Bia Bella's impenetrable granite curtains, lay rent and ripped asunder. Toppled and racked in ruin, she reeled with every possible kind of chaos under siege of the black artist's lion.

A knave had come to insure DeSeet his victory. It was Negare's lacky, toting the rind of his oft' slain sire in saddlebags soaked and dripping red. Baptized in the bath of bloody battle deeds, the yellow clay-born husk did breathe again, and live to lead his lion lord on to the throne of Mythlewild.

"Sovereignton trembled to see the sallow shell reborn. Her great greystone walls were but crumbled embrasures, ground into red dust under the brutish, bloodied heels and hooves of iron-cast rebel routs. The grand barbicon was breached; her gates lay splintered before a hundred scudding hordes of unwelcome violators. The placating moat was left a soggy, stagnant resting place, spilled bloody thick and dank with decaying martyrs and sullied valor. Folly's wine well bottomed under a murrey-tinted cesspool, choked and stinking with a more rancid, redder brew. But the lusting lion legions thirsted for other spoils than ale, and so swept the city streets away of life, and ran amuck with rank and ruthless atrocities. With cold, callous vengeance, the barbarians did brand and batter the fair town. Leaving naught but turmoil in their tracks, the lion looters slayed and sacked her valiant defenders. No shop or store, nor house or hut, was spared annihilation. All property and life were crushed, no matter their worth to the heartless ones.

The yellow ogre's swarms stormed toward the city keep, to its very heart —the palace, Bia Bella. Her elegant donjon, scuffed and chinked, was the last to fall into the insurgents mortal grip. Bloodthirsty and battle-brazed, the clay-born generals tramped at will along the flesh-paved pathways. The godless-guided souls basked in the debris of death and destruction, and filled their lifeless lungs with the cries of suffering citizenry which strewn each avenue, and lined the bloating town square beneath the hoarding of the gutted gatehouse guarding Bia Bella.

Constantio's son, Prince Agustus, agonized at the spectacle. He had readied his city in fine store. But for time and for knights was the gull prince left lacking— and magic too—for it was the blackest of the genre that took the sovereign town. Despite their stoutest efforts, the royal garrison and gallant townsfolk had not the muscle to withstand the combined atrocities of the ogre general and DeSeet. Armed with sword-edged sorcery and mantled in witch-cast armored amulets, their fell armies, once merged, bore unmercifully upon the belabored citizen-soldiery, mustered and commanded most ably by the pirate prince. Howbeit, with only mortal men and remnant palace guardians to defend her, the boar queen, Superbia, after harrowing weeks of well engineered though futile resistance, was left no choice except to see their holdings surrendered—lest the lion set torch to town and palace both, and none but death be victor. Although, to the embattled survivors' minds, the dead were envied for their escape. Those not so blessed were ushered into dungeons, dovecotes, or stockyard pens; there they were chained and trammeled, and forced to bear witness to their city's execution. The monster masses now mashed the townsfolk's last life's hope into the humiliating servitude of defeat. Sovereignton lay overrun and belly up to await the final ripping maul of murderous lions, frenzied and drunk with victory, and sniffing spoils to line their liveries.

With the ogre led slaughter of hearts and hearths complete, the jaundiced general, Negare, wallowed in the wealth of laden palace treasure troves. His lion liege, DeSeet, emerged serene and safe, and securely settled onto the High King's regal throne, smiling his crooked predatory smile. Never mind that skirted around the remnant city walls was the real seat of authority, King Constantio, with his surviving retinue entrenched, and enraged—and prepared to get it back!

Alas, when the sundered citadel saw at last its former master come across the scarlet waterway, it was too late for cheer. The monarch had arrived from Cinnabar in one night's crossing on Windy's canvas wings, while his fleet rode the Rollingway's swift current towed by Abraxus and Isolato's rapid breaths. All could only gasp from heaving decks to behold their bleeding bastion. From every parapet and masthead the Decima's royal standards struck—usurped by DeSeet's black and yellow banners. These cerecloths shrouded the lofty heights of Bia Bella's towers, blotting the grey smoky dawn and casting dismal dark shadows over the rubble that was her harvest. Sovereignton, the beloved hamlet Constantio had sired, was stricken and near death, beckoning for relief.

Nevertheless, Constantio's despondent forces were powerless to restore their stronghold. DeSeet mocked them by allowing the ragtag troops to march entirely to the city gates unopposed. His doors were open in welcome no longer—but closed and locked to bar the landlord from his manor. The lions taunted them further from the wall walks by tossing foodstuffs plundered from the city's larders, and petty coins of raps and halfpennyies from the royal vaults, as a baron would drop a bread crust to intrusive beggars come a knocking at his door. The hungry, haggard kingsmen responded not with craving, but with steadfast discipline and pride—and outrage!

The king's knights ranged into ragged lines of assault. Each contingent assumed their positions and gathered gallantly in a fetching display of force behind Constantio, who dispersed his columns—like his resolve—in tireless portions. General Affirmare, Admiral Honos, Siegfried Dragonheart, and even the gravely wounded king's paladin, Violato the Red, dug in around their lord, and land—and cursed the day DeSeet would sit upon the throne of Mythlewild. With ferocity and wrath did the proud warriors of Theland fling the food and farthings back into the tawny walls above them.

As the royal army's agitation swelled to tidal proportions, their monarch, Constantio, shook off the persona of grief which had overtaken him. Upon first sighting the ravaged remains of his city, remorse had numbed his senses. To confront how such a tragedy befell his subjects was a torment his crown could scarcely bear. He was their head, and he deserted them... left their homes unprotected, and so vulnerable to beasts. He had jilted his beloved home too—the Bella. What unthinkable misfortune had befallen his household? "Superbia, my dearest... and my son, Agustus..." It was for worry of his own that the head of Theland sorrowed most.

"Would you lose the Mythlewild entirely, to hold one town?" broke a soft, reflecting voice. "Does the enemy not inflict enough torture on you, Highness? Save your sorrow, Sire. Theland is not lost to you yet—nor is your town—would you yearn it back!" So spoke Constantio's consoling crystal lady.

The touch of Clarissima's clear, pristine wisdom on his thoughts was a mighty comfort to her king. Jo was with the glass seer, and the billiken's wide, pink-eyed smile of optimism equally persuaded the downcast monarch to furl his sadness and hoist his battered teakwood club along with his spirits. He squared his piercing, raven eyes to thank the grand sibyl and her wag. "It is all our homes that lie taken, is it not dear lad and lady? We shall both be better served to bear our arms instead of tears—and TAKE them back again!"

The pink-skinned brownie raised his sword to teakwood. Clarissima too brandished a borrowed blade. Others were quick to join: crusader's broadsword, Northman's too—Byne Un and Byne Tu together—and the bull admiral's saber, together with the king's captain. Soon, all soldiers' blades were drawn and pointed in rally of their high lord. Swords and spirits from the ten corners of Theland all meshed into one unified handful of hearts. Oaths were sworn on steel, to buy back their homes with blood, not booty stolen from their own purses.

Such a ceremonious boost of confidences stirred even through the heavy hanging clouds of despair and into the sky, which Folly patrolled in frantic loops and spirals, not knowing just which way to turn. Constantio had dispatched the valiant hippo on a desperate mission to seek help. But from Folly's vantage point, it was obvious that aid of any kind would not be forthcoming. From every direction that he could see, any flight would prove futile. There was no course left to take, no port of refuge or relief. Black plumes of destruction billowed from every hamlet, house, and holding across Theland. The whole winter face of Mythlewild was starkly scarred and blighted: from the Wild Wealds and Western Reaches, eastward to the seaboard and the high frigid firths of the North Holds; and down again into the Low Moors and deep South Swards. For hope, Theland looked heartward, past the commons of East Down, toward Middleshire—and the Serenity Plain—on this demesne did the extant fate of Mythlewild reside. Yet from every angle, every sight he saw, it was evident to Folly—that Fate was wearing black.

Meanwhile, below the battered gate of Sovereignton, Constantio's vociferous challenge had fallen short. From the gatehouse keep, viler salvos announced the lion count's arrival. When at last DeSeet emerged from out of the throne room, bedecked in boar hair and lion linen finery, and promenaded to the gatewall's highest standing rooftree, the powerful pierce-eyed king dulled and pursed away. All his ranks did lower their arms and raise their brows to gape in dismay; not at the treacherous lion, but because brought there with him were Superbia the queen, and the young gull prince Agustus, who together had mounted such a noble, though vain, defense. Each was bound fast, blindfolded and gagged, completely helpless and at the mercenary's mercy. He balanced them precariously on the battlement—to the very brink of death—at their throats, a dagger point. It was an edge which cut off the loudest cheer and bent every witness to silence while the cat count spoke in sharpest tones through crooked teeth.

"You've trod quite far enough, little liege, all trapped out in skins of lions. But now your prowl is done, and I, the king of beasts, have assumed the 'king of leasts' lair. Though your seat feels fine, I would give the crown you wear a fit before you lose your head, and title too—"

"Jackal! screamed Constantio, gathering all his remaining strength and beating the ground with teakstick. "Unscrupulous, usurping, butchering, coward! Deserting Cinnabar to stab at women and children!"

"Cinnabar has spared you too, king of squat!" gloated the lion. Now...tell me my mercy is unwanted here! You may ask your hogtied wife and wren. What a pity they cannot answer."

Constantio's anger hawked up the lofty precipice. "You're a cornered mongrel, DeSeet! If any harm is laid on my family—you shall soon be a dead one too!"

The jeering lion just stroked his plundered robes and laughed like a crazed hyena as he prodded the hostages with his knife. "You've surrounded my city with remnants of your 'runtling' regalia; but for all your tribe, it's you in the corner, drowning like a wog in a well... and wanting one last drink."

DeSeet jabbed his prisoners again ever so slightly, causing the portly pork queen to teeter on the gusty parapet heights. Superbia sent out a muffled cry, and her helpless husband far below choked his club as though DeSeet's throat.

Violato and Siegfried vied for the honor of shooting an arrow through his vile heart. Honos' voiced similar opinion. But wiser counsel was served on pink and crystal words. "The queen and prince's hearts are dear to us all, My King; but they are nearer now, in flesh, to DeSeet. We dare not miss so fine a mark with an angry, ill-shot bow." Everyone heeded Clarissima's words. Yet Jo was quick to catch the fuming enmity struck in Affirmare's eyes upon spotting his reborn bane, Negare was lurking under the turrets. The ogre's two-face ax was poised over the heads of numerous other hostages, among them, Elder Ambrose and his family.

"Upon my oath, that hulk will raise his ax no more beyond this day!" So he swore to Yang, his ever present squire. The crusader's stare would not stray from his clay-born adversary. Just as Constantio would not shrink from the boasting, bestial cur above the battlement looming betwixt the merlons which protected him.

"Take pride in your spouse and spud," DeSeet mewed. "Had they not been so understaffed of men and magic, who knows... you might be treading on your throne and not your grave. 'Twas a pity they found the dungeon more defensible than their fort. Still alive as you can see, they are, alas, like the rest of your possessions—mine! You're no more master here, King 'cub'—this house belongs to lions! Now summon up your strays, and begone before I give you back your litter, and join them to you at the basewall, with their lives, like your cause, lay forfeit. Another overzealous poke, and Superbia began to topple.

"NO!" Constantio cried out, helpless and gasping.

At that moment a third pawn, not so tightly wrapped or watched, owing to his slight and scroungy size, now leaned forward and nudged the queen safely backward from the edge of the blockhouse, where her balance was restored. The breathless throng below began to buzz and speculate on this new lag's identity. But the near tragedy had left its indelible mark upon Constantio.. Falling back on his cloud and searching for voice, the maligned monarch bitterly resigned his reign. "Lay back..." he commanded lifelessly. "All of you...back—"

"My King," counseled Clarissima, "it is not wise to leave our city in despots' jaws. 'Tis plain the count is quite insane, and the situation cannot but worsen..."

As his glass lady spoke of that which was unbearable to hear, Constantio looked up at his wife and son only a step away from their deaths. He could not imagine how. The gnawing, gnashing melancholy the king was feeling permeated into each of his command. Such a grueling mood stooped even the sky.

Watching from on high, Folly wept with his king. Frantic and inflated with worry, he paced the air in nervous scoots and darts, bow in hand and arrows readied, waiting for some chance to prove useful just one more time. The cherub archer wanted so to be beside his lord. Thus, with no place to flee, the hippo plummeted to the fight. His Highness needs his friends... I must get to him, thought Folly, descending as fast as a bulky barrel of lead towards the city gate.

He could see Constantio's generals mustering by their king as the loyalists regrouped to consider strategy. Also, Folly watched the lion man as he preened and gloated from the blockhouse in his victory, continuing to taunt his prisoners, and exchanging sneers with his ogre cohort below the turrets. "Oh poor, poor Superbia and little Agustus. How frightened they must be. And the other one—that scraggly one... Who pray tell might that one be?"

Folly broke his descent hastily upon sighting his own cherished wine well, now so woefully fouled by spilled blood. The proud gatekeeper was in turn filled with an ire unbeknownst to him before. "Murderers! Barbarians!" he bellowed.

Peering so intently below him, the floating hippo was unaware of the advance of new and present dangers, that is, until the blare of distant thunder stifled any further thought or moves. Faint at first, like wind, but foreboding in its tone—it was nothing natural. Suddenly, it was a tumult! It was a chest-pounding onslaught of wails and howls, like ghosts or shrieking banshees, striking the earth like a hundred bursting thunder claps.

Folly ducked behind a cloud in a start. He looked southward and saw a graveyard horde of demons, goblins, and ghouls roaring like a fiery eclipse over the plain. "Oh my!" shrieked the cherub. "It's the witch woman's clay-born cult...and Horros! That demon ape is leading them!" Folly opened his wide hippo mouth in an ear blistering scream. "SIRE! SIRE!... They're COMING!... LOOK OUT!" Constantio's chubby champion on wing continued to warn, "Your trapped! It's Horros... The bat is back! You've been lured to the city steps only to be set upon!" Unfortunately, as with most lessons in our lives, which are seldom learned until experienced, Folly's warning was past due. It was not blast enough to crack the din of gloom below, and not in time to be useful. Lust's champion bane had arrived, heading a host of surviving clay-born. The king's angel clambered back into the sky, as if to make his prayers more accessible to heaven. And while the heavens listened, Folly watched painfully, as Lust's mercenaries nailed their coffin trap shut around Constantio.

The king held to his ground at the foot of the city's walls, undeterred and unconquerable as grit. All the while, DeSeet baited him from the battlements above. Constantio's generals massed their dogged troops together in formation, building a defensive curtain of mail and men behind their king. But what a brittle and badly beaten wall it was, no more capable of withstanding Horros' attack than the city's brick and mortar buttresses had held against Negare and DeSeet. They were not combating mere armies as they had at Cinnabar—nor even simple magic. These were hell's elite, Luhrhollow's invincible soldiers of sorcery. To the cutthroat goblin, troll, and orge goths, add the clay-born carcasses who bore their death as armor. Constantio's flesh and battle-ragged knights were no match for any army manned and mantled thus.

When Folly had finished with his prayers, he recalled his well, and his king —and wound into a death-spiralling nose dive toward his floundering countrymen. He would abandon neither death, nor duty.

Suddenly, racing ahead of him by a nose, was a screeching condor. Folly pulled up dead in his tracks, as another condor appeared, and still another, knocking the lubberly hippopotamus topsy-turvy about the clouds until the sky became a churning, chattering, crowded nest teeming with raven-down and tearing claws and clacking buzzard beaks.

"I might've guessed that vultures would follow the luring scent of carrion," grunted Folly, bearing no fond memories of these flies of Lust's. The undaunted hippo held his air space courageously, and mounted a cloudy steed just like his leader. The cherub reached for his arrows, ready to die in arms—like a true kingsman!

But lo—the condors were not! In fact, they did not even pause to threaten such a feast as Folly, in such haste and havoc they flew. Then he noticed that these black fowls were not attacking at all—they were beating a retreat. And in a headlong hurry did they scuttle their sky. But from what could they be fleeing wondered Folly, scratching his unicorn stump.

Then an eagle appeared in their midst—a great bald eagle—and Folly knew. The heavens HAD listened! "Palladan!" he called. But Enduros' favorite paid no heed. Such was the intensity of his attack. And Palladan was not alone. A profusion of sousing golden eagles swept from the cloud banks, and the inky sky tinted gold, as the sun now dared to show his face. Eagles replaced vultures for dominion of the sky.

And on the heels of eagles flew providence, the warriors on the wind. Out of the north sky they stormed, like a welcome winter washing snow, on gold and silver chariots and monumental white-winged mounts. It was Enduros, lord of all earth, and godhead, fronting a hailing host of immortal knights. The mountain 'dotard' had sifted his ten realms of their godly gallants and, under stealth of Lust's own night, sallied them hither for this dawn blitz into Sovereignton.

Before Folly could comprehend the whirlwind around him, he had become one of their numbers. "I promised I would help!" It was Vero's voice. The king's white knight soon found himself flying alongside the prince of gods and men, and his stallion Paramount; but was too choked to speak amid his accompanying titan vanguard. Never in all his drunken dreams of wake or fancy had Folly imagined such a spectacle as this soaring and swirling around him now. What an honor!

The sky became a vibrant, shining sheet of pearl and platinum. And heaven's horns did sound the charge of earth-down deities to harken their arrival. Down they streamed in endless waves, on eagle wings and wakes of alicorn. Down poured the magic melting snow to quench the fire which scathed the land of lords and men and more.

Folly looked with awestruck wonderment at Enduros, glittering and brilliant as a blazing comet on his platinum-winged chariot, looking every bit the lord of legend: powerful, august, stirring, and inspiring supreme fealty among his divine following. The mighty lord of Mythlewild commanded his army of gods into the ash and anguish below.

All heads gazed skyward with shielded eyes; for such a luster they saw dimmed the sun to shame. Just as the sight of Horros on the horizon slew Constantio, the vision now espied resurrected him, and spurred his liegemen to cheers and swords.

Now it was the lion man's turn to stand and shudder. Stunned and immovable, DeSeet cursed the changing sky and swallowed his crooked teeth—and in this lapse, Constantio saw his chance—and grabbed it.

On command, his cloud pedestal bolted upwards, as did the king's thoughts. War is a madness which scars us all, DeSeet. But your sores will no more inflict my home this day. 'Tis time to lick the fatal wound my own cudgel can rend!

The powerful, little king hefted teakstick with trenchant sureness and cocked his steel will arm for all his worth. He thought only of his wife and son... and past failings. But he would not come up lacking this time.

The lion man looked down from his fit too late. He saw coming at him only one unremitting, chest-shattering blow. Constantio's club had been hurled with such a vengeful velocity that nothing would have stayed it from its target. Jarred from his loophole, death greeted DeSeet with bone-crushing ferocity, and insanity fell to a finer madness—love. The lion pretender was nothing but splinters and matted meat when he crashed earthward into the bloody mud behind the gate of Sovereignton. The dirt smiled a soiled and crooked crack as it consumed ambition's remains. In a befitting funeral, the count was further buried under other yellow fleeing feet. Negare sounded a farewell dirge, and cursed one last, relishing defilement on his former liege when he stomped the maned cadaver into his earthen throne—there to rule the worms with his witchy paramour.

"Is victory sweet, Governor? Is your realm rewarding? Rot in them then!" snarled Negare, pausing only to lay some final, freshly-cut aspersions on his count.

"Rot together, yellow dastard!" challenged Affirmare, poised in the gateway and barring any further retreat, thus trapping his arch foe into the dilemma of a fair contest.

So thwarted, the ogre hesitated again to ponder fearfully his fate, like a badger at bay. In desperation, the beast hurled his ax at Affirmare, and for the while it took to dodge the throw, the varmint made his break. Through the barbican he raced, but in the time he gained did lose the match. For there, under the hoarding, did the fallow fellow make his final, fateful pause. His last curiosity saw Sir Affirmare stanced at the gate sockets. "Byne Un," he shouted, before severing the chain which held the portcullis open. The massive, iron-spiked grid closed dutifully on the hulk that was once Negare. But though the king's doorway did have her villain spit and gutted, it remained for the crusader to lay the final telling blow. "Escape me not this day, Negare, for by my edge you'll die!" And with the heavy bladed steel of Byne Un, Affirmare did bring the butchered blood of citizens to bear upon the ogre's neck—and filled the lion's grave with clay-born sod. "No blood of massacre will you drink again to live; for now you lay without a heart—or head.

No lackey will unpack you from this death, Negare!" And with those words the crusader's loyal page dispatched the ogre's varlet, then together Yang and Affirmare clasped hands triumphantly.

"Well done, brave knights!" praised Constantio, still fresh from his coup. "But let us not linger here, lest we lose our edge as well." With his own family safe for the bye, their sire began to grapple tooth and nail to extricate his kindred hearts. Through the open gates of Sovereignton charged the courageous columns of the king to liberate their home from death. Shouts of "Affirmare" were heard, and some trumpets sang out in welcome to Constantio. Citizens, soldiers, all present men and immortals too—the ones that could—did lift their voice and arms for Mythlewild—and for those who would win it back.

When Enduros' host landed upon the Serenity Plain, victory seemed assured. It was gods against goblins. Ogres battled omnipotents as the awesome earth lord's army engulfed the field of war. With his titan son, Vero, by his side, the 'dotard' deity fought with the strength of a true earthshaker. "Lust!" shouted the aged god, "In your absence I will thrash your seeds!" And the mage's maggot minions scattered before her brother's might.

Folly lighted heavily on the enemies atop his gatehouse. Witnessing their leaders so decisively slain left the lot of them with no nerve to fight. Under a pelting curtain of arrows, they followed their stomachs in deserting the tower keep—many in the same stiff manner as their lion. Lofting next to the blockhouse, the fearless hippo freed Queen Superbia and Prince Agustus, and the other one—the frowzy little fleck—who had saved the queen. The group of them then lent further clout to the fray around them. Halting now, to gather arrows and a second wind, Folly took ecstatic notice of the reclamation of his town.

Once inside the outer curtain, Captain Violato managed to help free the captive citizens and so equip those partisans that were able to join in the melee's counterpunch. The bestirred townsfolk took up ogres' discarded weapons, and fought with intense rejuvenation, driving the disbanded invaders from their homes. Woman and warrior, knights next to knaves, and boys beside their heroes—all came to scratch in soldiers' shadows.

From the forebuilding, Ambrose and young Patrick bolstered the lines of retaliation along the gatewall surrounding the city's inner wards, and matched their foes blow for blow, like a pair of seasoned scrappers. And putting them all to shame was Celeste. Halo askew, the matronly archangel smashed heads expertly with the king's best; there was no counting the ogre carcasses that lay cleft and quartered in her footfalls. Valentina's mama obviously did not wear her chain mail apron solely for housework.

Folly's chubby, white cheeks brightened to see such a turnabout. He would not have been surprised to see their infant girl, Jing Jing, engaged in combat too; but instead, the elder's babe lay curled in Fearsome's protective custody. The pup's three snarling heads and slashing tail were effective warning to any dastard who would snatch a last fleeing life. For the most part however, the lion's scattering henchmen were more pressed to conserve their own lives than to steal others.

Outside the city curtain, Sir Dragonheart's command held position, lest the turn tail fiends make off, only to regroup some future day to haunt them. Admiral Honos meanwhile, laid back to his fleet. Aboard Miss Windy, any and all escape by ship was quelled. On the bridge was the pilot, Pax. The griffin controlled his helm, and still found hand enough to salute his friend, Folly, in a reassuring sign of confidence.

By this time, Affirmare paired with Clarissima and Jo at the palace keep, were brawling to retake their fortress. And when the Bella was won back they so signaled Constantio who held the blockhouse guarding the city's entrance. With their waving, the wan monarch felt the easement of a lifetime's burden. His wife and son were safe—and so too was his city, Sovereignton.

When the last rebel residue had been beaten from their city's walls, and royal standards of the Decima were raised again over Bia Bella, Constantio heaved a hearty, well earned sigh of relief, and gathered his friends and family around him in tearful reunion. Superbia smothered her husband in a massive ham hug, and praised Folly for this moment. "We all owe you eternal thanks, intrepid Folly!" pronounced the boar queen. "The heavens' aid you brought us has delivered our township back."

The albino hippo blushed a bulbous pink, his wings all aflutter. "Shucks... Enduros' advent was none of my doing," Folly explained.

Constantio next turned an eye towards his son—and the infested looking soul beside him who had risked his life for the queen. "Agustus, my boy! And this one?... Whoever you be, you saved my beloved—and my gratitude is yours for it!" Constantio studied the strange creature long and hard, but knew not what to make of the buggy little figure, who merely muttered incoherently to himself, seemingly ignorant of the day's deeds, and wishing for some blessed solitude again. "Speak up, lad!" bade His Highness. "Pray find some name or tongue for your king... Do I know you?"

The authoritative voice only served to chase the jittery thing away. He tucked his hairy head shyly behind Agustus, who draped a brotherly arm around him and began to explain to Constantio, who was left waiting for some response.

"Father... neither he nor I can answer you. His name is lost; except it that he is our kinsman. He has saved our lives—not only on this precipice—but in the dungeons, where he has dwelled all these years unbeknownst to us. Don't ask me how, but he survived, even thrived, in those environs... though it wears on him oddly."

The shaggy little lad unfurled a long, sticky bug tongue as if snapping at a flea, or maybe just in agreement with Agustus, who continued the tale as his father listened with keen interest. "When DeSeet imprisoned us, it was our friend here who provided food, foraged from his own home-grown stores. Roach and rats were the only fare, but it kept us alive and strong no less." Constantio scrutinized his son's new found friend with accelerating joy. Could his far-fetched thoughts possibly be true? Regretfully, he was not to know for sure—not yet.

Agustus' story was cut short as a gold-winged stallion streaked from the sky. Paramount came to a halt atop the block, where Folly measured his own wings against the divine steed's. "Vero!" exclaimed Constantio, bowing to the prince of gods. "Were the world mine to give, I would—for you and your grandsire have given me more!"

But the golden pride of deities dismounted silently, and his steps were mortally heavy. "Laud me not, great monarch of mortal hearts. Horros has escaped me," lamented the star-faced titan, who for the last hours had embattled Lust's prime demon. "The bat has shrunk into air, and blown away on some southbound wind..."

"Sensing certain defeat, all cowards shrink off," boasted the king.

"Or, in answer to a more urgent distress call for survival." Vero stared beyond the far horizon.

"High Prince... my lamb son, Christen? Have you news?" inquired Constantio with anxiety. "I'm told you took him under roof?"

Sensing the strong concern, Vero leveled a grim reply to the worried sovereign. "When my father and I set off, the lamb prince was safe atop Mount White... yet, still spellbound by the black queen's bewitchment. Lust departed you at Cinnabar because she saw a greater peril—the pilgrim boy, David, threatened her. As we departed Revrenshrine, the boy was leaving for a showdown with my estranged aunt. I believe Christen joined him and his companions in answer to the jinn's challenge, and to break the spell which strickened him—"

"In that case, we must rescue them!" exclaimed Constantio, boiling once more. "We'll move out immediately! You will join us, Prince?!"

Vero was reserved. "Good King... Would you leave your city again with the plague still frothing on its lips? Clay-born trailings wait this minute to return and finish their 'pig' roast!"

"But... we've WON, Lord Prince—the city is ours!"

"Won, have we? Look—look there; see how my father, Enduros is celebrating."

"Constantio and the others met the titan's sullen gaze and scanned the scene below them. The earth lord and his host persisted to battle the witch monster's minions. Gods and goblins both continued spilling blood. Black or red, the ground soaked it up in equal laps. Palladan's eagles still patrolled the air, as condors sustained menacing circles in a safer sky. And in prolonged skirmishing at the foot of the city walls, knights and rebels were ever knotted in mortal combat. Violato's reopened wounds had forced him to rest. Celeste nursed the red knight while Ambrose and Patrick helped shore up the gaping walls. Sir Siegfried faltered, and fell back behind the city portals, joining forces with Affirmare, else alone the one

653

might weaken. And left at Bia Bella, Clarissima and Jo did grand guardians make, though the crystal and the joker both were wearing thin. On the banks of the Rollingway, Honos was hard pressed to stave the surging exodus. Even the leviathan, Abraxus, was but an ocean drop unable to douse the fanning fire. Lust's malevolent power still flowed like blood in the veins of her clay-children.

"They have purloined some pluck from their panic!" Vero emphasized. "Look at your city, good King; its walls are still sponged with faults. How much blood can its stones absorb? Will your brave liegemen ever wring it clean again?"

Constantio milked his beard as he looked to disagree with the titan lord; alas, the truth would not serve him. "But, we had them on the run... Their lion head is dead... and their ogre musle too... Even that blue monstrosity has skipped the field."

"Who knows for what dark purpose Horros fled? As for your Count DeSeet, the lion is but one head—and a weak one—to lose. Negare had more tooth, but the tally still stands at two. There are legions more to fill their steps. And woe to count the clay-born, whose numbers will continue to swell as more are slain. Their yellow guts deserted them, but their brooding, black heart still lives to pump sustenance, brave Constantio—and beat us all into her ground's defiles." Vero stiffened now, and Paramount unfolded his set of golden wings. "Good King, the best help I can proffer is to advise: do not underestimate my aunt, the animus. You have seen the consequence of such miscalculation. You have your holding back again—but can you hold it? We have not lost, but neither have we won. As long as Lust has life, her poison's punch must be reckoned with." Abruptly the Titan Prince took flight again, to do his reckoning beside his struggling father.

Constantio was left to deal with his own reign. At the mention of Lust's name, his thoughts had turned to his adopted son, Christen—and his orphaned son, David—who at this moment bore the witch's wrath face to face. Only for the briefest moment was the doughty monarch permitted to reflect. The enmity in his thoughts aroused a solemn oath:

"I will fight you, Evil—my gods, and men, and me.

And right will win, though dead;

Killed, but not conquered

654

Buried, but not beaten—Never!

In the end, I will defeat you, Evil,

My gods, and men, and me..."

Then familiar, urgent voices called to him, and grim reality advanced upon the gate tower. Constantio retrieved his teakstick and hefted the increasingly heavy scepter again into arms; once again, squaring his thewy shoulders, the High King mounted his cloud steed and led his entourage once more into the pitch of battle.

Flesh was split and bones cracked, and the sun still cowered in some grey secluded sky. Try as he might, he could not shine, nor ward off the trenchant darkness. Least of all could any amber ray touch upon the secret, southernmost intimacy that was Luhrhollow. Nor could it, or any other gaze, penetrate its deepest, blackest pitfall.

CHAPTER 55

Most people believe histories hinge upon great events in distant lands, forged from the extraordinary acts of some select few, which we call 'heroes'. However, as you shall discover, the truly momentous wars of time are seldom waged on bastion or battlefield, nor joined by celebrated kings or transcendent immortals. The magnitude of profound conflict can be ruled by no measure, save for simple acts of brave men, facing impossible odds, with unyielding courage. Not the High King Constantio, nor divine lord of the earth, Enduros; neither the vast plain of Cinnabar, nor the towering city citadel of Sovereignton, could surpass in sum or substance that conflict being joined within the dismal dirt defile called Luhrhollow, by a small band of common souls, armed in valor, shielded with an iron-clad troth, and wielding nothing so deadly as an ordinary set of artist's colors. By any measure its outcome was unrivaled.

"I don't know the Egg's whereabouts, and that's that!" repeated David for the umpteenth time. The words only rang up from the crevasse and smote Lust's ears rudely. Dressed out in red gown and black slough, the wanton witch grumbled atop the fissure's rim. The lamb's spell broke on her impatience. A thorough search of her vaults left her wanting. The Glass Egg still eluded her. Such mysteries as those holed in these dirt cellars plagued the angel of black to the point of panic.

"Like your conquest, your magic too is failing!" twittered Niki at the top of her lungs. "Blame us if it solaces you, wench; you'll gain no Egg from our brooding!"

"Well! My flighty, pip-squeak pigeon... then it shall be mine to find, and mine alone to keep! As for you little nestlings, it's for sure you'll chirp no more this morn—nor any after! Your singed wings will burn off in my lava ovens to be served before my supping lion mate, who now celebrates his conquest of Sovereignton. Horse meat, mutton, lizard legs, and succulent sprite shall be his breakfast fare. Cackle... And you, you chittering, squawking squab, might slake my Horros' hunger —while this tough and gristly pilgrim portion will be MY feast!"

"Hee-haw," brayed the mule man, perhaps in pleading for a merciful favor or two of his former potentate.

But the loyalty of lechery is null, and Lust merely spat upon her past mistakes and turned her nose. "As for you, damn Vito, your meat—like your mettle —is too mealy and too stringy... And to hell with you all!"

"If you please, madam," spoke David, clearing his throat of all but pious frauds, while trying to foist the hag with courtesy. Lust was, after all, a woman. Though an ugly beauty blurred by seductive fronts, she was nonetheless prone to her own feminine frailties of vanity and flattery. "My friends and I freely admit that as of now, our cause is lost. You've an edge over us that we cannot hope to surmount. You've beaten us... and we submit—"

"Submit? My Tail!" steamed Fidius, before his aged composure and Peter's swift kick silenced his tempered tongue. The old lizard and his colt quickly fell silent, with fixed and sincere faces to match their companions, who strained to their limits in looking half as chaste as David sounded.

Lust lowered her skeptical eye into the dimly lit trench to scan its captives for any clues of contradiction in such a sudden striking of colors. Her stare fixed on Vito who, more than any other, stood remarkably rigid as one well-versed and varnished in the company of deception—and cowered only when the witch's eye was turned.

David cast a sly smile on the donkey deceiver. "I beg you, madam, indulge the doomed a final whim..."

"'Madam'? So now it's 'Madam' hag is it? Well curse my black soul, brat, if you're not flattering this woman, slinging manner instead of mud my way." Lust curled her thick ash lips at the pilgrim showering such unexpected amenity and resignation. "Possibly you are not so stupid, fleshling?"

"No, madam... I'm not! And to further prove the point, my compeers and I would pay homage to our queen conqueror, as befits a lordess of your 'rank'."

Lust's brows rose high before a wide slicing smile. "'Homage'?... a 'lordess' you say?" The jinn grew more enthusiastic on each bent word and crooked compliment.

And in turn, David's own zeal mounted with each new confidence gained. "Yes, Your Lordess-ship... it's a victory offering of a sort. Do the vanquished not typically render their betters some spoil? A bounty which may live after us who have been sacrificed before our queen? Or, consider it a tribute... our way of seeing you receive a fitting reward for your 'victory'."

"A tribute? To me? Why... I'm overwhelmed!" Steam drops escaped from Lust's remaining eye—or perhaps, for a moment, they might have been specks of tears from a lady unused to gifts since ages past. "What is it?" asked the lost angel eagerly.

"A portrait, madam," boasted David, tipping his canvas from the wall, then ducking quickly behind it as if it were a breastplate. "A fine portrait of you, Your Lordess-ship... so your true beauty may be exhibited for all times to 'reflect' upon. Won't you please come down and look at it," he coaxed. "You'll feel like a new woman."

Niki weaned, "It captures your charms perfectly, does it not, fellows!"

"A simply beautiful likeness," vamped Valentina, chewing her pale lips.

"'Beautiful' is not the word to describe it," smirked Christen.

"It's utterly indescribable," agreed Peter.

"You have ta lay eyeballs on it ta believe it—yes sirree," added Fidius flicking his tail for effect.

"Can't take your 'eye' off it!" blurted Vito, hoping no one had flung such a witty jab yet. The mule prince was proud to step forward in rally to his new friends' support—but cautious, as the others had been, to avoid actually looking upon Lust's image.

"A portrait, eh... of me? Why, artist, how flattering! Let me see it...cackle!" The witch began to dance about on the pit rim like a crackling fire as the pilgrims' wheedling took spark. "Vito! Be a dear and bring me my dues."

"B-But, mistress..." fawned the mule man, "... I cannot get out."

"Of course you can't, my mind is clogged." A purple blush found the siren's face as further proof of her mortality. "Toss it to me then, like a good ass—"

"Oh no—you mustn't!" exclaimed David. "That would ruin everything... er, the paint is still wet you see... only its surface is baked to a finish."

"So be it," grumbled Lust, growing rapidly thin-skinned under the ticklish toading of conceit. "I'll use my magic."

"You'll waste it in this hole, witch... I mean, bewitching one!" bleated Christen, trying so hard to hide his contempt. "Your charms desert you in these deep digs, black beauty," he said, and gestured to some familiar artifacts, "as your eye and shock of hair can testify. Could it be your audience of nestlings unnerves you?"

You've nerve in excess, mutton!" growled Lust furiously. "Bleat all you want; I'll soon tuck you in again to sleep—under death's covers this time!"

Yet for all her threats, the witch and her magic remained on the chasm rim. "Like the lamb said, crone—your parlor tricks don't work on us anymore!" Valentina blurted in uncontrollable anger. She refused to pander such an evil beldame a minute more. Soap and sweet-talk might trip her into their shaft, but ire would urge her harder, she thought. Lust paced the ridge in skittish frustration. She cursed and kicked and flailed the dirt like rain upon her prisoners, but took no steps into the trough. The truth was a sharp sword. Her magic HAD failed her in this pilgrim's presence, and wary would be her next move on him.

"The old witch withers with courage!" blared Christen, mocking the queen of defile for all the world to hear, now that their ruse was off. "You should blush her portrait's face in yellow, David—to the queen of COWARDS goes the spoil!"

To this new offensive flattery, Lust was ponderously unyielding—almost. It just so happened that the pilgrims had a pair of allies heretofore untapped: one being 'vanity', more lethal to ladies than any weapon; and the other, 'anger', the graveyard of reason. Both had a hand in landing Lust at last into the pitfall. From the furor of her rabid airs, ego's mistress balked into the cavity. It took less than a heartbeat for her to fall into their midst.

The ditch dwellers scattered in her presence. Her ebon shoulders nearly reached the rim as she loomed, out of fear perhaps, in massive proportions among her captives. With only a canvas sheet between himself and hell, David remained by his work, with Niki on his collar. The boy wanted so much to stand up to Lust. Though he lacked the height, his stature was immense, he was to be the only giant in this hole.

"Have all your friends left you, whelp?... with their words and wrath and wooings? I will have my homage now, cackle... Then dance upon its dead creator's bones until time's end! Give me your labors, pilgrim! And let me be gone to better business!"

As befits the supremely selfish, Lust's last living act was one of taking, and most dearly did it cost her. From their hidaways, the companions looked on increduously as David willingly surrendered his masterpiece. The fatal face turned into the witch's wresting grip, wherein its raw nature was exposed to Lust, who held it at arms length. Thereupon, the reflection assaulted its source—attached itself to her unyieldingly—and would not let go. Witched eyes locked onto each other and swelled hard and wide in horror. For the first time in life, Lust stood eye to eye with her own visage. There the soul and siren together froze in a dead match of vanities, and baked like bricks in evil's kiln. With all the powers of heaven and hell at her beckoning, the prime of prides could not shake its impasto gaze. The encounter was brief—mercifully so. Sin's angel cursed to crack and quake the hallow caverns. Her oily image cursed her back with even louder wailings, and all the earth trembled in their stead.

"Damn you, pilgrim!" was her screaming, scorching epitaph. Then Lust was silent forever more. Her soft, smooth, snakeskin turned to coal hard stone, a soul black gravestone so grotesque, the pitch darkness paled to bear it.

David too stood still as a rock. After an eternity of silence, soft cooing pierced the quiet. In sweet, tender tones Niki assured the boy... yes it was true. "Lust is dead, painter—it is done!"

David's friends now gathered around him to gawk—and even inspect—the stark results of his uncompromising toil: a forbiddingly lovely visage, chiseled into a cadaverous specter of repelling horror—such is evil's beauty. And when the nightmarish truths were realized by the band of brave souls, they cheered passionately.

"Bravo, artist! She's dancing to slower drumbeats now," bleated Christen. "The muddy mage has finally met her match!"

"Lust slew Lust," said David modestly, as if his triumph was just another sketch.

"Only because nothing less repulsive could turn the trick," quipped Peter.

"Yur durn tootin'," wheezed Fidius, comparing the cracks and chinks in Lust's crusty hide to his. "Even petrified, she's uglier than drool!"

"Statuesque," commented Valentina. "She's a brimstone bust, staring eternally upon her own flesh freezing face—a permanent monument to lust, and all who would crave it."

With no warning the after shock came. Luhrhollow grieved—or was it merely more applause for an ulcer healed. Whatever, as the coke and cinder floor pitched, and the pit walls rocked, the companions fought to maintain their balance. Then the cavern ceiling collapsed around them—but miraculously, not upon them. And when the earth had had its say, the dim unetheral glow of Luhrhollow was extinguished.

"Hee-haw... Where's the light!" whined Vito, scrambling around in a fright, kicking his heels and diving for cover under Lust's hair nest. Having little hearing left, he now feared his sight was lost to him too.

"No need to curse the darkness anymore, brother," calmed Christen. "This hell's fire has just died with its mistress."

"Even in her death the trench warden imprisons us," scowled Valentina. "How will we ever get out of here now. We're all as blind as bats!"

"Not bats," said David. A smile lighted his face as a bright glow began to illuminate their bleak hovel. "We're pilgrims!" And there he stood, with his amazing candle in hand. "I believe we've overstayed our welcome here. Shall we go! We've no time to lose. Mythlewild is in the hands of hellions, and we're still stuck in this trench!"

"Right—and WILL stay too, unless you can find us stairs as easily as light to take us out of our rut." Peter had been sauntering around and around the rubble in search of some means to escape. He was not at all cheered by the crumbled prospects.

"The walls ain't so steep as before, li'l' colt." Fidius cleaned off his specks and squinted past his upturned snout. "It's been sort a heaved and spewed around after the dugout's belchin'. We could still use a step or two though."

"The scree has left us stones enough to build a stairway out," suggested Val. "It's not rocks we lack, but time," said David, who sat upon Lust's toe, while pondering Niki as she skittered up to the stone witch's knee, and then on to her waist. Soon the little dove's antics caught the others' eyes.

"Well!..." she chirped from Lust's belly button, "...what're you all staring at? We can't step out whild sitting on our rumps, can we!"

It was an exuberant train of companions that filed up from their prison shaft on a sturdy staircase provided by—of all figures—Lust. "What a perfect hostess!" cracked Christen, as the lamb prince shimmied up Lust's leg just ahead of Vito who was the last to leave their hole, and did so very reluctantly. With his queen dead, the only master left to fear was his own father, the king. The mule man had no warm anticipation for what awaited his treachery at his step-sire's hands. For a talisman, he packed his prior mistress' hair along to bring him luck; and once atop her bare head, paused to bid her farewell.

They all stood clustered there to catch their breath as on a landing searching for some new steps. "Take care to avoid looking upon the painter's pretty picture," warned Niki. "You see how it admonishes admirers."

"I believe your model doesn't like your present, Davy," chuckled Valentina from Lust's brow. "She's not smiling!"

"Nonesense," said Christen from her nose. "It's such a perfect likeness, it has left her speechless!"

"She was never prettier," commented Peter, who sat upon her knobby head next to Fidius.

The leathery lizard wheezed heavily. "Lookit her skin... all turned ta tuff. An' it's still a mighty lot softer than it was, sure enough. Her heart too—fur she's helped haul these old dry bones outta this smudge pot—yes sirree!"

"All of you, save your gratitude and glibness," peeped Niki tersely. "Lust's kindness has again fallen short... on steps that is. We're still a good stone's throw away from out—and with no means to climb!"

So there they all remained, adorning their hostess' bald, onyx head like a crown cluster scanning the shaft's walls for any new settings or footholds. All that is, except Vito. The scrawny donkey prince, so wearied from the climb, napped in Lust's ear upon his billowy, red-haired cushion—that is, until Christen pulled the long lush tresses from under him. "Vito, good chap! What a splendid idea you had —bringing your crone's crop along to use when needed!"

From flat on his back, Vito brayed as though he knew just what his brother was talking about. "In death, Lust serves us better yet." As Christen spoke, he braided the supple red locks into long strands, like threads, until at last he displayed a large coil of red woven rope. "How many yards of yarn have weavers spun from my ram sire's wool? So shall the weaver of vice oblige us now!"

Everyone's spirit took a boost when the lamb boy twirled his lariat far and fast, clear to the rim, around a secure stalagmite. He then bound up and out of the abyss in a jiffy, as though spring-footed. "It helps to be part goat," he said with a wave from the top. "But for anyone eager to be out from that tuff queen's crown, such a climb will be a joyous toil."

Well, joyous, it was not. However, for the tested and tired, it was toil. By the time David, who was the last to clamber out, had joined his band, they all lay sprawled with fatigue, immersed smack in the middle of Luhrhollow's cavernous blackness. Were it not for his candle orb, even the boy's nose would be lost to him. The past night's ordeal had left them all weary, weak, and worn to a nub. The painter especially was drained beyond any conceivable limits. It was more than hunger or exhaustion which bore on him, it was despondency. In the shadow of his greatest triumph, and for all his other victories tallied, the pilgrim's quest was incomplete. Battles still remained; and the Egg—that elusive Glass Egg—was still lost.

"Oh my gosh! Niki—what about the Egg? It must be near; Lust's last thought was that it lay here, with us. We can't leave without searching..." As David exerted for breath enough to underscore his point, Sir Fidius filled in with wind enough to spare.

"Humph!" puffed the lizard. "How many rocks are you willin' ta turn in lookin', li'l' feller? This gulch's dry-heaves left us lots a hay fur yur needle ta hide under."

"Perhaps we already have your glass bauble, and just don't know it," remarked Valentina. "If its appearance is as misleading as Niki suggested earlier, then we may be as gullible as Lust was—"

"Yeah—that's it, Davy," agreed Peter. "I've been suspect of that miraculous candle you carry since seeing it at the outset of our trip. Could that candle be your shifty Egg?"

"Haw!... It's the witch's eye that's glass," laughed Vito at his joke. "For it found no cure for her, but death!"

But Christen saw no humor here. "No! What prize I held that night in Fairlawn was not an eye or wax—but a sphere. I could mistake it for nothing else, and would know it if beheld again."

"Well, if you ask me, such a highly touted knickknack as this must surely be beyond our grasp of it," griped Valentina impatiently. I doubt it was even meant to be found by anyone less than a god—we're only mortals for pete's sake! Anyway, what does it matter now? The shadow in this chase is dead... It's all over now, isn't it?

All this time Niki had been chattering under her breath, for the dove could supply no answers either. "Mayhap the Glass Egg is nothing more than the troth we share, or courage by another name... Whatever shell our Egg assumes, it has fooled the lot of us—I'm sure of that. And fools we are to think we're done while our homes are under siege. Furthermore, we're hardly out of this predicament either— especially, painter. If any, 'tis he who's done—completely done in. Our first task shall be to him, and then to home... And who knows, along the way, we may hatch ourselves an Egg!"

Wherever the truth lay hidden, David was losing his ambition for hunting it. Lust's near mortal duel had deadened him to any trivial discomforts. And the forenight's labor had sapped all remaining energies. Divested of all but an insufferable despair, it took his last ounce of strength to pull himself free of Lust's trappings.

He succeeded only on Christen's persistent jogging and support. Even now the lamb prince collared himself with David's limp body. "Well, artist, it seems we're up, but not out—eh! Which way do we go? Come on... that's a good sort. Your light is our best hope."

"And your shoes, painter," peeped Niki sorrowfully. It pained the tiny bird to see her young ward despirited so, and now of all times. "Your shoes can guide us out of this cavity and back to the surface world. After all, they brought us here."

"Niki..." gasped David, struggling for any breath that would come to him. "It's the shoes... My feet make me weary, so heavy... I can't explain it, but I don't think they're helping us to get out... For some reason they do not feel like budging from this rim. Is it the Egg which impels them so? Help me, Niki..."

Niki listened to her painter, then flapped at herself fitfully. "Oh! How could I have been so stupid!" At that the fervent dove leaped into the air and, had her singed wings been fully healed, would most likely have darted away to scout for escape. As it was, she mustered everyone up and proceeded to set them on their weary way again. It was now—when they began to grumble with doubt—that David's dancing taper flickered, then dimmed, bowed out—and died.

"NIKI!" shouted David in the darkness. "What's happened?...HELP! I can't see!"

"Oh but you CAN, painter! We all can! Perhaps some slippery 'lump' in the dark still holds you here—or it may be the light urging you out." Niki tested the darkness just to be sure. She was not disappointed. "Yes... it's time to pack the magic, and start relying on ourselves again," noted the dove. "It's dark, sure... but not black!"

"Niki's right!" bleated Christen. "There is light... but where is it coming from?"

"Up there!" cried Valentina, pointing in the distance at a faint spindle of light far off and above them.

"An opening!" guessed Peter. "But how on earth? Did Lust's belly ulcer, or have we been this close to freedom all along?"

"As a matter a fact, we could've been," said Fidius. "That upsettin' quake must a ruptured the ol' lizzy's hole—yes sirree! Why don't you hop on, li'l knight, an' we'll skedaddle outta here 'fore she retches again."

"Thanks, Sir Fierce, but I can't..." David took a big gulp of thick air, climbed to his feet, and helped Valentina onto the centaur's shoulders instead. "My trek is not completed yet, my friends. And my steps are not that much heavier than yours... I'll walk!" And so, it was David, with Niki perched proudly on his shoulder, that led the pilgrim band over the ever brighter scree and lava bed, through the narrowing shafts and tunnels and craggy corridors, into the light of the surface world, which for an eternity was denied them.

Vito, as usual, lagged far behind. He desired to have his witch's hair; but in bending down over the brink to pluck it back, he cringed to see his stone widow, and thought better. It was, after all, hers to keep. Thus spurned and spurred by fright, the mule man trotted to the forefront of the departing troupe.

His lead was short-strided however. As they met the light, the donkey stopped abruptly. It was here, in the cooler hot air, that the horseflies again picked up his scent. It was also here that the gleam was greatest, at the cavern mouth, where freedom was but a footstep away—that Luhrhollow's sentries' giant shadows fell across their path, barring the opening with their stark, clay-cold presence.

David was the first to see them, sulking in the silent sooty passageway, and spread the alarm. "Our luck is up!" he cried. "The witch has watchmen after all!"

But the pilgrim's shoes were anchors. In fact, none among them could find feet to flee or hide. But no matter, they were exposed and wholly at the mercy of the mammoth row of clay-born sentinels, looming over the escapees like livid, lava pillars. Terror struck the fellowship completely numb, except for Valentina that is.

The fearless fairy promptly dismounted her mount and jaunted boldly to the very foot of the nearest brute, who also seemed too stiff to act, even for this death squad. But the lithe little pixie girl had zest to burn, and spitefully kicked the unmoving colossus on the iron greaves coating his shin. A clear clang rang on and off the cavern walls. Her companions gasped. But Valentina only laughed sarcastically as Lust's lethargic line of guardians toppled backward into a crumpled heap. Each in turn felled its adjacent armsman, which subsequently upended the entire clay column, climaxing in a tumultuous, crumbling bier of decaying hulks. Revealed in each hollow chest was a warlock pike. Valentina slapped her hands together in a series of shrill claps while wiping away death's dust.

"My 'welcoming' committee to Lust's lair!" she explained. "The witch mistook my affronted femininity for frailty, and so tossed me to her warlock wolves. Most grievously were they mistaken—and most grievously they paid the price of error. These are their remains—shells, shed of all life—stuck like gourds and hung like crumpled cerements impaled upon their own poisoned points by this frail, fairy child. No match were the witch's weary rows of dead feet against this spry-stepping nymphet. For this crime I was sentenced to swing like a side of pork under wraps."

"Humph! These blood-crusted banner crests make fittin' flags fur that ol' gammer an' her slew-skinned goons," snuffed Fidius, nosing about the elf maiden's handiwork, while she seated herself primly on Peter's raised back and heeled him onward at a brisk gate.

"Last one out's a rotten egg!" she sang capriciously without much to-do. Then, with her comrades still somewhat slow to set pace, it was the angel child who took the initiative. Sidestepping the fallen array of putrefying debris, she sped merrily along the rippling stream of light. It was Valentina and Peter who first stepped from Lust's dark hold into a wonderfully warm winter day. Everyone was out, except David. The morning sun, shining once again, peeked into the earth's cracked crust to satisfy his curiosity. And in celebration at what he saw, poured honeyed beams of daybreak over the dark, dreary defiles of Luhrhollow and stuck to all the hidden nooks and crannies like brightly dyed silk coating soily skin.

When David's head at last poked through, a euphoric cheer erupted. Joining the voices of the fellowship, were invigorating winter breezes, patting their backs in victory, buffing their spirits, and filling their lungs with fresh energy. The forested trees rustled in applause. Mythlewild was alive again. All around them the cold ground softened. Winter's clouds receded, so morning's sunbeams could ply their tender muscles with warm, welcome handclasps and caresses to spare the fairly dressed fireflies from December's chills.

"Father above!" praised Christen in gratitude. "The soothing sun is back with us—Lord Zeros must be roused and well from his slab!"

David's first act upon joining his friends was to kneel down and kiss the sweet, sun-tinted meadowgrass. He didn't even notice their new guest, who had been there to greet the band upon their emergence.

"Ahem..." came the teeny tiny voice by David's nose, "...I had hoped to be the first to congratulate you, but the season and the sky and the sweet grasses have preceded me."

David's eyes bugged open, and he knew his prayers were heard, and in thanks cried out, "Creta!... Creta, you beautiful, blessed butterfly!"

"Tierra bid me come," said the butterfly so softly in her glee. "Some hellos were in order after your journey up from the ashes—especially after our hasty goodbyes."

"Creta," interrupted Christen, "you must tell us, what has happened at Sovereignton... Is Lust's hearsay true? Has my foster king, Constantio met his end this morn? Is the Mythlewild lost?"

Peter, Fidius, Valentina, all—hung on the reply for news of home and family. Even Vito, out of habit, brayed for news. Only the sound of horseflies , the mule prince's welcoming party, disturbed the quiet which hovered over them.

"The sun no longer weeps, Prince of Lambs," sang the butterfly so gracefully, "and neither must we! Though casualties are not yet tolled, 'tis not

Constantio, but DeSeet that lies dead this day—and pray, none of your blood rest with him—and most certainly, not the Mythlewild! Even the sky lord, Zeros, has wakened from his leave. His brothers inspired him...Or perhaps it was your victory, pilgrims! The sovereign of winds swept onto the field of war fronting the fleet force of his sky-walking currents and cloud-armored hosts, thus relieving the press of Lust's lionaries upon his zesty brother, the earth, and upon the earth's king too."

"Zeros—alive! Praise be!" rejoiced Christen.

"Aye! But it was not deity that saved the day—it was David." stressed the butterfly. The scourge of troll and lion persisted only so long as their leader Lust lasted. Theland is ours again thanks to our talented 'orphan'."

David could only bask silently in the glow of the moment. Whether from humility or fatigue, or both, Niki understood. She cooed soothingly to him from her pocket nest and winked at Creta, as the butterfly continued with her telling.

"With their queen, the clay-born too are slain. Just as on the tip of victory they stood—bang! All across the Serenity Plain—bang! 'Twas not the clap of sword on steel that rang the wooded walls, but the bursting shells of goblin ghosts, and souless soldiers—all popping like bubbles. In death, each monster wraith and bane wasted away into the oblivion which spawned them... beaten when their black mistress' heart had beat its last. Thus, with only mortal monsters left to combat, it was a cakewalk for the likes of gods and king's knights, and the homeless stalwarts of Middleshire to fend them forever off. Quite a contest it was—an epic I should say —and will say it, in my history books! But say, David... that scrape you were in— Oooh! There was a match if ever there was one! Had I ink or page enough to do it justice, or time enough for that matter." Creta's wings strummed like a lively lyre with praising psalms. "But come, our journey's end lies far to the north. I shall extol what other news I can on the way to Middleshire. You'll warrant quite another welcome there I imagine."

Lust and lions were not the only losers in this story, languor also bent before the onslaught of good tidings. Thus it was a merry, mirthy band which followed gaily behind the rainbow-winged flight of Creta. It wasn't long before the butterfly had led the party to a narrow, meandering pathway which would eventually catch a road to the Rollingway. It was here, amid a huge, green glade, lush with wildberry patches and plum trees, spared by winter especially for these guests, that the pilgrims truly relaxed and made merry. They dined in the luxury of meadowed halls and clover tiles, and tree-lined colonnades rising into the bright blue cloudless canopies. No decor, nor fare, dared compare to the sweet, juicy berries served up by a thankful land to its hungry heroes.

Vito, who had found victory's glare a bit too bright to be comfortably digested, fasted from the fruits of triumph, and sated instead on self-indulgences and pity.

David also abstained. He languished far behind the company on the way and, quite contrary to the others, experienced increasing difficulty in relishing the bounty of his labors. Instead, after a meager helping of berries, he was content to plop himself down in a crop of soft heather, and prop his aching legs upon a plush, cushiony nob.

Niki was quick to investigate her partner's malaise. "Somehow, the road has dealt more harshly to you, painter... Yet you have no new or visible wounds. What is it that plagues you so? Has your load not been lifted?"

David just laid mum in the heather, sweat-drenched and shaking uncontrollably. His speech was faltering. "I-I don't know, Niki... I feel faint; my head is so light, but my feet are weights. I can no longer lift them to walk... I-I can't explain it..."

Niki too was lost in the quandary. She gazed at the winged shoes, but their tongues were lead. "Something IS amiss, painter. Omnus' gifts have always served you unerringly—saved your life and ours. Even in Lust's cook pot the wings were heard to sing. And your paints have just worked another miracle. How perplexing to have those charms hobble you now—"

"Niki!" David sat up with a start—clutching an empty satchel. "The paints—I left them in that pit! I must go back!"

The boy was up and across the field retracing his steps before Niki could stop him. She raced to catch up, to reason with him. Painter, this is nonsense! The tubes are depleted, their purpose is served... Why retrieve them?"

"What else could it be, Niki?" replied David without halting. "Maybe there is an Egg after all, huh? Well, whether there is or not, the last of my paints remain

670

down there. It must be them that tug the slippers back to Luhrhollow. My legs resisted every move out of that that grave site—but look now! Notice how the shoes react as I head back that way. At Ocean Bottom I was numb to their callings, though my paints were an ocean apart. Then I was trapped by the sea. But there's nothing that can stop me this time... I'm going back, Niki. I've got to! Have you counsel for me now? Are there any answers to this one under your hat?"

"Painter, use REASON—I implore you! You're too weak to travel more. Wait... Rest first with us. To attempt another climb so soon is suicide!" Niki was beginning to tire now, and much to her distress and astonishment, the impulsive boy outdistanced her effortlessly.

"My shoes will carry me through this turn, Niki... I'm feeling stronger. Wait for me here..." David was gone, whisked away by shoes so swiftly there was scant chance for anyone to argue. He vanished into a web of bare trees.

"Someone should accompany him..." repeated the harried dove as the others gathered around, finally. Everyone seemed to be rather torpid for some reason. "... After all, that IS still Luhrhollow which awaits him... Lust's lair—"

"No more, Niki," reminded Prince Christen, who laid down in the soft, soothing grass. "It's Lust's bier now—'twas your 'runaway' who nailed her there."

"The danger is past," yawned Peter, settling into a nap. "The witch's bubble's burst—Creta said so. C'mon, lay down... Relax..." Fidius snored smokey puffs of agreement, as he too slept off his plum and berry feast. A witch's brew could not have cast a more potent spell.

Nevertheless, Niki continued to balk at the idea of David's skipping off by himself. "He's not been all alone since we began, that's all... Creta, your word is sage. Is it also your advise for me to fold my wings and nest?"

Enduros' butterfly spoke from the complacent comfort of a snug stump hollow. "'Tis always wise for us flyers to go where our wings take us; for without, we progress not. Your artist's strides are wider now, in part to you, Niki. And his witch IS dead. So, unless your wings are healed enough to catch him, you'd best let your eaglet fly so that his pact may be concluded."

Only now did the harried dove crouch from lassitude. She perched upon Creta's stump, but did not lay. "I suppose you, most of all, are right. Rest would be so very welcome... But I'll sleep in no other nest except beside his heart..."

"You're not going to follow him?" asked Valentina desparingly.

"Would that I had his stamina," mumbled Niki. "But tell me, lovely one, who among us sleepy-eyed, full-bellied folks could keep the pilgrim's pace? As Creta said, let's let our dream chaser take his final victory lap alone. With that, Valentina also fell slowly among the others swooning in heir cozy clover beds.

Only Vito did not slumber. His belly was still empty, yet his mind was deliberately full. For the first time in the mule's life his head buzzed with other than flies. With the first turned back and last closed eye—he was gone. No one noticed the sinister slip as he capered unwearily away after his adopted chum.

CHAPTER 56

In all the world, no place on earth—or off—was more repugnant to David than that gaping, black cavity which leered back at him from behind the yawning jaws of Luhrhollow. The pilgrim's increasingly restless shoes had practically flown him back here, and allowed only a smattering of delay before bearing him past the cold, craggy coke and cinder cusps; and carefully cutting a wide swathe around the clay-born carcasses of Valentina's molding. The hollow sentinels watched passively as their conqueror crept resolutely through the cavern's ashen throat, drawn inexorably toward some uncertain confrontation within its earthen recesses.

"Just one last time," pledged David, carefully picking his steps. The fresh air scoured the stench, and sunlight bathed away the blackness permeating the subterranean aisles with purifying winter airs. Deeper and deeper it went, accompanying the young boy, much as Niki would have done. Diligently downward he trudged, ever farther from his companions, until even the sun and wind were left behind. Daylight gradually screened into darkness, but David was heartened to find his lamp alight to this new challenge. Thus inflamed, his pace remained steady as a ferret on the scent under night's moon shadow. Quiet was all around him, thick as pitch. Lust's castle belly mourned in the far off spaces of the vault's vast hollow halls. Grumbling could still be felt underfoot. Moanings and aftershocks plied an unsettling atmosphere throughout... and bat wings brushed the air close by—too close. David's skin crawled. It had been hours since this long corridor was passed, and yet the dense dread still hung on the walls.

Withal, David continued to follow his feet; shoe wings whistled, heels beat, and apprehensions diminished. What's wrong with me, thought the boy. "There's no danger here anymore—" he said to himself out loud, as he halted suddenly at the brink of the abyss, very nearly toppling in. With his heart in his throat, David leaned over the edge. The cord of red woven hair was still hitched to the stalagmite. He peered into the depths—then let out a chilling gasp.

There, waiting for him under muted, mellow, dye-tinged candleglow—was Lust—still. The siren beckoned, with her brimstone arms outstretched in a perpetual pose of greed. So real she looks, murmured David's heart. So 'alive' prodded his imagination, running wild. For a heartbeat, the onyx-set eye of Lust looked bitterly at her defiler.

Don't be silly, spoke his common sense. It's nothing but a fleshless statue now. Her own reflection's all she'll ever see from this day on. Bowing to logic, the pilgrim ever so cautiously crawled down the braided ladder. Stepping at last on the witch's coal hard head, he felt a cringe in his toes, or was it the slippers? Or was it Lust perhaps, shuddering at her painter's return? Shrugging off such concoctions to nerves, David stooped over Lust's shoulder and held out his candle, pouring its shimmering light into the pit's dregs. Whereupon he spied his paints, still strewn about the ashes, just as he had so hastily left them.

While making his way down Lust's arm, David was compelled to pause and admire his painting. It challenged him to look upon its face—and eyes. They were Lust's eyes, locked upon each other—Lust gripping Lust—and woe to him who steps between. Shielding his own eyes with good judgment, the young pilgrim was careful not to rest his gaze on any one section—and especially avoided the portrait's evil eye. David absorbed his masterpiece a portion at a time, in swiftly darting glimpses, lest in lingering to grasp it all, its whole would capture him again in payback. Niki would be proud of my wisdom, he thought. And so the dove's painter faced his challenge one more time. But, as artists are prone to do, he panned his work. "Ugh! Did I really do that?..."

For a second David cocked his head, as if a noise intruded on his critique. "What's that?... Who's up there?" he called out, but only in a whisper. For whatever it was might be better left 'up there' unmolested. Anyway, when no response except dead silence was forthcoming, the boy dismissed his scare as minor tremors... or a bat perhaps.

His attention sprang back to the corners of his painting. His jaw dropped. "Oh my!" he gasped. "Something's missing! How could I have forgotten—" David scrambled to the witch's waist, slid quickly down her statuesque legs, and there at her feet, assembled what artist's supplies remained. He stashed them all safely away into his satchel—save for a single loaded brush, which he tucked between his teeth as he shimmied back up the witch's stony skirts.

As he climbed, the winged shoes whined loudly once more, causing David great consternation. "Why are you still crying? We've got everything now: the satchel, and all of the paints—so hush up! You'll attract, uh... attention," though David couldn't say of what. But his slippers droned on even louder as the painter made his exit, and did so hurridly, for he was growing more and more apprehensive by the minute.

Having reached the statue's breast, the young boy turned and leaned across the crone's frozen arms, laying like an infant cradled tenderly in his mother's loving embrace. But there was no gentle affection between this slag madonna, or her child. David was merely signing his painting. "Perhaps I'm vain, but an artist should always autograph his work!"

675

The two black-fire eyes watched in helpless agitation as the pilgrim painter dangled from Lust's lava limbs. Her gaping mouth was an extinct volcano with wide lips locked open in an ageless curse, and her hair still a billowing, red-raging plume. Her last words erupted in David's ears: 'Damn you, pilgrim'. That volatile oath crawled up his skin. Your empty invocations carry no weight now, he thought. He then shook off the goose bump words like hailstones, and stepped backward to admire his work just one last time. Poised on the witch's shoulder, he leaned against her temple with hands on hips—and in his looking, failed to heed his slippers' urgent warnings.

"There—that's not so bad after all!" confided David to himself.

"M-Mmmmmm, not bad at all..." came the ugly, growling echo, "...except maybe for you, pilgrimmmmm!"

All of a sudden, David felt the torrid touch of winter ice. He dropped his brush even before looking up to the pit rim. And when at last he stared into the voice's candle-lit face, he quaked in terror, and let loose his flickering taper. Careening first off Lust's rock arms, the magic orb smashed finally upon the chasm's black brimstone bottom. Its destruction rung waxen, like a hollow heart's break. With the light quelled, darkness again descended upon Omnus' boy.

Even in the dark, fear's image boiled the blood in David's veins. On the pit rim it stood. More than a monstrous bat lurking in a cave, it was the shade of the Devil himself. It was Horros, massive and stinking, and gnashing his entrenched legion of teeth. His blue bulk blotched out even the blackness. His stench rotted the last traces of sweet December air which had briefly stolen some of Luhrhollow's foul. Two stabbing red eyes, swelling hot, slit the dark. A blistering black tongue smacked a set of grinning, lurid lips. Then hell's worst growled, "Why don't you paint MY picture... pilgrimmmmm!

David's face was dry and drawn, bleached wan and quivering violently all the way down to his shoes, which were strangely silent now, as if useless in their wearer's weeping. The young pilgrim's exhaustion took hold of him. Emotionally racked and bone weary, his legs gave way. "Oh Niki... What have I done? Is there no end for me but suffering..."

Grasping Lust's hairline, David struggled to maintain himself; but there was nothing left, nothing to fall back on. Niki was gone. He was alone, and drained completely—totally. No specking drop of resistance remained in him. In this encounter, the demon could have him—mercifully.

David grew violently ill as the cold blue shadow that was Horros reached downward. The boy's aching stomach retched its fill of hell's convulsions, yet the real sickness upon him was not disgorged. Instead, its groping malady lunged even closer. For a moment, Lust's icy hot lips seemed to crack wide in a grotesque, misshapen grin, as she watched her nemesis lose his grip, and plummet into her hold on top of his sickness and upon her ashen alter.

The long preying arm of Satan's twin swept across Lust's coke stone skin on its way down into the abyss in search of its quarry. "M-Mmmmm... My, my! What have you done to my mistress?" bellowed hades' voice. "Mmmmm... She's nothing but a rock. No wonder I was summoned home again. Too bad I'm late, mistress. M-Mmmmm... Methinks our war fares ill for you. How fortunate I was to escape with my life!"

David just lay in prostration where he fell, cringing and hiding among the fissures and shadows. He was alive, but bruised and hurting in ways no pain can measure. Too weak to move—and too disheartened to care—despair clenched the boy long before Horros' hand began its hunt.

In the pitch it groveled, inching closer and closer. The glowing bat eyes bored through the dark like burning beacons. The scent of oils and man sucked into the beast's flaring nostrils. "Sniff... Hard to find in this gorge, aren't we? Hmmmmm... But I'm not too blind to see that you're the bug in our butter... pilgrimmmmm." The life-wrenching voice continued, feeling the darkness under its claws as it groaned on. "Have you any color left in your cheeks for me? Better use it now, pilgrimmmmm... The war has fed me poorly. Blood aplenty, but my hunger is for younger, redder meat... Yummmmm!"

David remained absolutely still, not even chancing to move towards a cleft or rocky brace; he chose to lie breathing into lava dust, lest his heaving lungs expose him.

"Aahhh, she died happy..." The giant shade mistook Lust's cracked, cursing mouth for a wide, wicked smile. "Like a mother she was, to all of us in her shop. She weren't as pert or perfect as her packaging admittedly, but she's all we had. Hell's the place for her alright... M-Mmmmm, what's this?" Horros voice tingled as he lifted out a supple sooty handful and popped the odorous chunk quickly into his mouth and swallowed it whole.

It was David's satchel. The leather bag of oily, paint-stained rags was mistaken for artist's meat. The painter yearned to cry out, but was spent of tears and strength. "Uuugh! You taste of grease and poison, pilgrimmmmm!" snarled the huge demon, angrily spitting fire breath and expelling oil and bitter colors back down into the pit.

It was only a burst of flame, but it provided enough light to expose the real morsel. The caverns resounded with bellowing laughter as Horros' hand delved into the magma basin for another grab. "Har har... Lit my fire, didn't you... pilgrimmmmm! We must be near at hand, mustn't we... Hmmmmm! What a tasty little tidbit you'll make... Yummmmm!" The rasping, reaching voice groped again in coal blackness as the bullying cobalt shapes closed in on David, who could do nothing except pray for a quick and merciful end. What a blessed relief devouring would be, he was thinking—Then he heard it.

"Hey! Over here you stupid block!" brayed a spindly, squeaky voice out of nowhere. "Here I am, Oaf! Catch me if you can!" heehawed the mule again from behind the monster's heels.

Horros quickly jerked his arm from the trench and twisted awkwardly around its rim clutching at Vito. The donkey prince had snuck up from the rear, and now skipped feverishly upon the covert's lip to and fro about the demon's clumsy feet, like an annoying nipper.

"Quickly, friend—out of there! Let's be off!" Vito honked and hollered as he nimbly dodged Horros' lumpish, lunging fists which pelted the air around him like falling fragments of the night sky.

In all the commotion, and lacking ears as he did, poor Vito could not hear David cry out his helpless state. "Save yourself, Prince! I can move no further, up or down!" he shouted as he was able. But no more than voice could he raise from the pit bottom.

Yet Vito would not flee. His tireless scampering had begun to confound the peeved and slowly moving sloth, who could detect nothing in the dark but wild whickering, which for all he knew was but one voice—his oily prey. Thus the pesky and persistent prince of asses might verily have succeeded in wearing the sluggish hulk down—had it not been for the rock—all baked with dirt and soot, and laying underfoot in the blackness. Brave Prince Vito, in his haste, did stumble and fall to his knees with a whine, kicking the culprit clod into the pit, where it rolled to rest by David's feet and seemed content to be again underfoot. There it went unnoticed by the boy—but not by his shoes. They began to hum anew, even as Vito shrieked his last 'hee-haw'.

"M-Mmmmm... Now I've got you, pilgrimmmm!" boasted Horros. His red, ember eyes squinted hungrily. Pinching Vito by his donkey ear stubs, he plucked the prince of martyrs from the black crevices and gobbled him up in one bite, without pausing to notice his error. "Y-Ymmmmm... Chewy, and tough as leather, but better than I expected from a tender pilgrimmmmm!" belched Horros, devouring the last of the brave mule man. In all likelihood the blue horror would have abandoned the grotto with his appetite glutted, had not David called out in his friend's behalf.

"Vito?... Prince?... Are you there?"

After a perpetually long and bewildering silence, the demon answered. And two burning red eyes again peered down into the darkness to pry out another bite. "Yes... We're both still here, pilgrimmmmm... and lest you be a phantom quizzing the darkness, the greasy gobbit kicking my innards will soon have company... Hmmmm!"

"Oh lord!" gulped David. "Y-You ATE him?"

"Aye, ghost of a pilgrimmmmm... keep talking, and you may join us in a bite!" Guided by the high-pitched voice, and David's uncontrollable breathing and throbbing heartbeat, the blue mandible approached like a giant tarantula, reaching for one more mouthful.

"OMNUS!" implored David, crying his prayers' last rites. "In my failings have you forsaken me, Overlord? Am I no closer to your fruit than in the beginning... Am I not your egg too? Are we all lost to you? Or don't you hear your children crying up there in your Far Always... Is the last breath of a braying mule to be the only answer to my prayers?"

When David could speak no more, stark silence erupted—the music of miracles' composing. It was now that David heard the hums of his shoes' strumming wings. They did not whine this time, rather did they sing, as a gently playing harp. And shame chased his fears aside, to be replaced with the courage of mules. Poor Vito had sacrificed himself for David—a noble penance for an ass's life. If such a wretch could find valor in death, then so must he. Though too spent and fallen to fight, he could still resist.

"You've carried me rightly upon this pilgrimage," spoke David fondly, looking upon his shoes for stamina. "It is for some purpose you've carried me back into this place of death... So it must be life I'll discover following in Omnus' steps—I pray you will surely lead me out again." No tears of doubt remained to stifle the pilgrim's resolve. His decision was made, even as his own hands groped the ashes for solution.

"If it's true that good will conquer evil, then let this be the time," decided David. "Even alone..."

"Nay, child—no worthy servant of mine will ever face evil alone." The rich, resonant voice flooded the dark chamber with solemn, shining splendor. "I am with you, even now, to tell you that my Egg is no vagary—nor is it mislaid. The yoke of life and death may not be where you expect, nay, that does not mean it is lost!"

In the glimmering wake of the hallowed voice, the veiled image of the anima, body and soul, appeared abreast of David, and he knew its name. Temporarily shielding Horros' oncoming specter, the vision was brilliant bright, but cloaked in mist, robed and feature-hidden in modest, faded umber broadcloth. Around its neck was a brooch... no, it was a key! This was Omnus—lord of all, Overseer to Mythlewild, and grandsire to the gods. It could be no other visage manifest. But wait! Another image intruded into the fiber's cowl, pure white and downy soft... a dove... It was Niki! It was HER face beneath the hooded mantle—or was it?

"Until all the days of time I am with you..." the voice trailed away. "Believe..." the persona faded, but its impressions were lasting.

"I DO believe!" cried David, loud enough even for the stones to hear. And with the vigor such a troth invokes the pilgrim began to stand. In doing so, his hand inadvertently landed upon the nugget which Vito had tripped into the hole. Gathering this up in his hands, he felt the strumming shoes tingling his feet, then surging through his whole body as life coursed again into his limbs. Both hands vibrated now, imbued with new found strength and conviction. He clenched the dirt-caked chunk, even as another larger looming hand surrounded him. Its heart-piercing nails stabbed into his flesh to gnaw and grind his fidelity. David's eyes moved from horror to heaven as he felt the cold, clammy grip tighten and draw him towards two glaring red eye slits. A defiant smile spread across the pilgrim's face as Horros' black tongue spate across the fang infested mouth.

Rubbing the sweat and cuts of his palms into this wad, his only weapon, David cocked his arm. "I do believe!" he yelled, into the devil's face. Then, with the trenchant might of all pilgrims who have tread peril's steps, or reached into dangerous depths to attain those impossible yearnings non-believers call dreams, the orphan painter surrendered his life to faith. "I DO believe!" he screamed, right into Horros' face—and hurtled the crusty stone away and home. Unerringly was it propelled, unswerving in its flight, and its landing—true to the test—and straight into the devil's gaping throat.

It was when that missile was cast, when the pilgrim's words were loosed—and only at that moment—that David found his troth. And it was now that Omnus' hunter found his Egg—if only for an instant. Before his eyes, the object tossed began to glow, shedding cinder, dust, and soot. Lo and behold—It was not a rock at all! It was a sphere... a shining knuckle... a radiant bone! It was the fox's booty, which Vito had knocked into David's hands. Yet it was burning brighter on this flight and, ignited from its dormancy by words of fealty, the orb became a comet boring at the devil's jaw. But wait—it wasn't a ball at all! Neither bone, nor stone it was which struck its mark—It was glass. And it was real, let there be no doubt. It was the Egg—

the fruit of Omnus' labor—heaven's eye. Into greed's gullet it lodged. And when Horros' cold muzzle closed on his morsel, it was iniquity and debasement which was devoured.

Good will inevitably taste foul to that which is evil. Thus the poisoned pill broke tart upon the tongue of Lust's prime sinner. The Glass Egg so lapped, plagued the demon's palate. And once ingested wholly into the big blue haunts did swell incurably upon Horros' entrails, and in digestion was compulsively expelled again. 'Twas in one huge, kecking heave that death spewed back the powers of the universe into the dirt at David's feet. Therewith a great transformation occurred. But the pilgrim witnessed it not. Laying prostrate in the ash, the young boy collapsed in a dead faint.

CHAPTER 57

"I just knew we couldn't trust that treacherous rump!" grumbled Valentina.

"If he's laid even one mulish hoof on our li'l' knight, I'll have MY turn at his hide this time, missy!" snorted Fidius, his fireball breaths nearly scorched the pixie's honey hair. The lizard and the lady locked knees to Peter's back as the determined pony boy frothed to sustain full gallop under their taxing weight. Had Creta, the butterfly sought saddle too, the young mount would surely have broken in two. Running in bounding strides ahead was Prince Christen, whose sinewy lamb legs proved swift and supple. Beyond them all flew the high strung little dove, Niki, who would be beside her painter child right now had she full wing. It was nearly noon, and David had not returned from his foray. Alert from their famished sleep, the pilgrim band now scrambled helter-skelter to the voracious mouth of Luhrhollow, tracing after the cloven tracks which smeared the slippered steps of David. Vito, branded by the guilt of his absence, was thus tart on the tongues of his pursuers.

"The cave's jaws be broad as an ass... Were it Vito, I would smash it asunder!" promised Peter as he swatted at a zealous horsefly upon entering Lust's brimstone orafice.

"Shame on you all," scolded Christen, picking his way hastily over gravel-gummed tiers of jagged, pumice-coated cusps. "Friendship was our vow to Vito—not malice. It's conceivable my stepbrother returned to help David, in repayment for kindness shared."

"Returned like a virus more likely!" griped Valentina. "Ouch!... That confounded fly!... Peter, I do wish I had a tail like yours to fend him off."

"Vito's tail was a horsefly's bane, had you kept it, maiden—"

"Shhh!" prompted Creta. "Instead of harping at flies, why don't we give a listen to this vault's buzzing." Even swallowed in the earth, the butterfly's radiant wings shone rainbow bright.

"The whole of this crypt is flooded with light now," peeped Niki.

"The latest eruptions have split Lust's swarthy seed bed like a ripe melon," observed Christen, "in gratitude to us sod busters who have weeded out the dandy-'lions'!"

"Or, in tumult over some new death!" mulled Niki as she gazed upon the buried. The pace slackened but a bit as the companions filed one by one past the dust of the strewn clay-born tombstones. Valentina spat on their dust as she veered from the others, specifically to tread upon each decaying mound. "I'll not honor their graves with my silence. DAVY!... Davy!... Are you all right?" The elf maiden stomped her way deep into the wide and winding volutes behind the rest. Lagging echoes of 'Davy' trailed after them.

"This place'd give a fire-breather chills," grunted Fidius, after endless trekking had netted them nothing but frustration. The old lizard took a seat and squinted his eyes while buffing the one lens remaining in his spectacles. The rocks held neither hoof, nor print of shoe. The pit way was similarly lost under the most recent rumblings, earthshakes, and screes.

"It all looks so different in the sunlight... maybe if we shut our eyes, we could find our way in again," remarked Peter in all seriousness.

"We've not lost this dratted horsefly for sure!" said Valentina, slapping at the buzzing nuisance which molested her the entire way. But of the girl and her gadfly none took notice—except for Creta—who merely watched and waved her wings in silence.

Christen was scouting several paces ahead with Niki, when Valentina's scream drew them back in a bound. They found the trembling, pixie enfolded in Fidius' wrinkled old arms. "I-I saw it..." she quivered. "S-Something's moving... over there... in the shadows."

"Nothing!" snubbed Peter, pointing into the far clefts and crags of the overhangs. He smiled to see the gritty girl's knees knocking for once, almost like a fragile female. "It wasn't nothing but a little ol' bat, fazed by the light's intrusion, probably more scared of you than you are of it." The creature shrieked away in a whimpering fright as a keenly thrown rock hit home. "Or, maybe it was a great big 'killer' fly—Hah!"

"Must've been SOME bat to spook our iron-nerved maiden into a lizard's hug," noted Christen, while Niki followed Peter's stone toss. The dove fluttered in and out of the chambers' crevices poking for clues.

"Oh, it was—it was," dramatized the centaur. "As blue as her mood too—Ho! With dotted eyes, flashing red as our flushed figurine's blushing cheeks."

"Blue?..." said the dove circling back, "...with flashing red eyes, you say?"

While Niki pondered on the bat, Christen's attention was diverted from the elf maiden to the persistent horsefly hovering about her—and also to Creta, who's bemused and quizzical silence now struck the lamb prince. "Horsefly!" He suddenly bleated. "Creta, that's it! My stepbrother! Niki, it's Vito... He must be near!" And he hied off after the horsefly, who strayed at a spanking clip under the ensuing limelight. However, it was not flies, buttered or buzzing, nor bleating boys which culled Niki from the expanse of endless tuff and pumice passageways, and sent her fetching ahead of the others. It was a calling of another kind. It was the voice of binding affection which guided the dove's hectic flight—right to the very brink of Lust's most defiling ditch. It now glimmered with a light to pale even the sun. Creta fluttered after, bouncing in merry, whimsical loops and spirals like a harmonious note in rythmic melody, and bobbing in time to the tuneful murmuring emitted from the abyss. The companions formed a staggered ring around the pit rim. There they stood numbly, enthralled and bewitched again by what they beheld. It was David. He was humming. The audience he attracted peered down into the ash-floored stage from their lofty tiers, applauding with bulged eyes and elated faces—all were rapt with bewildered glee. None marveled more at what they saw than Christen and Niki—for none but Omnus' ilk knew what they espied. From the fissure's floor, The Glass Egg's intriguing light beamed up at them. David's complexion also sparkled with a sheepish, but chipper, grin. He sat in the pulverized lava with his satchel shouldered, and clutching this odd... 'rock' to his chest as though it were his soul enfolded. Then, like a well-exhumed hearth, the nugget dimmed. Only David was left beaming. His face was imbued with an ethereal, argent sheen that only heaven's hands could prescribe, but embellished now by the sight of his friends clustered above like twinkling star facets. Yet the boy moved not a muscle, except to smile meekly.

"I'm afraid I've botched things a bit," he apologized. "Fell into this hole again, like a ninny... though I can't quite recall how. I woke from my faint to find my foot twisted... and this!" David held the shining stone aurora aloft, displaying in his extended hand a grubby, grey, 'clump'. I found it, Niki! It's Christen's Egg—see!"

"Has he gone daft?" whispered Peter. "That's no egg!"

"Took a thump on the noggin' maybe," puffed Fidius. "It's joggled his noggin!" The lizard and the centaur could see naught but a piece of stone in their pilgrim's grasp. Niki, on the other hand, immediately plummeted into the pit where her painter lay. The Prince of Lambs dropped too—to his knees—and gave thanks for a world restored. "You and your foot found more than a twist in this grave, artist," emphasized Christen, now making his way hurriedly down the hair-sewn line, over the frightful frozen magma footholds, and arriving to embrace his friend ahead of the ensuing band. "'Tis my grandsire's fruit that you've plucked from this nasty nest!"

"The Glass Egg!... THAT?" Valentina leaped from Lust's hard hem and scoffed as she stooped and inspected David's swollen ankle, which concerned her most. In consternation she applied some soft linen wraps. "You've taken quite a fall," she said, looking at her suitor's bruises.

"Yes... I have," he admitted, looking back into his pixie's angel-flecked eyes.

"Does it hurt?" asked Valentina, referring to the foot.

"Yeah..." replied David, referring to his pitter-pattering heart, "...but it feels really good!"

"Pahh! Why it's nothing but a rock!" scowled Peter, refuting all previous claims to the contrary as he trotted over to scrutinize—but not touch—the lackluster clod which David cradled like a mother hen. "You don't mean this hunk of dirt is what all our sweat and blood was spilled for?"

"Surely is a sad lookin' egg," admitted Fidius, doffing his bifocals lest they deceive him. Even then, the Egg's true image remained a blur to the group's intense scrutiny, causing the lizard to summarize their disappointment. "Not even a gater mama would admit ta motherin' the likes a that ruddy wad—no sirree!"

"Tell us, painter... what happened? Do you remember?" cheeped Niki fretfully from over Valentina'a shoulder fearing another memory blank.

"The shoes brought you back here for finer purposes than recouping a few squeezed out paint tubes," surmised Christen, admiring the care David lavished on his 'find', and so left it in the boy's possession until such time as Fate decreed its return. "Just how did you stumble on this prize of yours, artist?"

But David was unable to answer the lamb's question. He could only exchange glazed glances with those surrounding him.

"If you please," spoke up Creta, "the boy has only just awakened from his faint. But we've another witness here to this event... one whose buzzing tongue has attracted naught but slaps and blows. Yet has, in his own fashion, born us all to this place and revealed the mystery to me, in 'insect' dialect!.

Without further fuss, Creta waved the horsefly to the front before continuing. "That 'ruddy wad', as you call it, saved David's life. Whatever it is you see in his hands—no matter its name or shape—indeed it has saved us all... as did

687

Prince Vito! 'Twas Constantio's stepson that delivered the Glass Egg into our pilgrim's hands—right when he needed it most!"

"Vito?" groaned Valentina, pressing a poultice onto David's ankle with a bit too much zeal.

"Ouch!" cried David, only to be ignored by his friends as they dwelled on this new, odd and offbeat hero.

"Where is that earless flytrap anyway?" wondered Valentina. "HE can't be our savior, surely!"

"In a manner of speaking—he is," said the butterfly. "Right, Vito?" At this, the horsefly buzzed eagerly in affirmation as Creta related his tale:

"The aggravating horsefly you've been rapping and cursing, is Vito! Feverishly he has attempted to lead us here, where David lay, a near victim of Lust's most savage scion, Horros. Twas that devil who entrapped him within this trench. And thus, the Vito that you all knew martyred himself by selflessly attacking the demon giant, who mistakenly swallowed the unfortunate prince thinking it was David. In the scuffle, the sooty Egg was dislodged into the pit where our boy lay helpless. With no other weapon at hand, David latched onto the Egg quite by chance, and flung it, as a stone, with his last ounce of strength. Like from a slingshot, the pellet slammed unerringly into Horros' muzzle, whereupon the beast collapsed and retched on Omnus' jawbreaker. And while the blue devil gagged on such a magical slug, Vito—the horsefly—emerged from the ruptured gullet, safe and sound... but a bug! Purged of his past, an insect's shape shall be his penance. Vito relinquished his mule skin so David might live!"

"A bigger sacrifice than we've credited him, I'm thinkin'," apologized Fidius, swallowing some smoke as he reached out to poke Vito the fly fondly. The lizard hardly comprehended Creta's tale; but then neither did the others.

"A fly's a finer form for you anyway, Prince," remarked Peter in all sincerity. "You'll not be plagued by your kinfolk now!"

For his part, Vito was happy just to be alive. He buzzed jovially from Fidius to Peter, and over to Valentina, where he was met with a warm, contrite kiss. "That's for saving Davy... But if you dare reveal this maid kissed a fly—so help me, I'll pluck out your wings, since you lack all else! Now, pray tell, whatever became of this cloyed giant, Horros?"

"Yeah! Where is that... thing?" asked David. Only now, under Valentina's touch, did he rouse from his romantic repose and wonder as to the truth of this fly's incredible deeds... and of his own too.

"Shall we say the greedy gremlin's stomach was 'cramped'," quipped Creta, who lighted on David's chest, lest the real hero be forgotten. "In convulsions, the beast was also shriveled most grotesquely out of shape—an improvement in my opinion. David's Goliath is now a teensy little bat!"

"The blue bat!..." chirped Niki, "...with the red eyes!" The dove's own eyes lit up to see her painter so revived. "He was probably lurching after poor Vito to impart some unfinished revenge. And when he came to us, we offered swats instead of service." Valentina flushed as she eased David onto his feet; and all cheered when she pronounced him fit.

"An extraordinary tale at the least," commented Christen. "But the most puzzling question remains unanswered, by fly prince or butterfly sage: Just what artful trickery dug up my father's Egg from the tussock in Hurst Meadow—where I hid it—and buried it in this field of ashes? Or is your reach that long, my friend?"

Such a question posed, no one could answer... Or could they? As they each took a turn pondering the stone pressed against his heart, David caught Valentina in the middle of a wry, pixie pert grin. "Val, you imp! You know, don't you?"

"Shhh—hush, Davy... We women are entitled to our intrigues. Besides, who am I but an elfish damsel to answer the inquiries of sage druids and deities—or a knave, a prince, or paladin?" Then she added matter of factly, "I HAVE seen that clod of yours before, since you ask. The soot must crust your brains as it does your 'Egg'. As anyone can plainly see, beneath the dirt is a bone. If you would know the answer to your mystery, ask Fearsome—for there lies the solution to this riddle."

"Fearsome!... You mean Patrick's dog?" David couldn't believe his ears. "What has that pup got to do with any of this I'd like to know?"

Just then a great rumble was heard, and the vast caverns shook its own reply. Everyone feared new, more thunderous earth tremors, would bring the cavern's magma walls crashing finally down upon them and yet seal their fate it they tarried longer.

"You'll have to question Fearsome yourself it appears," interrupted Creta. "And to do that, we shall have to ditch this slag-flecked fissure while we're still alive to ask. So let your pace be as prolific as your prattle, and as spry as your sport," added the butterfly with a flap toward Valentina.

"Creta's right," proclaimed Niki to one and all. This hole is still too near to hell, for my blood boils yet." The dove pruned her feathers and lofted to the top of Lust's coal head. Painter, I trust your feet will not dawdle now."

With nary a pause, and a quartet of willing backs to lean on, David and his friends scooped up the last of his paints before making their way once again up Lust's pleats. The boy halted only in retrospect atop the rim. "I pray there are no more of her brood about, Niki."

"Lust's larvae will always breed amid discards of the earth's bounty," said the dove. "Though their queen is dead, her own eggs will spawn. Her graven presence remains an eternal stone specter; and her horror bat survives through his bereavement to haunt pilgrims. But waste no weeping epitaphs on her demise; stone silent griefs are fitting drapes for Lust petrified. Let moss and lichen mourn her now; and let the cold, clay—her company—console her, until that time all lust crumbles in decay, brayed and rotted into mold and powder dust, with worms and maggots her worthy heirs. Now, let us delay no longer over her."

David sat musingly astride Peter, the Glass Egg under arm, and Omnus' loaded satchel strung snugly over his shoulder, as though primed for some future works. "Do you really expect you'll be needing those used-up paints again?" asked Valentina.

"Sure," sang David, gesturing into Lust's abyss, "but not on anything like THAT! Prettier portraits are my calling from now on. There's lot's of promise yet to be drawn from these tubes." The artist winked at his pixie. Hearts quaked, and so did the begrudging vault that was Luhrhollow. Its heaving outburst buried the spell of the moment.

The anxious band turned from this sunken nightmare, and into the daylight's embrace, wending their way briskly back towards the surface realities.

"Niki..." mentioned David reluctantly, "...while I prayed for my life, Lord Omnus came to me and... and I saw his face. That is, I saw YOUR image within his robes..." The boy contemplated these words briefly, then shook them off. He preferred to believe the Overlord must truly be a dove—for only such a pure creature could conceive of miracles like the Egg. Niki had been with David all along, even at the end, envisioned in the pit against Horros, just like Omnus said he would be.

"Indeed," cooed the dove in answer to the boy's question. "Mine is his image... and yours... and all his flock—as each child's face is seen in their father's eyes."

The last of their ascent was marked with quizzing and conversation aplenty, and heaping portions of unanswers—as well as anticipation of joyous times to come. But who among them could have predicted the welcome awaiting them outside the confines of Luhrhollow.

CHAPTER 58

The jawboning band of pilgrims filed from the cave's mouth to discover themselves unexpectedly aghast and among a myriad of cloud-cloaked colossals. These great beings were as numerous and eye-filling as clouds crowding the sky, and they beamed brighter than the light any sun could kindle, with stature and grandeur to match. The glimmering gallery of airy knights surrounded the fellowship. Shrouded in willowy white armor trappings, the misty multitude stood posted on billowing cloud mounts and moved nary a muscle.

"Skywalkers!" flapped Creta. The butterfly sounded surprised as she winged her way in circles around the tall, spiraling ranks. "Come on out, you long-winded old vagabond—and bend our ears!"

From the banks of rippled warriors, four fluffy figures, slight as children, emerged with wings tucked, and cloaked in damask wisps. David's chin dropped through his chest. He knew this foursome from his dreams—from his audience with Omnus Overseer. "These are the breaths of our overlord's life, painter," said Niki, "the four winds! They're servants of Zeros, sovereign of the skyways."

"The winds? Why, I thought they were only kids," said David.

Niki cooed, "You remember! 'Twas in the sky lord's household at Welkin High you met them first. Pallbearers then, they mourned for their stricken master, Zeros."

"HO!—but you see their grief is gladness now!" blustered a voracious, full-bodied gusty voice on the heels of the four winds. Like a whirlwind, he swept into their midst, bringing his white-blanketed retinue to their knees as he entered puffy, portly, and proud. He swaggered across the earth—touching it not with print of foot —but holding fast to the air of his domain, as did all the skywalkers in his service.

A dazzling crown caught David's eye. No, wait—it wasn't a crown, but a star! It was the mourning star which had shined dark before, but now radiated warmth to wane the winter, and light to frighten night. The lovely star coursed above the earth beside its frothy master. "That's my shady lady," whiffed the stout and swarthy deity. "She's always around—just like your shadow—only she casts bright shade! Shady is my girl, although she looks to be a 'sun'—Ho ho! As for me, I am Zeros." The large lord bent low to David and Niki, and very nearly blew the boy away in the wake of his windy words. "All of my griefs are smiling this day! I have inhaled the breezes of life and I can taste time's passing again, thanks to your brave and breathless deeds. Even as my sister, Lust, expelled her last poisoned breath, I woke from her death slab concoction, gulped a healing draught of ether and with my four boys partook of the nourishing elixir, liberty, in my airy domain." The sky lord bellowed through a full, frosty beard, and twitched his bulbous blue nose at the companions.

Niki invited Creta and Vito to take refuge in David's breastpocket, lest Zeros' drafty dialogue toss the frail comrades miles asunder. As for the rest, they huddled together with heels and hands dug in, and on their knees bore the brunt of homage introductions as best they could, wondering when Zeros' long-winded thanksgiving would wane.

Niki informed David that the zephyr sire was a weathered old lord, with wind and words to fill the skies if allowed to blow on unabated. "Lord Zeros, son of my grandsire!" hailed the dove presently, rather than wait for an opening. "So it was your tempestuous arrival that so shook the vaults below."

"Ho ho!" blasted the sky with gale-force sincerity. "Niki—and Creta—you two blessed pets! And..." Upon spying Vito, Zeros was momentarily wont for breath, as if horseflies and deities did not mingle. "...And Christen, nephew, playmate of my winds—nay. Nay, good friends, the ground trembles under none but its monarch. 'Twas my brother, Lord Enduros, which the earth applauded—"

"And you, my boy," interjected a solemnly softer squall. "For you, David, my realm does also laud." The cloud ranks parted for the stallion-drawn, platinum-plated chariot of the earth lord, Enduros. Shining straight and stately he stood, impressive in omnipotent glory as Zeros was commanding in his own, more brash, authority. Palladan, his eagle, adorned his sire's shimmering mantled shoulders, flanked by a dazzling convoy of golden titan guardians dispersed alongside the blinding, pearl-decked rows of Zeros' skywalkers. "Rise, David, champion of my sire, Omnus. Rise, Christen, Prince of Theland. And Creta, Niki... all of you—off your knees! This day your are revered. You are the answers to men, and immortals', prayers. We have found you safely out of Luhrhollow, and on behalf of all our subjects, my brother and I beseech you to accept our humble gratitude."

Temporarily deflated under a more articulated sough, Zeros smiled a whiffet grin of amity while waving his rolling brother on. "Now our sister is slain," sighed Enduros without tears. "And while I will not gainsay the dead, let it be known that our vengeance is smitten. When Sovereignton's last blood drop was spilled, each of her defenders knew it was ended here—by you, boy. Even the descent of my brother, the sky, onto the battle plain evoked no dread or despair in the infidels to equal that sight of their own allies' bodies bursting apart at their queen's destruction." Upward swept Enduros' firm right arm; his scepter raised to the high heavens in acclamation. "Hail David!"

Zeros too swelled modestly to the heights in wafty praise. "All hail the 'foundling' of gods!"

Palladan called out to the far borders of Mythlewild. The four winds fanned out in a swirling dance. Such a hearkening of jubilation was unleashed, that to this day the hosts of white-clad skywalkers carry this resounding squall of emotions upon their tempest breaths. And the earth's titans expel their raucous roars from time to time, erupting from the crowns of mountain peaks, or below in the lower quaking depths. Yet it is not in wrath the earth and sky explode, but rather, awe."

The companions gathered around David, and bore him upon their shoulders. "Yes, painter... it's really over!" chirped Niki, answering some past posed question.

"Sovereignton is saved, the realm secured, and the Mythlewild is ours again —to keep for future histories," sang Creta, who fluttered in cheery circles around Enduros' cascading, snowy hair. "Nature has risen with our sky master; listen how the birds and insects sing and hymn in odes to their waking lord. The sun is shy no more, but shines as winter falls back into spring."

"Come along, boy," bid the earth lord, offering David a place beside him in the platinum chariot. "Your noble king waits in his palace with another regal reception, and a warm welcome home for his adopted knight. And my realm too you've saved—and my brothers'. Destiny behests our gratitude as well. So, the honor of escorting the gods' best gallant to Bia Bella has been vested to us immortals, if it please you?"

"If it please me? Boy Howdy!" David gulped and got jitters all over. He couldn't wait to ride with the legendary lord of all lands... yet he hesitated.

His indecision brought broad smiles to the faces of the gods. "Come," prompted Enduros, extending a sinewy hand, "of course there's room for your 'friend' too!"

"Yippee!" shouted David as he hopped onto the seat of honor beside the earth lord, hand in hand with Valentina. The boy refused to sit, and instead propped himself up as tall as he could possibly stand. "All set!" he said, winking gleefully at Palladan.

695

The great eagle called shrill like a bugle's blast, to which Enduros' team of fleet winged stallions responded in gallop. Without so much as a jostle or a jar they all sped northward on the king's roadway—proud to feel the pile of the free earth under their feet. Creta and Niki each lighted on their own master's shoulder, while Valentina invited Vito to join them. Cloud-veiled skywalkers followed the streaking titan brigade, as Zeros drew alongside his ground brother—only slightly higher up. Christen accompanied his four fleecy counterparts in the sky lord's trainband, and remarked to his friends at their oddly listless lord.

"So still, Lord Zeros?...And quiet! Has your slumber stilled the mighty hurricane of winds?"

The sky's grand father mussed the lamb prince's fleecy scalp in jest as he replied softly, "Nay, Christen, not slumber—but a boy—David. What gale could stir a heart so firm as that spunky youth! The season is now his. I shall store my winter chills a while longer and stoke instead the warming sun until his joy is spent... and by my calm, celebrate his feats."

Fidius meanwhile, found Peter's back quite warm, and more to his liking than swirling clouds or rumbling chariots. They nonetheless managed to keep pace with their exalted escort, thanks in no small part to an extraordinarily hefty tailwind, and 'fast' company. The entire party basked in a common glory, and chorus after chorus of good cheer and song, and much merriment on their journey to Sovereignton.

David had never before felt so proud, or so sublime as now, tucked between a deity and an angel. Such an imposing throng of gaiety suddenly elevated him from dismally depressing depths, to peerless heights of mirth. Esteemed by friends and lords alike, the orphaned artist humbly held his head amid the grandeur and the glory, riding the zenith of preeminence with zealous restraint.

For some unfathomable reason however, David felt an uneasy qualm grip his flesh. A clammy sweat broke on his brow as the steely hand of Enduros pressed upon his shoulder. The land lord's hallowed eyes were transfixed on the object the young pilgrim clenched to his breast.

"Is it stone, or spoil of war you enfold as life itself?" probed Enduros in a knowing and suspicious tone. "Tell me true, boy."

"It's the Egg, Lord," blurted David as the old holy squeezed forth a numb reply. "It's the Glass Egg... I swear!" And so was the truth extracted unalterably from his lips.

"Ahhh... I see!" said the earth god without skepticism. "So... your boots and brushes worked their wonder, and found my Egg at last... May I have it?" When no response was forthcoming, the liege of lords asked again, in other words. "I will have my Egg now, boy—Give it to me!" Enduros' edifying voice, so waxen and consecrated before, now rose in timbre and commanded compliance.

Yet this different David dared to take issue and stand on his principles. "Oh great leader of gods, forgive me for refusing, but... there's been a mistake—"

"Mistake! Take care, boy—I am not prone to error!"

David bowed under Enduros' incontestable voice. He glanced to Valentina and Niki for support, but they seemed feign to notice the earth's arm twisting style. Creta and Palladan sat like aloof waxworks perched by their master's ears. Only Zeros, who tread close by, was attune to their conversation—though by propriety he kept his distance. Still, his very proximity bolstered David's confidence, and he returned the land lord's forceful gaze. "Granted, Lord Omnus did craft the Glass Egg for you, Your Lordship. But surely in your infinitely celebrated wisdom, you can best comprehend the import of restoring such power as this to its creator... Is that not so?"

Enduros scowled. His steep brow sank severely, and David held his breath. "In all honesty, it does not impress me; on the contrary, this Egg looks incredibly rock-like to my eyes."

"Oh, but Your Lordship," emphasized the boy, "we are living witnesses to its endowments—"

"Humbug! And Thunderation!" fumed Enduros, turning scarlet under his bristling mantle of whiskers. His entire majestic countenance twisted into violent rage under the influence of the Glass Egg. "Must you ALWAYS contradict me, underling! I fully know its power! It's that potency I would have! Rock or Egg—it was meant for me—not for your likes to hoard away! That Egg is mine by right—and I claim it now! Surrender my boon, do you hear!" Enduros' voice was double-edged and thrust fully at the pilgrim's throat; his fists were bludgeons pounding at the boy's rapidly fading resistance.

Suddenly, in the midst of such illustrious security, David felt horribly threatened and vulnerable—so much now, as in Luhrhollow, did danger press upon his breast. Here, in gods' hands, serenity seemed so certain. Alarmingly, it was here and now that the young heart's nerves shattered. "VAL!" he cried, hugging the elf maid close to be fortified by her warmth. "Niki!... He looked longingly at the pious dove on his shoulder. But neither fowl or fairy lass were invited to participate in Enduros' dialogue with the pilgrim. Their ears simply rang with song and laughter. Only Zeros observed the child's dilemma. He twitched his plumb-blue nose and smiled a calming breath, but otherwise kept sill.

Maybe it was this encouragement which spurred David to act so brash; or maybe it was the magic of the Glass he held which enforced his reason; or—it may have been because he was simply a brave boy. For whatever reason, he reacted as before—with bold, brazen courage.

"NO!" he retorted to the surprised earth lord. "I cannot relinquish the Overseer's Egg to you, My Lordship—that would be impossible! My mission isn't completed until this creation is in its maker's hands..." David paused to cringe. He half expected the earth to rise in wrath and swallow him up again. Yet, the road remained spread out before him, and Enduros stayed surprisingly civil, though his demeanor was still heated to steam his beard. Albeit, with the lid left on the kettle, the boy applied more fuel for his argument. "Besides, Lordship, Lust is no threat anymore. What need has the lord of all earth for some magic charm or talisman now?"

"One can always use power, boy... even gods." The deity's composure sulked over his features; he combed through his whiskers. "I want to be great again... esteemed," he explained, "celebrated as in the far gone past. I want to be invincible again, strong knit—an earth shaker—like when I was young, and troubadours would sing praises to my exploits... and bards boast of my glorious deeds..." Enduros' eyes lost their fire and fell empty and waxen on the ground.

"But, Your Lordship," said David, daring to take the earth by the hand, "are you not exalted now? You front a resplendent army in the vanguard of a hard won victory over your arch rival, Lust. Don't you notice the vanishing of years since you donned your platinum panoply, and resumed your proper throne? The Enduros I behold now isn't shrunk, or wasted away—but hale and hardy, every inch the indomitable idol the legends exalted in ancient verse. Minstrels will pen new songs. Poets shall portray new, more stirring epic tales to rhyme. Your afflictions are a pittance, as are the years, to an immortal of your stature. Youth is yours to command—as am I—and all the earth, which is YOUR domain, great and most noble Lordship. Unlike the hocus-pocus vagaries of your sister, who merely believed she was sanctified, your power is no momentary caprice—but a durable legacy to divinity..." David peeked up, trying to glimpse under Enduros' heavy brow and thought he saw a glinting eye, so he proceeded. "Heck!... will power is the only power you're lacking if you ask me. With such sand, you'll live as long as you can dream. Why, you don't need this measly clump of mine, you've something better—you have endurance! And furthermore, if it's the Glass Egg that goads you to welcome me into your chariot, then you can just drop me off this minute!"

Now it was David's turn to trounce. The boy stood frowning at the brooding deity. For a moment only silent thoughts were exchanged. Then, through the thicket of whiskers, an ingratiating smile surfaced. "Please... do not leave me, boy. You have my eternal gratitude, and sincerest apologies. If not for you, child, I would have lost my head, nay—my kingdom—for want of that Egg. So that I may never again forget who I am, or was, I beseech you... stay beside me. If not in flesh, at least in heart and prayer, until I call for you at life's end." With that said, orphan and omnipotent clasped hands, and David pledged to live under Enduros' shadow until his final days.

"And, if you would heed your godhead—old fool that he is—you would be wise to hide that troublesome dole away—beyond the scope of envious eyes. Even a gritty crust cannot long disguise such magic."

David hastened to pack his prize safely away inside his satchel. In doing so, he couldn't help but take notice of Zeros' tactful interest in the proceedings which had passed so unnoticed by all others. His thoughts were exposed to the god of skies. "An immortal's grappling with his more human falterings is no proper spectacle for fleshlings to behold," explained Zeros, so David might know.

"And you, Lord Zeros... is it the Egg's magic that brings you also forth in homage?" asked David flashing a hitherto unused tool of his new maturity—skepticism.

"Nay, boy!" huffed the sky lord, somewhat disgruntled. "By heaven, it was the Egg's bearer which called me hither. Such power as you tote was never cast for this windblown deity... though, admittedly, by its possession I would not have slept the season away—Ho!"

"No... you would have contracted an affliction far worse than eternal sleep, Your Lordship—absolute power! Does that allure not tempt you? Aren't you awed by the Glass Eggs' swaying potency?"

"Naturally, pilgrim..." spoke the sky, caressing David with gentle, admiring breaths, "... and even more by yours!"

"Hey, Davy!" called Peter, pulling alongside the swift-born chariot. "Come out of that daydream you're in! Get back down to earth and listen... Do you hear it? Troubadors! They're singing verses composed to us, and our victory. Imagine... me and you, and all of us—celebrated in ballads!"

"You too, Yur Holinesses," wheezed Sir Fidius, referring to the deities. "Us ol' timers are back on the lips of our heirs too, by golly... fur a spell leastways."

"Look there!" exclaimed Valentina. "In the distance you can see Sovereignton. Why... however did we arrive so quickly?"

"Gods are impatient travelers," mentioned Christen, winking to Zeros, who laughed boisterously.

"Like good news, your triumphs have preceded you here, David, on trails swifter than my winds—the tongues of men! You boys will hear songs and tales enough to turn even heaven's ear, and boasts enough to leave the likes of me breathless in raw wonder."

"And there are some surprises too," added Creta, who nestled in Enduros' plush beard, tickling her earth lord's fancy.

"Why, yes," he chuckled. "We mustn't forget the surprises!"

CHAPTER 59

By late afternoon Middleshire's bustling Southshire Road bulged with assorted clusters of haggard and homeward bound citizenry. Gentry and soldiers, dappled among yeomen, drovers, and serfs, together with whatever family or possessions survived to tow. But anon, the noon observed something which swerved these packs of peoples from their various paths and labors. They all flocked toward the platinum chariot which sat halted in a shallow dell at woods' edge. It was far back of the rest of the divine caravan which paraded ahead eager for news of sons and sires and countrymen, and had, by the merry sound of it, arrived through Sovereignton's south gate to a resounding reception. Cheers and shouts of 'Hail Sir David'!... 'Prince of Deities'!... 'Savior of the Shire'!... 'Champion of Mythlewild'! trolled off into the undulating countryside, and tingled David's ears, giving him pause to think. Valentina plied the impetuous roadside gathering's fervor with twinkling eyes and a radiant smile—and lots of fast talk—while the bashful recipient of their attention mulled at the feet of the lord of the earth, and under Niki's consoling wing.

"Are you afraid even here, painter?" cheeped Niki into the boy's ear. "You have surmounted defeat, now it's time to face the test of triumph!"

David sought refuge behind Enduros' robes. "Listen to them, Niki," he murmured, with jellied cheeks and quivering lips. "They cheer for their 'savior'; but all that's here is, me... David, somebody from who knows where. Who am I really, Niki... a nameless, homeless, hero? I'm no messiah—that's for sure!"

Niki only rolled her round head at the pilgrim. "For the time being, the world deems you to be 'Sir' David, slayer of devils, ennobled protector of Sovereignton, paladin to kings and gladiator of gods—and select among both. So— what's wrong with a few titles? Harken to the masses; be their idol, they deserve one —and a grand one Fate has provided. Accept the acclamation, painter. You are the keeper of their flame—the bearer of the Glass Egg. Yet I believe it is yourself that's been found, by discovering what you are not."

"Such devotion you command does make the heads of gods go green, young eagle," spoke Enduros out of reverence. "It is from their knees they shout; yet not for me their lord, but rather for you David—their brethren. I would savor such worship, and relish the rewards of my labors while they last. Memories of heroes are oft' time fickle—as I can attest. People, not deeds, mold heroes... and reluctance is no qualification."

"The choice is hardly in your hands anymore, David," observed Creta, fanning her wings to the adoring populace swelling around them,"it's in theirs!" Palladan cawed in concurrence. Even Vito the fly buzzed his support.

"Do make up your mind!" sighed Valentina. "I can appease your partisans no longer, Davy. Now it's your turn. Go on, 'champ'—your public cries for you. Or would you fain to have Lust's clay-born embrace you again, instead of your king and countrymen?" While her he-man waffled and waited, Val began to fuss and polish her young Galahad so lava dust not diminish his luster.

At last David looked from the cover of Enduros' garb, and turned his shoulder south—but only ever so briefly. Then, proudly did he rise and step forward, facing the roadside with uplifted arms—just like a natural-born hero.

From under the tumultuous bellows of praise, did Lord Enduros urge on his team of spirited stallions. But slower now did they trot, splendidly slower, all the way to the wide open gatewall of Sovereignton. Through the waving, riotous multitude lining the concourse, behind the reams of bowed heads and dipped banners, lay the less exhilarating scene of carnage and devastation which was Serenity Plain's battle legacy. On the Rollingway River, David sickened to see the skeleton that was the royal fleet. A rift and wounded Windy was beached beside the quay in the distance, yet the regal lady gallantly dipped the proud Decima Colors in honor of her former 'galley slave'. David saw neither captain or coxswain on her splintered decks—and noticed that her flagstaff was rigged at half mast.

The platinum chariot crossed the red-gouged river bank, rank with death, yet still flowing life. The morbid flavor of bloody water stuck on David's tongue, and in his thoughts of Windy's crew. Enduros' team drew to a halt beside the south gate wine well. Its effervescent spring clot with thicker, fouler juice than fruit. It would someday distill decay and yield again its sweet refreshing comfort to pilgrims venturing through the city's gates, Folly would see to that. But... where was Folly? Momentarily the taste and taint of dead men's anguish shut out the cheering throng's jammed on every lancet, rooftree, and portal along the city gatewall. Gapped and gutted by war's decimation, the city's quarried curtain still stubbornly housed its inhabitants with aged august dignity. Above its blood and tear-filled moat, the sundered south gate creaked open under the yawning barbican, and a thousand ecstatic welcomes poured forth from a thousand bursting, happy hearts.

As David halted by the gatehouse, awed and aghast while centered within the euphoric mob, he felt an icy, crooked curse creep up from the caking mud on which he stood. He looked down into the trampled sod grave which held DeSeet interred, and the boy's grief was gone—for his fear was dead too.

He gazed heavenward and saw the four winds brush back the gloomy shrouds, as the sun—in abeyance to its master, Zeros—burned through the grey, murky sky draped about the plain. Other residue would not be so easily dispersed however; behind him, the droves of people had scattered to carry on their tasks of laying to rest the wastes of war. Homeless and hardened, as well as happy, they streamed back into the hills and dales to repair their ravaged lives, and set to build again and to begin again. Valentina scanned the trudging, strife-torn masses as they passed. In their plight she found no joy; instead she cried, as thoughts of her own family welled through gladder tears.

"Do not weep for the dead, little one," counseled Enduros knowingly. "Their graves are platinum shrines this hour too, such is their honor. And do not salt your sympathy with concern for your own household, for yours are among the living honored." Valentina dried her grief in David's happy hug.

Enduros also noted Vito, who neither budged nor buzzed from his mounting woe. "Even you, Prince fly, would be proud of your queen mother and stepsire and siblings, who long to welcome their prodigal home." Vito smiled slightly, as only a fly could.

David meanwhile found it hard to shake his own sullen mood. Over his shoulder, the flags on masts and tower sticks were all flown at half. "Tell us, Lordship... who is it that has died? For whom do all the royal pennants weep?"

The lord of the earth then waved his arm across the fallowed field and over the wracked city walls. "There lies the casualty the standards grieve, my boy—not one death, but thousands, a tragic loss ruefully born by us all."

"Yet there is one..." spoke Creta, beaming brighter than her rainbow wings, "...one that death gave back to us so the living might rejoice." But she would say no more, leaving David to wonder who.

"Howdy, li'l' knight!" wheezed a grainy old voice known so well to David. "You comin' in, or ain't you?" Who should it be all stacked up by the gate, puffy and proud in a shiny new armor vest, free of all traces of swamp and soot, and brandishing his trusty javelin...

"Fidius!" gawked the boy. "What a quick and splendid arrival!"

"SIR Fidius, if you please, li'l' Davy... knight errant, and new Captain a the Gate. I'm a fur real knight again, just like when I was a young tad...an' looky here!" Though standing poised and rigid up to now, the mellow croc' couldn't help but dash from his post and display a gleaming gold key. "The 'found' prince gifted me with my new metal skin—an' gave me charge a this valuable key.

David was indeed impressed with his lizard's new rank. "Why, Fidius... I mean, Sir Fidius, you've been promoted from catacombs to catwalks. In place of prison keys, you hold the city's key—"

"Oh no, li'l' Davy... This key ain't mine—it's yurs! His Highness knighted you too—officially! All of us who drew sword fur his lamb son, an' fur you, is tin skins now. King Constantio wanted me ta present his city's key so your journey ta him might be hastened—and honored!"

David graciously accepted the accolade, and clasped it tightly like Enduros' scepter, holding it visibly high and with great respect. Then, as praise and plaudits showered down from the eaves and porticos, he cast a bewildered look at the lizard. "But, Sir Fidius... if you're the gate captain, where is Folly? His wine well is soured... and who pray tell is this 'found' prince of whom you spoke? Do you mean Christen?"

"Don't fret fur Folly, li'l' knight," assured Fidius. "'Hip' still oversees the city's wells—especially now. His position has been, how should I say... 'elevated'. In recognition of his airborne heroics, the king decreed Hip' ta be the royal air corps—an' its first appointed commander. How 'bout that! As fur the foundling prince? He ain't no lamb, no sirree!" Fidius snickered at the comparison. "C'mon, you can see fur yurself. He's waitin' ta greet you... again!" The armor-clad lizard scampered ahead to pave the way through the crowded streets without waiting for further queries.

"'Again'?" asked David anyway. But Valentina and Vito could not answer; while Niki looked to Creta, who would not. Palladan knew, but kept his secret, cawing. And Lord Enduros reined his winged team forward with tight lips.

Onward went the platinum chariot, beneath the streaming ramparts, winding through the delirious crowd, and under the wide raised portcullis whose creaking, spiked cusps revealed no riddles. The city lanes were cleared now, of all but elated townsfolk. Only the debris and wreck of broken buildings loomed over their mirth like shadowy reminders of the dark which prompted their dawn. Once inside, Fidius returned to his post at the gatehouse, assuming his soldier stature. "A gilded gate- keeper our old 'gator, huh, Niki!" commented David.

"As polished as your broad grin, painter," chirped the dove. "But you'll lack no luster after today I'm thinking."

"Have you ever seen so many people!" exclaimed Valentina, curling and craning her head this way and that so as not to miss anyone, least of all her dear family.

"This isn't any devastated city," marveled David, awakening to the shouts and cheers from the jubilant throng, and waving more gratitude right back at them. "Sir Fidius has unlocked the pearly gates of heaven, and the gods are escorting us into paradise!"

Through peals of brassy cornets, and under a flourish of raucous trumpets, the pilgrim paraded past the pearl-appearing granite walls and over elysium paths heralded and acclaimed by all present. Not on streets paved with gold he rode, but on cobblestone, yet bulging with cordons of gold hearts and stout souls, and red carpeted with exuding welcomes every inch of the way. Flags, banners, ramparts—all waved for David, and handkerchiefs too unfurled in moist and merry salutes.

Soon the towering spires of Bia Bella soared into view. Their numbers were thinned and tussled, but they bore her battle scars with unparalleled dignity and grace. Everywhere chinks and rents rutted her brick complexion. Her broad, stretching curtain was shambled and torn open, but withstanding and intact—and instilling hope and heart warmth to all who massed in her granite hems. She stood as always, etched with enduring grandeur—a proper bastion for her people—and a most gratifying sight to homeless pilgrims.

The platinum chariot guided its own way into the city square, where Lord Zeros was waiting to meet them, flanked by the four winds, which rustled as winds will often do when stirred. Overhead, Vero swooped into view astride the svelte and graceful Paramount. Also clinging to his father's back was Peter, who called to David as the sleek alicorn glided to a landing beside his mortal master, Violato the Red. The wounded red-beard saluted as the newest king's champion arrived. Flanking the palace captain at the royal gate was General Affirmare and his faithful page, Yang. "Well met, young Prince," addressed the crusader.

"Welcome home!" they all hailed, and David nearly cried.

Among the notables in the reception party was the most prominent and distinguished family of the kingdom, at least in Valentina's eyes. For there, peeking at her with a wide button-eyed smile, was her baby sister, Jing Jing, tucked atop her father, Ambrose's, squat shoulders. The gentle elder's round face glowed at the sight of his precious pixie daughter safe and sound. Feathers flew as a teary-eyed Celeste flapped her floor length wings in glee. Her halo lit up the day, augmenting her silvery hair. The stern angel matron jumped for joy as her little fay drew near.

"Hi ya, Davy!... You too, Sis," called Patrick, as if one pocket-sized boy could be heard above such enthusiastic babel and ballyhoo.

Nevertheless, David waved to his good friends—and their three-headed puppy, Fearsome, who resisted his tiny master's most ardent attempts at restraint. Each head out barked even the loudest of cheers; while his long, long wagging tail kept anyone close by hopping and on their toes.

"Humph!" grunted Valentina to David. "It seems your return excites my little brother more than I do."

"Ho!" laughed the sky lord uncontrollably. "Now do you know how I feel, fair one? Your suitor steals thunder, even from us gods. The sky has cheated death today, and yet the boy's brethren hold him even higher in esteem."

"Boy Howdy!..." flushed David.

"Creta agreed with her uncle. "Indeed, David, this is clearly your crowd—and your day. They will not let you live with your humility. Your deeds have dressed you with a god's glory that these admirers will not let you shed."

David couldn't help laughing. "All I started with was a pair of shoes. I doubt glory's garb could suit me better."

Niki chirped too. "Quite a change from your last entrance into Sovereignton, is it not, painter? That night we stole into town as scoundrels do, hiding beneath Folly, and dropped from the sky in secrecy like thieves' pokes."

As if to punctuate the thought, a rubber-tipped message arrow landed with a 'twang', smack on David's chest, over his heart next to Niki's pocket. Its feathers stuck under Valentina's chin, tickling her pug nose. There was no mistaking Folly's handiwork. The hippo cherub floated exuberantly above the young couple like an inflated cloud over a parade, flip flopping in and out of a dozen disfigured sorties, and flapping a dainty wing at David.

"So that's the royal air corps," giggled Valentina, "the whole of it—in one round, white lump?"

"More like cupid!" said David, recalling another popular myth from home, as he glanced off Valentina's puzzled look to read the note attached to the arrow. Its message was magic: 'You are loved' was all it said. "Folly! Have you been sipping strawberry wine again?" jested David.

"Oh no, sir!" responded the albino hippo in earnest from on high. "On my oath! I've sobering responsibilities now...commander of the air I am. The birds be my subordinates. You see, I'm going to train pigeons to carry my messages."

"Pigeon envoys—how novel!" David chuckled as he winked at Niki. "But tell me, Commander, can these carrier pigeons ever be as reliable as hippopotamuses?"

"Oh, indeed," countered Folly. "Though not as hardy, the tiny chippers are a bit faster and less likely to, uh... stray. But the really important communiques—like the one you're clutching, sir—are still MY responsibility. That note be from the king's subjects to you. Hope you get its meaning, sir."

"He does," answered Valentina, reading over David's shoulder. "And that goes for me too!" she added, kissing him sweetly on the cheek. Then, even before they ground to a halt at Bia Bella's huge portal, the sunshine-eyed elf maiden leaped from the chariot and skipped into her family's embraces grinning brightly, while her boy friend's jaw hung open, wide as the Bella's gate.

"Better close it, painter," peeped Niki, "else the abandoned Vito forage for a new nest under your inviting tongue."

However, David's mouth gaped all the wider, as his buoyant reception gained momentum. A familiar flood of prodigious faces issued from the palace gate. At its crest was the crew of Miss Windy. Admiral Honos, Pax, and Siegfried Dragonheart lead the cavalcade, as a hundred happy hearts swamped Enduros' chariot, hoisted their pilgrim onto a sea of shoulders and swept him across the royal courtyard on a tide of undulating jollity. The last David saw of the earth lord, his retinue and Zeros' joined in with the others, their divine elbows mixed it up with lesser lords and lowborns. All were peers, elevated to equality in the day's eyes by a boy, an egg—and a purpose.

"Another tossed sea has hold of you, laddy," roared the bull admiral.

"But we'll steer our floundering galley scrub to home port." squealed the gay griffin coxswain.

"Aye! And to a warmer welcoming water than that last one for our fearless demon slayer!" added the Northman.

David swerved from sea to shoulder, bathing in bliss, landing at last on the great hall's steps, whereupon the swaying, shouting ocean of bodies did hush and kneel. On the balcony above, their Royal Highness, the High King, Constantio appeared astride his cloud. His sheared and matted lion skin vestments still clung from a pair of sturdy, thick shoulders. Alongside His Highness, stood his queen, Her sublime Grace, Superbia. Like her husband, Her Majesty had found no time to groom in the space of their victory—and under her gnarled boar hair found a modest, resplendence heretofore missing from her armory of beauty aids. With the sires were their sons: Christen, Agustus, and someone else unbeknownst to David... yet somehow familiar. He was a handsome youth, with long, combed titian hair and garbed in exquisite jeweled ermine. Yet he was a small and fragile fellow, no taller than the billiken, Jo, who with his crystal lady, Clarissima, supported the frail lad between them.

Before the royal family, even the titans and divinities of lords of earth and sky did bow their heads out of supreme respect for a mortal, who would one day attain their station in the life beyond.

Constantio would not allow such adoration however, and bid they all rise. "Especially you, David, my boy—fidelity's most devoted servant—before whom your king does kneel in homage from this day on." From behind a war's ravaged face, Constantio bled joyous tears. And never was he more endearing, or more stately, as in his weeping. "For everything you have given us, young knight... I owe you most dearly. From death's crypts, you have brought my son back to me..." Constantio held out a knotted arm and beckoned that son to him. "By him, I welcome you into my house, David."

"Long live Christen!" shouted David all by himself. He was practically the only one present who expected the lamb prince to come forward. By now almost everyone else knew the good news. Thus David was the one left staring is shock, as on the balcony, it was not Prince Christen who stepped to the rail—but the smaller, runty one. This handsome slip of a youth fixed a big, bug-eyed gaze on David as he spoke in weird and withdrawn utterings, hesitating and obviously uncomfortable under so much attention. Yet his vested presence commanded respect, while his very survival earned everyone's admiration. The people listened eagerly to what he said.

A long tongue unfurled from his parting lips, nearly collapsing David in disbelief. "Do I shock you so even now, David?... Did I not share my hospitality with you once before, in a deeper room within my house? Listen closely... the walls are not weeping now—eh!"

Suddenly—shockingly—the taste of rats and roaches was recalled in David's throat, and he shuddered to think of that dungeon. But it was true. It could be no other. His manner was still 'buggy'. His gangly hair, combed and shampooed, and revealed two eyes not one, but there was no denying it. The shackles were replaced with royal robes, which were perfumed and cleansed of prison's stench. This majestic minikin was every inch a nobleman. "Candlemaker?" gasped David finally. To which the handsome young prince grinned.

"Desderado!" shouted Constantio to the assembled multitude. My eldest son—Prince of Middleshire, and future High King of Theland!" Now it was David's ears which perked as His Highness explained. "Behold my first born, claimed—not on the fox's hunt—but the lion's! Imprisoned to certain death by my ambitious chancellor, Count DeSeet, the helpless child was held insane under his hypnotic host. And there he stayed, until resurrected by more modest trappings, which—while slaying the consort Lust—did set my son's mind and body free again."

Desderado only nodded timidly in his father's shadow. He was stifled not so much by madness, as by fanfare. Any intended comment was quick to evaporate under a crescendo of cheers and bravos.

Like the rest of the citizens, David was enthralled. "So that's what Creta meant by 'One who death gave back'!" he mumbled to Niki.

"Or, was it you, painter?... Or was it each of us? Is the witch's thumb not lifted from all our necks!"

"But lo! My family is not yet complete," spoke Constantio again, his swarthy voice booming above the din, "nor are my knightly ranks." With that, Constantio anxiously unfolded a sparkling white tunic embossed with a rainbow-hued device: a Trigon, like one of the ten realms of Mythlewild. Except this one was unique. It was a pair of trigon shapes: one being white, which represented Middleshire; and the other bearing all ten colors of Theland—just like the royal rainbow crest of the Decima Crown. "It's a Duel Trigon, my boy," explained the king, "which I now confer on you. The white wing is your pilgrim's shoe; and it's paired with your loaded paint- brush. For my newest knight, one coat—like one color—is not enough. Gad—even ALL is not enough! Were it only mine to deal." Volleys of cheers held David numb and speechless. "Well? Come forward—Sir David of Pastel Park. 'Tis about time to kneel and receive your title, and your heraldry, so all may know you are my champion!"

Adulation erupted anew as David was ushered to a place of honor among the king's family. After donning his honors, and finding both title and tunic an edifying fit, he exchanged hugs with his brethren. They zealously bid their pilgrim-painter-knight speak as the audience did plead.

Well, David's heart was pounding so loud by now that the fly prince, Vito, was forced to desert his breastpocket niche, and was instantly attracted to his new found stepbrother, Desderado, with whom he felt an insect's affinity. However, his earnest attempts at affection were sorely misinterpreted by the prince's protective sow mother. Queen Superbia drew a bead on the pesky fly as David endeavored to speak.

Words evaporated in the pilgrim's dry throat. In his nervousness, he peeked into his breastpocket for prompting; but Niki ducked back under cover. This new nest of David's afforded even deeper refuge for the shy dove.

"My loyal subjects..." said Constantio, enfolding his young champion from his predicament. "...I think Sir Pilgrim has finally met his match!"

Peals of friendly laughter thundered up to ply on David's ears and ease his nerves. Its intoxicating merriment soon dispelled any fears and reminded the boy how soothing cheer can be. "How long it's been since I relaxed... It was in this very hall, Sire..."

"Aye, my boy—and will be again." Constantio quelled his public so they might hear him. "It is time we all relaxed. We've earned some leisure, have we not? Having endured immeasurable tests of our fortitude, let us now surrender to our foibles. Tomorrow we will bury war's ruins and begin to build a better future; but today, diversion shall be our toil. Set aside your shovels and sorrows, as our swords and strife have been laid down. Anon, Lord Zeros has invited the sun as a special guest to warm our victory. Celebration is in order—" Here Constantio's eyes glassed like polished onyx—at the memory his gathered family traced. "As I recall, a war intruded upon Mythlewild's first annual Octoberfest. We shall recommence our commemoration to fall, and take up our festivities tonight—with a smashing thanksgiving banquet. Zounds! I mean to have my Octoberfest—even if it is November!"

"December, Sire," corrected Clarissima, his glass seer. "We are well into a new month, Liege." Jo held up one stubby pink finger as if to prove his lady's claim.

"Zounds—Let it be July! We'll have the merriest, cracker jack carousal this realm has ever witnessed! 'Twill be a feast fit even for the gods! My sons are returned to me." The stout monarch hugged each of his children fondly, including David. "Would that Vito, misguided ass that he is, could be with us to share in this sweet occasion—"

"Oh!... But he is, Sire," said David.

"Infernal fly!" snorted Queen Superbia, as she prepared to thwart the bothersome bug hovering over the royal family, as if he belonged.

David intervened just in the nick of time, and explained in no easy fashion Vito's affliction—and his heroics. News of her son's valorous role in their victory delighted the entire royal house. "Understand, Your Grace, that no power exists greater than the Egg's," emphasized David. "Your son will remain a fly... well, forever maybe... unless he lands upon a more suitable station."

Despite the fact that his stepson was now an insect, the king nevertheless rejoiced to have his loyalty, regardless of the wrap containing it. "Man, mule... or midge—whatever! A fly, By Gad! What title better suits my 'gadfly' son than that of steward. You will be in charge of our house, fly. Bia Bella was never more yours than now. Everyone, no matter how illustrious or itinerant, is welcome under my roof!" proclaimed the king. Then, holding his speck of a son aloft on his finger, Constantio invited his subjects in. "Our city is my banquet table tonight, to accommodate all my guests. None shall be turned away this eve... or ever more, By Thunder! My November-December commemorative Octoberfest will also be a birthday party. My boys, Vito and Desderado are both born to me again; Christen is safely returned; and in the bargain, I've gained another shoot—Sir David of Pastel Park!"

A jubilant tumult then burst throughout Sovereignton town as word of the celebration spread. That night, not in the king's grand dining hall, nor in any palace part—nor anywhere in the entire city—but only in the great outdoors was there room enough to hold the happy, heart-strong citizens who laid aside their tribulation to partake and savor the triumph of the evening.

CHAPTER 60

As the uninvited dusk approached to attend the king's Octoberfest, fun and games and contests for young and old alike had commenced. Songs and music echoed throughout the rubbled lanes, enticing any remaining sour heart to shed their dower moods, slap their thighs and stomp their feet to the tunes in dancing revelry. By evening's shank, none were without felicity and good times to parley. Sumptuous and gala the celebration was not—not if your only measure be from pantries and casks. Food and drink were in short supply, but mirth and merriment were not ravaged, and no complaints were voiced. Not even the gods were disappointed. Fellowship and goodwill were not depleted by war. Gods and kings and masses mobbed together, mingling ear to elbow in a jolly stupor. Flasks and songs and voices were raised in toasts and boasts to each and every other. The congeniality abounded above the battle debris and slaked the heartiest appetites. The boisterous droves craved not meat or liquid substance, but more filling, flavorful fare. For lack of viand, some 'meaty' talk would tantalize. Though beverage be meager, spirits were brimming. The suppers gnawed on bones of bombast and bravura, the ingredients of tall tales. All were served aplenty at the festal boards tonight—and no one was left wanting.

"In Bia Bella's main dining hall were the exploits' helpings portioned highest. Under her towering rafters boasts and puffery were pitched to the ceiling; even Constantio's mounted menagerie unstuffed their ears take it in. Immortals vied with mortals' imaginations in embellishing a heaping main course of stirring heroes' stew. While stomachs starved, the ears feasted with wild and whetting yarns dished out with fervent relish. No wine or spicy sauces spurred their drunken appetites. It was ungarnished talk and waggle on which they gorged, and all present had their say. Bawdy, bloody battles fought again and daring deeds retold and enhanced, could not quench the thirsting multitude who would savor every last drop and syllable. This was Mythlewild's glory. Words were their brew. Constantio filled their horns of fancy as he and his family and generals and subjects, and even gods, each took their turn in pouring bold and frothy words onto the hungry ears— beginning with their host. By his imperial account, it was Constantio's brilliant generalship which won Cinnabar.

"Nay! 'Twas not brains—but blood—that won that round!" boasted Violato, who tore open his livery to reveal his hewn and hackled body as proof that victory is bought by pounds of flesh.

"Wield well the sword—and the flesh is spared!" argued Affirmare displaying his red-glazed broadsword, Byne Un. "Scarred steel repairs easier than severed limbs—as the headless husk, Negare can vouch!"

"It is victory that would be severed from us, had I not arrived in time to stem the tide!" acclaimed Siegfried Dragonheart polishing his story to a luster matching his metal.

But Folly was there to take issue. "You had company on your sally into Cinnabar, forget not, Sir Northman! And just who would have survived these campaigns without a sky watch to hearken all from preying condors, and retrieve rescue where there was none to be had?"

"What about me?" mentioned Pax, finally set to extoll himself in no small part. "Did I not also serve beside the Dragonheart in the chase of snakewood and Cinnabar—and with king's air corps against the condor flocks!"

"My brave helmsman also steered the king's fleet to great success upon the blue battle fields of Citrine and Rollingway!" bellowed Honos in his most bullish voice, so none present could slight the conflicts waged upon the waterways. "Would that my fearless ship were here, she would take the air from all your sails!"

"An' in defense a Sovereignton, Adm'r'l...ye would've swapped yer good eye ta see yer burly bosun ward off the infidels, buyin' time 'til the mainstays drew up." Agustus spat a sticky slab of tobacco onto the floor. The young shellback reveled among his old shipmates.

Queen Superbia snorted beside the king, overlooking her farrow's coarseness temporarily. "Had my husband spared us another cohort or two to hold our town, 'twould have fared far worse for the invaders than the Bella's walls—or the walls of our dear citizen's bodies who shored her defenses."

"And some mighty precious bodies they were too, who threw themselves under the sword!" Elderman Ambrose now stood and attempted to be brief—but wasn't. The long-winded statesman was now the king's newly appointed confidant and prime counsel; thus he felt obliged to speak in excess of his position. "My own beloved family was only one of many to take up arms for this shire of ours—and did so with unfailing devotion..."

"As did countless others, Papa," noted Celeste calmly to her children, preferring not to cross words with her better equipped spouse. "Were his sword as honed as his tongue, our foes would have gone down begging for mercy!"

"Our swords were keen enough to fend off a hundred scallywags from southgate, right Fearsome," Patrick's pup barked three times in vociferous agreement with his towheaded master. He then returned to his repast of bones, which were as abundant as flattery.

Valentina laughed at her little brother's big brag. "Ho, Patrick, next you'll have your baby sister slaying giants... which, I might add just happens to be my claim to fame! A dozen clay-born ogres fell victim to my wiles, a retaliation to those upstart kidnappers!"

"It's true!" insisted Peter, as the pixie's family raised their brows. "It's many a monster and crude we in Davy's company confronted..." The pony boy raised his voice a notch or two above the family level and tested the verbal waters spilling onto the great hall's flagstone free for all. "Even pain-racked as I was, I managed to stay afoot—at times even racing, in and out of one pitfall after another—"

"Durn tootin'!" wheezed Sir Fidius, in from his post to notch a boast or two shoulder to shoulder with a frequent antagonist, Siegfried the dragon slayer. But the vainglorious Northman tapped this occasion to attone for past indiscretions against the aged reptile, and those of his ilk. Thus, arm in arm, he gave ground—and listened to the gator's offering. "From the bite a giant tree squids, ta the mazard of morass, 'twas nip and tuck every step an' turn a the way fur some! An' after sluggin' it out tooth an' claw, this leather neck still managed ta dredge up the winnin' tool— the li'l' dauber's pouch! AN' what's more, on the way I saved this here razzle-dazzle deity, yes sirree—right, big feller!"

Vero nodded politely. "It is so, Sir Fierce. Your fame was also retrieved in that sink, where once it was lost." The sun titan was so absorbed in the exchange of tales between two of truth's best benders, that he said no more, preferring to leave the mortals' exaggerations on the lips of those most deft at their use.

However, the lordly eagle, Palladan was not so prone to discretion. The normally stodgy old bird had been sitting on an exceptionally heroic chapter to add among these yarn spinners. After crediting the Ill-timber's demise to Vero and Paramount, he fluffed up his chest and hastened to describe how he alone did dispatch Vexpurra, Odios, and Horros—Lust's whole litter—in one swift sortie.

"What a marvelous predator I have!" jested the earth lord. "Puts his feeble father's exploits to shame he does." And then a score of witnesses rose to remind the hall of Enduros' tally in the battle for Sovereignton.

"Such heroics! And right under my very nose... Lo! What a potent sleep I suffered through to miss it all," lamented Zeros to his four wind retinue. Of all the horns blowing on this night, 'twas this one roister that was missed the most.

"I too was spellbound, Uncle, and did sleep through much adventure," bleated Christen after recounting his abduction in detail. "Only for the most decisive of the duels did I awake. And a most 'hair-raising' climax to this Egg hunt it was, let me tell you..."

At its upteenth retelling, Creto, the catapillar, did cringe and crawl away to seek refuge in his mollusk shell. The venerable scribe was just too appalled at seeing Mythlewild's history rewritten so. Nor was it proper, in his view, for deities to take such temporal pleasure in crowing and vaunting themselves. He at least would retain his poise—though it was not easy, for Mythlewild's historian could have really spread it on thick if so inclined.

Clarissima also managed to keep a clear head. However, the crystal lady had her hands full restraining her wag. Unfortunately for her, even Jo lacked not for voice tonight. The rambunctious billiken eagerly sought to mince a mime or two in lieu of words, but the midget's size foiled him. About the only audience the tiny jockular could capture was Vito. If a mute could stretch the truth, so could he. Alas, as he flirted and buzzed about, the royal fly was more likely to be swatted than applauded. The two teeny giants therefore played on each other's patience. And so it was, the autumn's epic drama was enacted on scales, and accuracies, of varying dimensions.

"Would that I had missed as much as my colleagues in their slumber..." peeped Niki, who could hardly be heard above the more windsome voices. Yet the little dove's soft chirp soon had the entire hall stooped to listen. And the array of stuffed bestiary mounted across Constantio's walls tilted their heads to hear out the pilgrim's tutelary, on whom all else had hinged.

"Alas, my painter's fate and mine were cast together from that first push of mine. And such a curse that fall had proved to be. Some sweet sleep perhaps would cure its pain. But with the painter no one wanted I endured the trial—so that others, and others' children might sleep easier. Now, upon its conclusion, I bear no ill... only those memories that will not fade away. From mountain peak to murky moors, from beyond the Far Always to ocean's bottom... like some lewd and leering 'eyes' these visions linger in my mind:

Slithering wooden eyes which made no branches safe to rest,

Coercing lion eyes that trapped resolve and put my troth to test,

Bloodless reptile eyes cast my way in sin's conclave,

Or wanton yellow stares of squids from far beneath the waves,

Lifeless, lusterless eyes of walking dead,

The bleak, black sockets dug into a bone man's head,

A hungry set of feline eyes pouncing in some shanty cellar,

Or the stinging, sulfur-siren's eyes—Lust, the evil dweller...

But lastly—and most lasting—it is not the haunting stares of the vile, but the tortured, tear-filled faces of the more virtuous victims which grieves my heart. The most eternal of all are the innocent, agonizing eyes of a lost boy who was drowned, deceived, debased, and in every way defeated—except in despair—where he found triumph. Yet in all the versions of victory purged tonight, one remains untold. Some silent one has seen it all—and worse. His combat was with it all—and worse. He saw these same sore eyes as I—as each of us... and in Lust's defile, saw more! He looked upon the face of evil, and peered into the anguished, auburn eyes of death—and brought back to us the gift of life. In all your sagas his name is present—but always after yours. Who speaks for my painter, if not I? He will not! For he has already told his story during these past months. Has anyone been listening? You've feasted long and lavishly on words... Will you have some truth to top it all? His facts shall be more filling than your swollen fables were—"

Even before the excited dove could say her piece, the stupefied crowd, evoked with words and memories, shouted in thunderous volleys for their ennobled guest of honor. "DAVID!" they cried. It was David on their tongues now. The sky lord bellowed. The king commanded. The people pleaded. Jo clapped, and Vito buzzed, even Creto peeked from his shell of propriety—though he wore no smile. Instead, the catapillar was dismayed as the newly knighted David was jostled from his bench and pressed to stand above the dais all donned and dandy fitted in his freshly knitted coat of arms and pressed to tell the tale to end all tales: of how hell's queen was toppled with vanity, and her prime evil vanquished by the power of the Glass Egg. "We would hear it!" they shouted. "We would see this Egg!"

And now, even Niki's smile evaporated into a livid gasp; for she too saw the danger here. "The Egg... Oh my! Painter—you mustn't! Before another word escaped, a firm peck jabbed David's chest. From his breastpocket, words of caution put a lid on his legend. "Beware, painter," warned Niki, "the Glass Egg is not an object for party revelry or indiscriminate ears. Let the others brag. Let men and gods contest their own importance. But let us bear Omnus' Yoke with more respectful quiet—as its ignoble sire would deem. Leave it lying in your satchel tabernacle, painter... else we crack it open and its cursed promise spill over Theland again. The yoke you bear now is more fragile and more vulnerable than any prior cross, and—lest you forget—it's a burden left undelivered as of yet!"

David paused to think, while the dining hall hung in anticipation of the forthcoming account, which the boy decided would indeed be a worhty one—but not his. "Hear me, er...HEAR ME, all you admirers of valorous deeds. In truth, the greatest tale of all isn't mine to tell. This hall has heard each of us relive our past and recent glories this night. However, there is someone with us at this banquet table, whose past is neither recent, nor glorious; but rather an insufferable eternity of despair. Someone whose most illustrious feats were far removed from battlefields. His victories were reaped from war's ruins. His foe was starvation; his glory was surviving. The dungeon was his field of honor... and oblivion, his only future. Time became his only visitor, and coackroaches his only allies. His was a triumph more deserving than any of ours... Desderado—son of Mythlewild—rise, and tell this gathering what real bravery is all about. Come forward, Prince, and explain what it is to die and live again each day!"

The vast chamber rang with applause and screams for Desderado. "All hail the Prince of Mythlewild!" they shouted, and would not stop until the diminutive figure rose from his plate of roast roaches and bug beer. Natheless, a lifetime of pent up isolation had rendered the solitary speck much too timid and withdrawn, and slightly mad, to readily accept such accolades. Desderado merely turned to his friend and ducked under the table. "Never mind you lost my candle," he whispered to David, "I'll just spin you another..." And the shy-minded prince stuck out his long bug tongue and began to sew, instead of speak. It was this burst of silent valor that the throng found most heroic, and they so demonstrated.

The lord of the earth was first to stand. With his retinue and his titan son also rising, they applauded the heir to Mythlewild. The sky ascended next and thundered his adulation with the winds to back him up. The lamb prince was quick to follow suit, and so too their Royal Majesties the king and queen, and their court. Lords and knights, their pages, and peasants, and people—all of them stood in tribute to Constantio's courageous elder son. The ovation was deafening. It resounded off the ceiling like a luscious symphony upon a stage starved for joyous rhapsodies. Thereafter, when all the stories were rewoven in countless variations, it was melodies and paeans which drowned the crowing cocks and heralded the dawn, which today arrived more splendidly than ever before.

Over the choruses of celebration, no one heard the clarion announcing the arrival of one more very special guest. Such tidings could not penetrate the exuberance. So it was with obscure pomp and bubbling circumstance that Sir Fidius led the tall and slender stranger through the crowd. Berobed in some fine, pure and flowing fiber, the grace and silken steps bespoke a queenly countenance, though no crown, nor face, or feature of any kind lay exposed—save for an alder staff, which marked her gliding strides in precise elegance. None, not even the gods, paid the slightest mind to such a veiled visage. Sir Fidius bade her sit at the foot of the royal dais while he delivered her message to the lamb prince, Christen.

"Beggin' yur pardon, Prince, but there's a pale-clad lady come fur you... with this." After handing over the message, the leathery knight returned dutifully to his portal. But Christen did not have to read it. The Prince of Lambs looked down to see the persona of his grandame sitting in isolated repose. Spirits soared with gaiety around her, yet she indulged in no food, or song, nor swarthy conversation; but rather waited—waited patiently to see her offspring home.

Christen's good-byes were brisk. Constantio knew this day would come. "Desderado is returned to his father," said the lamb child to his mortal parents, "now I must venture home to mine."

"If only all the lost hearts on Serenity could be reunited as we with our loved ones," wished Constantio tearfully. "Your divine father can take pride in his stock."

One by one, Christen bid farewell to his earthly family and friends. None was more difficult to part with than David. "I woke to your friendship only recently, artist... yet you are close to me as my own fold, who yearn for me now." David cast a glance toward the satin lady, waiting in exquisite peace, serene and soft, amid the cock and bull, like a white rose among briars. "You've met my grandame, Shana, once before," confided the lamb boy, "when you visited my grandsire, the Overlord. On that night you were entrusted with a sacred task—and a most profound and perilous one. But it is over now—completely—as I return with the Glass Egg to my father. You can be truly free again. Who knows, perhaps relieving you of the Egg's burden will be the sincerest gift of gratitude my fold and I can bestow.

David could find few words as he reached into his satchel. "There were countless times I thought this day would never come..."

"My father's sentiments too, no doubt," smiled the lamb endearingly. "Had my aunt but recognized the power she held for such a precious, passing instant—but glory be, that witch was blind!"

"Like the rest of us, at times..." commented David philosophically, extracting Omnus' Egg, which still looked to be nothing more than a stone, or dirty ball... or bone. Such it was to Patrick's pup. Upon spying his morsel again, Fearsome barked impetuously from all his heads and carried on in such a fit that Patrick would surely have lost control, had the huge dog not froze dead in his tracks. All six ears perked and his trio of heads cocked.

The bewildered canine just stood and stared, as did the king and queen, and David, and some few others who were not too pie-eyed from their pluming to see what miracle had occurred in their midst. Fearsome's bone was gone. David's stone was gone. And the ball Christen once tossed among the sheepfold was also gone. In the son of Omnus' hands, these temporal things became a transplendent Egg of glass. For such a vital, fleeting second did they see—those that looked—and in such wonder, that none could speak thereafter. By the time David found some appropriate uttering, it was too late. Christen was gone too. And with the lamb, his lordly lady left. And the Glass Egg was no more to be seen.

Who at the king's table, where boasts of glories past belittled more essential poignant present marvels, could comprehend the worth of such farewells or such reunions? Even the gods were unaware of what wonder work transpired. But Creto made a note for posterity. And among the royal family, it was for Constantio alone to grasp, and his spouse and sons perhaps... with time. Clarissima and Jo paid heed, and knew; for the Egg was their fruit too. Valentina saw, but did not understand. She looked to David, who understood, but had no words that could explain.

Then—with a start—David looked nervously into his breastpocket. He heaved a sigh of relief when two big, bright pink eyes peeked back at him. "Niki! You're still here... I'm so glad! For a minute I thought you had gone home too."

"I AM home, painter. My dovecote is in your pocket, close to that skipping heart of yours. Christen and I agreed that you should not have to part with the poultry and the Egg both... so, the 'chick' is staying!"

David was so happy; he almost forgot about his winged shoes and case of art supplies. "What about these, Niki... doesn't your mentor want his amulets back?"

"Why, those are yours, painter—to keep," tweeted the dove. "No one else is so expert in their use as you. And besides, you earned them!"

"No way, Niki... I've learned by now that magic—any magic—doesn't suite me!"

The dove only chuckled. "Have you not also learned by now, whatever magic does exist, resides in YOU and not in your talismans—that is your talent painter. And, if that is not reason enough for you, let us call them... an engagement present!"

What magic words Niki had spoken. Valentina flung her nubile arms around David, and a most engaging, entwining, embrace ensued. Before the banquet's end, the occasion veered from a commemorative-birthday-Octoberfest, into a prenuptial shower. Constantio set aside his crown to conduct the sacramental vows himself which, according to Mythles' tradition, would lead to wedlock some months hence, when the youths would come of age. Thus it was decreed by none other than Creto himself, historian of the gods, that young David of Pastel Park, having just surrendered one sacred covenant, did enter into another.

As dusk woke red-eyed across the early morning sky, it was apparent that Constantio's November-December Octoberfest would wear well on into January; had Celeste, stout guardian angel that she was, not heeded the voice of reason and thereupon poked, prodded, and persuaded her clan into making leave. "We've work aplenty waiting for us in the Dingle, Papa. It's time for us to head back and discover if we've any home left to reclaim."

Patrick and Fearsome ran ahead to ready the ox cart, while Celeste took charge of Jing Jing, who slumbered peacefully as if nothing else mattered. Elder Ambrose bid good evening to the royal family and numerous others, eventually following his spouse into the palace bailey where Patrick and pup waited eagerly to go home.

But David's farewells could not be rushed; and when at last he appeared in the doorway, it was with teary eyes. Slowly he strolled down the walkway, his betrothed, in hand and Constantio for escort. "How I prayed for my ordeal to end..." said the boy wistfully, then paused to reflect

"Tosh!" blurted the king merrily. "Your 'ordeal' is just beginning, my boy!" He cast a wry wink towards Valentina as she stepped onto the ox cart.

"Well?..." said the pixie girl. "Are you coming, or aren't you?"

In a quandary David finally answered. "Uh, I don't know... Everything is so different now. I've waited so long to go home again that I forgot... I don't really HAVE a home... except the woods in Pastel Park; and I can't live there forever—especially now..."

"A palace roof would keep the rain off you, my boy," Constantio put forth a most generous offer. "As long as my family rules in Middleshire, you'll have a home at Bia Bella. What a prestigious courtier you could be—Court Painter, 'Artist of Aristocrats' I would title you. Nay—I would FATHER you—and with pride! Have I not already knighted you, and adopted you in spirit into this royal house? I could legalize it quick enough were you willing to have a royal roof, and all its obligations." David's chest expanded with heart-felt pride displaying his new, emblazoned tunic.

"Er, your pardon, Sire..." Elderman Ambrose was about to put his powers of persuasion to the test. Standing on the ox cart, he reached for his soft soap and went to work. "Imperial Highness, you've three fine heirs already, with estate enough to fray a lesser lord. Would you also claim a potential progeny of mine? Allow me to point out that Sir David is an orphan no longer. Moreover, your decree has practically imparted him into MY household... It is only fitting that he should come along with us."

Valentina agreed wholeheartedly with her father, and so did the rest of the angel's family, including Fearsome, who barked thrice in howling approval. Then

Chancellor Ambrose, newly appointed counselor to the king, continued 'counseling'. "Of course, David, if you would rather stay here in this big, overblown domicile and live like a fancy, pantsy prince, instead of coming along with your future family...a nd Valentina—" The elder's diplomacy was cut short as David scrambled into the ox cart between the elf maiden and a trio of yelping puppy heads.

"Well met, Sir Pilgrim!" laughed Constantio, raising his thewy arm in farewell. "I'll settle for a family portrait—and nothing less—when next we meet."

David waved to the Bella and her family, and all her friends. It was only now, as the cart shrank from the inner ward under the pale moon's subdued winter canopy and the waning lays of celebration, that the boy took notice of what had once been Queen Superbia's lovely rose garden, where once a treasured eve was spent. The sight touched David with sadness. The youthful romance fostered in the arms of rose and lavender bushes, now shed a departing tear. The exquisitely sculptured shrubs and meticulously manicured lawn, were now pruned and pitted with harsher tinted buds and branches under the more calloused yellow thumbs of Negare's ax-wielding hew and hackers. And the scarlet flecks dotting the dewy grass were not the roses' petals.

"Gardens can be grown again," remarked Valentina, sharing her suitor's secret thoughts, "and garden walls remade... and futures built as well. But what we keep in our hearts and memories need not, for they will blossom as long as we care enough to nourish them." David's heart suddenly basked in sunshine, even before the fully laden ox cart turned into the rise.

After twining their way out through the busy, waking, patchwork lanes of Sovereignton, they halted by the south gatehouse to exchange parting words with Sir Fidius, who stood chatting with his dragon son, Abraxus. The huge serpent lay sanguine in the city moat.

"My boy just come up from the 'Bottoms," explained the elder lizard. "Been keepin' his fishtail lordy, Isolato, company in his lonesome wing-ding down under. Even that ol' sea bass is on a toot; he's rolled up the carpet an' popped the cork fur this occasion... Anyways, they both bid you good tidin's"

David thanked the great sea drake for salvaging his life high in the Snowmass and also in the stormy North Salty. Then he turned his attention to the platinum chariot and its hitch of gold-winged stallions tethered by the river bank. The great eagle Palladan and the caterpillar scribe, Creto, perched within. Vero stood nearby rubbing down his father's team, a bit lonely perhaps, now that Paramount was again stabled in the Bella to be near Peter. Also present were the four winds, who paced the air around the Rollingway and played a game of tag with a single shady star.

"Why, what do you suppose they're all doing out here?" wondered David.

"Waitin'..." replied Fidius. "Their lordships glided over by the edgewater ta chew the fat."

David looked puzzled. "You mean talk?... To who? There's no one there but the river!"

Fidius nodded. "Yes sirree, an' the river is listenin'."

"I don't understand," confessed the boy.

"It's family talk, li'l' knight," puffed the seasoned lizard.

"You'll soon learn about families," added Ambrose with a fat smile. "Neither gods, nor mortal man are immune to kindred feelings. It's like love... sometimes, you just can't escape it."

"We had a humdinger of a time, didn't we, li'l' Davy!"

David nodded, wondering if Fidius was referring to the party. "It was a humdinger alright, Sir Fierce... but I'm awfully anxious to go home."

CHAPTER 61

The full-bodied moon, bundled up in layers of grey, winter clouds, politely relieved her retiring brother sun of his chore. From across the dell her pale, sympathetic shadow sprinkled over Hue Dingle and lit on David and Valentina. The couple sat comfortably atop the brown and thinly clovered knoll which used to overlook the beautiful fieldstone cottage. But now, all to be seen was crock and ashes, war's posterity. It came as no surprise to the elf maiden that their manor house lie among the casualties. She had often feared that statesmens' holdings would be among the first to feel the heat of invasion. This was their second night home however, and tears of remorse yielded to vivid memories of the past, which in turn gave way to the stark and determined realities of the present.

From a makeshift ox cart encampment, the entire elderman's family awakened early that morning, each and every member assigning themselves to the laborious task of rebuilding their homestead. Now, with a long day's work completed, they relaxed.

"For David and Valentina that meant being alone together, reposed in their favorite spot—the knoll. Zeros had finally permitted winter's chill to set its frosty foot upon the hills of Middleshire, yet there WAS warmth to be found. The pretty pixie sparkle was faded from the woodsprite's cheeks, just like the waning sunlight. In hopes of cheering his troth, David had begun a sunset painting. The painter's comfortable oily smock replaced the young knight's spotless coat of arms. Unfortunately, the sun proved too modest a model; rather than bask in the sky, he chose to hide in the dusk. In the wagon, Celeste sang soft lullabies to Jing Jing, who slept snug under her angel mama's downy wings. Of them all, only the baby fay appeared unscathed by the holocaust. Ambrose stoked the warming fire which crackled in the hearth. The yawning, brick fireplace was the lone survivor of the pillage; and even without roof or walls to hold her dwellers, it remained as the heart core of the household. Beneath their cart, on a plush mossy carpet, Niki occupied Patrick and his lumbering pup with more chapters of her pilgrim's adventures, lest the boy's curious appetite intrude on the knoll's privacy.

David unveiled his incomplete sunset painting, but Valentina only looked down into her barren yard with reminiscent eyes. "Val? It's a beautiful sunset painting..." admired the artist, practically to himself, "... even if it doesn't have a sun in it."

Although David's jest failed to light a smile, the pixie did manage an emotional reply. "We have a beautiful home too... if only we had a...H-H-House in it!...sob!"

"Please don't cry, Val, you're a soldier too, remember. You still have a beautiful home—better than any other place. Only the dwelling is gone. Its pitch and timber frame is gone, and its thatch roof may be ashes; but you still have stones and a firm foundation on which to build. Only the house is cinders—your 'home' is still standing. It's down there... in the ox cart with your family, and your belongings, and all their love. With that base, we'll soon build a new house—a prettier house—just as full of feelings as the old, and even more!"

Valentina's red sunset eyes were pulled from the yard to settle on David's smiling face. "It will have to be bigger too," she added. "The family's larger now you know!" Her spirits began to rise, and she squeezed her admirer's hand hard, which turned his face into crimson. "Will you miss your other home?" she asked.

David only laughed. "The woods?... Nah, not a pittance."

"No, not the woods... I mean your other REAL home. You know, before you came to Pastel Park and Mythlewild. Patrick says you talk about it sometimes, when you can remember. Don't you ever wish you could go back there?"

The angel girl waited for the longest time while David pondered her question. Of his prior life, only brief and random scenes would come to mind—and at their whims, not his. On whose orders will last night's dreams return? Fate had once picked a few choice pictures from his past, but they were smears upon his canvas now. And Creto gave yet another glimpse of yesterday's life; the name was Tommy, but who was he? Certainly he was no one David recognized. Do I think about him, or his home... do I miss it? That was no easy question to answer, and the words came out in pieces too. "Sometimes... often... most recently when Horros' hungry red eyes stole into Lust's defile and his black tongue crept across my skin... I wanted to be home then. The stench of the beast's breathing sent me longing backward..." Then the boy found the words that had eluded him."... But that was the last time—and will be!"

"I'm glad you stayed, Davy." Valentina's cheeks flushed with amber again, in memory of the sun.

"Me too," replied David through a sheepish grin.

"Were you an orphan in this other land of yours?"

"Yes, as I recall."

"And so you left... Why? What made you do it, Davy? And what was it that made you look for the Mythlewild?"

"I don't know... just wanted a family I supose. I never knew mine... Anyway, it was just a notion I got. Guess notions sometimes make us do inexplicable things."

"And once you got this 'notion', how did you ever find your way here?"

"A caterpillar told me to follow my road toward the sunrise side of the horizon... When the pavement ended, I was here—in the Otherland, you call Mythlewild."

"Could you find your way back, er... if you ever wanted to?"

"Hmmm, I don't really know... I never actually tried." David tugged at his chin, then shook his head. "Nor will I! This is my home—I'm a Mythle now!"

"With a family!" added Valentina.

"Well, your folks will disown me fast if we don't get back down to that hearth before this cold night air grips us."

"But, Davy, it's such a crispy clear night, the moon is practically inviting company. And I feel so much better now... and warm. Papa will understand; just like he did in the queen's rose garden, remember? I gave you my tiny portrait, the one you painted on this very spot." Valentina's glowing face now glittered with pink moonrise.

David looked at the locket around his neck. It smiled up at him too. "Yeah, I remember that night. I carried your memory with me everywhere—even before you gave this to me... I wish it was bigger."

"Davy! Make it bigger. Paint my portrait again... Now."

"Now? But, Val... it's dark!"

"It was dark in the queen's rose garden too. And, you've just painted a magnificent sunset—and did it without the sun. You even painted Lust in her dark pit. Oh, I know you had a candle then... but the moon can be your light now, like it was in the garden. Come on, don't you think it's MY turn!" One more generous squeeze of the hand was all the persuasion the young artist needed. How long he had waited to paint Valentina's portrait for real. Now, in pastel pale night light, David's picture sat in perfect pose with that winning smile unsheathed. "I won't turn to brimstone, will I?"

David laughed. "No—sugar maybe!" The fairy's irresistible image sweetened the artist's heart-thumping muse, and both of them swayed into the brushstrokes as his canvas came alive, lit with lovely pastel moon-coated colors.

Presently, another one of David's patrons appeared on the scene. Patrick, who had a sweet tooth curiosity for tasty tales of questing, came running up the hillock barely ahead of Fearsome, and only slightly behind Niki, who lighted on her painter's shoulder by way of announcing the youngster's arrival.

"Whatcha doin'?" asked the boy. "Still paintin'?"

"Uh-hum" grunted David, who was much too preoccupied to do more.

"That supposed to be Sis?"

"Uh-hum."

"Whadda ya want to paint her for anyway?"

"Patrick!" snipped Valentina. "Isn't it your bedtime, young man?"

"Supposin' it is. Mom said I could come up here an' say goodnight to you guys."

"Good night!" his sister said briskly.

"'Night, Patrick," chuckled David.

Valentina frowned to see her little brother still glued to their knoll. "Thought maybe you could tell me just one more story, Davy... Will ya?"

"I can't begin to answer all his questions, painter," panted Niki. "He's so incurably curious."

Putting aside his paints, David gave Fearsome a large pat on each of his three heads. The huge puppy then laid down by the winged feet and rolled over onto his back wagging his mile long tail. "As friendly as the day we first met, aren't you big fella."

Fearsome yelped three times as though he remembered chasing David and Niki into the nettlesome ebony tree back on that September night. Like his moppet master, the boy's dog begged for another yarn.

The pair's enthusiasm brought a condescending laugh from David. "Well now, I'd be delighted to tell you a bedtime story. What would you like to know?"

"Tell us how you really found the Glass Egg, Davy. Nobody's told us that one yet, not anyone—not even Niki. She says no one knows, but I'll bet you do—don't ya?"

David began to shake his head. "Well, as a matter of fact... No. I don't guess any of us will ever know exactly how the Egg turned up in that pit..." David then glimpsed the pugnacious glint in Valentina's eyes and recalled their discourse upon escaping Luhrhollow. From the smirking elf, his gaze fell upon the fawning puppy stretched out at his feet. "... Or DO they?!"

"Yes," snickered the sprite smugly, "someone knows. In all the excitement, you all forgot that I have a story to tell too!"

David and Niki tuned their ears attentively. But Patrick was skeptical. "You, Sis?... YOU know how Davy found the Glass Egg?"

"Of course," she boasted, "and Fearsome knows too—don't you, boy!" Patrick's pup barked enthusiastically, as if pleased of his accomplishment, but he wasn't talking. "Need I remind you boys that WE are part of this adventure too." Patrick's sister continued, thrilled at the opportunity of finally revealing her secret. "Remember how Vito and that nasty vixen kidnapped me and stole me away into the witch's hands?"

"Yeah, we heard that already; so what?" grumbled Patrick.

"So... along with me, that filching fox fancied one of Fearsome's bones, and took that also. She took it all the way into that black madam's lair and laid it right at her feet—so close Lust nearly fell over it. Even holding the Glass Egg under her nose, the witch could recognize it, not for what it was, but what it wasn't—not an egg, but a plain, tooth-riddled morsel of Fearsome's!"

"Fearsome!" squawked Patrick. "You mean ta say ol' Fearsome had the bone... I mean the Egg, all along? But how?"

"Just you wait a minute more, young man!" emphasized Valentina as she completed her tale at Luhrhollow. "None, except Christen and Niki, did know their grandsire's Egg to look upon it. Yet both were in the pit bottom and unable to see atop the rim. Even while the Egg sat in our very yard at the outset of the journey, it went unnoticed. Niki was hidden away in David's breastpocket, and he was not yet aware its appearance—"

"But my shoes knew," inserted David, only now beginning to unravel the mystery. "They spoke to me from the start, in your yard, just as they did when urging me back into Luhrhollow; only then I was excited upon starting my adventure and mistook my shoes' warning for zeal, like mine."

Reflecting back on that note, Niki felt the urge to add, "How ironic that we embarked upon our odyssey only to find something that was right at our feet from the very beginning!"

"But how'd the Glass Egg get in our yard in the first place?" Patrick wanted to know. "How'd Fearsome ever dig it up anyway?"

Valentina took particular delight at answering her brother's persistent questions. "You should know, little brother—YOU had it the day you brought your runaway dog home from the bog, with David and poor, nearly drowned Niki."

"Huh?"

"Fearsome had it all along," explained David, with Valentina's permission. "It was his 'treat'! He 'dug it up' in the grassy tussock in Hurst Meadow, by the ebony tree root—right where Christen hid it the night of his abduction." David gave his pal's pup three more solid pats. "It was Fearsome who found what everyone else could not! We went wandering all over Theland in pursuit of what we already had!"

The three-headed canine seemed oblivious to his accomplishment and all the recognition, preferring instead to roll under the delight of the boys' vigorous pats and hugs. "Why you ol' mutt, you're a hero!" exclaimed Patrick. "And all this time I thought we had missed out on all the action."

"Well, now that you know how important you really are, young man, maybe you'll find it easier to sleep," said Valentina. "Why don't we say good night to David now. It has been a lo-o-ong day!"

"You guys go on ahead, I'll clean up and be right down. We ought to have lots of time for portraits from now on." David smiled as he watched his pixie princess glide down the dewy hill. He then cleaned his brushes and put away his paints. Niki tucked herself in for the night, safe inside her painter's warm breastpocket. Storytelling had left her quite tired and she was still a bit wary of the huge, three-headed puppy who had once given her such a scare. For the time being, Fearsome frolicked with another friend: a flirtatious butterfly

David whistled to himself as he shook out his dirty rags, then tucked everything tidily into his satchel. Just as he was about to start down the knoll to join Valentina and her family, the faint sound of fluted music sifted through the glade. It was a familiar chord. Next, a lamb hobbled from out of the thicket, and Fearsome let out three exuberant howls, rushed up to the skittish creature, then lunged after it, baying to beat the band.

Niki woke in a fright. "Oh, that dog!"

By and by other lambs appeared on the rise from the woods; soon David was in the middle of a flock of sheep. Then he knew just where the music originated. "Niki, look—it's our old shepherd friend, Liberato."

The sleepy dove poked her head out of David's pocket, and sure enough, there was the tousle-haired goat man who had saved the pilgrims from the condors far up on the Snowmass.

"Hey, buddy!" hollered the faun from behind his flute. "You seen my sister around here anywhere?" Fearsome was now beside himself as to which of the many bouncing, bounding bodies he should chase. "Guess she's still out roundin' up strays."

David worked his way through the mutton and greeted his shaggy friend warmly. "Liberato, how good to see you again! What brings you down this way? I thought you were a mountain goat man these days."

"No more, guy, not me! Let me tell you, those mountains are too dang moody for my gentle bones. Such a commotion we heard for a 'ternal long spell. A rukus ain't good for my woolies' nerves; spooks 'em somethin' fierce. An' that mad mountain's colder'n a brass crook staff; dang near froze my horn off in the gol' darnedest blizzard you ever saw. We was herdin' a flock a 'snowballs' for a week after! The sun ain't shown his face until just this week. Glad to see it too, by golly; don't like cold, dreary skies... turns my mutton's milky fleece all dingy an' dull. Now the sun's returned to bleach 'em white again, so's we're headed back to the Downy Meadows. My partner, Pandas, is down in the Commons now, locatin' some choice, sun-ripened sweetgrass for us. Says things've gone back to normal again an' it's safe to return."

"I think the worst weather is already behind us," added David.

"You don't say? Well, like to gab some more, but I gotta rustle up Milly. It's mighty late, an' Sis's still out fetchin' strays when she's got camp to pitch, an' vittles to cook, an'—"

"Why not stay with us tonight!" suggested David. "I'll warm up some comfits and ginger. We're kind of homeless too, temporarily. But we can all camp out together... and we DO owe you a favor! You're all welcome."

"Lambs too?"

"Especially the lambs! Say... aren't you still worried about foxes in the South?"

"Foxes? Nah, can't never get away from the foxes. Long as there's sheeps, there'll be varmints lustin' after 'em. Guess it's best to just hold your ground an' have it out with 'em. Funny though, Pandas said the last fox he saw turned plumb stiff at the sight of woolies. Hey—looky down there! Danged if Sis ain't already made herself to home. Looks like you folks got burned pretty bad here. Maybe we could lend a hand in buildin' things back up... Say, I notice you still got that dawg. He's sure a fine one—make a good sheep dawg. You're mighty lucky!"

"Yes, I guess I am... Very lucky!" agreed David. His breast chirpped in accord as they headed into the fire-lit dell. The three-headed dog and the many-headed sheepfold barked and bleated at each other on their way down the hill, until Fearsome stopped to snap at the dancing butterfly which hummed a merry good night. "Careful, fella, that's not another 'bone' to nibble on." David smiled and looked skyward as he gave the pup a pat on his snouts. Evening's clouds replied with fleecy smiles of their own.

The End

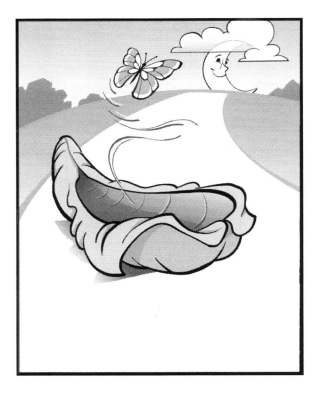

EPILOGUE

'Keep alive a place in your heart where dreams may grow.' What a fine moral that would make for my allegory. And since most any story worth its words should have a moral, you could settle for that one. Or, you might just prefer to find your own. That's what I did. I learned how to become a butterfly!

My story is much like the Glass Egg itself: real, and waiting to be grasped by anyone of troth willing to act upon that irresistible notion, and venture after it. It is a gift recognizable to those wary, wondering ones ready to investigate magic places, like the 'Otherland'. Any lessons gained from such adventures depend on what you're looking to find.

What is your wish? Mine is to bring into your life a metamorphosis... or perhaps a simple thought, or smile of joy. As for morals? Well, since each and every man, woman, child—and mythle—of us is unique and very special in our own inimitable way, you may wish to sort out your own conclusions, or you might not. Mayhap you'll discover a Glass Egg, a ball, a bone, or stone... or nothing at all!

For my part, I shall close my tale as I began—as all stories begin —with a notion, a dream; and for you, my readers, a wish: For those who have found their Glass Egg—cherish it. For those still looking—relish the hunt. And, if there are any who have never yearned for an Egg ... Faretheewell!

Yours sincerely in history,
Creta (the butterfly!)

Well, there you have it. This is how my one night's 'note' turned out.
Over the years, the Glass Egg has hatched numerous other stories. There are 64 in fact, one tale for each of the Glass Egg's characters. I call these stories, 'Fairly' Tales. They're kind of like fairy tales, only a little more *grin* than Grimm. You can find them on Amazon should you care to have a look. Even better, step in… maybe you'll leave happily ever after!

T.T.